They're tall, d
...but are th

MEDITERRANEAN
Tycoons

MEDITERRANEAN Tycoons

Michelle REID
Kate WALKER
Sarah MORGAN

MILLS & BOON

All the characters in this book have no existence outside the imagination of the author, and have no relation whatsoever to anyone bearing the same name or names. They are not even distantly inspired by any individual known or unknown to the author, and all the incidents are pure invention.

Harlequin Mills & Boon Limited, Eton House,
18-24 Paradise Road, Richmond, Surrey TW9 1SR

MEDITERRANEAN TYCOONS © by Harlequin Books S.A. 2011

The De Santis Marriage © Michelle Reid 2008
The Greek Tycoon's Unwilling Wife © Kate Walker 2007
The Sicilian's Virgin Bride © Sarah Morgan 2007

ISBN: 978 0 263 88522 4

024-0211

Harlequin Mills & Boon policy is to use papers that are natural, renewable and recyclable products and made from wood grown in sustainable forests. The logging and manufacturing processes conform to the legal environmental regulations of the country of origin.

Printed and bound in Spain
by Litografia Rosés S.A., Barcelona

THE DE SANTIS MARRIAGE

Michelle REID

Michelle Reid grew up on the southern edges of Manchester, the youngest in a family of five lively children. Now she lives in the beautiful county of Cheshire, with her busy executive husband and two grown-up daughters. She loves reading, the ballet and playing tennis when she gets the chance. She hates cooking, cleaning and despises ironing! Sleep she can do without and produces some of her best written work during the early hours of the morning.

CHAPTER ONE

THE WHOLE pre-wedding party thing was revving up like a gigantic engine and Lizzy had never felt less like partying in her entire life.

Now a night at La Scala, dear God, she thought heavily. For here she stood surrounded by luxury in this posh Milan hotel suite, about to put on a posh designer dress that must have cost more money than she dared let herself think about, so she could look the part for a posh gala evening spent at La Scala, while back home in England the family business was about to go under taking everything they owned along with it.

She had not wanted to come to her best friend's wedding but her father had insisted. Her brother Matthew had gone a whole step further and become really angry. 'Don't be stupid,' he'd snapped at her. 'Do you want Dad to feel worse than he already does about this mess? Go to Bianca's wedding as planned,' he'd instructed, 'and while you're there wish her all the damn best from me with her super-rich catch.'

It had been said with such bite it made Lizzy wince to recall him saying it. Matthew was never going to forgive her best friend for falling in love with another man.

Then Bianca and her parents had put even more pressure on her to come to Milan and in the end it had been easier to give in and do what everyone wanted her to do when all *she'd* wanted to do was to be at her father's side supporting him.

But instead she had to shimmy into this dress, Lizzy told herself, puffing back an unruly curl when it flopped across one eye as she settled the straps onto her shoulders then turned to the mirror to check out the finished effect.

What she saw reflected back at her sent instant horror pouring into her expressive face. The dress was way too clingy in all the wrong places and the silver-grey colour looked awful against her pale skin! And it was not for the first time in her twenty-two years that she wished with all her heart that she were a delicate and sweet fine-boned brunette like Bianca.

But she wasn't. She was a long curvy redhead with an unruly long mop of glossy chestnut curls that just refused to stay confined no matter how much torture she put herself through in an effort to pin them up. Add skin so startlingly white it looked dreadful against the silver-threaded grey silk and it was like looking at a ghost!

When Bianca had bought the dress a couple of months ago to wear to her betrothal party she'd looked fabulous in it— pure sensation on legs. Yesterday she'd tossed it at Lizzy in disgust. 'I don't know why I bought it. I hate the colour. The length is not right and my boobs don't fill it.'

Well, there was no chance of that problem here, Lizzy thought, small white teeth biting down into her full bottom lip as she hitched the tightly fitted basque top further up the pale plump slopes of breasts and grimly thanked the boning in the bodice for helping it to stay put.

The rest, she saw on second inspection, didn't cling quite as badly as she'd first thought it did and—Face it, Lizzy, she then told herself firmly, beggars cannot be choosers, girl, so you should—

The sudden knock sounding at her suite door diverted her attention. 'Are you ready, Elizabeth?' Bianca's mother called out. 'We must not be late for La Scala.'

Certainly not, Lizzy thought dryly. 'Just one more minute!' she called back.

La Scala waited for no man, not even the higher echelons of Italian society she was about to mingle with, she mocked as she slid her feet into a pair of high slender heeled silver mules, then turned to apply a coating of clear gloss to her lips. She refused point-blank to use the seduction red colour Bianca had supplied along with the dress.

Standing back to give her reflection the final once-over, she suddenly found the humour in standing here in her ill-fitting borrowed feathers and laughed for the first time in weeks. All she needed now was for her best friend to toss her that fabulous diamond ring her betrothed had presented her with and she'd be sorted. All family debts paid via the first pawn brokerage she could find.

But Bianca wasn't quite that giving—not that Lizzy resented her for that. Bianca Moreno had been her closest friend since the day they had both found themselves stuck in the same strict English boarding-school feeling like a pair of aliens dropped in there from outer space. Bianca had come to the school directly from a carefree lifestyle in Sydney with her Italian born parents. They'd gone from ordinary to mega-rich overnight when an uncle in England had died suddenly making Bianca's father the main beneficiary of the London based Moreno Inc.

Whereas Lizzy, well, she had been sent to the same school after her mother had caused a terrible scandal by having an affair with their local, very married MP. She had been so mercilessly teased and bullied at her old school about the affair that her father had decided to remove her from the situation by placing her in a school hundreds of miles away from the fuss.

Did it stop the teasing? No, it didn't. Did she tell her father that? No, she did not, because he'd already been too cast down by the scandal and the fact that their mother had walked out and left them taking with her what funds she could grab. So Bianca had become her close friend and confidante. They looked out for each other. Bianca was the black-haired black-eyed spitfire with a solid grounding in good Australian spunk and Lizzy the much quieter one with her natural spirit squashed by the bullies and a mother who'd never bothered to get in touch again after she'd walked out.

From the age of twelve to their present twenty-two, she and Bianca had rarely done anything without the other one knowing about it. Now her friend was about to marry into one of Italy's finest families and, despite not wanting to be here, Lizzy was ready to shelve her own worries and do whatever it was going to take to help make Bianca's wedding day next week absolutely perfect. It was Bianca's family who'd paid to bring her over here. They had provided her with everything from room and board to clothes to suit every glittering occasion, even if they were Bianca's cast-offs.

And she was grateful to them—she was, because she could not have afforded to come otherwise, no matter what her father had said. So here she was, one week into a two-week sabbatical from family troubles, joining in the partying run-up to Bianca's glossy marriage to her super-rich, super-sophisticated beau.

Luciano Genovese Marcelo De Santis, the thirty-four-year-old supreme head of the great and vast De Santis banking empire—Luc to his very close friends.

A tense little quiver made a sudden strike down Lizzy's front and in pure self-defence she snatched up a silvery silk crocheted snug from the bed and hurriedly tied it across her front while wishing to goodness that she didn't experience that same crazy tense quiver every time she let herself think about him.

He was strange—a truly intimidating mix of smoothly polished cool sophistication and lean, dark, sexy good looks. Bianca purred around him like a sleek kitten, which seemed to amuse him, but then Bianca was Italian and as a race of people they were like that, open and warm and more touchy-feely than the British—*her*, Lizzy thought, making the rueful distinction.

She'd never purred around any man and couldn't envisage ever wanting to—which made the way she quivered around Luc De Santis all the more disturbing to her peace of mind. He wasn't her type. He was too much of everything. Too big and tall, too lean and dark, too sexy and handsome—too crushingly cool and terrifyingly enigmatic, she decided as she hooked up her little silver beaded evening bag and headed for the door.

They'd met only once before she's come to Milan, in London several months ago at the private dinner Bianca's parents had held to introduce their future son-in-law to their English friends. Luc had come as such a shock to Lizzy that she had not been able to stop her eyes from constantly drifting in his direction because he was so far away from her idea of the kind of man her friend liked.

'What do you think?' Bianca asked her.

'Intimidating,' she said, because that evening was the first time the tense quiver had struck. 'He scares me to death.'

Bianca just laughed, but then she'd been laughing at everything. Happy—in love again—high as a kite. 'You'll get used to him, Lizzy,' she promised. 'He isn't nearly as awesome once you get to know him.'

Want to bet?

The next time she'd met him had been just a week ago, she

recalled as she pushed the button to call the lift. He'd arrived here at the hotel looking for Bianca and found Lizzy standing in Reception having just arrived in Milan. He'd come over to her—of course, he would do with impeccable manners like his, she reasoned. Yet she still had not been able to stop the next quiver from making its strike.

He'd been angry that Bianca had not been at the airport to meet her—she'd seen the anger snap at his handsome dark features just before he'd blanked it out. When she'd said quickly that she hadn't been expecting to be met, his wide, sensual mouth had tugged into a telling flat line of disapproval.

Cool, calm and used to ordering people about, he'd then taken it upon himself to organise her arrival by making sure she had a nice suite of rooms and had even gone as far as to escort her up here to check the suite out for himself.

It had been the moment when his hand arrived at the base of her spine to politely usher her out of the lift that the next quiver had struck, shooting down her front like a flaming arrow and making her jerk away from him like a scalded cat, only to feel really foolish for doing it. Other than to send her one of his cool, steady looks, he'd let his hand fall to his side and thankfully made no comment.

Now here she was waiting to ride the same lift down to the mezzanine floor of the hotel where they were all gathering for drinks before they left. And if she'd avoided Luc De Santis like the absolute plague for the rest of this week Lizzy had a horrible suspicion she was not going to be able to do that tonight. The party was too small, the reserved boxes at La Scala too intimate. Her only hope was to manage to wangle it so she sat in a different box from him.

There was a mirror hanging on the wall by the lift and she diverted her attention to it to push the stray curl off her brow.

It flopped back down again like a renegade. She should not have decided to pin it all up because it just wasn't going to behave, she predicted. But giving in and letting her hair hang down around her shoulders in a tumble of loose glossy cork-screws had only made her face look paler and her grey-green eyes look too big.

Like a frightened rabbit, she likened, wrinkling her nose as she gave the errant curl a teasing tug and watched it spring back into place again.

It had to be that precise moment that the lift doors slid open to reveal none other than the great man himself. Their eyes clashed for a startled second. Knowing he'd caught her pulling silly faces at her own reflection was enough to flood colour into Lizzy's cheeks.

'Oh,' she said, just too disconcerted to keep the dismay from sounding in her voice. 'Are you staying here too? I didn't know.'

Brief amusement lit the unusual gold colour of his eyes. 'Good evening, Elizabeth.' He always called her *Elizabeth* in that dark, deep, slightly lilting Italian accent of his. 'Are you coming in?'

Coming in—heck, she thought, letting her eyes run over him. He was wearing a conventional black silk dinner suit and was leaning casually against the rear wall of the lift, which should have helped to diminish his daunting height a little and that overwhelming sense of presence he always carried around everywhere with him—but didn't.

And the idea of stepping into a lift with him again did strange things to the nerves in her legs as she made them move. Finding a tense smile to flick his way, she then turned her back on him to watch as the doors closed them in.

Silence hummed as they waited. She could feel his eyes on her. Tension made her bite into the soft tissue of her inner lip.

'You look very beautiful tonight,' he murmured softly.

Lizzy had to fight down an inner wince. She knew what she looked like and she knew what he was seeing—the poor best friend decked out in the dress his betrothed had worn a couple of months ago at the party in London.

So, 'No I don't,' she therefore responded curtly.

It was a relief when the lift doors opened onto the elegant splendour of the hotel's mezzanine lounge bar. As she went to step out that hand arrived at the base of her spine again and this time she froze where she stood.

It just wasn't fair. Why did she always do something like this around him?

'Shall we?' he prompted smoothly.

Lizzy made herself walk forward, stingingly aware how his hand remained exactly where it was this time—as if he was taunting her silly reaction to him. The first person her eyes focused on was Bianca's mother, looking stunning in sparkling diamonds and unrelieved black.

'Oh, there you are, Lizzy,' she said, hurrying towards them with an anxious expression threatening to ruin her perfectly made-up face.

'Luciano,' she greeted, her dark eyes skimming warily over her future son-in-law's face before she returned them to Lizzy. 'I need a quick word with you, *cara*,' she begged.

'Of course.' Lizzy smiled, automatically softening her tone for this tiny, elegant woman whose nervous disposition made her worry about everything—and everything usually encompassed her beautiful daughter. 'What's Bianca done now?' she asked.

Meant as a light tease, it was only when the man standing behind her said coolly, 'Nothing, I hope,' that she realised she'd spoken out of turn in front of him.

Sofia Moreno went pale. Lizzy got defensive on Bianca's

mamma's behalf because she'd noticed before that Sofia was not comfortable in Luc's presence.

'It was a joke,' she said sharply—too sharply by the sudden stillness she felt hit the man behind her and the flick of tension she felt play along the length of her spine until it gathered beneath the light pressure of his hand.

Next second he was leaning past her to brush kisses to Sofia's cheeks. Having to stand here, trapped between the hard warmth of his body and Sofia's delicate one, Lizzy felt a twinge of remorse because his gesture was so obviously offered as a gentle soothe to his future mother-in-law's frazzled nerves.

'I will leave you both to—confide together,' he murmured then, and his hand slid away from Lizzy's back.

He strode away towards the bar to greet some friends, the loose-limbed elegance with which he moved holding Lizzy's gaze though she didn't want it to.

'Lizzy, you have to tell me what's wrong with Bianca,' Sofia Moreno insisted, setting Lizzy's eyelashes flickering as she moved them away from Luc. 'She is behaving strangely and I cannot seem to get a pleasant word out of her. She should be down here by now standing with Luciano to greet their guests, but when I went to her suite after I knocked on your door she wasn't even dressed!'

'She had a headache at lunch and went to her room to rest,' Lizzy recalled with a frown. 'Perhaps she fell asleep.'

'Which would explain the rumpled bed,' Bianca's mother said tensely, 'and the way she looked like she'd just fallen out of it *and* the way she snapped off my head!'

'Give her a few more minutes to get herself together,' Lizzy suggested soothingly. 'If she still hasn't put in an appearance, I'll go up and chivvy her on.'

'In the bad mood she's in, only you dare to do it, *cara*,' Bianca's mother said tautly.

Not Bianca's betrothed? Lizzy wondered dryly as she linked her arm through Mrs Moreno's and led her back to where the rest of the guests were gathered. A few seconds later she was being warmly greeted by Bianca's father, Giorgio, and introduced to a cousin of Bianca's she hadn't met before.

Vito Moreno was about her own age and blessed with the Moreno dark good looks and a pair of laughing blue eyes. 'So you're Elizabeth,' he said. 'I've been hearing a lot about you since I arrived here this afternoon.'

'Who from?' Lizzy demanded.

'My dear cousin, of course.' Vito grinned. 'Bianca insists you are the one person who saved her from a life of rebellion and wickedness when she had to leave Sydney to live in the UK and attend the "stuffiest school around".'

Ah. 'You're one of the Sydney Morenos,' Lizzy realised. 'I recognise the accent now.'

'I used to be Bianca's partner in crime before you took my place,' he explained.

'You're *that* cousin?' She laughed up at him. 'I've heard all about you too.'

'That's my pulling power shot to death.' Vito sighed.

A long fluted glass of fizzing champagne appeared in front of Lizzy and she glanced up as she accepted it to find Luc standing over her like some dark towering giant.

'Oh—thank you,' she murmured.

He just nodded his dark head, sent an acknowledging nod towards Vito and drifted away again leaving Lizzy feeling—odd.

Then Vito said something and with a mental shrug she pushed Luc De Santis to one side and wished to goodness he would stay there for good. The minutes wore on, the mezzanine bar slowly filled with guests and still there was no sign of Bianca. Eventually people began to get restless, checking the time on their watches.

Lizzy's gaze drifted towards Luc De Santis. He was standing apart from everyone else talking into his cell phone—and was not very happy by the stern look on his face.

Was he talking to Bianca? She would not be surprised because she'd seen him angered before by Bianca's habit of always being late.

Well, get used to it, she told him silently as she watched him snap shut his mobile and slide it into his jacket pocket. Bianca's blithe lack of awareness to time and space was the constant bane of her mother's and Lizzy's lives. He could count himself lucky if she managed to turn up on time at the church next week.

As the minutes dragged on, though, even Lizzy found she had to fight the need to keep checking her watch, and Sofia Moreno was sending her pleading looks. She was about to excuse herself to go and find out what Bianca was doing when there was a sudden stir by the lifts.

Everyone turned to look as one. The following silence held like a shaken heartbeat because there, at last, was Bianca, looking an absolute vision dressed in billowing gold silk. Her long dark hair was up in a dramatically simple style that showed off the sweet perfection of her face and the slender length of her creamy smooth neck. Diamonds sparkled at her ears and her throat.

Thread a tiara into her hair and she could be a princess, Lizzy thought fondly as eyes like huge pools of liquid dark chocolate scanned her audience, then her soft mouth took on an apologetic tilt.

'Sorry I'm so late, everyone,' Bianca chanted quietly, and the mezzanine bar stirred to the sound of a beautifully directed indulgent response.

'That's my brave girl,' Lizzy thought she heard Vito murmur beneath his breath and she glanced at him sharply, but saw nothing in his expression to warrant such a strange remark.

Then Luc was striding forward to take hold of Bianca's slender fingers and lifting them to his lips. Whatever he said to his betrothed brought a sheen to Bianca's eyes and a vulnerable tremor to her oh, so beautiful mouth.

He loves her, Lizzy realised in that moment. An odd little sensation clutched at her chest. Frowning slightly, she turned away from the two lovers and was relieved to feel the sensation fade.

They were ferried to the opera in a fleet of sleek limousines. Vito Moreno was obviously meant to partner her tonight and he made her laugh, which made her relax more and more as the evening wore on. La Scala was fabulous, an experience Lizzy really enjoyed—mainly because she'd successfully managed to avoid being placed anywhere near her best friend's disturbing fiancé. Afterwards they moved on to have dinner in a beautiful sixteenth century palazzo on the outskirts of Milan.

It was all very stylish, very much a glimpse of how the richer half lived. There was dancing as well as dining, and because Vito kept on filling her wineglass Lizzy was tipsy by the time Luc De Santis arrived by her chair to invite her to dance.

There was a hovering second while she hunted around for an excuse to refuse him, then his hand arrived beneath her elbow to propel her to her feet. 'Come on,' he said dryly. 'It is expected that the groom dances at least once with his bride's maid of honour.'

Lizzy thought that was supposed to happen after the wedding, but the telling quiver struck again making her too tense and too breathless to say it as he drew her against him on the dance floor and smoothly urged her to dance.

The lights were low, the music a slow romantic ballad accompanied by a female singer with a stirringly deep and sensual voice. She felt her heart begin to pump to a heavier beat as they moved together and she absorbed the full disturbing impact of his masculine warmth and his muscular hardness pressing against her tense, softer shape.

'Relax,' he prompted after a few seconds. 'This is supposed to be an enjoyable pastime.'

Lizzy looked up, caught the mocking glow in his eyes and felt the sting of heat flush her cheeks. 'I'm just not used to—'

'Being held this close to a man?' he mocked.

'Dancing in these shoes!' she corrected hotly. 'And that wasn't a very nice thing to say.'

He just laughed, the sound low and deep and disturbingly intimate the way it resonated against the tips of her breasts. 'You are an unusual creature, Elizabeth Hadley,' he informed her then. 'You are very beautiful but you don't like to be told so. You are tense and defensive around me yet you can completely relax with a serial womaniser like Vito Moreno.'

'Vito isn't a womaniser,' Lizzy rejected. 'He's too laid back to be a womaniser.'

'Ring any telephone number in Sydney and just mention his name.'

And that was cynicism, not mockery, she noted. 'Well, I like him,' she stated stubbornly.

'Ah, I see he is beginning to reel you in.'

'And that wasn't very nice, either!'

His dark head suddenly dipped, bringing his lips very close to her cheek. 'I'll let you into a secret, *mia bella*—I am not very nice.'

He was so close now she could smell the masculine pull of his tangy scent. Lizzy jerked her head back. 'Well, you had better be nice to Bianca,' she warned loyally.

He just laughed as he straightened up again, then drew her even closer so he could control her movements with a cool, casual strength. He was taller than her by several impacting inches, which put her eyes on a level with his strong, chiselled chin. They didn't speak again, and as the dance wore on maybe it was the fault of too many recklessly consumed glasses of wine that made her so aware of everything about him. Even the smooth feel of his silk lapel beneath her fingers fascinated her, and the bright whiteness of his shirt against the natural olive tones of his throat.

He was gorgeous. There was just no use in trying to deny it. Everything about him was so perfectly presented from the neatly styled gloss of his satin black hair to the length of his very Italian nose and the truly beautiful shape to his mouth.

And the singer droned on, low and soulful. Lizzy felt the sensual pull of the melody percolate her system as potently as the wine she had been drinking all evening and like a fool she closed her eyes and just let the sensation carry her away. One set of his long golden fingers lightly clasped her pale slender fingers, the other set rested low in the arch of her back. She had no idea how her fingers were stroking the silk lapel of his jacket or that she had moved in so close to him that her breath was softly feathering his throat. She just moved where he guided her, aware of the tingling tension affecting her body but unaware that it was affecting him too. His fingers moved slightly against her clasped fingers, the hand at her back glided upwards to the centre of her spine and gently urged her into even closer contact with him.

It was—nice. Kind of tingly and floaty and she hadn't a clue as to how much she had relaxed into him until she felt the living warmth of taut skin brush against her lips and tasted it on the tip of her tongue.

With a jerk of shock Lizzy flicked her eyes open and pulled back her head. Dismay instantly curled its way through her body accompanied by a wave of mortified embarrassment that flooded like fire into her face when she realised what she had done.

She had just brushed her lips against Bianca's fiancé's throat and tasted him with her tongue!

CHAPTER TWO

'OH, MY GOD,' Lizzy gasped in skin quivering consternation.

They weren't even dancing any longer! And he was looking down at her with one of those dreadful mocking smiles tugging at the corners of his mouth!

Dropping her eyes to his throat, Lizzy wished with all her pounding heart that the ground would just open up and swallow her whole.

'I'm so sorry!' she whispered, stepping back from him so violently she almost went over on the spindly heels of her shoes.

'In truth I was rather flattered by the—compliment.' His hand snaked out to steady her. 'Fortunately I sensed it coming, which is why we are now standing outside on the terrace away from curious eyes…'

Outside—? Glancing dizzily around her, sure enough, Lizzy discovered that they were indeed standing on a shadowy terrace she had not even known was here! Realisation hit as to how engrossed she must have been in him that he'd been able to manoeuvre her through a pair of open French windows out into the cooler evening air without her even being aware!

Once again she took a shaky step backwards—right out of his reach this time—and thankfully managed to remain safely upright. The music still droned somewhere in the near

distance. Mortification riddled her blood. She wanted to die
and she couldn't look at him—didn't know what to say in her
own defence!

And he was so relaxed, his hips resting against a heavy
stone balustrade, his arms lightly folded across his wide chest,
and she had the sickly feeling he was thoroughly—thoroughly
enjoying himself.

'Blame the wine,' he offered gently.

Lizzy nodded, pathetically grateful for the miserable excuse.

'I'm not used to drinking so m-much.'

'No,' he agreed.

'And Vito—'

'Was constantly filling up your glass.'

She hadn't been going to say that, but hearing him say it
brought her eyes flickering up to his face. 'He wasn't!' she
protested, then swallowed and added helplessly, 'W-was he?'

'Poor Elizabeth,' the cool brute murmured. 'Caught by the
oldest trick in the book.'

Then she remembered what she had been doing with him
and she dragged her eyes away from him to wave a decidedly
uncoordinated hand towards the French doors.

'I th-think I should…'

'Go back inside to him so he can intoxicate you some more?'

'No.' The waving fingers tightened into a fist and dropped
to her side. 'You have a very nasty sense of humour, *signor*.'

'And you, *signorina*, have a very moist tongue and a warm,
soft pair of lips.'

That was it, Lizzy couldn't take any more of this, he'd had
enough fun at her expense. Spinning on her heel, she turned
towards the doors.

'What are the two of you doing alone out here?' a new
voice suddenly intruded.

And nothing, nothing in all of her twenty-two years, had ever made Lizzy feel as bad as she felt then when her friend—her beautiful, happily in love *loyal* best friend—stepped through those same French doors.

'Your—maid of honour was feeling the heat,' Luc responded evenly. 'She needed to breathe some fresh air.'

Barely holding herself together, Lizzy felt her insides squirm with guilt and shame when Bianca looked at her and said, 'Are you okay, sweetie?' with genuine concern. '*Dio*, you do looked flushed, Lizzy.'

'Blame your cousin,' Luc suggested. 'He is the one who's been topping up her wineglass all evening.'

'Vito? Oh, the wicked boy. And I told him to take care of you for me...' She floated across the terrace to place a comforting arm across Lizzy's shoulders. 'With your sternly temperate papa you're just not used to late nights and partying are you, *cara*? In fact you are *not* used to drinking alcohol at all!'

'My father isn't that bad,' Lizzy mumbled, feeling more uncomfortable by the second.

'No, he's worse,' Bianca said curtly, doing nothing to hide her dislike of Lizzy's father, the man she still blamed for breaking up her love affair with Matthew two years ago. 'I'm still surprised that he actually allowed you to come here knowing you would have to enjoy yourself! I even had to provide you with clothes so you were not forced to turn out in those terrible modest sacks he prefers you to wear!'

Wanting to curl up inside her own skin now at this small piece of insensitivity, Lizzy wondered helplessly if this was punishment for what she'd been doing with Bianca's man.

Surprisingly it was Luc De Santis who came to her defence, 'That's enough, *cara*,' he said to Bianca. 'Modesty is not a sin. And your friend has a—headache,' he offered up.

'Hearing you chatter on about things she would rather not discuss in front of me is making it worse.'

'Oh, sorry, Lizzy. I'm such a mean mouthed thing,' Bianca said contritely. 'Tell you what, why don't I take you back to the hotel? We could both do with an early night and Luc won't mind, will you, *caro*?'

This could only get worse if a rat jumped over the balustrade and told Bianca the full gruesome truth about why her best friend was out here with her man, Lizzy thought as she suffered Bianca's contrition with a lump in her throat that was threatening to turn into tears.

'Of course not,' the smooth-voiced man himself agreed.

'N-no—really.' She was almost consumed by self-hate, 'I can't let you leave your own party. Vito said he was going soon to catch up on his jet lag. I'll—I'll go back to the hotel with him.'

'No, I won't hear of it,' her wretched best friend said firmly. 'And Vito can come back with us so I can tell him off for getting you sloshed. Luc will organise a car.'

Dutifully, Luc De Santis straightened out of his relaxed pose against the balustrade. Lizzy cringed inside and refused to look at him as he strode past them to go inside.

She should confess, she *needed* to confess—but how could she? Bianca would be shocked. She might never forgive her. Their friendship would be over for good.

But what if Luc told her first? What if he thought it would make an amusing story to relay to his betrothed? How was she ever going to live with it if he did?

They were about to step into the limo when Luc touched Lizzy's arm. 'Don't do it, she will never forgive you,' he warned so softly that only she could hear him, shocking her further that he could read her mind. 'And if you have any sense you will steer clear of Vito Moreno,' he added grimly.

Then he turned to his fiancée to offer her a brief kiss good-night.

Vito's company in the car made the journey a whole lot easier for Lizzy because she could pretend to doze while he and Bianca talked. It vaguely occurred to her that the conversation was hushed and heated, but she assumed Bianca was keeping her promise to give him a hard time for the trick with the wine so she didn't listen.

And anyway, she did have a headache, one of those dull, throbbing aches that came when you didn't like yourself and knew the feeling was not going to change any time soon. When the two cousins decided to have a last drink in the bar before they went to their rooms, Lizzy made her escape and spent the night with her head stuffed beneath her pillow, trying not to remember what she had done.

But she should have listened to what the other two had been saying, she discovered early the next morning when hell arrived with the sound of urgent knocking on her door. If she'd listened she might have been able to stop Bianca from making the biggest mistake of her life.

As it was, all she could do was stand and listen in growing horror while Sofia Moreno poured it all out between thick, shaking sobs.

'She's gone!' Bianca's *mamma* choked out hysterically the moment that Lizzy open her door. 'She just packed all her things in the middle of the night and left the hotel! All this time and she never showed a single sign that they were planning this between them! How could she? How could he? What are people going to say? What about Luciano? Oh, I don't think I can bear it. She has thrown away a wonderful future. How could she do this to us? How could your foolish brother just turn up here and steal her away?'

Having assumed that Mrs Moreno had been referring to Vito, *'Matthew?'* Lizzy choked out in disbelief. 'Are you sure you meant my brother, Mrs Moreno?' she prompted unsteadily.

'Of course I mean Matthew!' the older woman shook out. 'He arrived here yesterday afternoon, apparently. He was *hiding* in Bianca's bathroom when I went to see her yesterday! Can you imagine it? She wasn't dressed and the bed was rumpled! *Dio mio*, it does not take much to guess what had been going on! Did you know about what they were planning to do, Elizabeth—did you?'

The fierce accusation straightened Lizzy's backbone. *'No,'* she denied adamantly. 'I'm as shocked about this as you are!'

'Well, I hope that is true,' Mrs Moreno said coldly. 'For I will never forgive you if you played along with this inexcusable thing!'

'I thought you meant she'd gone away with Vito,' Lizzy murmured dazedly.

'Vito? He's her cousin! Are you trying to make this situation worse than it already is?'

Thoroughly chastened by the appalled response, Lizzy could only mumble out an apology.

'Now someone is going to have to break the news to Luciano,' Bianca's mother sobbed. 'Bianca has left him a note but Luciano went to his Lake Como villa last night to prepare for our arrival tomorrow and my husband has left for the city to see to some business this morning—he doesn't even know yet what his wicked daughter has done to ruin our lives!'

The Villa De Santis stood on top of a rocky outcrop, its pale lemon walls kissed by the softening light of the afternoon sun.

Lizzy's stomach gave a nauseous flutter as she stepped from the water taxi onto the villa's private jetty with its newly painted ribs standing out in the brilliant sunshine against the darkness of the older wood. Another boat was already moored there, a sleek, racy-looking thing that completely demoralised the water taxi as it nudged in beside it.

Bianca's father had arranged for a car to bring her as far as Bellagio. They'd discussed if they should ring Luc to break the news to him, then decided he should be told face to face. At first Giorgio Moreno was going to make the trip himself, but he'd looked so ill that Lizzy had offered to come in his place.

His heart wasn't good and she felt responsible. How could she not feel responsible when it was her brother who'd caused all of this? But after her own utter stupidity of the night before the last thing she wanted to do right now was to come face to face with Luc De Santis.

The old quiver struck as she walked towards the iron gates that she assumed would lead to steps up to the villa. Behind her, she could hear the water taxi already moving away, its engines growling as it churned up the glinting blue water, leaving her feeling as if she had just been marooned on the worst place on earth.

A man appeared from out of the shadows on the other side of the gate, stopping her in her tracks with his piercing dark eyes that looked her up and down. She had to look a mess because she certainly felt one with her hair hanging loose round her pale face. And she was still wearing the same green top and white capris she'd pulled on so hurriedly this morning when Bianca's *mamma* had knocked on her door.

'May I help you, *signorina*?' the man questioned in coolly polite Italian.

Passing her nervous tongue across her lips, 'I've come with a letter for Signor De Santis,' Lizzy explained. 'M-my name is Elizabeth Hadley.'

He nodded his head and produced a cell phone, his dark eyes not leaving her for a second while he spoke quietly to whoever was listening on the other end. Then with another nod he unlocked the gate and opened it. 'You can go up, *signorina*,' he sanctioned.

With a murmured thanks Lizzy was about to step past him when a sudden thought made her stop. 'I-I will need a water taxi back to Bellagio,' she told him. 'I didn't think to ask the other one to wait.'

'I will see to it when you are ready to leave,' he assured her.

Offering another husky 'thank you', Lizzy continued on her way to discover a set of age-worn stone steps cut into the rock face. At the top of the steps she found soft green lawns and carefully tended gardens and a path leading to a stone terrace beyond which stood the villa with its long windows thrown open to the softest of breezes coming off the lake.

Beautiful, she thought, but that was as far as her observations went. She was too uptight, too anxious—scared witless, if she was going to be honest.

Another man was waiting for her on the terrace. He offered her a small stately bow and invited her to follow him. It was cool inside the villa, the decoration a mix of warm colours hung with beautiful tapestries and paintings in ornate gold frames. The man led the way to a pair of heavy wood doors, knocked, then opened one of them before stepping to one side in a silent invitation for her to pass through.

Needing to take in a deep breath before she could make herself go any further, Lizzy walked past the servant into a beautiful room with high stucco ceilings and long narrow windows that flooded the room with soft golden light. The walls were pale, the furniture dark and solid like the richly polished floor beneath her feet. Shelves lined with books filled narrow alcoves; a heavy stone fireplace dominated one wall. As she spun her gaze over sumptuously ancient dark red velvet chairs and elegant sofas she finally settled on the huge heavily carved desk set between two of the windows—and the man who was standing tall and still behind it.

Tension instantly grabbed hold of her throat and sent her heart sinking to her toes. He already knew about Bianca, Lizzy realised. It was stamped right there on his grimly cold face.

'You have a letter for me, I believe,' Luc De Santis prompted. No greeting, no attempt whatsoever to make this easier for her.

But then why should he—? 'H-how did you know?' Lizzy dared to ask him.

His eyes made a brief flick down her front, then away again. 'She was to be my wife. The position made her vulnerable to a certain kind of low-life out on the make, so of course I had a security team watching her.'

But they didn't stop her running away with Matthew? Lizzy would have loved to have asked the question but the way he was standing there in a steel-dark razor-sharp business suit and with his face carved into such cold, hard angles, the question remained just a thick lump in her throat as she made herself walk forward, feeling as if she were stepping on sharp needles all the way.

Coming to a halt in front of the desk, she set down the letter. Her heart was pounding in her ears as he held her still with his gaze for a taut second or two before he reached out and picked the letter up, then let yet another few seconds stretch before he finally broke the envelope seal.

After that there was nothing, just a long, long numbing silence while he stood behind his desk reading the words Bianca had used to jilt him with, and Lizzy stood with her eyes fixed helplessly on his lean dark face, aware that the power of his innate pride had to be the only thing stopping him from diminishing to a used and broken man.

'I'm—sorry,' she mumbled, knowing it was a wincingly inadequate thing to say but—what else was there for her to say?

He gave a curt nod of his head, eyes like gold crystal set between heavy black eyelashes still fixed on the single sheet of paper even as he slowly set it down on the desk.

'You were offered no forewarning of this?'

Lizzy felt her nails bite into the tender skin of her palms as she closed them into tense, anxious fists. 'Nothing,' she answered.

'Her family?'

She gave a helpless shake of her head. 'Y-you were there last night—she looked radiant. She—'

'My future bride basking in the glory of her good fortune,' he drawled in a cold, mocking lilt.

Pressing her lips together, Lizzy lowered her gaze and said nothing. It was so obvious now that Bianca had been putting on a fabulous act aimed to fool all of them last night. Now it all felt so horrible, the extravagantly romantic glitter and gloss just a huge cruel con. She'd floated around like a princess in her gold silk. She'd clung to this man, smiled at him so starry-eyed and in love. And everyone had smiled as they'd watched her, everyone had remarked on what a fabulous couple they made. Even Luc with his rather sardonic way of looking at everything had smiled for his beautiful betrothed. In some dark corner of her being, Lizzy had been dreadfully envious because not many women got to live their childhood dream of falling in love with and marrying her prince.

Not that Luc De Santis was a prince, because he wasn't. He was just formed from the same mould handsome princes came out of, with his tall dark good looks and his perfectly constructed body and the added kudos of inherited vast wealth that had come to him down through centuries of careful De Santis bridal selection.

Dynasties, Bianca had called it. 'I'm marrying into a dynasty because I have the right name and the right genetic fingerprint.'

It had been such a cynical thing to say that Lizzy had been shocked. 'But you love him, don't you?'

'Are you joking, *cara*?' she'd laughed. 'You've seen him. What girl in her right mind wouldn't fall in love with Luc? Even you if you were given the chance.'

Lizzy's slender shoulders twitched in guilty response to the sound of that airy challenge ringing inside her head, because she knew she had already developed a kind of fascination for this man and it nagged her conscience to death—especially after last night. But she also frowned because it was only now as she stood here having to face the fallout from her best friend's stunning deception that it was occurring to her just how cleverly Bianca had skirted around the question of her loving this man.

She watched as Luc picked up the letter again, long brown fingers lifting up the single sheet of snowy white of paper to re-read yet again what Bianca had written to him. His face remained cold—completely expressionless—yet Lizzy discovered that she couldn't breathe. It had something to do with the way his lips were being held in such a steady flat line and the way his nostrils flared as he drew in a breath.

He was angry, she realised, and she didn't blame him. Whether his heart was devastated was difficult to tell. The few occasions she'd been in his company—even last night—he'd always struck her as someone who did not feel much of anything.

Cold, hard, unemotional, arrogant, she found herself listing as she stood here waiting for him to speak. She supposed she could tag on other words like tall, dark and disgustingly gorgeous but all those words did was to describe his potently masculine outer shell. It was the first description that really said it all about the inner man.

The long silence dragged until it picked at her nerve-ends. In one part of her consciousness Lizzy knew she should be getting out of here now that she'd delivered the letter, but she was oddly reluctant to leave him alone.

She still felt responsible—though her common sense told her she wasn't. She felt—pity for him, though she knew he would probably be utterly contemptuous of her for daring to feel it.

Strange man, she thought, not for the first time, as she stood on the other side of the desk unable to take her eyes off his face. For all of his wealth and his power and high standing in Italian society she had never seen him as anything other than a man who stood alone. Even when he'd been with Bianca she'd sensed a reserve in him she had never been able to adequately explain.

'I…I suppose you're wondering where your engagement ring is,' she blurted out, needing to say something to fill in the unbearably tense empty space, and the ring had come up in discussion when Bianca's mother had said the same thing.

'No,' he denied without any inflection whatsoever. 'I would imagine that running off with a poor man has already sealed the ring's fate.'

Lizzy winced, cheeks heating at this cool reminder of the other issue in all of this she was having to deal with—the fact that the man Bianca had run off with also happened to be her very own brother.

'Matt isn't poor.' She felt compelled to defend Matthew's middle class earnings. It was, after all, the only thing about him she felt she could defend right now.

'In your estimation or mine?'

Oh, that was so very arrogant of him. Lizzy felt anger begin to rise even though she knew she didn't have the right to let it. 'Look—' with a tense twist she turned to the door '—I think I had better leave you to—'

'Running away like the other two?' he mocked her.

'No,' she denied that. 'I just think it's better that I go before I lose my temper.'

'So you have one?'

'Yes.' She swung back round only to find that he had come around the desk so quickly and silently she hadn't heard him move. Now he was leaning against it with his arms folded across his chest, Bianca's letter lying discarded on the desk behind him.

Surprise brought a soft gasp whispering from her throat. And a new kind of tension flared in the pit of her stomach at the way he was studying the little green top and white capris she'd pulled on so hurriedly this morning, and the wildly unruly state of her hair.

Last night she'd made a fool of herself with him. This morning she'd been awoken by hysterics and accusations from Bianca's parents that still rang in her head. Now this— this deeply unsettling man she'd been sent to face because Bianca's parents couldn't bring themselves to do it—and he was looking her over as if he couldn't believe she would dare to walk out of her room looking as she did.

Well, you try applying make-up when your fingers won't stop shaking, she told him silently as she suffered his cool appraisal that was so spiked by the glint of contempt. You try wondering what clothes to wear for an audience with a jilted man when your nerves were shot to death at the very prospect.

'During the week you have been here in my country I've watched you play the straight man to Bianca's high-strung and volatile temperament,' he said so suddenly it made Lizzy blink. 'I've watched you soothe her, calm her and even humour her. But I do not recall seeing you threaten to lose your temper with her even when she took it upon herself to mock or embarrass you, so why do you feel the need to lose your temper with me?'

'Y-you attacked my family.'

'I *attacked* your brother,' he amended. 'You don't believe I have the right?'

Of course he had the right. This time yesterday he had been one half of a glittering couple, his marriage to Bianca only a short week away. It was supposed to be the wedding of the year here in Italy, now it was about to become juicy fodder for every media outlet and it was her very own brother who'd turned it into that.

Lizzy moved jerkily, offering a small conciliatory flip of one hand despite feeling as though she were being whipped by his smooth cutting tone. 'I give you the right to despise my brother,' she acknowledged. 'I will even give you the right to be angry with me because I'm the sister of the man who ran off with your bride. But I will not—' and her chin came up, eyes sparking with challenge '—stand here and let you deride the fact that we are not rich like you.'

'I did that?'

Lizzy pressed her lips together and nodded. He wasn't the only one around her who'd had his pride battered today. She'd had to put up with some pretty mean observations from Bianca's parents about her brother that had been difficult to swallow down.

'Then I apologise.'

Lizzy didn't believe him. Facing up to him like this, she didn't see or hear so much as a hint of apology in his tone. But, 'Thank you,' she responded politely anyway. 'Now if you don't mind, I'll leave you to—'

'How did you get here?'

Once again she was about to turn away when he stopped her. 'By water taxi across the lake from Bellagio,' she said.

He nodded. 'Then it seems to me that you're stuck here until I arrange your return across the lake.'

'Y-your man on the jetty said he would see to—'

'It's a case of priorities, Miss Hadley,' he cut in. 'My instructions take precedence around here, you see.'

He was pulling rank, Lizzy recognised, lips parting to say something then snapping shut again when it suddenly struck her that he was burning for a fight.

Did she take him on? The question lit up her brain while her common sense told her to just get the heck out of here because she wasn't up to his weight. He lived in this fabulous villa on the banks of Lake Como, he owned a beautiful apartment in Milan, which was why she'd been so surprised to find he'd taken a suite at the hotel last night, and at least three more fabulous homes Bianca had mentioned set in different parts of the world. He lived the high-powered jet setting lifestyle of the world's business heavyweights. He even flew the world in comfort in his very own executive jet.

And just out there tied to his private jetty floated his sleek glinting white private power boat that could spin her back across the lake in ten minutes—but he was refusing to give the order because he felt the need to kick someone around a bit and she happened to be conveniently there.

Lizzy looked away from him then back again, not at all sure

what to do next. 'You do know you're being petty,' she sighed out finally.

'Green,' he murmured.

'Green—what?' she flicked out, completely thrown by the comment.

'Your eyes when you're angry,' he provided. 'Most of the time they are a soft placid grey.'

'They can spit pretty sharp daggers too when I'm cornered,' she reacted.

'Let me test that,' he offered. 'You have known all along what they were planning.'

It was not a question. 'No,' Lizzy insisted. 'I *told* you I did not know.'

But even as she said it her insides were creasing guiltily because perhaps she had seen it coming only it had been so much simpler to just block it out.

'I did not have you down as a liar, Elizabeth,' he said coolly.

'I'm not lying!' Frowning—annoyed with herself as well as with him *and* this horrible position she'd been put in, 'I did not see it coming,' she insisted a second time, 'but I admit I feel some responsibility because I think I should have done.'

'Because you knew they were lovers?'

Did he have to put it as calmly as that? Shifting her tense stance, 'Yes,' she answered, deciding to be blunt with him since he didn't seem to possess a single sensitive nerve in his body. 'For a while, several years ago.'

'Childhood sweethearts.' His hard mouth flicked out the semblance of a smile.

A bit more than that, she thought as she pinned her lips together and made no comment at all. Then, because she couldn't take the probing glint in his eyes, she let out a sigh.

'You were right about the wealth difference meaning something. He's never going to be good enough for her you know.'

'Whereas I hit all the right criteria for a Moreno?'

Lizzy offered a shrug this time—what else could she do?
He did hit all the right criteria. He was everything the Morenos
expected their beautiful daughter to marry. Matthew wasn't.
Matthew came right out of middle class England. He'd
enjoyed the necessary public-school education to give him a
great kick-start in life but that was about it. Until this recent
financial crisis her family had survived comfortably on its
small business income—no more, no less. Matthew was
expected to take over the business from their father one day
and to marry some nice middle class Englishwoman who
would not demand more from him than he was able to provide.

Bianca on the other hand was always going to expect more.
She was always going to have what she wanted in life even if
it meant providing it herself. Matthew wouldn't be able to
cope with that. His ego would take such a hard knocking he'd
never be happy, whereas this man had so much money of his
own he wouldn't give a toss as to how his beautiful wife spent
her own money, and *his* ego would stay firmly intact.

'She will come back,' she promised. 'She just needs time
to—sort her head out.'

'Not her heart?' The dry distinction made Lizzy wince.

'I'm sure she loves you,' she persisted. 'She's just not ready
to commit to marriage. If you just give her time, then I—'

Black eyebrows with a fascinating silken gloss arched her
a curious look. 'Are you actually standing there, Miss Hadley,
suggesting that I should wait for Bianca to sort her head out?'

Well, was she? Lifting her chin, 'If you love her—yes,'
she insisted.

'Then you are a romantic fool because it is not going to

happen.' He moved suddenly, straightening away from the desk. 'There is a wedding arranged for next Saturday morning and I intend to make sure that it goes ahead.'

Without a bride? Lizzy stared at him. 'You mean—you're going to find her and drag her back to marry you?' A silly kind of laugh left her throat at the very image of Bianca being dragged by this man down the church aisle kicking and screaming.

'No.' Reaching behind him, his long fingers picked Bianca's letter up again—this time to fold it with slow, neat precision. 'I mean to replace her with someone else.'

She was pretty much held in his thrall by now. 'Just like that?'

'Just like that.' He nodded and made her gasp as he ripped the letter into small pieces, then calmly dropped them into the waste-paper basket standing by the desk.

It was such a cold act of dismissal of Bianca and everything she should mean to him that Lizzy began to feel slightly sick.

'You will have to move quickly to put your life in order, of course, but with my assistance I think it can be achieved in time.'

She dragged her eyes up from the discarded pieces of paper. It took a few seconds for his words to actually sink in— then they did sink in and Lizzy took a jerky step backwards.

'M-my life is fine as it is.'

'I don't doubt it,' he acknowledged. 'But will it be *fine* by tomorrow when I inform the authorities that your brother has emptied your company bank account?'

CHAPTER THREE

'TH-THAT was not in the least bit funny,' Lizzy husked out, her heart beginning to thump heavily against her ribs because this conversation had just taken a sinister turn for the bad. 'I know you're hurt and angry, and I accept you feel the need to kick someone around in response. But that doesn't give you the right to lie about my family!'

'Your *brother*.' Once again Luc made the distinction. 'I restrict my accusations to only one member of your family. The rest I will honour with the benefit of the doubt—for now.'

He was losing her with every cool word he threw at her. 'You suspect my *father* of being a crook? Where do you get off believing you can say something like that?'

'I "get off", as you so nicely describe it, by being a banker,' he responded. 'And being a banker I am not prone to let my heart rule my head.'

'You've lost me.' Lizzy stared at him in bewilderment.

'Then let me explain. Bianca is a very wealthy woman.'

'I know that,' she snapped out.

'A little—shall we call it family ingenuity?—and she could be misled into believing that her childhood sweetheart had hit it rich.'

'I think you need time on your own for some quiet contemplation,' Lizzy told him curtly, and did what she should have done minutes before and turned on her heel to leave.

'Your—close relationship to her made me curious,' he continued smoothly as she walked. 'So I decided it would be wise to have you and your family checked out.'

'Checked out?' Once again she swung round to stare at him. 'So where the heck do you get off *now* thinking you have the right to do that?'

'The right of Bianca's future husband who was—er—puzzled by your close friendship to her. You're not her type, Miss Hadley,' he stated bluntly. 'Anyone with eyes can see that Bianca comes from a different side of the fence, yet here you are, staying in the best hotel in Milan paid for with her family's money, wearing clothes she has bought for you so you would not look out of place in the company of her rich friends, and about to play the honoured role at her wedding as her chief bridesmaid.'

'*Was* about to,' she hit back, infuriated by the nasty slant he was putting on everything.

'Was,' he acknowledged with a cool dip of his dark head. 'So I decided to do some checking, and guess what I found out? Hadley's is not merely enjoying a temporary cash crisis as I was given to believe, it is about to go under altogether. Your father is in debt up to his neck. Your brother hates the whole engineering scenario and resents the fact that he is expected to stay in the business.'

Lizzy flushed. 'Matthew wanted to be an artist.'

'Oh, how romantically right for him,' her persecutor mocked. 'With his golden good looks and his ravaged sensibilities he makes the perfect rescue for an impressionable thing like Bianca—whereas you,' he went on before Lizzy could say anything, 'you make the perfect level-headed foil to keep Bianca's starry eyes blinded to what your brother is really about.'

Lizzy straightened her trembling tense shoulders. 'Have you quite finished slaughtering my family?' she demanded, wanting to slap his face.

'Haughty,' he remarked. 'I like it.'

'Well, I don't like you!' she hit back. 'Bianca and I have been friends since we were twelve years old—her wealth or my lack of it has never been an issue between us because that's not what true friendship is about! *My* family works hard for its living, *signor*,' she defended proudly. '*All* of us work hard! *My* father did not waste his life swanning around the world enjoying the useless life of an overindulged playboy from a filthy rich but totally dysfunctional family from which you, sadly, were the cynical end result! And *if* my brother is different from the rest of us at least he knows he is loved! Whereas you, *signor*, with your untold wealth and your inherited arrogance, can't ever have been loved to be so cold and suspicious of everything and everyone that you have to dig into their lives behind their backs!'

'Dysfunctional?' His glinting gold eyes narrowed on her. 'You have a very cynical view of *my* family history, Miss Hadley. It makes me curious as to where you collected *your* information and, more interestingly, why you did.'

Lizzy tensed as if he'd shot her. She'd walked herself right into that prickly trap. 'I...Bianca,' she said, hating the hot rush of colour that mounted her cheeks because she knew she'd been guilty of spending hours looking him up on the internet. 'She described marrying you as joining a dynasty because she had the right name and the right genetic fingerprint,' she crashed on. 'It sounded so cold and businesslike to me that I thought she was joking at the time, but now I see that she wasn't joking at all or you would be standing there too over-whelmed by your broken heart to even think of putting such a cold suggestion to me!'

'Finished?' he asked when she finally ran down to a breath-less choke.

Shaking all over now, Lizzy pressed her trembling lips together and nodded.

So did he, and straightened from the desk. 'Then with the character assassination over we will return to the subject of our wedding,' he said.

'I am *not* marrying you!' Lizzy all but shrieked at him. Was he mad?

He moved round the desk. 'You kissed me last night.'

The reminder forced her into dragging in a sharp intake of breath. She'd hoped he'd forgotten it. She'd prayed all night long that she'd just dreamt up that awful, shocking stolen kiss.

'I was drunk—'

'You appeared to be.' He was opening a drawer now and taking out a thick folder which he placed on the desk. 'Of course, you could have been playing with me as diversionary tactics to keep my eyes blinded to what Bianca was up to.'

She was so stunned by that cynical slant on her stupid be-haviour, when she opened her mouth nothing came out of it.

He smiled—coolly. 'Everything is open to misinterpretation, Elizabeth. When you—came on to me like some very tipsy sweet, shy virgin, I was—flattered. Now?' He flipped open the file. 'How different things can look in the cool light of day and with common sense re-established. Come and take a look…'

It was not a suggestion. Lizzy felt a tingling prickle spread across the surface of her skin as she forced her shaky legs to move back to the desk. He twisted the file around, then stabbed at it with a long finger to draw her eyes down.

She found herself staring at a bank statement—a bank statement with the Hadley name printed at its head. 'H-how did you get hold of that?' she whispered.

'I'm a banker,' he reminded her—again. 'With the right contacts and the right strings to pull I can get anything I want.'

There was a double meaning in that remark that did not pass by Lizzy.

'Look where I'm pointing,' he prompted.

She looked, then stilled as if turned to stone.

'The date shows that your company account received a heavy injection of funds just two days ago,' he spelled out what she had already seen.

Five and a half million…Lizzy had never seen five and a half million written down in black and white before. To her it was a gasping amount.

'If you look at the next entry,' her tormentor persisted, 'you will see that the five and a half million pounds was withdrawn again on the same day.'

'No,' she breathed, refusing to believe what it was he was implying here.

Then she jerked out of her shocked stasis. 'I need to ring my father.' White as a sheet now, she turned dizzily and headed for the door.

'You will not call anyone,' that ruthlessly calm voice instructed. 'At this precise moment I have control of this situation and I mean to hold onto it. Bringing someone else into it will risk that control.'

'Control over what?' Lizzy swung around to stare at him.

'You,' he provided. 'Until you brought me Bianca's letter I was still puzzling as to why your *father* had successfully negotiated the loan he needed to save his company only to instantly remove all the money and put it somewhere else.'

Lizzy suddenly needed to sit down somewhere. The only chair handy was the one placed several feet away from the desk. She sank into it. Her head was swimming, the complicated puzzle of what was really going on here beyond her stunned capabilities right now.

'Your brother is the only other person besides your father authorised to access this account. Put it all together, Elizabeth,' he encouraged. 'It does not take much effort to calculate that your brother has taken the money to fund his romantic elopement with Bianca. If you did play a part in their disappearance then I hope you have taken into account that you have been left here to carry the can.'

At that precise moment Lizzy didn't care what position she was sitting here in. She was worried about her father. If—*when*—he found out what Matthew had done he was going to—

'Of course, I must also point out that if you are genuinely innocent of any role in this, then you are still about to carry the can,' that oh, so hateful voice injected, 'because *I* want reparation for being taken for an idiot, and if that means putting you into Bianca's wedding dress and marrying you in her place, then that is what is going to happen.'

'For goodness' sake!' She jumped to her feet. 'Don't you think this situation is bad enough without you trying to fly to the moon?'

He *laughed*! Lizzy couldn't believe she was hearing it! 'You have a quaint way of expressing yourself.'

If the desk hadn't been between them she would have thrown herself at him in fury! 'I am *not* marrying you!' she had to make do with shouting out.

'Why not?' Throwing himself into the chair behind the desk, he arched her a challenging look. 'Is there something wrong with me?'

'Don't ask me to make a list,' Lizzy muttered, wrapping her arms around her body and glaring at him while her mind shot off in all directions trying to find the sense in this mad situation. 'You've got the eyes of a lion,' she then heard herself murmur out of absolutely nowhere!

'Lions mark their territory, jealously protect their women, but they do not hunt,' he responded lazily.

'Is that supposed to mean something?' Lizzy snapped, wishing she'd kept her silly mouth shut about his eyes.

He offered a shrug. 'I am ready to mate. I want—cubs. I did not have to hunt for Bianca because she's always been there in the background of my life ready to claim once she'd grown up. Now here you are.' Those damned golden eyes fixed on her face. 'You don't need hunting either because I have you caught and shackled by your brother's stealing tendencies and an attraction for me you find impossible to hide.'

'I am not attracted to you in any way, shape or form,' she denied stiffly.

'Then why the sweet, tender kiss?'

'Oh, for goodness' sake.' He was like a dog with a particularly juicy bone to gnaw on. 'It wasn't a kiss! I accidentally brushed my mouth against your throat! *And* I was drunk!' she added for good measure.

'Tipsy on months of guilty lusting,' he taunted. 'Your attraction for me has been right there in your body language from the first time we met in London and you couldn't stop yourself from hungrily drinking me in,' he declared arrogantly. 'It was there when we met in the lift in Milan. It was definitely there last night when we danced together and I gave in to temptation and waltzed you out onto the terrace. And it was absolutely there in that dizzily irresistible brush you allowed your lips and the tender moist tip of your tongue to make against my throat.'

Feeling as if she were drowning in the hot steam of her own embarrassment, Lizzy struck back. 'You are more than ten years older than me, and that makes you really old in my eyes, *signor.*'

'Thirty-four to twenty-two is a good difference, *cara.*' It was the first time he had used that endearment to her and it quivered down her spine like a terrible sin. 'It means I can offer you experience and fidelity, having worked out my studding period when I was your age. Whereas you will give me your youth, your beauty, your wonderful smooth, tight, creamy white body—and your *loyalty* when you switch it from your friend and your brother to protect your father from the worst scandal you can possibly imagine if his name gets dragged into this.'

'How cold you are.' Arms tightening across her body, she shivered.

'Not between the sheets.'

'And that's it?' Lizzy flashed. 'Between the sheets I get your warmer side and your fabulous experience while out of them I get to play the role of your very rich, very pampered, *young* trophy wife and face—saver? No affection offered, no *love?*'

'Love is an overrated fantasy.'

'Coming from you I expect that it is.'

'Are you digging at my dysfunctional family again?'

'I'm digging at the fact that I don't like you very much.'

'But you desire me like crazy,' he confided silkily.

Lizzy made a tense movement of her body, a frown like a dusky cloud settling across her face.

'You're turned on just by looking at me,' he continued relentlessly. 'You have this instinctive knowledge that the sex is going to be so good between us and it nags at you like a persistent ache. If I stepped round this desk right now and drew you into my arms you would go up like a Roman candle.'

'Without the bed and the sheets?' The sarcasm was out before she could stop it. If she'd meant it as a slap at his horrible self-confidence all it did was to make him laugh— softly, deeply, a seriously disturbing, huskily attractive sound that came from somewhere low down in his chest. 'I can be adaptable, *bella mia*, if encouraged.'

Hating his lazy, laid-back superior poise and self-assurance, she was riled into taking him on. 'So if I decided one day to, say, stroll into your office and demand sex with you while you're busy on the phone making more millions?' she challenged.

'Is that one of your fantasies?' he quizzed, bringing a flush crawling up her throat. 'Then, of course, I would do my best to accommodate you—just make sure you arrive wearing no tights.' He ran his eyes down over her. 'Panties can be dealt with, tights demand a distinct lack of finesse, and if your fantasy forces me to make millions while I accommodate you then, the easier you make it for me, the more pleasure you will get out of it.'

'God, you're insufferable.' Lizzy spun her back to him, barely able to believe the calm insolence with which he'd said all of that and despising herself for giving him the chance.

'Just more experienced at this game than you are,' he told her. 'Though sex across my desk while I talk on the telephone is novel,' he admitted. 'Maybe we will try it.'

Her slender shoulders hunched and she lifted up her hands to grab at them as if doing so would keep his outrageous suggestion out. It didn't matter that she knew she had started it. He was right and he was so much more experienced at this game so all she'd managed to do by taking him on was to walk herself right into his tormenting trap.

'Do you know where the runaway lovers have gone?' The question came at her right out of the blue.

'No.' She shook her head.

'Do you know, then, how your hair catches fire in the sunlight coming in through the window behind you?'

That oh, so silky spoken observation flared her hair around her face as she spun around. 'For goodness' sake, will you stop playing this crazy game now?' she shrilled out.

'No game,' he denied, and he was lounging in the chair now, so damn sure of himself and everything he'd dared to say to her that she couldn't take her eyes off him, couldn't *not* be aware of the sensual pulse emanating from every part of his long, lean body—like a man with his desire on the rise. The half-lowered eyelids, the low burning glow of gold in his eyes. The mouth that had softened to show its capacity for enjoying the pleasures of the senses and the challenge in his expression that wasn't really a challenge but a heat-seeking message of absolute promise.

'Marry me next week and I will lift your sex life from the disappointingly mundane to the bone-melting exciting,' he offered.

Lizzy gaped. 'Who told you my sex life was—?'

'Bianca, who else?'

Her best friend, *Bianca,* had said that about her—to him?

'She gave you two different lovers, neither of which lasted beyond the first venture between the sheets. Englishmen, of course,' he said, 'with a fumbling lack of finesse.'

'And you think speaking to me like this shows finesse?' The heat of dismay and the sharp sting of hurt were crawling all over her. She had never felt so let down by Bianca in their ten year friendship! How dared she speak to him about Lizzy's personal life—how dared she tell such wicked lies about it? 'Well I don't,' she said grimly. 'And I am not going to listen to any more of it.'

She turned—once again to leave.

But that relentlessly cool voice was not going to let her go. 'Marry me next week and I will bail your father out of debt, pay off his *loan* and send in my own team of experts to help oversee the recovery of his company,' it continued, bringing her to yet another quivering standstill. 'Which,' he added, 'I will fund until it can stand on its own two feet. *Don't* marry me next week, and I will light the litmus under an embezzlement scandal then just stand back to watch it go up.'

The bottom line, Lizzy recognised, the very lowest point he was prepared to go to to save his pride.

'Someone owes me, Elizabeth,' he went on grimly. 'Either you pay the debt or your family pays that debt. The fact that I desire you is the only thing giving you the luxury of choice.'

'This is just revenge,' she whispered.

'Revenge is a form of passion, *mi amore*. My advice would be to grab my offer while the passion for revenge still rides hot in my blood.' Words…he was clever with words. So clever he was tying her head and her emotions into knots. Moving in a daze, she went to stand in front of one of the windows, staring out at the glittering lake backed by the misty grey mountains in the distance and the town of Bellagio just a simmering cluster of white on the opposite bank of the lake.

So near yet so far away, she thought bleakly. She could be marooned on an island with Luc as her jailor. As he'd already pointed out, she wasn't going anywhere without his express say-so.

And Matthew, she considered. Why had he done it? He was older than her, but only by eighteen months, and he'd had good reason to resent their father for his strict refusal to accept that his son had a right to choose what he wanted to do with his own life. Had he taken the money in an angry desire to hit back at their father? Had Bianca encouraged him to do it because it was his father who'd put a stop to their romantic plans to marry two years ago?

Mrs Moreno had told Edward Hadley that he was tackling their romance the wrong way. Ban them from seeing each other and you will create Romeo and Juliet, she'd warned in her dramatic way.

Dramatic or not, it appeared now that what she had predicted had come true—or at least partly true. Lizzy hoped to goodness that the two of them were not going to go the whole hog and drink poison.

But to take things as far as they already had done seemed fantastical to Lizzy, especially when she knew that both of them had been involved in other relationships since their break-up—the most important one being the one involving this man sitting here waiting for her answer.

And, she was going to have to admit it, she was hurt that neither of them had confided in her. Though maybe that part was not so fantastical because she would have tried to stop them and they would have known it.

'What will happen to them when they eventually resurface?' she questioned huskily.

'Bianca has done nothing wrong other than to change her mind about marrying me—a woman's prerogative,' he dryly pointed out. 'As it stands for your brother right now, it has to be up to your father and the bank to say what will happen to him.'

Smooth, blunt and honest. He didn't even bother to repeat that he was the one holding the axe suspended over Matthew's head.

Or she was.

'I won't wear Bianca's wedding dress,' she whispered. 'I won't marry you in a church. I won't let you buy me anything that isn't absolutely essential for the role you want me to play for you. And I won't stop working, because I need to earn money to pay you back every penny you invest in Hadley's.'

'You *will* marry me just as everything has been arranged already,' he countered. 'You *will* accept with grace anything I choose to bestow on you and you will *not* go back to work.'

Lizzy swung to face him and was shocked by the kick she received low in her gut because he was so— 'Y-you can't just slot me into Bianca's place just like that,' she said as she attempted to override over what her body was trying to make her feel. 'The authorities won't allow it!'

'At the risk of sounding boringly repetitive, money talks.'

Money talks. And so it did. 'I think I hate you,' she whispered.

'Nevertheless you will take up Bianca's place with pride and dignity and fool the world into thinking it was you and I and not them who discovered they couldn't live without each other. And you will *not* pay me back anything other than with our first child seeded in your womb. With that goal in mind you will come to our marriage bed with warmth and honesty—which means you will not fight against what we both desire.'

'Can I please go now?'

She was so close to tears she was barely managing to hold herself together and, the choked request brought a soft curse biting at the back of his throat. He came to his feet, made a move as if he was going to come towards her, then abruptly pulled himself up.

'In a moment.' The lean, handsome shape of his face had drawn into a cold, hard, impenetrable mask again. 'We have a few more details left to discuss.'

'Discuss?' Lizzy picked up. 'Doesn't that imply that I'm allowed an opinion?'

'Probably—' he grimaced '—but seemingly you are not,

because I was about to say that I prefer to speak to your father before you do. Not up for discussion,' he added when she went to speak. 'Also, you will not be returning to the hotel in Milan because you will be living right here from now on.'

Lizzy pressed her fingers to her lips to try and stop them from trembling. 'Like a prisoner.'

'No,' he denied that. 'I can protect you here from the fallout about to hit us when I make the announcement later today, whereas the hotel in Milan will be put under siege. I also have an itchy suspicion that the Morenos are not going to like this turn in events. You will feel sorry for them. I, on the other hand, will not.'

'What a joke.' She laughed thickly. 'Why do you think they delegated the job of coming here to me?'

Surprise momentarily lit his golden eyes up. 'So they're scared. Good, that works in our favour.'

'Will you stop talking as if this has anything to do with me when it hasn't?' Lizzy choked. 'I'm just the pawn here you're using to salve your wounded arrogance!'

'Pawns are very powerful pieces on the chessboard.'

'Oh, shut *up*!' she flared up. 'Have you *no* idea how infuriating it is that you have a slick answer to everything?'

'Seemingly not.' A hint of a wry smile touched the corners of his mouth. 'I will try to curb the habit,' he offered.

Pulling in a deep breath, Lizzy let it out again. '*Now* can I go?' she repeated.

Reaching out for the telephone sitting on his desk, he stabbed in a set of numbers, then began shedding instructions in Italian to whoever was listening on the other end while Lizzy listened and wished to God that she didn't find the rich smooth tones in his voice so attractive when he spoke his native language.

'Did you understand any of that?' he asked a moment later.

'Some.' She nodded. Having Bianca as a friend meant she'd learned to speak Italian pretty well over the years. 'You were arranging a room for me.'

'It will be ready in a few minutes.'

Stepping around the desk, he began walking towards her. Lizzy immediately tensed up, sheer instinct placing her onto the balls of her feet like a runner waiting for the sound of the gun.

'W-what?' she said warily when he pulled to a stop in front of her.

He said nothing, just held her eyes with one of his disconcertingly steady looks and lifted up a hand to her cheek with a crazily disturbing gentle touch. Lizzy released a broken little gasp, one part of her wanting her to jerk back from him, but another part refusing to let her give in to it when it would only tell him things she didn't want him to know.

And he was beautiful, there was just no denying it even though she very much wished that she could. For all of his coldness and his arrogance, his ruthless determination to have his way and the grim anger she instinctively knew was still stirring away behind the control, Luc De Santis possessed a physical beauty that was just so dangerously compelling.

His eyelids drooped as he moved his fingers to gently touch the corner of her mouth. 'I will make you a deal,' he said in the husky dark tones of a man about to get really personal. 'You can pay me back the money you owe me with kisses. Let's say—one kiss a euro,' he suggested. 'Starting from now...'

His dark head lowered and his lips parted, his fingers sliding to curve around her nape beneath the heavy fall of her hair.

Push him away, her one single working brain cell was screaming at her, but she remained perfectly still, tingling inside and breathlessly fascinated by the expression on his face as it came ever closer to hers.

A soft, helpless breath prized her lips apart, he scooped it away with the lick of his tongue, then he was kissing her, crushing his lips against her lips, warm and soft and undeniably—nice.

Then he was drawing back a little, searching her eyes to check out her response. 'Grey,' he murmured and grimaced. 'I am going to have to do better than that.'

He lowered his head again, long fingers guiding the tilt of her face to accept his second kiss and this time the sensual thrust of his tongue. Heat flared inside her for a second, and she was dimly aware of making a helpless groan.

Once again he withdrew. 'Almost green,' he said, 'and that makes two euros repaid to me.'

Then he smiled a brief smile, let go of her face and turned to stride away, pulling the door open and closing it behind him again, leaving Lizzy standing there, numbed by the knowledge that she'd just given him, free and for nothing, all the proof he needed that what he'd said about her wanting him was true.

She had no resistance to fight him with. She had been struggling with her attraction to him for weeks. And she did go up like a flame when he kissed her. Even if the flame had been only brief—it had happened. He'd felt it. As far as he was concerned their deal was sealed.

CHAPTER FOUR

THE MEDIA went into a frenzy. Lizzy learned, reluctantly, to be thankful that Luc had shown the foresight to move her into his home. No one was allowed near the villa without his express permission. No one was allowed to contact her by phone.

Except for her father. When Lizzy was eventually allowed to contact him she found him hurt and angry and confused. He couldn't believe that she of all people could put herself between her best friend and the man Bianca was supposed to marry. He was disappointed in her. 'I tell you, Lizzy, I hope you're not taking a leaf out of your mother's book.'

It had been the ultimate criticism that made her cringe in shame.

Matthew, on the other hand, had at last done something to earn their father's respect because—apparently—he'd chased over to Milan and taken poor Bianca away before the scandal hit the press. No, he had not heard from her brother. No, he had no idea where they'd gone.

And, most amazing of all, he hadn't a clue that Matthew had emptied the company bank account. 'An error,' he called it when she dared to broach the subject, 'which the bank put right the very next day.'

Even Luc came in for her father's reluctant respect because

he'd been so ready to apologise for the distress they had caused so many people. And, of course, Luc was going to make recompense helping Hadley's to get back on its feet.

Only Lizzy was to be left out in the cold and his comparison to her mother told her why. But, yes, of course he would be there to give her away on Saturday. Luc expected it.

Good old Luc, Lizzy thought bitterly.

And as for the Morenos, they had a field-day talking to the press and telling them how their poor daughter's best friend had stolen Luc away.

'I'm a marriage-wrecker,' she informed the root of her character assassination via the telephone while she paced angrily up and down in front of his desk. She was speaking to Luc via the phone because after he'd walked out of here three days ago he had left the villa altogether and had not bothered to come back. 'Matthew is the saving knight on the white charger. Bianca is the betrayed damsel he saved. And you,' she told him, 'are the absolute epitome of man's idea of a man. Big enough to acknowledge your mistake in your choice of bride and arrogant enough to grab the one you decided you wanted instead!'

He laughed. Lizzy wanted to fly at him in a rage but he wasn't here and—what difference would it make if he were? She would still be all the bad things people were saying about her and...

'When you said I would be the one to carry the can, you really meant it,' she whispered.

'Once the fuss has died down you will become the envy of every woman out there, trust me,' he drawled.

'Because I've been fortunate enough to catch you?' That was just so typically arrogant of him! 'Well, I don't feel fortunate. I feel unforgivably used. So if you're expecting me to sign this prenuptial contract your lawyers have just delivered here, then you go to hell, Luc, because I'm not signing anything!'

With that she slammed down the phone.

He arrived at the villa a short hour later. Lizzy was in her room. It was a beautiful suite with views over the lake and a balcony she dared not step onto because of the million cameras trained on the windows from the ton of boats moored out there on the lake.

Curled up on a sofa reading a book that had no words printed on the pages as far as Lizzy could tell, she said 'Go away,' without looking at him.

He slammed the contract down on her lap. 'Sign,' he commanded.

Lizzy ignored him. She was wearing a short blue cotton skirt and a little lemon top, the sunlight coming in through the long window behind her setting the twisting mass of untidy curls on fire around her shoulders and face. She wore no make-up and she wore no shoes. And if any man was used to seeing his women primped to an eyelash it was Luciano Genovese Marcelo De Santis.

A really impressive proper fountain pen arrived on the top of the prenuptial contract. 'Sign,' he repeated.

Toying idly with a spiralling curl, Lizzy shifted her lips into a stubborn purse.

On a heavy sigh he turned and strode away from her. She heard the rustle of clothes. Reluctantly allowing herself a glance in his direction, she saw the jacket to an iron-grey suit land on the back of a bedside chair. By the time he turned back to face her, his tie had been loosened from around the collar of his blue striped shirt and her stomach muscles curled and stung.

The man meant business—she could tell by the look of determination she glimpsed on his lean, sleek honey-gold face before she quickly looked away.

He came back to where she was sitting with her long bare legs curled beneath her and the contract still resting across her thighs. Glancing around him, he reached out for a pretty pale blue brocade chair and brought it close to the sofa, then sat down.

'Listen,' he said, leaning forward to rest his forearms on his elegantly clad knees. 'I cannot marry you unless you sign the prenuptial agreement.'

'Shame,' Lizzy drawled, unperturbed, 'because I don't agree with it.'

He pulled in a breath. 'It is purely a business necessity,' he explained, keeping his voice deliberately level and calm. 'I am the head of a very prestigious bank. I am also worth more than a king's fortune. If you don't sign this my shareholders will lose confidence in me for being too weak to protect myself.'

'Then don't tell them,' Lizzy said rationally.

'They will find out. Things like this inevitably get out,' he reasoned. 'You will be judged a greedy gold-digger and I will be judged a fool.'

'So I will be judged a greedy gold-digging marriage-breaker.' Lizzy shrugged. 'What's one more label when I'm already covered in them?'

His hand snaked out. He took the book from her fingers and grimly tossed it aside. Next he picked up the fountain pen and held it under her nose.

'Sign,' he insisted.

Lizzy stared at the pen but didn't take it.

'Please,' he added.

She released a sigh. 'Strike out the bit about who gets the children in the event of a divorce,' she said heavily.

Without uttering a single word in protest Luc picked up the contract, found the relevant clause and struck lines through with the pen and even added his signature in a bold, sure, elegant scrawl.

'Now do the same with the one about me getting—whatever amount you've had put in there,' she murmured.

'No,' he refused.

'Take it or leave it,' Lizzy warned stubbornly.

'Then I will leave it.' He stood up with the contract and walked away. 'Our marriage is off. You have an hour to pack your things and get out of my villa, Miss Hadley,' he informed her. 'Take my advice and leave by the servant's entrance if you don't want to be swamped by the waiting press. Oh, and don't forget to tell your father that he owes me five and a half million pounds and the bank another five and a half million pounds.'

With that he hooked up his jacket and headed to the door.

Lizzy shot to her feet. 'All right, I'll sign!' she snapped, furious with herself for taking it so far that she'd lost the higher ground.

He paused, all lean, dark, sexy male with a way of holding himself that made Lizzy hate the trickle of awareness she felt heating up her insides.

He turned, that, oh, so clever face revealing absolutely nothing but cool authority as he walked back to her, dropped his jacket on the back of his vacated chair, then silently handed her the contract and the pen.

Spinning away, Lizzy stepped up to a little table by the window and scrawled her signature, then spun back to hand him the contract and the pen.

He took them in his long brown fingers—then calmly dropped them on the floor. The next thing she knew she was locked in his arms. Her shocked exclamation earned her nothing but the fierce pressure of his mouth and the hot, hard, probing thrust of his tongue. In the dim distant swell of her own pounding heartbeat, she was aware of the hunger he fed into that kiss and the tension locked into his hard-muscled frame. One of his hands took rough hold of her hair while the other was a clamp on her hip that kept her pressed tightly up against him.

And if she had never experienced the full force of a man's passion before, then she was learning all about it now. He kissed her deeply until she whimpered; he let her feel the growing power of his desire. He muttered something when she trembled against him, then he swung her off her feet and carried her to the bed.

'Don't,' she choked out when he lowered her down there and looked as if he was going to follow.

But he didn't follow. He stood there looking down at her, making her feel small and weak and very vulnerable as he flicked the burning gold heat of his gaze over the hectic rise and fall of her breasts and her tensely curling bare toes.

Those eyes came back to her eyes, then dropped to the reddened swell of her mouth. 'That's three euros paid off your debt to me, Miss Hadley,' he informed her coolly and turned, went to recover the prenuptial contract, his pen and his jacket, and strode out of the door.

But not without Lizzy seeing the heat that streaked across his high cheekbones, or the visible signs of his arousal he'd found impossible to control. Curling up on the bed, she hugged herself and wished she understood what was making her tick these days. Wished she understood why watching him lose his unflappable control had excited her so badly she had to press her thighs together in a futile attempt to smother the sensation.

A helicopter arrived to transport her to her wedding. Shiny white and sparkling, it landed on the stretch of lawn that overlooked the lake. That morning a famous designer had arrived from Milan bringing her wedding gown. He was the first person she had seen besides Luc and the household staff for a week. She knew her father was here in Italy because she'd spoken to him on the phone. She knew that Luc was staying not far away because she'd seen a different helicopter with the De Santis logo glinting gold on his tail fly over the villa twice a day.

And she knew she was still the centre of a media frenzy because a maid had told her, giggling and excited about it, whereas all Lizzy could think was—how was she going to cope when her secure haven here in the villa had been taken away?

The gown bore no resemblance whatsoever to the one that Bianca had been going to wear, she was relieved to discover.

And it was truly beautiful. She hadn't a clue how the designer had managed to make it to fit her so perfectly and refused to ask the question, but the romantic drift of floating white silk made in the Grecian style disturbed her oddly when she viewed the finished effect in the mirror because she looked so soft and sensually curvy and—vestal.

Luc's idea of how a bride should look?

'Don't chew your bottom lip like that, *signorina*,' the designer advised with a critical frown. 'Your mouth is ripe enough to drive Luciano crazy without you plumping it up some more.'

Lizzy released her lip from her anxious white teeth and slithered her eyes over the silky fall of her hair. Carla the giggly maid had done it for her—washed it, conditioned it, actually almost tamed it. And the barely there hint of make-up applied by Carla's steady fingers made her look—

'It is now no mystery to me why he risked ridicule to replace *la bella Bianca* with what I see standing here,' the designer said.

'Don't,' Lizzy responded, her voice sounding shaky and thick the way it left her tense aching throat.

Her loyalty to her best friend would not allow anyone to mock Bianca. And she missed her. She wanted to see her, talk to her, find out why she'd run away with Matthew, and if what Lizzy was about to do had her blessing because if it didn't…

Lizzy swallowed, the ache of tears threatening her eyes. A knock at the door revealed Luis the major-domo who'd first led her into this villa a long week ago.

'It is time to leave, *signorina*,' he advised.

Her father met her at the church. He looked younger than he had when she'd left him in Sussex two weeks ago, the strain of worry having gone from his face, but the cold disappointment she saw in his eyes made her want to cry all the more.

'You look beautiful,' he said. 'Just like your mother.'

Just like her mother, Lizzy repeated bleakly as he bent to press a cool kiss to one of her cheeks.

Then he walked her into a church packed with curious witnesses. The rippling hiss of softly voiced comments accompanied them down the long stone aisle towards the man she could see standing tall and straight at the other end.

He was wearing morning grey—formal like her father, like the man standing beside him whom she vaguely recognized, but that was about as far as her ability to think about anything went.

And she wanted Bianca. Bianca was supposed to always have been here with her for her wedding just as she was supposed to have been there for hers.

And she wanted to stop and turn to her father and say sorry, beg his forgiveness because she couldn't bear knowing that he was walking beside her likening what she was doing here with what her mother had done ten years before.

The marriage-wrecker, the greedy little gold-digger only out to please herself. Being aware that she was just being silly believing her own press didn't help.

Then Luc turned to look at her, his lean, dark, sombre expression fixing on her like a magnet that pulled her the last few faltering steps to his side. Her father offered her hand to him, he took it, long brown fingers firm as they closed around the trembling state of her own. After that the rest became a hazy glaze of traditional solemnity wrapped in a muffling shroud of beautifully toned Latin that eventually joined them as man and wife.

And the kiss Luc pressed to her lips was somehow piercingly poignant if only because it sealed this mad, ill thought-out union in front of a few hundred fascinated witnesses.

Four euros, Lizzy found herself thinking as Luc lifted his mouth away again. It's going to take me a lifetime to pay back what I owe him.

As if he knew what she was thinking he grinned, all gleaming white teeth and mocking arrogance.

The next thing Lizzy became aware of was stepping out of the church into brilliant sunlight and a cacophony of sound. Cameras flashed, her heart fluttered into sudden panic, the man standing beside her drew her closer into his side. Two rows of dark-suited security men formed a barrier to hold back the curious onlookers and Luc hurried her down through this corridor of safety to a waiting limousine, his arm not leaving contact with her until he had seen her safely shut behind the car door.

The car sped off the moment he'd settled beside her. The hazy glaze lifted from her eyes. Silence stung. It was over. She'd done it. She'd married her best friend's fiancé. The air sounded choked as it left her lungs.

'So you do remember how to breathe,' Luc's quietly sardonic voice said beside her.

Seems so, Lizzy thought without attempting to offer a reply.

Instead she looked down at her hand where a traditional gold band now adorned her slender white finger. Across the gap separating them a matching band glowed against the brown of his skin. She hadn't expected him to wear a ring too, it had come as a surprise when she'd been quietly instructed to place it on his finger.

But, like the church and its packed congregation, she presumed the rings were the same rings he had bought for his marriage to Bianca.

'I am not that insensitive,' he said coolly.

So he was reading her mind as if he owned it too now. 'And at least the dress was mine.'

She sensed his sharp look, the slight tensing of his muscles as he caught the bleakness threading her tone. 'You don't like the dress?'

Was he blind? 'I love it. It's the most romantic and beautiful wedding gown I've ever seen.'

'And you look beautiful in it—*bellissima*,' he extended huskily. 'No one watching you come down the aisle to me was left wondering why it was you I married today.'

'One more goal on your pride-saving agenda successfully accomplished?'

Lifting her chin, Lizzy looked at him for the first time since they'd kissed as man and wife—then instantly wished that she'd kept her eyes lowered because he looked so bone-shiveringly breathtakingly devastating and perfect—the true handsome prince she had bagged for herself by foul means.

A bitter little smile caught hold of her mouth. 'Well, don't look to me for congratulations because you're not going to get any,' she told him, turning her eyes away.

'You feel cheated,' he murmured.

Of what? Lizzy wondered. Of choosing her own wedding

dress? In truth she felt cheated of a lot of things today, not least the given right to choose her own husband, or having her best friend there to share her day with her, or seeing pride, not disapproval, on her father's face.

A sigh shot from her. 'I've hurt and disappointed my father with all of this.'

'And now you are in danger of disappointing me.'

It was the way he said it that made Lizzy look back at him, wary tension uncoiling inside her when she saw the almost savage glint of anger hardening his face.

'We made a deal,' he reminded her grimly. 'One where neither of us would deny the one basic ingredient that will make this marriage work.'

He meant the mutual attraction. Lizzy pulled in a breath, her lips parting in readiness to say something cutting about that, but he stopped the words by reaching across the gap to press a set of cool fingers over her mouth.

'Be careful, *la mia moglie bella*, that you don't talk yourself into trouble with that unruly tongue of yours,' he advised. 'Your father will recover from his disappointment once he begins to consider the good fortune our marriage has blessed him with,' he assured with hard cynical bite. 'Just as you will learn to get over your disappointment in me as your husband because I intend to see to it that you do with the first bed and opportunity we get. And,' he continued in a dark driven undertone without letting her eyes break contact with his, '*I* will recover from my disappointment in you when you stop feeling sorry for yourself and remember just who you are now, *Signora De Santis*. For this name makes you my wife, my lover, the future mother of my children and the gracious custodian of the De Santis good name.'

Wow, was all Lizzy could think when he finally fell into a

simmering silence. Somewhere in this strange conversation they'd been having she'd hit a raw nerve when she hadn't thought he had any!

Lifting up her hand, she caught hold of his fingers and pulled them away from her mouth. 'That was really good,' she commended. 'Quite breathtakingly arrogant and rightfully proud of your mighty fine self, in fact, and it should really have put me squarely in my lowly place.'

'But it didn't?' He raised a questioning eyebrow.

Lizzy shook her head, aware that her heart was pounding erratically, but unaware that she was still holding onto his fingers—or that those fingers had curled around hers.

'You are still the guy who blackmailed me into marrying you to salve your ravaged pride and I am still the woman you *paid* to salve that ravaged pride!'

'You believe that there are no other women out there who would have jumped eagerly into your shoes?'

'I would imagine there are hundreds,' Lizzy said coolly. 'But aren't you the one that told me you could not be bothered to hunt?'

'Quick.' He smiled—then tugged on her fingers. Next thing she was lying in a slither of bridal silk across his chest. Her surprised gasp had barely broken free of her lips before she received the full passionate onslaught of his kiss. And this time it was hot and hard and deeply probing, as if he was deliberately piling on the passion in each kiss by carefully calculated degrees. By the time he raised his head again Lizzy felt dazed and shaken, her breathing fast and thick. Her lips felt bruised and the way he ran a finger across their warm, pulsing surface was a source of mockery in itself.

'As you see,' he murmured softly, 'I still do not need to hunt.'

It was such a slap at the way she'd gone into the kiss

without putting up a fight that Lizzy paled and scrambled off
his lap. Her dress was dishevelled, and as she tried to smooth
it with unsteady fingers she felt the sultry burn of his eyes as
he watched her, felt the drumming pulse of his sexual domination and the worst feeling of all—his amusement.

'I did warn you once, *cara*, that I am more experienced at
these games than you are,' he reminded her from his languid
sprawl on the other side of the car. 'Be a little wiser and stop
trying to take me on.'

The car slowed then, sending her eyes to the side window
to see that they'd arrived back at the villa without her noticing.
Though her biggest surprise was that she hadn't known there
was a different way into the villa other than via the lake. Now
a huge pair of heavy iron gates were in the process of swinging
open. The car glided through them and on through extensive
gardens to pull to a smooth halt beneath a covered portico to
the side of the house.

She hadn't dared to come outside while she'd been staying
here because she hadn't wanted any members of the press to
snatch a picture of her from their siege position on the lake.
But glancing towards the lake now as Luc helped her alight
from the car, she was stunned to see that it was no longer
there! All view of the lake had been totally blanked out by a
wall of sturdy white canvas that had been erected along the
cliff edge—she assumed to frustrate greedy camera lenses
from taking pictures of the wedding celebration about to
take place.

The whole celebrity-style over-the-top show intimidated
her from that moment onward. If Bianca had been here Lizzy
would have taken it all in her stride with a dose of healthy
humour to help her along. But then if Bianca had been here,
she would have been the bride at this wedding and taking the

sparkling centre of attention as her due, with Lizzy happy to fade into the background, as she liked to do.

As it was, she wasn't allowed to fade anywhere. She had to stand beside her new husband and welcome their guests in from the church.

His guests, she reminded herself. *His* wedding day. None of her friends had been invited, just her father, whose disapproval still showed when he arrived and gave her a stiff hug.

Her eyes pleaded with him for understanding, but all he saw when he looked at her was a woman like her mother, and there was no forgiveness in him at all. It was like being deserted by her only ally and she found she had to fight back the tears as she watched him turn his back on her and walk away.

'Explain to me what the hell that was about,' the man standing beside her demanded.

But Lizzy just gave a silent shake of her head and blinked the tears away. A man like Luc would never understand what it felt like to be crushed beneath the weight of someone's disapproval. The feeling would be as alien to him as—as feeling uncomfortable with the sensation he'd caused with his quick change of bride! In all the years since her mother had left them, Lizzy had tried her best to show none of her wayward traits. But as she stood here now in this beautiful villa, wearing this beautiful gown, feeling so rejected by the one person she should have been able to rely upon for support, she had to ask herself if spending her life trying to earn her father's approval had just been a useless waste of her time.

And her now very crushed heart.

The endless stream of elegant guests kept on coming. She smiled, she endured the looks of cool interest, the polite comments and the sometimes not so polite. Hurt clung heavily to her chest while her face maintained its placid composure and Luc kept her close to him, with his arm strapped at an angle across her back so his hand could rest in the indentation of her waist.

Eventually they began to circulate. No one got to speak to either of them individually. His hand remained a firm clamp at her waist. He was showing a united front and no amount of teasing from his closer friends about his possessive attitude to his bride could budge him from her side.

They ate from a beautiful serve-yourself banquet—Lizzy nibbled sparingly, held her untouched glasses of bubbling champagne and endured the amused, mostly ironical speech from Luc's best man with her eyes carefully lowered, Luc with a wry but complacent smile on his face.

Nothing touched him, she noticed. The man had nerves of steel and no emotion at all. Yet she knew by the changing grip of his fingers on her waist that sometimes something violent erupted inside him, especially when they caught the edges of hushed conversations discussing Bianca and the fact that the poor jilted bride seemed to have slipped off the face of the earth.

Was his response due to anger or pain? When she glanced up at his face, it, of course, revealed nothing.

She caught fleeting glimpses of her father in the crowd and wanted to go and ask him if he'd heard from Matthew, but every time the thought hit, Luc was guiding her off in the opposite direction.

The afternoon wore on with agonising slowness until she began to really feel the strain of maintaining her smile. So when Luc bent his head to tell her quietly that it was time for her to go and change out of her dress, she was so pathetically relieved to be given an excuse to escape she didn't even bother to ask him why she needed to change.

Carla the giggly maid was waiting for her when she reached her bedroom. She provided the answers as she helped her out of her wedding dress.

'It is such a shame that you must remove this beautiful gown so soon, *signora*.' Carla sighed wistfully. 'But with your new clothes all packed in your bags and already on their way, it must be so exciting and romantic to be swept away by the *signor* to your secret honeymoon destination.'

Honeymoon—?

CHAPTER FIVE

OH, PLEASE don't, Lizzy thought helplessly, so horrified that Luc was intending to take this romantic stuff that far that her lips came together with a snap to stop the groaned protest from slipping out.

But the protest glowed in her eyes as she came back downstairs dressed in a soft green wraparound dress that clung lovingly to her figure and swirled around her knees.

Luc was already waiting at the bottom of the stairs for her. He had changed too, into a soft coffee-coloured linen suit and a simple tee shirt that made him look cool and casual and superbly stylish and just too darn sexy to be fair.

He looked up at her and something flared in his eyes that made her steps falter as her heart gave a fluttering stir. Then the expression was gone and he was holding out a hand in a silent command for her to continue down the rest of the stairs.

When she came close enough, he took hold of her hand and drew her towards him. His lips arrived at her temple; she felt the heat from his body warm against hers.

'Beautiful,' he husked.

So are you, Lizzy thought helplessly, but she didn't say it. 'Where are we going?' she whispered instead, sharply aware of all the people standing around watching them.

'Where all newly married couples go.' He took the cream jacket she had draped across her arm. 'Somewhere we can be alone.'

'But I don't want to be alone with you.' She frowned as he draped the jacket across her shoulders.

'You don't? I am devastated.'

He just sounded sardonic to her. 'I thought we would be staying here. Can't we just stay here?' She glanced up at him anxiously. 'I'm used to being here now. It's—comfortable.'

In the process of gently releasing her hair from inside the jacket, Luc paused to look down at her, a strange expression swirling around in his dark golden eyes.

Then the smile was back. 'It is traditional to change venue.'

Lizzy stepped a little closer to him, her voice a hurried confiding whisper aimed at the taut solid skin at his throat. 'It's silly.'

'What is?'

'The rest of this.' Her eyes gave a quick restless flick of the waiting crowd. 'If we're supposed to be leaving, won't *they* all be leaving too?'

'You want me to throw our guests out?' He sounded incredulous.

'Your guests,' Lizzy corrected.

'Watch it, *cara*,' he warned quietly. 'You don't want to talk yourself into yet another tight corner with me—especially with so many witnesses.'

'All I'm saying is that we might as well stay—'

He moved so smoothly she didn't sense it coming. One second he was smoothing the jacket across her shoulders, the next his long fingers crushing the slender bones, and with a controlled strength he pulled her tight up against his chest and the rest of her argument was being thoroughly crushed by the kind of kiss that locked the breath in her throat.

She was only dimly aware of the murmuring ripple that spread around the hallway as the first tense quiver to hit her in days made its fierce stroke down Lizzy's front. Pleasure flared out from its edges, sending her hands up to press hard against his chest in an attempt to push him away. But he was going nowhere and neither was the kiss, the heated force of it sending her body into a straining arch against him. The so carefully draped jacket slithered from her shoulders to land on the ground by her feet and his arms folded her even closer—someone murmured something mocking, someone else uttered a dry laugh.

Luc eased the pressure on her mouth by slow degrees and with tender stroking caresses. 'The show must go on, *cara*,' he murmured softly.

Too shaken up by the whole public reminder, Lizzy just swallowed tensely and nodded. Then the slow-rolling swell of applause took off around the gathering as Luc was stepping back.

Stooping down to recover her fallen jacket, he tossed it casually over his shoulder as he straightened again, then turned to offer their audience a wry mocking bow. Laughter joined in with the clapping. Lizzy kept her eyes lowered and hated the wild blush that burned her cheeks.

It wasn't until he'd captured her hand and led her outside and she saw the helicopter standing on the lawn again that she remembered her father.

She turned quickly to Luc. 'I can't leave here without seeing my father.'

He tensed beside her. 'He has already left here to catch his flight back to Gatwick,' he informed her coolly.

For a whole minute Lizzy couldn't breathe. The sense of

rejection was so total she just stared blindly at Luc as the colour slowly drained from her face.

With a soft curse, he drew her across the lawn and bundled her into the helicopter. A few minutes later and they were rising up above the temporary wall of white canvas and swinging round to face the lake where a whole armada of different sailing crafts clustered a short way out from the jetty, with their army of little media people scrambling, no doubt to get a picture of them leaving.

Beside her Luc made a tense, restless movement with his body. 'Ignore them,' he rasped. 'They will soon get tired of playing this game and move on to the next sensation.'

Oddly enough she didn't care any more how many silly photographs they managed to snatch.

'He left without saying goodbye to me,' she whispered.

That was what mattered.

'He has a business to rescue.' He didn't even try to pretend he did not know who she meant. 'You must accept that Hadley's has to take priority with him right now.'

Oh, yes. 'Thank you,' she said, 'for that very thin excuse.'

After that they finished the journey to the accompanying sizzle of his frowning impatience and her numbed silence. Lizzy stared out of the window as they skimmed over the top of the glistening blue lake. An hour later they were crossing the tarmac at Linate Airport to a private jet wearing the De Santis logo on its shiny white fuselage.

The interior was a luxurious statement to corporate living. Luc saw her seated, said something to a hovering steward, then strode off to check with his pilot.

Two minutes later he was back, and the engines were running. He took the chair next to Lizzy and clipped home his seat belt, instructing her to do the same thing.

They took off into pure blue skies and she still hadn't got a clue as to where they were going. In truth she just didn't care. Today had been the worst day of her life and right now she felt like a traffic accident, one of the walking wounded that functioned by sheer instinct and nothing else.

'I sent him away while you were changing,' Luc rasped out suddenly, bringing her face around to stare at him.

He was lounging in the seat beside her, the absolute epitome of casual nonchalance, but Lizzy saw the tension around his mouth.

'Why?' she breathed.

His golden eyes flickered over her. 'He upset you.'

He upset her? 'He's my father,' she snapped out. 'He's allowed to upset me!'

'I am your husband,' he countered. 'I am allowed to remove all upset from your life.'

Lizzy threw him a look of burning dislike. 'You upset me. Does that mean you're going to remove yourself from my presence?'

'Not while we are flying at ten thousand feet.' He grinned—then stopped grinning and sighed instead. 'Stop spitting hatred at me, Elizabeth, and explain to me why your father believes he can treat you the way that he did today.'

So she told him about her mother in a cool, flat, dignified voice, unaware that he watched every fleeting expression that passed across her face because she refused to look at him as she talked.

'So you see,' she concluded, 'he sees his worst fears for me materialising in our wedding today.'

The steward arrived then with coffee and sandwiches, bringing a halt to the conversation while he transferred everything from a tray to the low table in front of them. Luc waved the steward away when he went to pour out the coffee and leant forward to do it himself.

'Do you look like your mother?' he asked curiously.

Lizzy nodded. 'I'm like this constant reminder to him of what she did.'

He handed her a cup of warm dark coffee. 'And where is she now?'

'She—died, two years ago.' Her voice had turned so husky she took a sip at the coffee to cover it up—then frowned at the bitter sweet taste. 'You've put sugar in this.'

'You don't take sugar?'

'No,' she said—then, curiously, 'Do you?'

Sitting back in his seat, he took a sip from his own cup. 'We don't know very much about each other, do we?'

No, Lizzy thought bleakly, we don't. 'Well, do you take sugar in your coffee or don't you?' she demanded.

'Strong, black and sweet,' he answered, then turned his head to look at her, his golden eyes darker than usual and re-flecting an expression she could not quite read.

But she felt it make its old strike at her solar plexus and frowned as to why it had. They couldn't be discussing a safer subject unless they switched to the weather.

'It seems to me, *cara*,' he then said ruefully, 'that your family is as dysfunctional as mine, which makes us more in tune than you would like to think.'

Opening her mouth to argue with him, she closed it again, because she realised he was probably right. 'I still don't like sugar in my coffee,' she said firmly, and put her cup on the table.

He just laughed, and rang for the steward to bring another cup.

For some unknown reason her mood lightened. She even ate a couple of sandwiches and felt herself begin to relax.

'Where are we going?' she finally decided to ask him.

'Well, that took its time,' Luc mocked, getting up to stride down the cabin. 'The Caribbean,' he enlightened as he opened up what turned out to be a drinks cabinet and selected a bottle from the row. 'I have a place there, hidden away on a paradise island with only pelicans for company—want one?'

He turned to show her what looked like brandy. Lizzy shook her head.

'Scared you will get tipsy again?'

'Scared I'll fall asleep.'

'Fortunately for you—' he came back with two glasses and sat down again '—falling asleep on board this plane is not a problem because we have a bed to sleep in through that door you can see at the other end of the cabin.'

Expression as bland as he could make it, he waited for her nervous glance towards the door set into the bulkhead, then silently offered her a glass.

It was either take it or endure another round of sarcastic comments from him, Lizzy knew that.

'With a nine-hour flight ahead of us, with or without the brandy, you are going to discover a need for that bed.'

'With or without you?' It was out before she could stop it.

His golden eyes lit up. 'Was that an invitation?'

'No, it was not!' she denied.

'Then take the brandy,' he said. 'You are safe with me— for now.'

It was the *for now* that made her feel edgy, but it was the lazy challenge in his tone that made her take the brandy from him and defiantly toss it to the back of her throat.

'Not a good idea, *cara*,' he said as he watched her fall into a fit of gasps as the brandy burnt like fire all the way down to her stomach.

He was right and it wasn't. The brandy went straight to her

head. She lasted a full long hard-fought-for hour before she succumbed to the need to lie down and close her dizzy eyes.

Luc offered to help her down the cabin. She refused with a stiff dignity that cost her plenty to make it all the way into the small bedroom without stumbling over her own feet.

A few minutes later, wearing only her bra and panties, she was curling up beneath a soft duvet covered in the smoothest linen, and dropping into a muzzy sleep with what felt like the world playing drumbeats on her head.

For hours she slept, she didn't know how many, before she came drifting upwards into semi-darkness with the muted sound of the plane's engines to remind her where she was.

Her head had cleared and she felt so much better than she'd felt when she'd come in here. She was hungry too, but the idea of getting up out of the comfortable bed and getting dressed to go out there and face Luc had her turning over in the bed with the intention of staying right where she—

Shock froze the air in her body when she saw him. He was lying on his front right beside her with his dark head resting on the pillow next to her pillow and his wide naked shoulders glowing bronze in the soft light coming from the lamp on his side of the bed.

From being completely relaxed to the point of a wonderful bonelessness, she was already in the process of tensing up when she realised he was asleep and she let the tension seep away again on an inner swirl of tingling relief.

The black satin crescents of his eyelashes were resting peacefully against his high cheekbones and his mouth was the most relaxed she had seen it, its sensual shape all the more beautiful in repose, and his hair was ruffled, revealing a hint of a glossy black wave she hadn't ever noticed before.

Held by a curiosity she knew she should not be giving in

to, Lizzy let her eyes roam over his arms, thrown up against the pillow, the width of his shoulders and long bronzed back exposed because the duvet had slipped down so low.

Her fingers scrambled at her own part of the duvet, inching it carefully over her shoulder because his nakedness reminded her about her own near nakedness.

Was he naked—as in completely naked? The intimacy of the situation struck like a feather being drawn across the surface of her skin. Her nostrils flared and she picked up the warm scent of him, clean yet so irresistibly male it sent the moist tip of her tongue sliding on a slow circuit of her warm lips for a reason she refused to examine.

And the skin covering the muscles she could see shaping his body wore a sheen that made her think of suntan oil, though she knew the effect was due to his own natural oils conditioning his skin while he slept.

Her husband, she thought, trying the title out to see how it felt, and still found the concept as alien to her as having the two of them lying here together in this bed.

'Grey,' a deep, dark, slumberously warm voice murmured.

Lizzy started, her eyes leaping up to his face. He was awake. She tensed, her fingers gripping the duvet. She would have dived right out of the bed if she weren't aware that she was wearing the sheerest leaf green bra ever fashioned and matching panties that made a mockery of the name.

'Sexy soft smoky grey—no, don't move away,' he said when she went to do just that, and with a lithe shift of his body he rolled onto his side and propped his head on the heel of his hand so he could look down into her wary face and the scented fire flow of her hair where it spread across the pillow.

'*Bellissima*,' he chanted softly. '*La signora bella De Santis.*'

'No,' she denied. 'Will you stop calling me beautiful?'

'Strange creature.' He smiled, reaching over to stroke the stray curl from her brow. 'You have the most exquisite face I have ever seen on any woman and the most fascinating determination to deny it. I would love to know why that is.'

'I won't respond to your kind of flattery—' the curl flopped back again and Lizzy swiped at it frowningly '—just because you…'

Her voice trailed away, teeth pressing into her bottom lip when she realised what she had been about to say next.

Moving that bit closer to her so she felt the tingling sting of his chest hair prickle the skin on her arm, he prompted, 'Because I—what?'

'Because w-we're married and—here,' she finished—then shook out an unsteady gasp when one of his legs arrived across both of hers. 'W-what do you think you're doing?' she demanded.

'Getting comfortable with my wife.'

Her fingers let go of the duvet so she could use them to push him back again, but it came as a tingling shock to her racing senses to feel the solid heat of his muscled body and the crisp warmth of his chest hair prickle against her palms. The whole situation was a tingling shock, she decided, snared by the living warmth of his leg weighing heavy on hers and the expression in his eyes as he continued to look down at her, tender and soft and still sleepy enough to make those shadowing eyelashes diffuse the hunter-like gleam from the gold.

She could even feel the steady beat of his heart where he pressed against her arm. He leant down and kissed her, not passionately or anything, just light and gently, yet she still jerked her head back, feeling besieged by his heat and his strength and his close proximity.

'Stop panicking,' he chided softly. 'I am not here to hurt you.'

'But I don't—'

'And it is customary that you kiss the man you wake up with.'

He was expecting her to kiss him? No way, she thought, and gave him her response with a shake of her head.

'You mean you expect me to do the kissing? Not very fair of you, *cara*, but—okay,' he said, and his mouth found hers again, only this time he traced the outline of her lips with his tongue, then gently probed between until she gave in and parted them for him. She let him taste her with a sensual slowness, her breath trapped in her chest. By the time he pulled away again her heart was thumping heavily and her lips trembled in protest at the loss of his.

'Not a bad way to start the new day,' he murmured.

'It—it's still dark out there,' Lizzy managed to whisper.

'But past midnight,' he said, drawing back a little to rest his head on the heel of his hand again. 'You were asleep for hours. You missed our first dinner together as man and wife and left me alone to contemplate the folly in urging my temperate bride to knock back brandy like a fully-fledged alcoholic.'

Lizzy flushed. 'Being unused to drinking brandy does not make me temperate.'

'Intemperate, then?'

Meaning she'd behaved like a hot-headed fool? He was probably right, she accepted reluctantly.

'Well, I'm hungry now,' she said with what she congratulated herself as sounding near normal with her heart still thumping against her ribs. 'S-so if you would just move your leg away I'll get up and...'

Her voice faded into nothing at the slow shake of his head. 'Relax,' he encouraged. 'I am not going to seal our wedding vows here in this very unromantic place, but I do want some more of what we have been sharing…a lot more,' he husked as he lowered his head again, and this time there was nothing slow or gentle about it.

His mouth claimed her mouth with deep, sweet, sensual male hunger, and he pressed her back into the pillows with the weight of his body, driving the breath from her lungs. Heat poured into every skin cell, the taste and the scent of him and the ravishing passion making her lose her death grip on the duvet so her hands could clutch at him for dear life.

His husky assurance that he was not going to turn this into something she wasn't ready for gave her the excuse she needed to just let go of restraint and she began kissing him back with an eager fervour, her body arching into the pressure of his. She barely noticed when he stripped the duvet away altogether; she just writhed with pleasure when she felt his hand stroke the length of her pale naked thigh.

Dragging his mouth from hers, he burned a dark golden look into her eyes. 'You feel like silk,' he breathed, the words deep and excitingly unsteady.

Then he made her groan when he reclaimed the kiss, his hand stroking upwards over the thin line of her panties to the flat of her stomach, the warmth of his skin against her over-sensitised skin making her quiver and cling as he blazed a trail of burning possession over her taut, slender ribcage to the rounded thrust of her breasts.

Panic arrived in a self-conscious rush from her exposed thighs to her throat as he gently cupped his fingers around the firm, rounded fullness of her breast barely covered by the green flimsy mesh of her bra. She tried to push his hand away, but he caught hold of her wrist with his other hand, making the flurrying sound of her breath shiver from her body as he gently lifted her hand out of the way so he could sear a path of warm, moist kisses down the arching column of her throat and over the hectic pant of her other breast.

She cried out and went wild beneath him as the sensual lap of his tongue located her nipple, sending a clamouring shock of heat piercing sensation screaming through her head.

With a softly uttered tense expletive he came back to her mouth, his hand sliding beneath her to draw her up against him. The next thing she knew the clasp of her bra had sprung free and he was lying her back against the pillows again and the scrappy bit of mesh was being trailed away.

'You are exquisite,' she heard him rasp through the hazy mists of her ravaged senses.

Then he was taking her mouth once again, crushing the pulsing hot softness of her lips and dipping deep and hungrily with his tongue at the same time that his hand closed around her breast again, naked now and so alive to his touch she cried out in half protest, half sense spinning pleasure, and grabbed blindly at his head, her fingers clawing into the glossy thickness of his hair.

He kneaded and shaped and kissed her breathless. She could feel the tremors attacking him, feel the fevered flush of his body and the tension in him, trapped his groan with her tongue when he pressed the distended tightness of her nipple against his palm.

She should have stopped it there, but she didn't. She should have known that if you arched and writhed and quivered against a man you were going to tip him over the edge. But she liked what he was making her feel, too much, and was much too greedy for more.

And his hands were gliding everywhere now, caressing and learning what made her cry out and what made her writhe in shimmering pleasure. And his skin was like hot satin against her anxiously restless palms. She had never felt so totally out of control of her body and senses. She was panting and whimpering against his mouth and he was breathing fast and unevenly.

Reality should have arrived with the burgeoning thrust of his powerful erection pushing against her thigh at the same moment as he slid his hand between her legs and made that final intimate claim—but reality was nowhere. She was lost in a storm of heated pleasure. It sang along her veins and her flesh and it was all she could do to cling to him as his long fingers cupped and moved against her, his other hand buried in her hair, and the heat of his kiss was so deep and potently passionate she was almost beyond recovery when he lifted his mouth to mutter, 'I knew you would do this to me,' and eased her last scrap of mesh out of his way so he could glide the length of a finger inside.

Nothing prepared her for the power of this heated intrusion. There was just no way she could control her response. She arched and squirmed and found her mouth locking onto his as if it were the only way she was going to survive what was racing through her blood. He was whispering things she couldn't hear, and filling her with sensations she hadn't known she could feel.

Then he moved to strip the panties from her body and it was the rasping curse he uttered that brought her crashing back down to earth.

Panic erupted from her like a heaving monster, and she pushed him away from her with the agonised strength helped by the stinging shot of adrenalin singing through her blood. She caught a glimpse of his face, his shocked confusion, then she'd slithered out from beneath him to land in a mess of shaking limbs and whirling senses on her feet by the bed.

The pulsing silence that followed held the small cabin in a death grip except for the sound of her broken breathing. Her eyes felt so big and dark and glazed she was barely even able to see him through them.

'Y-you said—' she finally just about managed.

'I know what I said,' he coolly cut in.

Lizzy blinked, her eyes daring to focus on him still lying there with his long body so magnificently naked to his long brown feet. He had covered his eyes with an arm and the mouth beneath it was closed and tight. Unable to stop her eyes from raking over him, she stared at the potent evidence of his desire thrusting up from a thick cluster of virile dark hair.

Shocked by the blinding rush of heat that burned through her, she turned dizzily away with absolutely no idea what she was going to do next.

Jump on him, a wicked voice inside her suggested. 'Oh, God,' she choked, lowering her head to cover her burning eyes with her hands. She couldn't believe she'd ever let it go that far—she couldn't believe she'd trusted the promise he'd made!

'You have the sexiest backside,' he drawled suddenly, making the tumble of her hair slither down her spine as she arched upright. 'Creamy white and smooth and tight and deliciously framed by the lace edges of your pretty useless pants.'

Feeling the sting of total embarrassment, Lizzy reached behind her to hook the green mesh back into its rightful place.

'You think that helped?' he mocked.

She shook her head and wished she still had her bra on, because she just might have found the courage to turn around and spit something vile at him. But she didn't and her breasts felt heavy and throbbed, the fiercely distended tips stinging like aliens with the power to reach down deep inside her and pluck at other senses she wished she didn't have.

'You think, then, it is good fun to call a stop when things were becoming—passionate?'

He was angry. It hit Lizzy like a blow that arched her aching spine some more. 'Y-you don't understand.'

'I know a tease when I encounter one,' he said cynically.

She heard movement behind her to say he was getting off the bed, and like a wild thing she snatched up the only thing she had available—her wraparound top, which she dragged on. He too was pulling his clothes on; she could hear the rustle as she wrapped the top around her and tied it in an angry, tight, finger—trembling knot.

'A man who can't honour his promises deserves to be switched on—and off,' she responded once she felt safer to do it with her upper body covered up.

'No natural instincts at work in you, then,' he scorned that.

Snatching up her skirt and shimmying into it, she finally felt brave enough to turn around. He was standing on the other side of the bed, with the bulkhead almost touching his broad shoulders. And he was still so boldly naked she wished her ravished senses would just curl up and die. The soft light from the bedside lamp played across the flexing muscles in his shoulders as he pulled on his trousers, the taut clench of stomach and his hair-roughened chest.

Dragging her eyes away from him, she missed the way he lowered his own eyes to the burgeoning fullness of her breasts moulded by fine knit fabric so the tight peaks of her nipples pushed against the cloth.

'I'm not going to apologise for calling a stop to what you said was not going to happen,' she tossed back her hair and said.

He hooded his eyes, the old cold cynicism back with a vengeance. Bending down towards the bed, he picked up something. 'Here…' He tossed it at her. 'You had better put this on before you walk out of here, or my steward will suffer an apoplectic fit.'

With that ruthless cut into her bravery, he pulled the black tee shirt on over his head, then strode towards the door. It didn't slam—it wasn't designed to slam, Lizzy realised as she watched it seal into place.

But he'd wanted it to slam, the grim, spoiled, arrogant devil.

Then she looked down at the bra she now held in her fingers, glanced at her body and blushed to the roots of her hair.

They finished the rest of the journey in a state of cool withdrawal from each other scattered with super-polite snatches of conversation now and then. Lizzy ate, he didn't, instead he drank coffee, and no hint of alcohol in any form put in an appearance.

Eventually he produced a bulging briefcase and settled into his chair to concentrate—Lizzy wished she had something similar so that she could do the same thing.

But she didn't. She was now the pampered wife of a very rich man and her job as her father's secretary had gone. Her new role in life was to look the part of a rich man's wife—learn to look the part, she amended. And to be quiet when the rich husband was concentrating, because the look on his stern profile told her that was what he expected her to do.

Eventually she dozed again, curled into her seat with her shoes slipped off and her feet tucked beneath her and her head resting against the corner of the chair. When she awoke it was to find herself covered with a soft blanket and Luc was still sitting beside her working away.

She watched him for a while, sleepy eyes following the sudden flick on his pen when he scrawled something on the document he was reading, long fingers deft and supple and precise in their link with his brain. It was the same fountain pen she'd used to sign the prenuptial contract, she noticed, black, with a ring of gold circling its slender body, the platinum tipped nib feeding ink onto the paper like liquid silk.

'You've spelt indecisive wrong,' she murmured without knowing she was going to say it, or even that she'd been reading as he wrote.

The pen stopped and lifted. He turned to look at her, golden eyes not angry any more, just coolly detached. 'I do not misspell,' he informed her arrogantly.

'You've used an "i" instead of an "e",' she insisted. 'The sentence says, "This attitude is indecisive and unacceptable."' she read aloud. 'It loses impact with the misspelling.'

'You can read my writing from right over there?' Setting his shoulders against the back of his chair, he looked at her curiously. 'To the point that you can distinguish an "i" from an "e"?'

Lizzy nodded, still curled beneath the blanket. 'Not if you were writing in Italian,' she felt she should point out. 'My Italian spelling isn't good enough.'

'Nor is your English.'

Lizzy glanced at his face. There wasn't a flicker of uncertainty in his expression, yet she hadn't seen him look down to check if she was right. Which meant that either he was too confident for his own good, or she had made a mistake.

Uncurling her feet from beneath her, she pushed aside the blanket and reached out and took the page from his lap. She read it carefully, then handed it back to him without uttering a single word.

His eyelashes flickered, uncertainty darkening the colour of his eyes, and she laughed softly, couldn't help it—it felt so very good to be right.

He looked down, couldn't help himself, then a rueful smile stretched his lips. 'You aggravating ginger haired witch,' he said, having to carefully turn an 'i' into an 'e'.

'My hair's not ginger,' Lizzy protested.

'What is it, then?' Tossing the work down on the table in front of them, he sat back and looked at her again.

'Chestnut,' Lizzy answered, and combed a set of fingers through it to push the curls away from her face. 'With a will of its own,' she added as a curl flopped down onto her brow.

'Much like its owner.'

'So you noticed.' She gave the errant curl another hopeless swipe only to watch it spring back down again.

'I noticed,' he answered evenly.

'Have you also noticed yet that I'm a virgin?' she asked him casually.

CHAPTER SIX

IF LIZZY said it to shock Luc out of his cool composure, then she certainly succeeded, she saw, as burning dark colour swept across his high golden cheekbones and he launched to his feet sending paperwork scattering as he accidentally knocked against the table.

'Is that your idea of a damn joke?' His eyes flashed out a blaze of blistering fury that made her reach for and pull up the blanket.

'I just—thought I should mention it before things go too—heated again,' she explained, blushing herself because now that she'd said it she felt silly and stupid and—

'A virgin,' he snapped out from between his clenched teeth. 'Where the hell did you get the idea to throw something like that at me from out of nowhere?'

'Well, what would you have preferred me to do?' Lizzy reacted hotly. 'Have it written into that stupid prenuptial contract so you could take your time getting used to the idea?'

He was pale with anger now, not flushed. 'We just almost made love—'

'No, I stopped it,' she reminded him, 'being such a horrible tease.'

Grabbing the back of his neck, he spun away from her.

Lizzy huddled in her seat. 'I was going to tell you before in—in the bedroom but you turned nasty. Now I wish I hadn't told you at all!'

'So do I,' he muttered, striding off towards the drinks cupboard.

'Well, if it offends you this much, then why don't you do your usual trick and chuck this bride out and put another more experienced one in her place?'

'It does not offend me,' he denied stiffly. 'And I did not chuck Bianca out, as you so charmingly put it. She left me.'

'Wise girl,' Lizzy choked, fighting hurt tears now because hearing him say that made her remember that she wouldn't be here having this conversation if Bianca hadn't walked away from him.

Bianca, his first-choice bride!

'Well…' getting up, she began picking up scattered papers because she desperately needed something to do '—I am what I am, and you are what you are, which says to me that we don't have m-much going for us in this stupid m-marriage. But I know I can't bury my head in the sand and pretend I'm going to stop you every time you touch me because we both know I like it too much!'

'Elizabeth—'

'No,' she choked out. 'Just sh-shut up, because hearing you toss out one of your clever answers right now will just m-make me sick!'

He actually looked startled. 'I was not about to—'

'Yes, you were. You don't know how not to.' Swiping the tears from her eyes and that annoying stray curl from her brow, she gathered in his papers with trembling fingers, then came to her feet. 'I don't know how to deal with a man like you and it's making this situation very difficult for me.'

'You think I know how to deal with you?' he hit back. 'You are nothing like any woman I've ever encountered.' He knocked his drink to the back of his tense throat. 'You are quiet and shy and unbelievably sensitive in one disguise, then a flaming mix of defiance and passion in another!'

'Well, now you know why.' She put the papers on the table.

'Yes, I know why,' he accepted. 'You're a virgin—'

'Trapped in a marriage I didn't want.'

'By a man that you *do* want.'

Lizzy swallowed thickly because she just had no defence to that. She did want him, even though she wished that she didn't. She had wanted him for so long the guilty feeling still creased her insides.

'I'm not going to fool myself that you really want me,' she responded unsteadily, hunting around for her shoes now, though where the heck she thought she was going to go in them she hadn't a clue. 'Like you so love to say, you don't hunt and I'm here. But if you're daring to think that because I'm attracted to you I can't m-mind that I come in second best for you, then forget it, because I do mind.' She swallowed again. 'And the fact that I'm not being given the choice as to who I give my virginity to hurts enough without you responding as if I'm offering you some dreadful social disease.'

'I apologise if you feel I gave you that impression.'

He was coming over all cool and stiff now, which, Lizzy supposed, was typical of him.

'You—surprised me,' he added.

I surprised myself, Lizzy thought bitterly. I should have kept my big mouth shut.

'And if the—sex between us is such an issue to you, then perhaps we can take it more slowly from now on.'

So he didn't even want the sex with her now, Lizzy took

from that smooth toned offer. 'Thank you,' she responded with chilly politeness.

The 'fasten seat belts' sign beeped into action then, saving her from the risk of sinking to the floor in a puddle of wretched tears. Instead she sat down, fastened her seat belt and occupied her trembling fingers by folding up the blanket.

A tinny voice came over the speaker system. 'We will be landing in five minutes, Luc. The weather is dry with humidity at seventy-five degrees. The time is—twenty-one thirty-three. Santo is waiting with your car.'

Luc closed the drinks cabinet with a telling snap, then came to sit down himself. They didn't look at each other as the plane began to make its descent and the silence between them was sharp enough to cut glass.

His hand still made that possessive anchor to her spine, though, when they left the plane, and the tense little quiver still made its strike down her front.

Formalities were swift and efficient. The night air was hot and heavy with the seductive aroma of spice. The car was a sturdy four-wheel drive with plenty of room to stack their luggage in the boot. And their driver, Santo, greeted them with a set of wonderful white teeth and the kind of warmth Lizzy didn't think she was ever going to feel penetrate to her bones again.

'I thought you said there would only be pelicans here,' she said as they skirted above what looked like a pretty town clustered around a horseshoe-shaped harbour where she could see the yachts swaying gently in the moon-washed night.

Luc didn't answer for a moment—long enough to inch up the tension between them some more. Then, 'I was being sardonic.'

It was death to any vague hope Lizzy might have had that they could return to some kind of normality after the ugly scene on the plane. Pressing her lips together, she said nothing else, just stared at the shadowy shapes of an alien landscape sweeping past her window. It was only as they turned in through a pair of gates and she saw a beautiful sugar-pink plantation house standing in front of them that she suddenly wondered if this was where he'd meant to bring Bianca too.

Then—*Don't!* she told herself angrily. Stop playing this pathetic torment with yourself. Aren't things bad enough as they are?

A swarm of staff came out to meet the vehicle. Doors were opened for them, the still heat of the night became filled with warm smiles and even warmer congratulations that included hugs and happiness on their behalf until Luc gave the order for it to stop.

The house itself looked as if it had been transported here right off the set of a period movie. Lizzy could almost see the ladies in crinolines gliding out onto the front porch.

She could hear and smell the ocean though she couldn't see it, and the heavy scent of tropical jasmine hung like a drug in the air.

'Come,' Luc said, making another one of those small hesitations, then rested an arm about her shoulders—for the comfort of the staff, Lizzy realised, and didn't push him away.

But those hesitations were beginning to speak volumes. He didn't want to touch her. Her silly confession about her lack of sexual experience had given him the biggest turn-off of his life. Now a wall was up and the detached cool was back, and it showed in the way he walked and the way he spoke so smoothly and quietly to the milling staff.

Inside the house was just as beautiful as his Lake Como villa, but decorated differently in cool pastel shades.

Lizzy stepped away from him as soon as she dared to, to

glance around the huge open hallway with a white marble staircase sweeping upwards to a galleried first floor. A huge fan hung from the ceiling gently humming away and disturbing her hair as she spun slowly on the heels of her shoes.

'We will do the proper introductions tomorrow, but this is Nina, *cara*…'

Swinging to face Luc, she found him standing with his eyes carefully hooded and his face like a blank golden space. Her own eyes flickered slightly as she moved them sideways to where a tiny creature with beautiful dark brown skin stood smiling shyly at her.

'Nina manages the house and the staff,' Luc's carefully modulated voice explained, 'so if you need anything go to her.'

Finding a smile from somewhere, Lizzy stepped up to say hello and to offer Nina her hand.

'I am very happy to see you here, Signora De Santis,' Nina returned with a smiling formality that made Lizzy feel like a fraud. 'May I offer you both our delighted congratulations on behalf of all the staff here?'

Considering the rush of congratulations they'd just received outside, Nina's carefully rehearsed speech kind of fell flat. Still Lizzy managed an adequate reply while sensing the tension that hit the man standing at her side.

'My wife will want to go upstairs to—freshen up and change,' he said calmly, with the 'my wife' sounding hollow to Lizzy's sensitised ears.

'I will show you, *signora*,' Nina said. 'Please,' she invited, 'this way…'

Lizzy walked in Nina's wake, aware that Luc remained standing where he was watching her. She was halfway up the stairs when she heard his footsteps echo off the tiled floor, but refused to look down and check where he'd gone.

The bedroom suite was beautiful, a soothing melody of pale blues and ivory and soft eau-de-Nil. Two maids were busy unpacking their bags for them. Another fan spun quietly above a huge mahogany four-poster bed, and yet another one hummed across the room above the French windows in front of which a table and two chairs stood, already set for two.

'There is a bathroom, *signora*, through here,' Nina was saying, pulling Lizzy's attention to the door she was holding open to reveal soft gold and cream tones of Italian marble. 'Would you like one of the maids to draw you a bath?'

'Oh, n-no—thank you,' Lizzy murmured shyly. 'I think I'll just—explore first if that's okay.'

'Of course. You want to settle in.' Nina nodded, let go of the bathroom door, then clapped her hands at the two hovering maids. 'Come, both of you, we will leave the new *signora* to catch her breath.'

Well, that was one way of putting it, Lizzy supposed as she kept her smile fixed until all three had left the room.

Then she wilted like a dying flower into a chair, shoulders sinking, face paling, eyes feeling suddenly very empty as she stared at the huge four-poster bed with its drapes of fine white silk.

One huge bed, two large dark mahogany wardrobes—her gaze drifted over to them next—and two sets of fancy luggage standing half unpacked in front of each. One large very classy bathroom—from what she'd glimpsed through the gap when Nina had held the door open—and a table set for two by the window with a single red hibiscus flower standing in a tiny white vase, and two ivory-white candles floating in frosted glass bowls of water, just waiting to be lit.

Plus one wilting bride sitting here and a reluctant groom

out there somewhere, probably downing brandy by the glassful while grimly ruing his lot.

The perfect honeymoon in paradise.

Getting up, she walked over to the suitcases to check which set belonged to her. She recognised nothing either in the cases or from what was hanging already in the wardrobe. She was a bought bride with just about every detail of her old life stripped away from her—except for the one thing he didn't want to have and wished weren't there at all.

Bending down, she flicked through a stack of soft designer lingerie. Sexy, every single set—purchased to seduce—plus bikinis in different styles and colours but no modest one-piece. Then there were the clothes that shrieked designer at her—bright, modern, chic and sassy to reflect current fashion trends.

Great.

Sighing, she turned and headed for the bathroom, then stood looking around it. One wickedly decadent deep plunge bath with optional whirlpool, two big shower cubicles, one toilet bowl and two white porcelain basins standing side by side above which hung mirrors and several glass shelves filled with bottles and tubes and jars of every beauty aid a woman could wish for.

And she refused—absolutely—to let herself question if all of this had been meant for Bianca.

Instead she stripped off, picked a shower cubicle and stepped into it.

Ten minutes later she walked back into the bedroom, wryly unsurprised to find that the maids had been in and finished the unpacking while she'd been showering.

Wrapped in one of the towelling bathrobes she'd found hanging behind the door, she rubbed at her wet hair with a towel as she wandered over to the window to look out. On impulse she tried the handle and found that the window was unlocked. Pushing it open showed her a bleach-boarded veranda with white slatted rails. The wood was warm beneath her bare feet as she stepped onto it, the heat of the night kind of soothing, and she stood leaning lightly against the rail and rubbing her hair while she tried to make out what the view in front of her was like.

It was truly pitch-dark out there but she caught the frothing white roll of a wave as it came into shore. It wasn't far away, perhaps a few hundred yards at most. And as her eyes grew more used to the darkness she managed to make out the shape of a white-painted gazebo not far from the beach.

It was then as she strained to focus on it that she captured a brief glimpse of Luc's face. He was standing beside the gazebo, nothing more than a shadowy bulk.

'You will get bitten by mosquitoes if you stay out here for much longer,' his cool voice drifted up to her.

'Don't be such a spoilsport or I'll go and find myself a large bottle of brandy and enjoy myself.'

He laughed; it was deep and sardonic. 'I might join you.'

This was crazy. Lizzy sighed. 'Is all of this macho sulking because I've spoiled your honeymoon plans?' she demanded. 'Because if it is I hope you are enjoying yourself!'

With that she turned and walked back into the bedroom closing the window with an angry click.

He arrived through the bedroom door as she was fastening her damp hair back with pins. Pushing a wide shoulder against the door frame, he slid his hands into his trouser pockets.

Tall, dark, handsome—sexy. Lizzy wanted to take her eyes off him but the flair that was happening in the pit of her stomach was stopping her from looking away.

'Do we try to bring this crazy marriage back on track or

do we crack open the brandy bottle?' he asked in a cynical mocking kind of voice.

'Crazy just about says it.' Lizzy shrugged, turning away so she could put down her comb. 'I think the only reason we made it this far was because we hardly made contact during last week.'

'Hell of a week for me, *cara*. I was juggling weddings and brides and fathers-in-law and the media.'

'Thank God for pre-prepared honeymoons in paradise, then.'

It was out before she could stop it, but it wasn't just what she said but the way that she said it that made her go still with her shoulders slumping wearily, and made him as silent as the grave.

'This isn't going to work,' she whispered shakily. 'I think I want to go h-home.'

'To your unforgiving father?'

Oh, that was just deliberately cruel! Lizzy winced. He released a heavy sigh.

'Bianca wanted to visit her relatives in Australia so we were going to spend our honeymoon living out of a hotel that overlooked the opera house,' he informed her flatly. 'She would not have liked it here—too quiet, and there is nowhere for her to show off and shine. I'm surprised she didn't tell you all about her Sydney plans, since she informed me that she tells you everything.'

'As we both now know, Bianca didn't always tell the truth,' Lizzy murmured, referring to the huge act her friend had put on while planning to run away with Matthew. 'I'm—sorry,' she said then, 'for constantly jumping to the wrong conclusions.'

Luc just grimaced, as sombre as hell now. 'Nina has prepared us a light supper. Would you prefer to eat here or downstairs?'

End of subject, Lizzy recognised, her gaze drifting over to the romantic table set for two. 'Downstairs I think,' she said as she looked back at him.

He just nodded and straightened up from the door. 'Five minutes, then,' and he walked away—and if he glanced at the table by the window, Lizzy didn't see him do it.

Five minutes later she walked down the stairs to find Nina waiting for her. 'Signor Luc is in the small dining room, *signora*,' she said. 'I will show you the way.'

He was sitting at a round dining table idly pinching prawns from a steaming bowl of pasta while he waited for her to arrive. Another red hibiscus flower stood in a tiny white vase in the centre of the table and the candlelight came from several sources, flickering across the white tablecloth and against fine crystal wineglasses and his lean dark face.

He came to his feet when he saw her hovering in the doorway, his golden eyes shadowing over as he scanned them down the short dusky mauve empire-line dress she'd decided to wear. Nerve-ends fluttered in response to his sombre scrutiny, and Lizzy hated the self-conscious bloom she felt warm her cheeks.

It didn't help that everything about him was so sense-crushingly elegant. Somehow in the last five minutes he'd managed to change into a white shirt left open at his throat and a pair of black silk trousers that accentuated the powerful length of his legs.

'Pre-planning,' he said, using her word from earlier with a dry cut to his voice.

'I wish you would stop reading my mind,' Lizzy complained as she walked forward.

'Your face is—expressive.'

Oh, I really needed to know that, Lizzy thought helplessly and muttered a husky thanks when he politely held her chair for her.

'I know you are probably not hungry,' he said in a lighter voice as he returned to his own seat. 'But try to eat some of this for Nina's sake. I think she's confused enough about what's going on between us, without us offending her by rejecting her food.'

Lizzy nodded. She had seen the anxious expression on the housekeeper's face when she'd come down the stairs. For a honeymoon couple supposedly so wildly in love with each other they'd been willing to take on the censure of the world just to be together, the way they were behaving had to look strange.

So, on a deep breath that pulled in a bit shaky, she reached out for the bowl of pasta and spooned a few helpings onto his plate, then did the same for her own. Luc produced a bottle of champagne from an ice bucket set by his chair and popped the cork.

'More pre-planning?' Lizzy mocked.

He just sent her a brief smile as he poured frothing foam into two crystal flutes. 'You don't touch this until you have eaten some pasta,' he instructed.

Lizzy uttered a small laugh. 'You sound like my father.'

He stiffened. 'That was not my intention.'

Staring at the carved lines on his face, she realised that she'd touched that raw nerve again in this man with nerves made of steel.

He didn't like to be compared with her father, she realized. It offended him. Nor did he always recognise a tease.

And he didn't like virgins.

The supper continued in near silence after that, his withdrawal from the sparring arena as obvious as the stern expression he wore on his face. And Lizzy had killed her own chances of managing light conversation when she'd let herself remember what was supposed to come next.

Her main problem being—she didn't know what came

next. She'd known on the flight over here. For the whole week before the flight over here she'd known exactly what was going to come next because Luc had spelt it out to her in cool, precise language.

Marriage, sex, babies—little De Santis cubs.

'It's late.' She stood up, with no idea why she picked that precise moment to throw in the keeping-up-appearances towel. 'I think I'll—go to bed.'

She didn't look at him, but she could feel his eyes on her, feel his sombre mood. And he didn't say anything, just sat there lounging in his seat twisting a champagne flute between his fingers as he watched her make her retreat.

The pale blue curtains had been drawn across the window and the intimate table for two had been cleared. The bed had been turned down and the lights in the room had been reduced to a misty glow either side of the bed. As she stared at the bed Lizzy hugged herself and shivered as if she were standing in the coldest place on earth.

Slipping out of her clothes and into the smoothest white silk nightdress she'd ever run her fingers over, she tugged pins out of her hair until her scalp stung with the angry, frustrated violence she used.

She didn't look in a mirror—she didn't want to see what was written on her face. She just crawled between the cool linen sheets, punched the pillow with a clenched fist, then laid her head on it and willed herself to go to sleep.

It took hours—hours of lying there willing and wishing, and replaying the events of the day through a revolving door of spinning images and arguments and…waiting. At some point she must have accepted that her wedding night was going to be the same sterile event her wedding day had been because she finally managed to relax and drop into a deep, dark sleep.

She was warm and relaxed and beautifully comfortable dreaming about gentle waves rolling into a soft sandy shore, when the feel of a set of long fingers gently massaging the silk covering her stomach brought her awake.

She opened her eyes, felt the lazy moist warmth of a pair of lips taste the sensitive hollow by her ear—and tensed.

CHAPTER SEVEN

'NO, BE STILL,' Luc's dark husky voice commanded.

But the vibrating rush of sensual panic made Lizzy's heart beat a fast tattoo against her ribs and on a soft breath she flipped onto her back, eyes wide and staring up at him through the darkness.

'I thought you—'

He kissed the words away, sealing his lips to her lips and gently teasing the tiny tremor with his tongue. 'We are going to rescue our wedding night, *amore*,' he told her, 'and we will take it very slowly, so slowly you will not remember to be scared.'

Lizzy wanted to say that she wasn't scared but she couldn't, the hand at her stomach awakening her senses to the message being relayed to them by the slow, sensual caress his fingers made across the slippery silk. And she could feel the heat of him as he leant over her, feel that the full length of his body pressing intimately against hers was naked and aroused.

She closed her eyes and parted her lips for him, felt his sigh as he took the invitation and sank his tongue into her mouth, gently at first, then with deepening passion as she responded, catching the increasingly erotic rhythm of his tongue stroking against hers. Her hands lifted up to clutch at him, her finger-nails digging into the muscles braced like stretched satin in his arms, her body arching upwards in a compulsive need to press against that massaging hand.

As if the telling movement triggered something inside him, he slid the hand lower, skimming over her hips and her thighs to reach for the edge of her nightgown, then with a smooth, swift, experienced efficiency stripped it all the way up to her throat.

The loss of his mouth and the slick, lithe way he removed the scrap of silk over her head set her shivering and gasping, then the kiss was deep and hungry again, the massaging hand gliding now, over her newly exposed flesh. He stroked her thighs, the gentle contours of her hip and the indentation of her waist. When she whispered something into his mouth, he rose up and looked down her length to watch as his fingers moved on over the flat of her stomach to skim across the top of one pale rounded breast.

Lizzy closed her eyes when she felt the possessive claim that hand made and was ready this time for the burning wave of pleasure that drenched her as he stroked, then cupped, then grazed the aching tip with the pad of his thumb. Her nipples sprang out in a blatant leap and she squirmed in embarrassment.

He wasn't embarrassed. He just used his long fingers to shape the quivering globe in preparation to take that tight dark rosebud into his mouth. A piercing hot sting struck from the centre of her nipple and shot all the way down to her thighs, bending her body like a wand. Once again he lifted his dark head and looked at her, then strung a gentle line of slow, tender kisses along the line of her jaw. Lizzy closed her eyes and endured until at last he stopped teasing and gave her what she wanted—the warm, seductive pressure of his mouth on her own.

She kissed him as if she would die if she didn't. She floated on a sexual high. When he tried to calm her, she ran her finger-nails into his hair and scored them down his back.

'*Il virago inglese,*' he accused on a rough shaken shudder.

Lizzy didn't care. She wanted his touch, she wanted to toss herself back to where they'd been on that other bed, before she'd chickened out and called a stop. And she wanted to feel every sensual sensation she knew was still waiting for her to experience.

So the tense curse that left his chest meant nothing to her until he used the superior strength in his arms to bring her tumbling halfway back down to earth.

'I said slowly,' he husked at her. 'I will not ravish you, Elizabeth.'

But she didn't know the difference between fast and slow. Her own wild senses were ruling her actions; the sweet, tight pulse of desire was controlling the pace. The fingers she sent spearing into his neck so she could bring his mouth back to hers were fierce and urgent. 'I want to be ravished,' she whispered to him.

His kiss-heated lips twisted into a grim smile. 'You don't understand the concept and I will not give you an excuse to accuse me of ravishing you once it is done and your conscience decides to torment you.'

Her eyes widened in protest. 'I w-wouldn't do that—'

'You would,' he insisted. 'You want me but you don't want to want me, you have simply allowed yourself to forget that. In fact,' he added, sending a sardonic gleam to her liquid green eyes, 'I predict you will take great pleasure in accusing me of anything that might come to mind.'

'How can you be so cold and detached that your mind can even think of these things right now?' she threw at him helplessly.

'I am not cold and detached.' But his dark face clenched. 'I am just trying to play this as fairly as I can for you!'

'Me?' Lizzy choked out a laugh, feeling the whole wretched, glorious wash of pleasure swirl into bitterness. 'You haven't been fair to me since you met me.' Clenching her fists, she used them to try and push him away. 'You're a lousy lover, Luc,' she added in thick frustration when she couldn't budge him by even half an inch. 'The kind that sounds like he wants me to sign another contract before he condescends to move this marriage on!'

Once again her tongue had outpaced her common sense. Lizzy knew it the moment the cutting accusation was out. Her breathing disappeared, her eyelashes flickering as she took in the look that had frozen his face. Teeth burying themselves into her full bottom lip, she waited, heart pounding, her foolish stubbornness refusing to let her take the words back before it was too late.

And she knew she should have done—his complete stillness told her that she should. Yet he didn't move, didn't speak, he didn't make any really visible sign that she'd managed to cut into him at all. It was just there in the pulsating silence, in the way she was suddenly feeling the difference in their age and experience, and in the tiny quivers stinging her muscles in places they should not be doing at a tense moment like this.

'S-say something,' she breathed when she could stand it no longer.

He moved then, like a man who had just come to a grim decision. One of his arms snaked outwards and suddenly a light switched on, bathing them both in a soft golden glow that did nothing to lessen Lizzy's tension one bit. She actually felt her eyes turn black. Yet he still just continued to look down at her, into her huge wary eyes and the silken tumble of chestnut curls rippling the pillow around her delicately featured very pale face.

And her heart wasn't beating fast now, it was thumping slow and thick. His face, his beautiful, beautiful face was still so expressionless it just didn't go with what he did next.

What he did was to spear his long fingers into her hair, then curve them around the back of her neck. As she gasped he tilted her head back so it arched her slender white throat, then lowered his dark head and buried his mouth in her taut, smooth flesh.

Nothing in her meagre experience with men helped to warn her as to what was coming. It was seduction at its most deep and determined level. It was the man of experience making no concessions for her foolishly defiant innocence. He made love to her with a grim and silent precision; he dragged each and every sensually erotic sensation to the stinging surface of her pale, smooth, receptive skin. He moved his mouth in hot, sensual glides until he reached her parted, trembling mouth, then he kissed her long and deep and without mercy until she was dizzy with it, throbbing and drunk. And he used his hands and his mouth and his tongue in ways and in places she hadn't known could be so deliciously good.

The quiet command of his voice worked her like a puppet. She was trapped, enslaved by the string-pulling power of his knowledge and her own desire to feel whatever he decided to bestow on her too-responsive flesh. He caressed each curve and hollow and soft warm crevice of her body; he drew her taut with exquisite sensation with his hands and his mouth and his teeth. He kneaded the rounded, swollen fullness of her breasts and sent her teeth into his satin, taut shoulder when he teased and sucked their eager tips.

She even felt him tremble once or twice when her restless, untutored fingers scraped across his flesh. And when the downward glide of his trailing fingers finally took control of the pulsing ache between her legs she flailed in a morass of hot feeling, lost to reality because her own heady consciousness had locked onto the will of her body and the way he slowly, relentlessly brought her climbing and crawling and panting and needing to a whimpering, pleading peak.

No single part of her did not know what it was like to be caressed by him—no nerve-end, no muscle, no velvet dark place of intimacy, until she pulsed and throbbed and breathed out his name in a helpless, breathless, sensual chant.

She hadn't opened her eyes in ages, not since she'd lowered her eyelids in surrender and let him do this to her. But as she felt his weight easing down on top of her and her thighs being urged apart her eyelids lifted, her eyes making deep, deep contact with the heavy gold darkness in his.

Everything about him was heavy gold darkness, the breadth of his shoulders blocking out most of the lamplight, the long, hard-muscled torso pressing down on her with his hips. She felt the presence and the power of his erection nudge against her carefully prepared warm and wet and swollen flesh. His mouth was still somber, but it was tender when he took her mouth in yet another deep, drugging kiss.

Then it was there. His hands cupped her bottom to lift her and he made that first smooth, blinding thrust with his hips. Her body throbbed and stretched to accommodate him; she felt him like a burning shaft of fire in the innocence of her sheath. Her breath caught, her fingers dug into his shoulders and sensation poured in a swirling wave of fear and anticipation down the pulsing length of where they had joined.

'You are sure you want this?' he husked at her.

The fact that he'd even asked the question after so much pulsing macho male domination made tears sting the back of her throat. The point surely was—did *he* want it?

Lizzy nodded, her mouth just a breath away from his mouth, her eyes clinging dark and vulnerable and helplessly needy to his. It was his eyes that closed when he made that final invasion, his mouth that quivered tautly as she tried to choke back a cry of pain. It was his hands that trembled as he pushed the hair away from her face, then kissed it, kissed it in soft, soothing touches until he felt the tension slowly seep out of her. Then she felt him go deeper, felt the singing dance of her nerve-ends clamour to his probing force. His hands were gliding down the silken thighs to her calves then, and lifting them until her legs circled his waist.

The action sent him even deeper, he shuddered and whispered something in Italian she did not catch, then he was folding her into the strong embrace of his arms and moving— moving, feeding them both into a sensuously searing rhythm that throbbed like a living entity inside her. Her fingers clung to his back as he increased the pace with each hot, pleasurable thrust. She knew where she was going but didn't know how to reach it. She whimpered anxiously against his mouth.

He caught hold of her hair again to push her head backwards. 'Look at me,' he said, and she lifted heavy eyelids she hadn't been aware of closing, to be trapped in the burning dark flames in his eyes. Then, like that, he made it happen for her, made her body quicken and finally surrender to the bright and sizzling accelerated rush.

Her first cry broke his rhythm from deep and slow to short and fast and she lost it—lost whatever it was she'd been desperately hanging onto as she shot on an explosion of fierce pleasure into wild white pulsating light, while he held her and watched her and orchestrated each wave as it battered into her, each helpless cry, each quivering, broken, convulsive tremor that just seemed to go on and on and on…until with a low, thick groan he joined her, spilling heat on the flames with a sharp stabbing movement that sent an ecstatic pleasure rippling through every muscle and bone and sinew he had.

Seduction, she acknowledged long minutes later when she finally drifted back to earth again. I've just been completely, beautifully, thoroughly and ruthlessly seduced.

He still hadn't moved and his weight was heavy on her; she could feel the still-pounding beat of his heart against her crushed breasts. She became aware that her legs were still wrapped around him, though their bodies were no longer intimately joined.

Still, she knew the image of the two of them like this was going to live with her for the rest of her life.

Coupling, she named it.

It was that physical and basic.

Releasing the still trembling tension out of her limbs, she slid them away from him. As if her movement made him also decide to move, he levered himself up onto a forearm, reached out and switched off the light.

It was so abrupt, so stunningly final. He didn't release her when he shifted his weight onto the bed beside her, but there were no words spoken between them, no clash of eyes. It was as if now it was over he was expecting them both to just fall asleep.

It hurt. It made vulnerable tears sting the backs of her eyes and her throat. She was damp between her legs and the lingering tremor of pleasure still worked within her as her stretched muscles slowly contracted back to their original state.

When she couldn't bear it and tried to speak he just put his hand to the back of her head and pressed her face into the prickly dark warmth of his chest.

He fell asleep like that—holding her. Lizzy had never felt

so wretched in her entire life. Had she brought it on herself? Was this grim silent aftermath her reward for persistently taking stabs at him—at his irritatingly unflappable control, at his prowess as a lover? She wished she knew why she did it. She wished she understood how she could resent him so angrily yet want him so badly. She just didn't understand herself at all.

She tried to move away from him, but his powerful arms held her fast. Oddly—again—she found she liked being held by him and slowly let her muscles relax.

It didn't occur to her that he was lying there with his eyes wide open, and that each time she moved against him he was having to fight to keep his response in check.

And she didn't know that while she was seeing what they'd just done as a basic coupling, he was seeing it as the most soul-stripping experience of his cynical sexual life.

Lizzy drifted asleep in the warm cocoon of his arms and awoke late the next morning to find an empty place beside her in the bed. In a way it was a relief. No awkward moments having to face him while her defences were down, no stumbling around trying to think of something to say that wouldn't come out sounding silly and vulnerable and gauche. She could shower at her leisure and get her act together.

No, she couldn't. Instead she sank down on the edge of the plunge bath and let the whole high octane event of her wedding night rush through her head and her body in small explosions of remembered feelings, few of which made her feel good about herself—or about him.

What were they doing to each other? *Why* were they doing it? All Lizzy knew as she sat there remembering the hot tempo of their passionate coupling was that somehow, in the last week leading up to last night, she had allowed Luc De Santis to become a terrible fever of desire that had built and built inside her until it had taken her over.

Because she loved him—?

No! She stood up with a jerk. *No*, she didn't love him. She didn't *want* to love him!

Dear God, don't let me go down that no-hope route.

Coming down the stairs half an hour later took courage because she still hadn't reconciled last night in her head. And she ached all over, in places she didn't think it was possible to ache, places that made her feel sensitive and self-aware and—yes, scared of what to expect from him when they met.

Unsure where to go once she reached the hallway, she followed her instincts and found herself back in the room they'd eaten supper in the night before. It was late, almost lunchtime by her reckoning, though her body clock was so up the creek, she wasn't sure if that meant lunchtime in Italy or lunchtime here because she'd forgotten to put on her watch when she'd changed before she'd left the Lake Como villa.

The room looked different in the daylight. Bigger and bright, with the sun shaded from streaming in through the wide open windows by a huge striped awning she could see rippling softly in the breeze outside. Beneath it was a smooth stone patio stretching out to the glinting blue of a large swimming pool, and beyond that the lush colourful growth of a lovingly tended tropical garden leading right down to the edge of a blinding white sandy beach, then the rich turquoise-blue of the Caribbean sea. No sign of the gazebo from this side of the house, she noticed, and the waves that washed the shore lapped gently as if they were too lazy to foam and roll.

A sound from behind her made her turn sharply, expecting to find Luc, only to watch Nina come hurrying into the room with a beaming smile on her face.

'Ah, so you have surfaced, *signora*. Mr Luc said to leave you to sleep your jet lag away, but I was beginning to worry that you would never wake up to this beautiful, beautiful day!'

The housekeeper's gushing bright chatter eased some of the tension out of Lizzy's body. Within minutes she was sitting in the same chair she'd sat in the night before, sipping freshly squeezed orange juice and eating slices of delicious fresh fruit with Nina still fussing around her like a mother hen taking care of a brand-new chick.

'Please call me Lizzy,' she said after the *signora* began to grate. She didn't feel like a *signora*, she didn't even feel like *Mrs*, though the gold ring on her finger told her she was.

Which then asked the question—what did she feel like?

'Mr Luc went out after his breakfast to check on his farmers, as he always does when he arrives here,' Nina was saying, gaining Lizzy's attention quicker than anything else could.

'His farmers?' she prompted.

Nina gave a nod, pouring steaming coffee into her coffee-cup. 'He didn't tell you? This house and the land belonged to his grandmamma. Her portrait hangs in the main salon. I will show you later, if you like. Mr Luc spent a lot of his childhood here, during the school holidays. His grandmother was a forceful lady who pioneered the concept of collective farming on the island. Mr Luc has continued her success in the wake of her untimely death last year.'

Last year? Lizzy had not known that Luc had suffered such a loss so recently.

Nina nodded. 'We still miss her—Mr Luc most of all. She made him human, he once told me.' The housekeeper paused to offer up a sigh. 'It is the downside of being born into great wealth and responsibility, I suppose, that you switch off your softer instincts so you will keep yourself strong.' Then she showed Lizzy her wonderful smile again. 'Now you are here to make him feel human, heh?' The gleam in her rich brown eyes made Lizzy burn. 'His grandmamma would like you. You have a look of her, and you are stubborn like she was, and—'

'English,' a different voice drawled.

Lizzy froze in the process of picking up a juicy chunk of fresh pineapple, her eyes skittering towards the door where he stood leaning against the framework, casual as hell dressed in pale chinos and a blue tee shirt, his hair ruffled as if by the breeze. Every inch of him was long, lithe, so spare of flesh it was like looking at a breathtaking study of firm-muscled, lean golden strength that set her senses responding with tight little pulses deep down in the intimate place between her legs.

'Virago.' The housekeeper turned to smile at him, seemingly unaware as to how the tension in the room had just rocketed. 'You called her the English virago.'

'*Il virago inglese,*' he softly translated, then watched, his eyes mostly hidden beneath the heavy fall of his soot-black eyelashes, the telling dark flush march up Lizzy's throat and cheeks.

He'd called her that last night, when she'd buried her teeth in him. He'd said something similar to her on the plane. Stifled beyond speech by the endearment's link with one of his close family, she dropped the piece of pineapple back onto the plate and came jerkily to her feet.

'*Buon giorno, la mia moglie bella,*' he murmured smoothly then, the hidden gold in his eyes flaring briefly as they took in her tiny white vest-top and her short blue skirt.

Lizzy was suddenly excruciatingly aware of the pinprick sting of her nipples inside the flimsy white cups of her bra, and the amount of leg left on show by the shortness of the skirt. Her hair was tied back and she wished that it weren't as a fresh layer of heat seeped into her cheeks. She wished she were standing here in a full-length woollen coat despite the overwhelming Caribbean heat.

'No reply for me, *cara*?' he mocked her numbing silence.

No, she thought, because I just can't speak yet. Instead she used her tongue to soothe the sudden tremor that had developed across her lips. He watched it happen, and there was nothing on his face to tell her what he was thinking, yet she sensed a tension in him that literally picked at her flesh as he dipped those eyes down her full length once again.

'So my sweet virgin bride is robbed of speech,' he mocked her. 'Perhaps there is some hope left for my lousy technique.'

Lizzy tensed. *'Don't,'* she shivered out, mortified beyond bearing that he could say something like to her at all after last night and especially in front of his housekeeper.

'We are alone.' He smiled briefly at the way she flicked her startled eyes to the place where Nina had been standing. 'She beat a hasty retreat when you blushed so charmingly. And it is too late to keep your virgin status on our wedding night a secret, *amore*. There was blood on the sheets.'

The shockingly abrupt announcement froze the colour out of Lizzy's face.

'You did not notice?' Levering himself away from the door, he started moving towards her. 'One of the maids surely will have done when she remade the bed after you left it.'

Lizzy flinched when the sleeve to his shirt brushed her arm as he reached past her to pick up her discarded piece of pineapple.

'No comment,' he mocked when she still said nothing. 'I admit, when I saw it, it made me feel positively medieval.' He put the pineapple into his mouth. 'I half expected to arrive back here this lunchtime to see the evidence hanging from the window as proof of your chastity and my undoubtedly—'

With a stifled choke, Lizzy turned and ran, switching the cruel battery of his words off like a flick of a switch. As she made it into the hall without throwing up she wondered bitterly if the heavy crash she heard behind her was a sign that he was angry he'd been left mocking a lost audience!

Outside the heat was so intense she almost changed her mind and went back into the coolness of the house. But—no. Burning alive was a better option than going back in there, she thought painfully as she took off across the grass, heading for—she didn't know where or care.

She did not understand what made him want to be so constantly cruel to her. Twenty-four hours as his bought bride and already she did not know how much more of it she could take.

Dropping down on the stone steps of the gazebo, she hugged her knees to her chest and stared out to sea. She was trembling, her mind filled with lurid images of giggling maids whispering their secret to the rest of the staff here. Luc had called it medieval, Lizzy wanted to call it—

A step sounded close beside her, shutting off her painful thought patterns to replace them with a whole aching set of new ones.

CHAPTER EIGHT

'I'm—sorry,' Luc murmured tautly. 'That was unforgivably brutal of me.'

So he was aware of it? Lizzy supposed it had to mean something at least. Though thinking that did not stop the glaze of hurt from washing across her eyes before she blinked it away again.

'When you've had enough of punishing me for being the wrong woman you married,' she whispered, 'do me one small favour, Luc, and arrange my flight home for me, please.'

His sigh was carried away on the light breeze coming in from the ocean. When he dropped down into a squat in front of her and gently touched his fingers to her pale cheek, she refused to look at him and still just wanted to break down and weep.

'I was shocked,' he said gruffly, 'when I saw the—evidence myself this morning. I felt I had stolen something from you that did not belong to me.'

'That's your only excuse?' Lizzy still would not look at him.

'No. I have others,' he admitted, 'though I don't think you're ready to hear them right now.'

He was probably right. She'd heard more than enough of his cynical view of everything. Her heart was breaking into little pieces in her chest and her eyes were still stinging.

'I will not take the stick you should be beating Bianca with,' she told him thickly. 'You spoiled last night for me—twice, counting your performance just now—and I think you did it deliberately.'

'I attack when I am on the defensive.'

Doesn't everyone? Lizzy thought painfully.

'I expected you to throw some deserved accusations at me just now, so I got in first.'

'You know what you are, Luc?' At last she turned her face to look at him, and felt no sympathy whatsoever for the now penitent expression she saw on his handsome dark face. 'You're so cold and cynical about everything you don't recognise feelings in others. You believe you can treat me with contempt because I made it so obvious from the start that I'm—attracted to you.'

A strange smile touched his tense mouth. 'Not contempt,' he denied.

'So there was blood on the sheets,' Lizzy continued unsteadily. 'A sensitive man would have gently pointed it out to me, but not you. You stride off into the day without a care as to what the embarrassment was going to do to me.'

'I thought you would have noticed it for yourself.'

'Well, I didn't.' She turned away again. In truth she hadn't dared look at the bed once she'd scrambled out of it. 'And what is it you find so wrong with my—inexperience?' she challenged suddenly. 'Why do you believe it's okay to mock it, *make* a mockery of it?'

'I can do better.'

Too late for Lizzy.

'Yesterday I was—angry about a lot of things,' he disclosed. 'Things I should not have brought into our bedroom and should not have carried with me out of it this morning.

Now I am asking you to accept my apology and my promise that I can and will do better from now on.'

Quite a speech for the sardonic man who believed himself above such things.

'You're hunting,' she murmured absently.

There was a sharp moment of shock, then the soft sound of rueful laughter, then his fingers returned to her cheek and firmly turned her face.

'I am hunting,' he agreed with a real smile that actually relaxed his tense features, 'which makes this a bad day for male lions, *cara*, because it means they must be feeling desperate.'

That was a message, Lizzy recognised, a serious hint wrapped up in a new kind of rueful warmth. She drew in a breath, wishing she could decide if this was just another one of his clever strategies aimed to keep his life running on its nice even keel.

'Make me feel ashamed of you once more,' she said finally, 'and I walk away from this marriage no matter what you threaten me with.'

To her surprise he just nodded, no clever quick counter-attack, face still serious, the dark golden eyes wrapped in luxurious dark eyelashes, an even shape to his beautiful mouth. He'd dropped the cool mask, Lizzy realised, and all she was seeing now was the too handsome, worryingly alluring man.

Then he was rising to his full height and holding out a hand for her to take so he could help her up. Lizzy stared at that hand for a few seconds, still hesitant to take what she knew it was offering, yet too aware of the tingling sting of entice-ment at work in her blood to stop her own hand from lifting and settling into his. His fingers closed around hers and he drew her upright. When she tried to take her hand back he held onto it and used it to bring her even closer until she was standing a mere breath away from touch-close to his lean, hard, now very familiar length.

Her heart began to thump. He was going to kiss her, and she couldn't make up her mind if she wanted to be kissed right now. Tension inched up along the length of her spine and made the air shiver as it left her lungs.

'I n-need some things your wonderful style team forgot to pack in my luggage.' She went for a diversion on a quick agitated rush of speech.

'Like what?' he murmured.

The murmur was disturbingly husky. 'A gentleman doesn't ask that question,' she responded distractedly.

'I thought we had already established that I'm not one—a gentleman,' he added.

She looked up, at his mouth, saw the hint of a grimace taking control of it, felt her own lips tremble and part. 'A s-sunhat, then, and a truckload of sun screen,' she compromised her answer, trying so hard not to sound as unnerved by his closeness as she actually felt.

But maybe he knew, maybe she even quivered. It was difficult for her to tell any more because tense inner quivers around him had become such a permanent thing she was learning she had to live with. Anyway, he gave a tug at her hand. The thin gap between them disappeared altogether, the warmth of his body heat stimulated every nerve-end she possessed and sent her eyes lifting up to clash warily with his.

Whatever he saw reflected in her eyes sent a strange kind of grimace moving across his lips. Then he did it—he kissed her.

It was such a brief embrace that it had gone before she could even think to react to it.

'Then let's go shopping,' was all he said.

Lizzy knew then that they had just sealed yet another deal

between them, though heck if she had enough sense left to work out what this one was about.

And he was back to playing it cool again, being the guy who liked to be in control of everything—including his renegade wife. He drove them into town in a soft-top sports car with the roof firmly in place to keep the heat of the sun off her fair skin. They strolled in and out of small shops painted in different pretty pastel shades, each one carrying the kind of interestingly individual things that made Lizzy want to linger and browse.

He chose her sunhat while she wasn't looking, a wide, floppy-brimmed thing made of bright pink straw that he paid for, coolly put on her head, then walked her out of the shop without giving her the chance to object about the colour and the way it had to be clashing with the colour of her hair.

'Arrogant,' she muttered.

'All of my life,' he answered smoothly, and walked her into a pharmacy and proceeded to pick out the highest factor sun screen he could find and Lizzy let him because—

Well, why not? she told herself. He'd taken command of every other decision in her life, like her clothes, her wedding—her wedding night. So she left him to it and went off to find the other female-type items she'd wanted to buy that she'd left off her list back at the gazebo.

He paid the bill.

And she began to feel like a very mute, very pampered female with just enough resentment burning inside her to stop her from liking it.

As he walked beside her his hand was always in touch with her somewhere—her hand, her arm, the base of her spine—until they bumped into some people he knew, when his arm became that angled pressure across her back and the hand a long fingered clamp in the indentation of her waist that drew her in very close to his side.

Making a silent statement as he'd done at the wedding or being protective of his new bride? Lizzy didn't know but she leant into him anyway for protection as he introduced her as, 'My wife, Elizabeth.'

She could tell from their expressions that the news about their scandalous marriage had even reached as far as this tiny island in the Caribbean.

'*Cara*, this is Elena and Fabio Romano, friends of mine,' he completed the introductions.

Elena Romano was young and slender and extremely beautiful, but she wore the kind of curious gleam in her dark eyes that made Lizzy think of a black-eyed witch with long sharp nails. Fabio Romano was tall and tanned and middle-aged with a languid boredom about him that had her wondering if that was where Luc was going to be by the time he reached his middle years.

They said they were cruising the Caribbean on their yacht and invited Luc and Lizzy to join them for the afternoon. Luc was beautifully suave and gracious with his refusal. Fabio Romano was beautifully suave and gracious in his acceptance of it. His lovely wife was not. Her black eyes sparked with irritation, which she vented on Lizzy.

'Such a sweet hat, *cara*,' she murmured, 'very cute and— pink. How do you dare to wear that shade with your hair colouring?'

'Luc chose it,' Lizzy answered smoothly. 'He likes cute and pink.'

Elena's light laugh tinkled off into the sunlight. Lizzy felt the press of Luc's fingers as they bit into her waist.

'Ah,' Elena hadn't finished, 'that explains your wedding

photograph in this morning's papers—' she nodded '—and the positively dramatic image you made of the pale young virginal bride standing next to her sternly reformed rake.'

Well, the cruelly perceptive bitch, Lizzy thought breathlessly. 'My style team managed to get it just right, don't you think?' She smiled through gritted white teeth.

She hadn't been around Bianca for years without learning how to respond to such a woman. And even if the floppy brim to her cute pink hat hadn't been blocking him off from the shoulders upwards, nothing on earth would have made her look up at him as she felt Luc's fingers bite into her again.

'And with so little notice.' Elena slid her eyes down to Lizzy's stomach, the suggestion she was implying shocking Lizzy into releasing a gasp.

'Gosh,' she rallied. 'It never entered my head that people would think poor Luc had been *forced* into marrying me!'

'They don't.' Surprisingly it was Fabio Romano who pulled himself out of his boredom to put a stop to this. 'Elena is fishing for information. She is always fishing for information—it is the staple diet for a professional bitch.'

Well, he said it, Lizzy's eyes told the other woman while Elena flushed. A few minutes later they'd made their polite farewells and were walking back to where they'd left the car.

'You were a great help,' Lizzy said, stiff with anger and a very bruised pride.

Luc, on the other hand, was coolly indifferent. 'You will learn soon enough that it is safer to say nothing at all around people like Elena.'

Well, Lizzy didn't want to learn to *be quiet*. If that was a brief taster of what was waiting for her when they returned to Italy, then she didn't want any part of it.

'She's attracted to you, which is why she got her nails into me.'

'Now you are being fantastical.'

'An ex-lover, then, with a grudge because she didn't end up your dramatically pale virginal bride.'

'You would have to go back a long way into Elena's past to find the virgin,' he laughed. 'And why are you angry with me when you were more than capable of handling the situation without any help from me?'

'I don't like your lifestyle,' she muttered.

He didn't say anything to that one. He just opened the car door for her and waited for her to get in. Lizzy pulled off her hat and placed it on her lap, then watched in simmering silence as he dropped her purchases at her feet before he shut her door and strode round the car bonnet to get in beside her.

'I want to see the photograph she was talking about,' she told him.

'No.' The engine vibrated beneath her on a low growling leap into life.

'Why not?' she persisted. 'Have you seen it?' she then demanded sharply.

All she got back was a view of his profile set in stone. Her head suddenly began to buzz as he swept them back up the hill towards the villa. Like little pieces of a jigsaw falling into place, Lizzy began to link that ugly scene he'd orchestrated this morning with what Elena Romano had said.

'You have seen it,' she declared in a hot, husky voice filled with fizzing resentment. 'It was the reason why you were so nasty to me this morning. You saw that photo and didn't like what it fed out there for everyone else to see—namely me, looking all pale and interesting, and you, looking like some poor rich guy who'd been caught by the oldest trick in the book.'

'You possess a wild imagination,' he drawled casually.

'I want to see it,' Lizzy repeated.

He said nothing, just pulled the car to a stop outside the sugar pink plantation house and climbed out of it. Lizzy did the same thing, glaring at him across the car's soft top. He was frowning, grimly ignoring her as if she were an irritating fly he would like to swat away with his hand.

Well, that was fine, she told herself as she stalked around the car and into the house. She wasn't a complete air-head. She knew a man like Luc didn't go anywhere unless he had a reliable connection to the internet.

So she began stalking the huge hallway, opening doors and glancing inside them before she moved on to the next.

'If you want to see over the whole house, *cara*,' his hateful voice murmured, 'I am happy to show you around without risking the paintwork on all the doors. Go away, Nina,' he added as a mere calm aside.

Lizzy turned in time to see the housekeeper disappearing towards the back of the house. *He* was standing in the middle of the pale marble floor looking so darn together against her sizzling anger that she wanted to fly at him with her nails unsheathed.

Instead she balled her fingers into tense fists by her sides. 'If you and the rest of the world can see a picture of me at my own wedding, then *I* want to see it!' she insisted furiously.

'I assure you, you don't,' he said, smiled, then dropped the smile and shot out an impatient sigh when all she did was to spin her back to him and move on to fling open the next door. 'Why is it,' he snapped out, 'that everyone else gets to enjoy your placid side while I only get the—?'

His voice just stopped. Lizzy didn't notice. She was too busy taking in the room she had just stepped into filled with the softest light and gentle shadows—and a huge gold-framed portrait hanging from one of the pale blue walls.

'The virago,' she murmured, just too stunned to remember that she was supposed to be hunting down some kind of office in this many-roomed mansion. 'Dear God,' she added on a thick shaken swallow as her feet took her further into the room.

'La Contessa Alexandra De Santis,' Luc's deep dry voice fed to her from behind. 'Grande Dame, matriarch, bad mother, wonderful grandmother, and my other *virago inglese.*'

'She looks like me,' Lizzy whispered.

'I believe Nina said so,' he returned evenly.

'But you don't?' She was staring up at the face of a breathtakingly beautiful creature who could have come straight out of a Titian painting.

'Your hair is darker and your eyes are grey, not blue.'

But the shape of her mouth and the small pointed chin and the hourglass shape of her slender figure inside a gentian-blue gown that could only have been fashioned by the finest haute couture looked like Lizzy.

'How old is she here?' she asked on a reverent murmur.

'Forty nine,' he replied, dragging another gasp from Lizzy's shocked lips because she looked barely eighteen. 'My grandfather commissioned the painting as a gift for her fiftieth birthday. He claimed that her beauty was the only thing about her that kept them together. She claimed they stayed together because she allowed it, despite the countless affairs he enjoyed during their long marriage.'

'She loved him, you mean.'

'I like to think so, though I don't believe he deserved such devoted loyalty—and divorce was not heard of in Italian society in their day.'

'And she made him pay in other ways.'

'Now that was astute,' he said after a startled moment.

Because I feel like I know her outside and in, Lizzy thought breathlessly. And I'm standing right here with a man I wouldn't trust as far as I could pick him up and throw him.

'You think I am like my grandfather,' Luc murmured.

And *that* was astute of *him*. 'You take what you want,' she responded, 'because you believe you have a right to and you don't play fair while you do it.' Turning around, she pushed her chin up. 'I want to see that photograph now.'

His eyes took their time shifting from the portrait to the determined tilt of her face. What he was thinking didn't show. If he was still trying to compare her to his grandmother, it didn't show. If he had decided to marry her because she reminded him of probably the only person he had ever really loved, even that didn't show.

Hard, tough, unemotional, arrogant, she found herself listing all over again while she stood waiting for his response. The fact that she'd just realised he had a title attached to his name, though she'd never heard anyone use it, only added more reason as to why he was like he was.

Her heart began to thump oddly because he still wasn't saying anything and she was damned if she was going to back down now—even if there was something going on in those implacable golden eyes that she did not quite understand or like.

'We keep fighting,' he said finally.

Lizzy nodded, lips pinned together.

'And you persist in believing that you can win.'

Well, give up on that belief and she might as well lie down and let him trample all over her. 'I can use a computer, so if you just point me in the right direction...' she prompted.

He smiled. It wasn't a condescending smile, but neither was it pleasant. If she could see herself she'd probably be backing off, but she could not see how the defiant tilt of her chin was making her spiralling hair flame around her face or that the rounded shape of her breasts was moving too fast inside her top, nor was she aware that her nipples had sprung into two tantalisingly tight teasing buds.

He was aware, though, aware enough to allow his body to respond to temptation, aware enough to enjoy drawing out the tension between them until her eyelashes feathered down on her cheeks as she dropped her eyes from his.

She found her gaze settling on his throat. It was that taut golden throat that had been the cause of all her problems, she reminded herself. And the still vivid memory of her lips brushing against it made her suddenly burn to place her lips there again. It was a shock—her whole fascination with his throat was a bewildering puzzle she just could not understand. Yet it was there pulsing away with its bad temptation for her to just lean in and—

Maybe a retreat was sometimes a good idea, she heard herself think in a tense, anxious backtrack. 'I think I'll go and—'

'Coward.' He laughed softly—and moved so fast she didn't see it coming until she was already locked into his embrace and his mouth was hungry on hers.

It was a hot kiss, a long and demanding and seriously, seriously deep kind of kiss. When it was over she was breathless, the front of her body pressing into him with a soft and needy intimacy that brought a flush to her cheeks, and her only comfort was that she could feel the sense drenching evidence of his response pressing against her.

'I wish you would stop just grabbing me like this!' she managed to push out on a stifled whisper.

'I don't play fair,' he reminded her dryly, and captured her mouth again. By the time this one was over she was trembling against him and her fingers were clutching at the back of his neck.

'Fast or slow?' he husked, still toying sensually with the cushion soft heat of her mouth. 'Fast means we rip our clothes off and get very basic right here against the wall or down on the floor. Slow means we try to make it to the privacy of our bedroom. You choose.'

Choose? 'I don't know,' Lizzy mumbled helplessly. 'I'm not very good at all of this.'

'Trust me, *cara*, you are very good at it,' he responded harshly, though harsh in this case was very sexy.

So sexy she gave in to, and leant in to let her tongue make a half-clumsy slide on his taut golden skin. His rasping curse was exciting. The way his hands took hold of her by the waist and put her away from him brought a whispered, 'Sorry,' shaking from her lips.

He just grabbed hold of her hand and began trailing her behind him into the hallway, the decision apparently made for her as to where the rest of this was going to take place. He towed her up the stairs and into the bedroom. Shutting the door behind them, he then towed her over to the bed and propped her up against one of the posts.

'Don't move,' he said as he took a step back from her.

Lizzy only wished that she had the power to move, but she didn't. She just leant there and watched as he began to strip his clothes off. Dark olive skin wearing the gloss of warmth and the taut muscle formation that rippled as he moved was revealed to her in swift degrees. His tee shirt—gone, his long fingers dragging her eyes down the cluster-dark arrow of hair on his torso to watch, in churning anticipation, him unfasten his trousers and strip them away. He wore flat loafers that he heeled off and kicked to one side, no socks to cover his long brown feet. Only one item of clothing was left on his body, and her breathing grew piercingly tight as he stripped that away too.

'You like what you see?' he demanded silkily.

Lizzy glossed her lips with her tongue and nodded.

'You wish to lick me some more?'

'Yes, please,' she breathed.

He took that step back towards her, so impossibly beautiful and arrogant and powerful he made her heart pump deliriously.

'Enjoy,' he invited, and she couldn't believe how quickly she moved towards him, she couldn't believe it was she who was so eagerly touching him with her fingers, tasting him with her tongue and grazing his flesh with her teeth, while he stood there, passively allowing her with his hands grasping the bedpost so she was trapped in the circle of his arms.

Though he wasn't really passive—he flinched and flexed and breathed tautly to every move she made on him. When she stretched up for his mouth he gave it, when she bravely dared to run her fingers down through the mat of hair and explore the length of his erection, the velvet-smooth length jerked and pulsed.

And he was breathing as unevenly as she was, the tension in him clenching his muscles tight. When she flung her arms around his neck and just clung, he seemed to see it as some kind of surrender because he muttered something in Italian, then took control. Her skirt ripped because he couldn't be bothered to find the zip on it. As she gasped in shock it landed in a warm heap at her feet, and he was already bending down to strip away her panties. The hungry intrusion of his tongue between her legs before he straightened up again drew a keening cry from her throat. Her top went next, sliding over her head and disappearing out of her line of vision, her breasts bouncing as he released them from her bra. He caught them up in the cups of his long fingers, nothing prepared her for the hot wave of pleasure that danced through her as his mouth ravished their tender, tight peaks.

If this was slow in his estimation, it wasn't in Lizzy's. It was hot and passionately fast. Her fingers bit into the solid strength of his biceps, and she trembled and writhed, and kept her eyes closed because that way everything felt so much more powerful. When he finally tumbled her down onto the bed her slender legs parted so she could feel the full impact of him when he stretched himself out on top of her.

For a full sense-locking second she thought he was just going to take her right now like this, and she was shocked by how much she wanted him to. But he didn't. Slow came in an agony of new experiences; she was a physical, sensual, trembling wreck by the time he decided it was time.

And this was no coupling, she found herself thinking hazily as he came inside her with a long, slow, probing push that took the breath from her lungs. It was a hot, deep, passionate lovemaking where the two of them became one single unit moving and breathing and finally reaching the agonised beauty of perfect pleasure, which left her skin and her nerves and her muscles and even her bones a livened, quivering, warm liquid heap.

And his kiss this time lingered, his arms the tower of strength she clung to as he slowly brought her back to earth. I will never be able to let another man do this to me, she thought hazily, and had no idea that she'd whispered the thought out loud.

She only knew that something made him begin the whole, long, sensual journey all over again. They spent the whole afternoon like that—making love. They did not dress. They did not leave their room. They showered together and lazed together and stroked and kissed and made love together and eventually slept together in an intimately relaxed tangle of limbs.

CHAPTER NINE

HE WAS STRANGE, Lizzy found herself thinking again, as she watched Luc stand out in the hot sunlight deep in discussion with one of the island farmers, while she sat on the shady porch of a tiny blue-painted farmhouse, sipping at a tall glass of something cool and slightly odd-tasting the farmer's wife had brought out for her to quench her thirst.

He had three definite settings as far as she had been able to work out in the two weeks they'd been on the island. Cool and sophisticated, as on the couple of occasions he'd condescended to let her into the company of friends he had here. Or serious and deep, as he was being now while he listened intently to what the farmer was explaining to him. Then there was so hot and passionate she'd sometimes wondered if she was going to survive the demands he made on her body and her senses. Especially in the warm dead of night when he would wake her up because he needed her there and then with no space given for her to refuse.

If she could refuse, which she'd discovered she couldn't.

She was hooked on Luciano De Santis, she mused satirically as her eyes drifted over his wide shoulders pressed against the white of his tee shirt that hugged his torso all the way down to the narrow band of his cargo shorts. Naked, he was—colossal. Dressed, he was just too sexy to be real, even in a pair of baggy knee length shorts that had seen better days.

The old sting set up its usual flurry low in her abdomen as she slid her gaze down what was left on show of his long tanned legs. A man's legs, she observed. Strong and sturdy, peppered with dark hair and tightened by the muscular formation she knew for a fact was capable of crushing her in two.

Moving her eyes all the way back up him again, she saw the slight twitch he gave with his shoulders and knew he knew she was looking at him. It was like that between them now—a constant awareness that flowed across space like a magnetic vibration. Taking another absent gulp at her odd tasting drink she wondered if it all would still be there once they returned to reality the day after tomorrow.

Milan, not her other comfort zone on the shores of Lake Como. The real world in which Luc would slip back into his busy life and she would...

The chain of her thoughts stopped right there because she didn't know what she was going to do. She didn't know what they were going to go back to. Luc had kept the real world out of their time here, probably because he too was unsure himself as to what to expect out there.

She didn't even know if Bianca and Matthew had reappeared. She hadn't spoken to her father at all—hadn't wanted to and Luc hadn't encouraged her to ring him. And after their altercation about their wedding picture on their first day here she hadn't bothered to bring up the subject again because—well, she'd discovered that she preferred to pretend that all of this was the true reality and out there was the fantasy.

He turned to look at her then, so deliciously gorgeous she felt her heart squeeze to an aching standstill. He'd been in an unusually sober mood all day, and that mood still reflected in the golden eyes he lowered to the half drunk glass in her hand, then lifted back to her too expressive eyes.

I love you, she was thinking, and just hoped to goodness he couldn't read *that* as he walked towards her, the farmer having been distracted by his mobile phone.

'Would you mind if I finished that for you?' He took the glass from her without waiting for an answer and downed what was left of the drink before she could tell him that the farmer's wife had prepared a glass full for him too.

Beautifully polite and arrogantly insolent all in one sexy package, she thought as she watched him grimace as if the drink had tasted odd to him too.

He had taken her everywhere with him during the last fortnight. She'd met very rich friends and very poor farmers and to a man they'd all treated her the same way, with warm smiles and welcomes that reflected their feelings for him— and his grandmother, since everyone had also commented on how much she looked like the late Contessa De Santis.

The farmer's wife came out on the porch and started chatting to him in Cajun while Lizzy sat and listened. She didn't care that she couldn't understand a word they were saying, she just loved to listen to the attractive dip and flow of their voices—especially Luc's.

'How many languages do you speak?' she asked him later as they drove away in the open-top sports car with her pink hat firmly in place on her head.

'I don't know,' he answered casually. 'I pick languages up easily.' He added a throw-away shrug as if it didn't mean a lot.

But it did mean a lot. It *said* an awful lot about him. He was the true international high-flying businessman, cultured, educated, refined—supremely comfortable inside his own skin. Curling her legs beneath her on the seat, she turned to study his honey-gold profile, a smile playing with her mouth.

'What?' he said, turning a glance on her.

'Arrogant,' she murmured.

'I thought we had already established that.' He looked back at the road again.

'Conceited, then, if you think it's okay to shrug away the fact that you're fluent in a million languages.'

'A million?' He sent her a sexily lazy grin. 'You have a quaint way of offering me a compliment, *cara*. And you have your own amazing talents.'

'Like what?' Lizzy scoffed. 'Wearing hair-clashing hot pink because you like it?'

'That is certainly one of them.' He nodded with a grin. 'Then there is your talent for being quiet and unobtrusive when we are with other people, which only adds to your air of mystique.'

'Mystique?' Lizzy grimaced. 'I'm just shy, you know that.'

'Except with me…' the sunlight glossed his dark hair as he sent her a grin '…which is when another of your amazing talents puts in an appearance—the wildly passionate and sometimes downright provocative you, like you're being now.'

'I am not being provocative!' Lizzy protested.

'What would you call the way you are sitting there curled in that seat like an innocent kitten when you know your skirt has ridden up to the tops of your thighs?'

'You have a one-track mind.' She tugged the skirt down.

'You make sure that I have. And,' he went on without any noticeable alteration in his tone to warn her as to what was coming, 'you have another amazing talent that really impresses me because I don't know another person who can knock back more than one mouthful of Martha's rum punch and still walk a straight line, never mind have a sensible conversation.'

Lizzy's eyes widened and her mouth dropped open only to close again when her tongue made a searching curl of the taste buds inside her mouth. 'So that was the odd taste I detected?'

'Martha's very own home-made rum.' He nodded. 'Now I am sitting here driving the two of us back to the house as quickly as I can so I can get you into bed before the full effect kicks in.'

'Rum,' Lizzy repeated, and even as she did she felt the first worrying stirrings begin to seep into her blood. She'd had rum once before—and only once because the effect Luc spoke about had been so—

'You are not coming anywhere near a bedroom with me,' she said, straightening out her legs and sitting up straight.

'But we had such a fabulous time, *cara*,' he taunted softly, 'with you losing touch with all your inhibitions and me gaining the sweet benefits of it.'

'It didn't taste like the rum I had that time.' She frowned.

'There is light years in difference between carefully refined rum set down for decades before it is bottled, and the kind of rum Martha makes,' he informed her. 'The first has the same fine quality of the best French cognac, the other is more like a witches' brew—slow to work but lethal once it gets going.'

'You drank half my glass,' she reminded him.

'Mmm,' was all he said, but Lizzy understood exactly what the lazy *Mmm* was meant to represent.

Sure enough she couldn't get her legs to support her when she tried to get out of the car. Luc laughed as he came around the car and gathered her into his arms and kept on laughing as he carried her into the house. She was already tasting his throat as if her life depended on it, her arms like two slender snakes around his neck.

'You taste of De Santis,' she mumbled luxuriously.

'I will take that as another compliment.'

'Mmm,' she responded and licked.

The bedroom door fell open, he carried her to the bed and dumped her on it, having to tug her clinging arms from around his neck so he could turn back to shut the door. By the time he turned again she was already half naked, kneeling in the centre of the bed like a mermaid floating on a sea of white linen.

'You've got too many clothes on,' she complained as he walked back to her.

'You think I don't know this?'

He lost his clothes while she wriggled her top off, set her breasts free from her bra, then arched her body in a fine, lithe stretch.

'I feel so sexy I want to crawl all over you.'

'Later,' he muttered, climbing on the bed and catching hold of her to lift her up, then bring her down again so she straddled his thighs in a warm blending of soft womanliness and strong, hard male.

Her arms went around his shoulders again, her mouth already searching out his, and she moved her hips against him until she caught the thrust of his erection just where she wanted it, her quiver of pleasure making him gasp, the firm clasp of his hands to her slender ribcage there to support her so she could set her own sensual pace.

And she rode the road of pleasure without a single care that she groaned and gasped and even laughed, it was so glorious. She strung out the sweet agony for so long it almost hurt when she finally fell over the edge.

'If you ever drink rum in the company of others I will shoot you,' Luc muttered into her hair as he held her limp body against him.

But all Lizzy could do was whimper because, 'I want you again already.'

Passion was everything in paradise, Lizzy concluded much later when she lay stretched out on her stomach with her eyes closed and feeling as if there wasn't a cell in her body that hadn't been rejuvenated.

Luc came out of the bathroom—she picked up the clean scent of his recent shower. When he came to stretch out beside her and ran his fingertips up the length of her spine she smiled. 'I think you're gorgeous and sexy and a fabulous lover,' she told him.

'And I think you are still intoxicated,' he countered dryly, 'which means that later, when you recall saying all of that to me, you are going to hate yourself.'

'Not good for your ego,' Lizzy agreed—then, 'Oh,' she breathed, 'do that again—it felt just wonderful.'

But he didn't. Instead Luc rolled onto his back and stared at the ceiling, his mood suddenly sombre again. 'Elizabeth,' he said quietly, 'I need you to concentrate for a moment because I have something I have to tell you…'

When she made no response he turned his head to look at her, his mouth easing into a grimace when he realised that she was asleep. The alcohol-induced sensuality he had been enjoying for the last few hours having now dropped her like a stone into a deep, restful stupor.

He sighed, and went back to staring at the ceiling. The news he'd picked up on the internet this morning and put off telling her all day was going to have to wait a little longer.

A little longer, however, was swallowed up by the speed of events.

Lizzy came awake to find herself alone in the bed—if she didn't count the heavy thump taking place in her head. Rum, she recalled, the tender ache of her muscles as she dragged herself into the shower reminding her of how her afternoon had been spent.

The moment she went to look out of the window while she combed the damp tangles out of her hair she knew something was different. She could see two men pacing the sugar-soft sand on the beach and it only took a second for her to realise that they weren't just pacing, they were patrolling.

Losing the comb, she turned and walked out of the bedroom. Two harried looking maids passed her on her way down the stairs. They murmured hurried greetings as they continued upwards and their normal smiles were missing.

Puzzled and curious, she continued down into the hallway, following the sound of Luc's voice sounding grim and terse. She found him in the small dining room, standing by the table pouring coffee into a cup while he talked on his mobile phone.

He was dressed in the same shorts and tee shirt he'd stripped off so hastily earlier, but other than that everything else about him had changed. The stern look on his face, the sharp clip to his voice, even the way he moved was sharper, as if he'd switched on a fourth setting—that of grimly focused, fully charged, alpha tycoon.

'What?' she demanded the moment he turned to look at her, catching her first step into the room.

The mobile phone snapped shut, he tossed it onto the table. 'Our hideout has been discovered,' he told her without bothering to dress it up at all. 'Elena Romano decided it would be good fun to publish it on the internet, with a charmingly acid piece about the softer side of Luciano De Santis.' He grimaced. 'Your pink hat put in an appearance, via a photograph she must have taken as we walked away from her that day.'

'But—why would she want to do that now, almost two weeks later?' Lizzy frowned as she walked forward.

'Fabio has thrown her out,' Luc enlightened her. 'He caught her in a—comprising situation, apparently, with one of his deckhands. I presume she decided to use her meeting with us to divert media attention away from herself.'

'And has she?' Lizzy had reached the table.

'Yes.' Luc handed her the cup of coffee he'd just poured. 'The media mob is piling onto the island as we speak, which means that we are going to cut our stay here short.'

When he said short, he meant short, Lizzy realised a few seconds later when a helicopter swung over the top of the house and landed on the lawn by the pool. Walking across to the window to watch it settle, Lizzy saw just how efficiently Luc had thrown a ring of security around the property—tough-looking men had been stationed everywhere her eyes drifted.

'Is all of this really necessary?' she said with a cold little shiver.

'Yes,' he responded, his voice deep and tight. 'I have other news,' he said then, and waited for her to look at him before he added, 'The runaway lovers have re-emerged. Bianca is at Vito Moreno's home in Sydney, your brother is back in England.' There was a pause in which Lizzy held her breath because she could tell from the gravity of his expression that something bad was coming. 'He was arrested at Gatwick airport and is currently being interviewed by the police.'

She went pale. 'But I thought you said you had—'

'He confessed, *cara*,' Luc cut in grimly. 'He made a voluntary confession about taking the money from Hadley's and blew my cover-up to bits. Now I am expected in Milan to explain myself. We leave here in ten minutes.'

Ten minutes to get ready to leave was nothing to the nine long hours it took to fly back to Milan. Luc wasn't talking. He'd withdrawn behind a wall of icy courtesy, and Lizzy couldn't blame him. His pride had been hit, his integrity. Lizzy didn't think he was ever going to forgive any of them for it.

And the only slither of comfort she could glean from it all was that Matthew's arrest had not leaked out into the public arena. Luc spent most of the flight on the telephone working to ensure that it remained that way.

They arrived at Linate airport early in the morning to dark clouds and heavy rain. A limousine with blackened windows picked them up and transported them into Milan.

Luc remained on the phone throughout that journey too, the monotone flow of his voice never tiring, though Lizzy had switched off from it hours ago.

Half an hour later they were in his Milan apartment. Luc was checking his mail. Lizzy moved off, looking around her, aware that he was watching her, his eyes flicking her glances between reading the envelopes. He knew as well as she did that this was it—the hard reality of their marriage kicked in right here.

And as if to punctuate that he was wearing a suit, the first suit she'd seen him wear in two whole weeks. It was a smooth and elegant dark suit that enhanced just about everything about him from the breadth of his shoulders to the length of his long legs and even the sleek-styled darkness of his hair.

'I will show you around in a minute,' he murmured.

Lizzy turned to offer a fleeting smile. 'I've been here before.'

Then she turned away again. Even his voice sounded different, quiet and level and—cool.

The one time she'd been here—to a party he'd given the first week she'd been in Milan—his voice had sounded like that. And he'd worn a suit, something designer-cut to look casual. He'd moved through his guests with the smooth, silent grace of a satellite circling outer space. He'd barely noticed her in the crush—though he did pause to speak to her once, she remembered. *Ciao, how are you? Having a good time?*

Did he even remember her name?

Then she smiled because of course he'd remembered it. He was the man with a million languages logged in his brain, so one small name wasn't going to escape him.

'We will be spending most of our time here, so feel free to change anything you don't like.'

Lizzy nodded and moved through a wide opening into the vast cutthroat stylishness of the lounge. What was there to change? she mused as she wandered over to the window to check out the view. The pure silk grey curtains with that dramatically simple dark brown line threaded through them, or the matching cushions tossed so perfectly casually against scrumptious brown leather?

She could throw chintz at it all, she supposed—just to irritate his very good taste—or change a painting or two and put up some of her own rough sketches done in bold strokes of charcoal during one of her crazy moods that had used to erupt without warning when being quiet and placid had got on her nerves.

She turned away from the window, to find him standing in the opening through to the hallway. His expression was—unreadable, she decided described it best. Gorgeous, she allowed, as in gorgeously handsome and gorgeously tanned and even gorgeously unreadable.

'Can I have my own room?' Lizzy didn't even know she was going to say it until the words left her tongue.

'Own room as in what kind of room?' he came back smoothly.

Own room as in I don't want to sleep with you any more, she thought, but was so shocked by the discovery she didn't say it out loud. Instead she shrugged. 'My own bit of space.' She hedged for a compromise because she was going to have to seriously think about the other thing before she dropped that kind of bombshell. 'Somewhere I can put all my junk when I get it delivered.'

'You like junk?' He raised a curious eyebrow, but it wasn't really curious—it knew what it was she was hedging around.

So she nodded, pressing her lips together because they'd started to tremble and she could feel the threat of tears stinging the back of her throat. There was a great yawning gap opening up between them, which had nothing to do with the length of the room. And she was suddenly intensely aware of the age difference between them, the twelve long years that gave him the control to stand there and look beautifully at ease with what he was about to face, while she—

Lizzy swallowed. Her heart was pumping oddly, heavy and thick, because she knew that the yawning gap had started to widen the moment the helicopter had landed on the lawn in the Caribbean.

It had stretched even wider during the long, grim journey and then wider again when he'd come out of the bedroom on the plane just before they had landed dressed like that, and quietly suggested that she might like to change.

So here she was, standing in a neat pale grey suit that had somehow appeared without her knowing how on a hanger behind the bedroom door. And she felt like a stranger—to herself—a person carefully fashioned to suit *his* image when really she was—

'What's wrong, *cara*?' he prompted huskily and the tears in her throat almost beat her up in their rush to reach her eyes.

'Nothing,' she managed, though she didn't know how she managed it. 'I just feel strange here—out of place.'

'You will get used to it.'

Reassurance or an order?

'It's the—'

The telephone began to ring then, sounding so shockingly shrill after weeks without hearing one that both of them started in surprise. Luc went to answer it, striding back through the opening and across the hallway. Lizzy tried to pull herself together and followed him. He was standing in what looked like his study with the door swinging open wide. She diverted towards the back of the apartment where she remembered the kitchen was situated and made herself busy hunting down the necessary things needed to make a pot of coffee.

When she heard him come in the room, she didn't turn to look at him. 'I have to go out now,' he told her.

She nodded, pressing her lips together again because she wanted to say something about Matthew and the whole wretched mess her family had placed him in, but she just couldn't seem to find the right words.

'I don't know when I will be back, but I have arranged for an employee of mine—Abriana Tristano—to come here to—advise you as to how to respond to any fallout that may occur.'

'Like a PA?' she turned to ask him.

He nodded. 'She's good. Let her take care of everything. She has my mobile number to liaise with me if she needs to—clarify anything.'

I don't like this, Lizzy thought, standing there looking at him. 'I w-would prefer to come with you,' she said. 'Be seen at your side.'

He smiled for the first time in hours and hours, one of those sensually amused, very intimate smiles that softened the harshness out of his face, and it swam through her blood as potent as Martha's home-made rum.

'*Amore*, having you by my side will be too much of a distraction—as will coming over there and kissing you for suggesting it.'

Lizzy moved, she just had to do. 'Then I'm coming to you,' and she covered the space between them, lifting her slender arms around his neck so she could give him the distracting kiss whether he wanted it or not.

He tasted warm like the man of the Caribbean, and smelled expensive like the man of Milan. When he didn't pull away and even slid his hands beneath her jacket to mould her against him, the silly uncertainties she'd brought with her into this apartment melted away.

'Don't let them bully you,' she murmured as their lips reluctantly separated.

'You see this happening, with me?'

No, she was just delaying the moment when he walked away from her and her liquid grey eyes told him so. 'I'm just scared,' she confessed on a husky whisper.

'Don't be.' He touched his lips to hers again. 'I know what I'm doing.'

The doorbell pealed then, and he moved away from her. As she watched him stride down the hallway she saw the change take place in his whole mood and manner as the man from the Caribbean was cleared away.

Abriana was nice, though Lizzy had been ready to dislike her. She arrived wearing jeans and trainers and armed with fresh pastries from the local patisserie. Her warm, friendly nature kept Lizzy's anxieties damped down to a minimum. And she dealt firmly with every phone call and visitor that tried to gain entrance into the apartment.

It took twenty-four hours for Lizzy to realise that she'd been carefully isolated again, much as she'd been at the Lake Como villa. And she was being carefully protected from this new wave of media interest that had hitched its wagon onto their lives.

No phone calls, no newspapers for her to read what was being said, but even Luc couldn't stop the television from reporting on the burning question—had Luciano De Santis, President of the De Santis Bank, misused his position of power in connection with a loan given to his father-in-law?

'Luc advised you not to watch this,' Abriana said worriedly when she saw Lizzy turn pale. 'He did not do anything wrong. He used his own money, not the bank's money, and he has clear proof of that.'

'Yes,' Lizzy said, trying—trying to believe what Abriana was saying, but she knew more than Abriana did, just as she knew that Luc would not be called to answer questions if it were as neat and tidy as Abriana said.

She hardly saw him during the next long week. Although he came home to the apartment each night it was late, and he was tired and uncommunicative. As the days crawled by she watched the strain of it all inch tension lines into his face.

And he didn't sleep in her bed. He said it was because he didn't want to disturb her when he retired very late and got up so early the next day, and she understood that—she did.

But she missed him, meanly and selfishly she missed him and almost welcomed the miserable fact that she did.

Then, one week after they arrived back from the Caribbean, the feel of the mattress moving beside her brought her swimming up from a fitful sleep. By then a familiar pair of hands was taking hold of her and turning her into the burning heat of his hungry kiss.

The moment he let her up for air she searched his face through the semi-darkness. He looked different, relaxed, the strain and the tough self-control had gone.

'It's over?' she asked.

He nodded, levering himself up on his side so he could look

down at her. 'Your brother is off the hook because the bank has decided not to press charges since the money went missing for only twenty-four hours,' he said. 'And your father simply told the truth and maintained he knew nothing about any of it.'

'And you?' she asked.

'I talked my way out of it,' he answered, 'By deciding on my story and sticking to it. So long as I continued to insist I knew nothing about the five and a half million your brother took, they could prove no wrongdoing on my part.'

Lizzy lifted a hand to touch her fingers to the rueful twist at the corner of his mouth. 'But what you did was—wrong?'

He didn't answer for a moment, his eyes dark on her anxious expression. Then he took hold of her fingers and kissed them.

'Morally, yes,' he said.

Tears spread like a film across her eyes. 'I'm sorry, then, that you felt you had to do something wrong for my benefit, but—thank you,' she added. Then, because she knew she just had to say it, in fact she'd been burning to say it throughout the long, hard week, 'I love you, Luc,' she whispered to him.

It was the first time she had allowed herself to say it and even hearing it fall from her lips set her heart pounding in her chest because she knew she couldn't lay herself more open to him.

Yet he said nothing—nothing for ages, just continued to kiss the tips of her fingers and look down at her through those dark golden, utterly unreadable eyes of his.

Then he smiled. 'Loving gratitude from my worst critic,' he mocked lightly. 'It was almost worth it.'

It was like receiving a kick in the teeth. Lizzy tried to get up, but he stopped her.

'No,' he husked, 'forget I said that. I'm still stinging from being forced to explain myself and that was unbelievably generous of you.'

Was he trying to make her feel better? Because he wasn't succeeding. She felt broken in two.

'And I love you too, *bella mia*,' he added huskily. 'Of course I do. Why else would I put my reputation at such risk if not for the woman I love?'

Why else indeed? Lizzy thought bleakly. Desire? Anger? Wounded pride? A determination not to look the fool Bianca had turned him into, no matter what it cost him?

She could have made the list grow and grow, if he'd let her, but, 'Now all I want is you, so badly I ache,' he roughed out, and the warm crush of his hungry mouth took away her ability to think.

For the first time since their wedding night they made love with a grim, silent intensity that pounded her wounded emotions and left her satiated but with tears on her cheeks.

He gently licked them away and said nothing. He continued to hold her close and said nothing. And when she woke the next morning he had gone from their bed leaving her with an ache that dragged on her insides.

It was an ache that was not going to go away any time soon, and indeed was about to become a whole lot worse.

Though Lizzy didn't know that when she crawled out of the bed that morning. In truth she would have preferred to remain in it, with her face buried in the pillow and the covers pulled up over her head. She did not want to face whatever the new day was bringing, but Abriana was due to arrive and she needed to get herself together by then.

There was a note waiting for her when she walked into the kitchen. It was propped up against the kettle and her fingers trembled as she picked it up and read Luc's precise bold scrawl. 'Dinner at eight' he had written. 'I will book a table somewhere special. Wear something fabulous. It will be our first date.' And he'd signed it, '*Ti amo*, Luc.'

Ti amo, Luc...

Thick tears crushed the muscles in her throat as she stood there trying to deal with the impact the endearment was having on her.

Ti amo, Luc...

She wished he hadn't written it. She wished with all of her aching heart that he'd just pretended the words hadn't come up between them so she could try—try to forget how stupid she'd been and maybe manage to move on.

But '*Ti amo, Luc,*' told her he was feeling bad about his reaction to her when she'd said it. '*Ti amo*, Luc,' said he was attempting to make amends. '*Ti amo*, Luc,' reminded her that they had a marriage to continue whatever else had happened and '*Ti amo,*' was, she supposed, a basic part of it, even if it was offered without the sincerity of truth.

She crushed the note in her fingers and wrapped her slender arms tight around her aching ribs. The phone began ringing out in the hallway. It took six long echoing rings before she could bring herself to answer it.

'Yes?' she whispered.

'Elizabeth?' Luc questioned sharply. 'Why are you answering the telephone? Where is Abriana?'

Why was he the only person in the world who called her Elizabeth? she found herself thinking. Why did he have to be so painfully different from everyone else?

'Sh-she's not here yet,' she answered.

There was a buzzing silence. She wished she could think

of something to say but she couldn't, and her voice was shaking—she'd heard it for herself when she spoke.

'Are you all right, *cara*?' he husked out then.

So he'd heard it too. Lizzy pressed her lips together. It was mad how one small endearment had the power to turn her into this much of a pained, quivering wreck. *Cara*, she could deal with. *Cara* was lightweight and familiar.

'Luc, I think I m-might catch a flight home to England today. Go and see—' she swallowed '—m-my father and—'

'The hell you will,' he bit out harshly, then followed it up with a blistering curse. 'What is the matter with you? Why are you choosing this moment in particular to do this to me?'

To *him*? She was doing it to herself! 'I just thought—'

'Well, *don't* think!' he rasped at her. '*Por Dio*, I will never understand women for as long as I live! I am on my way back to the apartment. You will do nothing until I arrive. We should not even be having this conversation! Abriana should be there to answer the damn phone!'

'Why are you on your way here?' Lizzy asked frowningly.

There was another sharp buzzing silence and she could almost see him seething inside his chauffeur-driven car. 'I will tell you when I get there. Our plans have changed. We will be going to the Lake Como villa. Use your time packing a suitcase for a stay there instead of packing one to leave me!'

The phone went dead. Lizzy stared at it in a state of blank disbelief. He never got angry—not fire-breathing angry, anyway. He preferred the icy kind that could freeze the blood in your veins.

The doorbell sounded its ring then. Replacing the telephone receiver, she went to let in her PA, with her head still whirling over too many things to make her stop and think before she turned the lock and opened the door.

The person she saw standing there dressed in unrelieved black sent her gasping in shocked disbelief.

'Bianca!' she breathed.

CHAPTER TEN

BURNING BLACK EYES spitting murder at her, Bianca Moreno took a step forward and threw her hand against the side of Lizzy's face.

'How could you, Lizzy?' she sizzled at her. 'How could you just marry him like that?'

The whip-crack sting sent Lizzy staggering backwards, her hand jerking up to cover her cheek. 'But y-you ran away with Matthew,' she stammered out. 'You left Luc—'

'I didn't leave him!' her best friend spat at her scathingly. 'Luc sent me away, because he said he'd found someone else and he didn't want to marry me any more!'

She was repeating her own press, Lizzy realized. 'But that isn't true. You know it isn't, you—'

Bianca stalked off, a shimmering mass of hurt tears and anger that Lizzy had to follow with her insides still shaking from the shock angry slap.

'Matthew rescued me.' She continued to use the press line from a tragic position in the centre of the living room. 'I called him up when I saw what was happening between you and Luc—'

'But nothing was happening!' Lizzy insisted.

'I needed Matthew to come and take you away before you

ruined my life!' Swinging around to face her, Bianca let Lizzy
see the pained tears in her eyes. 'He was going to do it too,'
she said thickly, 'the very next morning after that—fiasco
w-when I caught you and Luc together on the terrace. I saw
your face, Lizzy! I knew what you'd been doing!'

The cringing guilt of that incident coming back to haunt her,
Lizzy opened her mouth to say something, but nothing came out.

Bianca burned her a scathing look. 'I got you away from there
as quickly as I could,' she went on. 'Your brother wanted to go
to your room then and there and drag you home by the scruff of
your traitorous neck, but it was already too late.' Her voice broke
down into a choke. 'Luc arrived only minutes after we got back
to the hotel. He told me it was over—right there in front of my
cousin Vito and your brother, Lizzy!' she cried. 'He finished it
between us and I have never been so humiliated in all of my life!'

None of this was true—not the way that Bianca was telling
it anyway, but what Lizzy couldn't work out was why she was
persisting in telling it to her as if it were!

'You know you're lying,' she husked out shakily.

'I'm lying?' Bianca seared out. 'Did you or did you not have
the hots for my fiancé from the moment you set eyes on him?'

'Oh, God,' Lizzy choked in shuddering answer.

'We were friends—*best* friends! And you betrayed me in
the worst possible way that you could! Well, now you're
going to know what it feels like to be hurt beyond bearing and
be humiliated, Lizzy, because I'm pregnant with Luc's baby
and I want him back!'

With those final words ringing in the silence that followed,
several things suddenly happened at once. Luc appeared tall and
tense in the opening through to the hallway with Abriana standing white-faced at his side. Bianca saw him and on a broken sob
she ran towards him and threw herself against his chest.

'I'm sorry, I'm sorry,' she kept sobbing over and over while she clung to him, and he just stood there with his handsome face cold like frozen marble and his golden eyes fixed on Lizzy's face.

He had to have heard what Bianca had said because she'd been shrieking loud enough to drown out the sound of him coming into the apartment. And he wasn't denying it could be possible. He wasn't pushing Bianca away. He was just looking at Lizzy—looking as if waiting for *her* to say something, but what was there for her to say?

And, anyway, it was as if someone had just switched on a light to make her see reality for the first time in weeks of self-denial. It was crazy and she knew it, but not *once* had she so much as considered that Luc and Bianca would be lovers. She'd just blocked the now sinkingly obvious out. Having to face it now, though, having to stand here with Bianca's finger marks still stinging her cheek and her stark eyes fixed on Luc's sternly controlled expression—glass case or not—she knew she was going to have to get out of here as fast as she could before she threw up.

Bianca was still sobbing into his chest as Lizzy managed to get her shaking legs to walk forward. She was vaguely aware that he'd muttered something at Abriana because she disappeared out of sight and the growing horror of it all throbbed like an invisible monster in the air surrounding her. The closer she came to them, the worse the throbbing felt.

When she finally drew level with them, Luc snaked a hand out and caught her shoulder. She shuddered so violently he bit out a curse.

'*Don't,*' he said in a dark husky rasp.

She paused to look at him, then at Bianca held against him, then back into his eyes, and a strained, pale, helpless smile twisted her quivering lips at the tableau they made—the man, the jilted betrothed, the wife.

Maybe he was reading her mind again because Luc moved his hand on her shoulder as if he was trying to use it as plea. *'Don't,'* he said again. 'I will deal with it.'

Deal with it... Thick tears wrapped themselves around her throat. For what was there for him to deal with? A near-hysterical ex-betrothed? A stung and stunned and stupidly naïve wife? Or a baby, which totally, utterly overwhelmed the importance of everything else.

She shrugged off his hand and walked away from him. Hidden away inside the bedroom, she found herself staring at her own image reflected back at her from the full length mirror hung on one of the wardrobe doors. It was like looking at a stranger, a long and curvy total stranger with grey eyes and chestnut-coloured hair and an errant curl that insisted on flopping over her brow.

It was over. It had to be. It didn't matter any more if most of what Bianca had screamed at her was the detailed fabrication put out there to save Luc's face. What mattered was the child Bianca claimed that she carried.

The first De Santis heir.

She was the infiltrator in this little trio, Lizzy told herself, which meant that she was the one who was going to have to leave.

Maybe Bianca was right and she did deserve what was coming to her. She certainly felt that she did as she carefully turned away from the mirror only to find herself staring at the bed. Then with a race-quick spring of nerve-dragging agony the panic erupted, the desperate need to get out of here now—while she could!

It took very little to do it, she realised painfully as she

turned to yank open the closet door and dragged out the first suitcase she could lay her hands on. What she flung into that suitcase showed no sign of logic. Nor did the way she suddenly diverted halfway through and pulled open the wardrobe door to snatch at the first outdoor garment she saw. It was a black linen jacket she had never worn before. She dragged it on over the white tee shirt she was wearing with a pair of denims, then hunted down her handbag and rummaged through it with tight, trembling fingers to check that her passport was still in it along with her credit cards, then, finding everything in order, she completely forgot about the half-packed suitcase and spun to open the bedroom door.

All was quiet in the hallway as she walked along it. Even Abriana was nowhere to be seen. And the door to Luc's study was shut tight into its housing, telling her that he must have taken Bianca in there.

Outside it was still raining—raining—raining. She waved down a cab and climbed inside. Linate airport was busy. It was always busy but she managed to get a seat on a flight about to leave for London. Three short hours later she was walking through the arrivals gate at Gatwick.

And the first face she focused on was her father's. Tears once again started to threaten. 'H-how did you—?'

'Luc called me,' he explained, then nodded his head at someone standing behind her.

Lizzy glanced round, then withered out a smile as she turned back to her father's sombre face. She had been followed from the moment she'd stepped out of the apartment, tracked every foot of the way here by one of Luc's security team.

She didn't know why her tears picked that moment to break, but she threw herself sobbing into her father's arms.

'It's all right, Lizzy, you're home now.' Her father patted

her back awkwardly. They were not a hugging, sobbing kind of family. 'Let's go and find my car.'

They were halfway home before she asked about Matthew. 'He's okay,' her father said. 'If nothing else, he learned a few hard lessons in life with his crazy escapade, the main one being that taking something that doesn't belong to you might be exciting while it's happening, but there has to be a point where you accept you're going to have to pay.'

Was he talking about Matt stealing Hadley's money, or her stealing Bianca from Luc? Lizzy didn't ask the question because she didn't want to know the answer.

'Where is he now?' she enquired instead.

'In one of those expensive rehab clinics paid for by Luc—didn't you know?' he said to her gasp of surprise. 'I thought Luc would have told you.'

If there was one thing Lizzy had taken away from her very short marriage it was that Luc only told her what he wanted her to know. 'Why rehab?' she questioned.

'Your brother had got himself into some messy stuff long before this thing with Bianca came up,' her father said grimly. 'I blame myself,' he added heavily. 'I should not have been so determined to make the two of you be the people I wanted you to be instead of the people you needed to be... Matthew owed a lot of money to a lot of unsavoury people,' he continued heavily. 'The idea of *borrowing* some of Hadley's loan to pay these people was where the rest of his problems began. One bad idea exploded into a damn foolish thirst for revenge on me. The rest you know. He took off with Bianca for Australia to learn his real lesson in life, that the greatest love of your life is not always the sanest love of your life—as you have no doubt just found out for yourself.'

Again Lizzy said nothing. She didn't want to think about

the insanity she had shown around Luc. All she wanted was to walk back into her own home and into her old bedroom and be miserable in there for the rest of her life.

Only it wasn't going to happen quite like that. The telephone was ringing even as they stepped into the house through the front door. Her father picked it up.

'It's Luc,' he said, holding the receiver out to her.

But Lizzy just pressed her lips together and walked into the kitchen. She didn't want to speak to him—probably ever again.

He rang again the next morning, and again she refused to speak to him.

'We owe him a lot, Lizzy,' her father chided her cold stubbornness, grimly stretching out his hand and the phone.

'Not me,' she denied. 'I've paid my debt to him.'

The fact that she knew Luc must have heard her say that didn't touch her at all because she had paid her debt to him with kisses and heartache and by believing too many of his lies.

So where did he lie to you? a little voice in her head challenged.

Stop it, she told it. Leave me alone with my complicated misery. I like it. And she picked up her coffee-cup and took it with her back to her lonely bed.

He didn't call again for the rest of the week and she hated him for it. Hated and hated and *hated* him with a poison and a fierce vengeance so when he did finally turn up on the doorstep late one afternoon, she was more than ready to leap on him and hit him—just as Bianca had hit her.

Trouble was, you didn't lash out at a man who looked about as bad-tempered as Luc did, Lizzy accepted, unable to stop her eyes from greedily tracking over him from the top of his rain wetted head to the tips of his wet handmade leather shoes. He was wearing a long black woollen overcoat and like his hair and his shoes, it was speckled with its share of the rain that had been falling relentlessly across all of Europe for the last week, and the stern stark expression on his face was—tough.

'Can I come in?' he asked. 'And before you answer that,' he then put in darkly, 'let me advise you to remove that frosty pout from your lips, *cara*, or I might just decide to remove it for you.'

And he wasn't bluffing. Lizzy could see by the way he'd fixed the glinting gold of his eyes on her mouth that he was quite prepared to carry out his threat. And what was worse, she felt the burn, the old tempting vibration grind into action to spin out its link between the two of them. It brought her chin up, her eyes flashing out a green warning that clashed head-on with the gold.

'I don't know where you get off thinking you can just arrive here and start ordering me about,' she returned angrily, 'but let me tell you that you lost the right to—'

He took a threatening step forward, forcing Lizzy into taking a quick backward step. Her heart leapt, so did her breathing as six feet three inches of black-clad very grim male took the door from her clinging fingers, then replaced it on its latch.

Stifled by his closeness as his full intimidating presence filled the small hallway, Lizzy slid warily around him and walked into the living room and didn't stop until she reached the fireplace with its fire burning warmly in the grate.

He came to a halt in the doorway so they ended up facing each other across a twelve-and-a-half-foot gap.

The light was soft in here, the ceilings lower than those in his homes, so he suddenly looked taller and bigger, his face not quite as pale as it had looked on the doorstep a moment ago with the autumn cool to help blanch the colour out of it. And—tired, Lizzy noticed for the first time, the grim lines of tension he'd worn on his face throughout the week before Bianca had turned up well and truly back in place.

'You've lost weight,' he said, making her aware that while she had been studying him he had been doing the same thing to her.

'No, I've not,' she denied, but wrapped her arms around her body all the same as if they were going to disguise the pounds she knew she had dropped.

'And you look—tired.' He ignored her denial. 'Missing sleep over me, *cara*?'

'Oh, isn't that just typically arrogant of you to say that?' she snapped back.

To her surprise he grimaced, '*Sì*, probably.' Then with a sigh he lifted a hand up. 'May I remove my coat? It is—warm in here.'

Lizzy wanted to tell him that he wouldn't be staying long enough to bother, but in the end she pressed her lips together and nodded because—dear God, she didn't want him to go.

His fingers worked free the buttons and she watched every one of them separate from its buttonhole until the coat eventually came off. He was wearing a suit beneath it, another sleek dark suit that shrieked Luc in business mode and—

'Here, give it to me,' she said, walking towards him when he looked around for somewhere to put the wet coat.

Their fingers brushed as the coat exchanged hands, and he closed his around hers for a second—until she froze up like a statue and on a sigh he let go of her again.

Refusing to look at him, she took the coat out into the hallway. By the time she came back he was standing in front of the fireplace—more or less where she had been standing, only he had his back to her and his wide shoulders were rod straight and tense.

And the crazy, weak tears started to threaten the back of her aching throat because he was staring at a framed photo-

graph of her taken at the age of eighteen when she had gradu-
ated from school. She was smiling, shy for the camera, that
errant curl flopping over her brow. Bianca, had taken it. There
had used to be another similar picture of Bianca but Matthew
had removed it, her father had told her.

'How is she?' she asked thickly. 'Bianca, I m-mean.'

'She is well.' He turned to look at her. 'She's back in
London with her parents. Elizabeth—'

'M-Matthew is out of rehab,' she quickly cut in.

'Yes, I know. Elizabeth—'

'He won't come home. This is a small market town where
everyone knows everything about everyone and he just can't
bring himself to face them all so he's staying with an old
school friend in Falmouth... They're planning to take off
round the world together—backpacking... He means to—
find himself, and I suppose if anything good came out of
w-what happened then it has to be that my father has accepted
that he had been too tough on Matthew, so he's—'

'There is no baby, *amore*,' Luc quietly interrupted.

CHAPTER ELEVEN

LIZZY JUST STARED at him, her eyes like twin grey pools of blank incomprehension that made Luc grimace. 'I thought I would tell you before you ran out of innocuous things to say and resorted to telling me about the lousy weather,' he explained. 'Bianca *lied*, Elizabeth. She is not and never has been pregnant. She is just angry with everyone—you, me, your brother— angry with herself for making such a mess of her life…'

'You mean she—came to your apartment and said all of that just to hurt me?'

'And me.' He nodded. 'Though it has taken the full length of this miserable week to admit it.' His golden eyes glinted. 'She knows you well, *amore mia*,' he said softly. 'She knew just what to say to make you run from me. So now I am standing here wondering why it is you are still standing over there instead of throwing yourself at me in gratitude and relief!'

The sudden burst of his anger made Lizzy stiffen. 'G-grateful for what—?'

'That there is no child,' Luc elaborated. 'That I am not about to become involved in a heavy paternity suit and that you are still the woman I made my wife—and you should have stayed in Milan and supported me until this truth came out!'

And there it was, Lizzy realised, the reason why he had

arrived here looking bad-tempered and tough. He was angry because she hadn't hung around to be mocked by everyone for a second time. He'd expected her to fall on him now he had given her the good news that it wasn't going to happen!

'You have a twisted sense of self-belief, Luc, if you truly expected me to fall on your neck with relief!' she informed him. 'Or have you forgotten I was already planning to leave you *before* Bianca put in an appearance?'

'I have forgotten nothing.' He moved, beginning to close the gap between them. 'I was merely giving you the opportunity to allow that small incident to fade quietly away.'

'Well, I don't want it to fade away,' she said, backing as he kept on coming, 'and don't you *dare* touch me!' she warned as she felt her spine hit the door. 'You've lied to me, bullied me, squeezed every last drop of feeling out of me, but what did you ever give me back?' she asked, a sudden onset of tears bringing him to an abrupt halt. 'Your wonderful body and the pleasure of using it is all that you gave back to me, Luc,' she informed him jerkily. 'And you dare to believe that that should be enough to keep me loyal and supportive to you?'

'No,' he sighed out, turning away from her to grab the back of his neck with a hand. 'You deserve better from me.'

And having him admit it did *not* make Lizzy feel better. 'Well thank you for that small crumb,' she said, wishing she were dead now because she just couldn't stem the sudden urge she had to throw herself at him anyway.

Then she remembered the note, the brief throw-away *'Ti amo,'* and she threw herself round to drag open the living room door. 'That said, then I know you will understand that I w-would like you to leave now,' she said, hating the telling tremor she heard in her voice. 'My father will be home in a minute and I would prefer it if you—'

'No, he won't.'

Lizzy stilled in the doorway. 'Won't what?' she demanded.

'Be home soon,' Luc extended. 'He knows I am here,' he explained huskily. 'He thinks I am taking you out to dinner.'

'Dinner?' Her shoulders wrenched back. 'I don't want to have dinner with you.'

'It is the only way you will get rid of me, *cara*,' he said.

It was the cool way he relayed that that made her twist back to look at him. The moment she saw the way he was standing there looking as contained as hell, she knew he had turned back into the cool-headed Luc De Santis who did not play fair in a fight.

Tall, though, lean, sexily handsome. Lizzy found herself nervously moistening her lips. 'Explain that,' she instructed.

'Dinner,' he repeated. 'That is all. I have already reserved a table. All you have to do is to sit down with me and eat.'

Never in a million years was that all he was expecting her to do.

'Or I will call in your family debt…'

Ah, *now* he was talking, Lizzy thought. She understood this Luc so well! The unreadable expression, the arrogant tilt to his head that had once made her want to fly at him across the width of his desk.

'Dinner…' She folded her arms. The heavy sweep of his eyelashes dropped low as he watched her do it, and the tense quiver struck down her front. 'Where?'

'My hotel. I'm staying at Langwell Hall.'

Langwell Hall, Lizzy repeated silently. Only the best would ever be good enough for Luc. Langwell Hall was the finest hotel in the area—once a spectacular stately home left to go to ruin, now beautifully refurbished and transformed into a hotel.

And she knew exactly what he was doing with this oh, so

polite, spiked-with-threat invitation; he was taking her out of her comfort zone here in her own home and putting them in the perfect place for him to feel comfortable in.

'I don't have anything fit to wear for dinner at Langwell Hall,' she informed him coolly.

Those gold eyes made yet another sensual dip down the front of her plain linen shift dress with its limp, shapeless shape. 'Come as you are,' he responded carelessly. 'We will be eating, not putting on a fashion show.'

And Lizzy was feeling angry enough to do it, resentful enough of his bullying tactics to just call his bluff and let him walk her into Langwell Hall's fancy dining room wearing a dress she'd had on for two days because she'd been too upset and depressed to bother changing it, but...

'Dinner,' she said again, with a different emphasis. 'That's *all*, then you bring me home again and leave with no more threats?'

'*Sì.*' He nodded—and he had to switch to Italian to make *his* emphasis.

Without another word she turned and walked into the hallway, chin up, eyes sparkling as she strode up the stairs to her room. Maybe she should have looked back because she might have caught the telling way he ran his palm over his face as if to wipe away the tension in it.

When she came back down again she was wearing a full-length black raincoat over the only half-decent dress she had here in England, which was a very modest knee-length matt-black jersey thing with long sleeves and a high neck.

Luc was already waiting for her in the hall with his coat back on and a sublime patience strapped to his face. His hire car was a Bentley Continental. It was like floating in luxury as they drove through the pouring rain.

They didn't speak. Like the dreadful calm before the violent storm, the static electricity played tunes on her nerves.

Langwell Hall lived up to all her expectations with its oak-lined and hushed great hall and grand oak staircase and its many reception rooms filled with beautiful old furniture, fine porcelain displayed in glass cases and its priceless works of original art.

They were shown to a table set into a corner of the elegant dining room. Someone invisible had taken their coats. Soft lamps instead of candles refined the atmosphere, sparkling crystal and polished silver and fine bone china graced the pure white tablecloths.

Luc waved the *maître d'* away to personally attend to Lizzy's chair. 'You need diamonds,' he murmured as he saw her seated.

'Not a good way to soften me up,' she drawled.

She was thinking of Bianca's diamonds. By the time he sat down opposite her she knew he was thinking about them too by the grimace she saw on his lips.

'Emeralds, then,' he recovered smoothly, 'to compete with your eyes.'

'That was corny,' she chided. 'And my eyes are grey.'

'Not right now, they are not,' he drawled softly, and smiled as the heat of an angry blush warmed her cheeks because they both knew her eyes only turned green when she was lost in the throes of heated passion.

Seemingly it didn't matter what kind of passion it was that was driving her.

The *maître d'* returned to offer Luc the wine list, but he just waved it away and ordered what he wanted. And because Langwell Hall was that kind of place, the order was taken with barely a glimmer of uncertainty that they could provide it. Menus were set down in front of them instead.

Lizzy opened hers and pretended to study it cover to cover. Luc just sat back and studied her.

'Stop it,' she said, without glancing up at him.

'I like looking at you,' he responded levelly. 'Sometimes you take my breath away.'

'Sex.' She named it dismissively.

'You want more than sex from me?'

That focused her attention, though not her eyes, on him; she kept them carefully lowered. 'My French isn't good enough to read most of this,' she murmured, indicating the menu. 'You are going to have to translate.'

'Ti amo,' he said. 'It means I love you.'

The way Lizzy jerked in response she almost knocked the glasses over. 'That was Italian.' Her eyes lifted, wide and wounded, to his. 'And don't make fun of me, Luc—' even she could hear the pained shake in her voice '—or I walk.'

But his face didn't wear a hint of mockery anywhere, neither did his sigh sound mocking as he reached into the inside pocket of his jacket, then leaned forward to place something down on her menu.

Needing to swallow the lump in her throat now because his eyes were so dark and intent on her, Lizzy looked down—and froze.

'Tell me,' he said quietly then, 'which part of this note upset you so much that you screwed it into a tight ball and threw it to the kitchen floor.'

Lizzy shook her head, the tears gathering. 'I—didn't know I had dropped it there.'

'This part?' he persisted as if she hadn't spoken, pointing with a finger at the bit where he'd written, 'Dinner eight o'clock.' 'This part upset you because you believed I was issuing one of my arrogant commands instead of a request?

Or was it this part, *cara*,' he went on gently, 'where I was insensitive enough to point out it would be our first date?'

He knew which part it was that had upset her—he'd just teased her with it before he produced the evidence!

'I'm not playing this game,' she breathed and jerked to her feet.

He stood up also, catching hold of her wrist as she went to leave. '*Ti amo*,' he said.

'No,' she whispered and tried to pull free.

But his fingers tightened. '*Ti amo*,' he repeated yet again, tensely. 'I will keep saying it until you listen to me.'

'In the same way you made a joke of it in bed?'

It was out there in the dining room before she could stop it, her impulsive tongue throwing out the biggest hurt he had ever wounded her with. People stopped eating to look at them; the dining room fell deathly silent.

'I tried to put it right in this note.' He held her eyes with the burning intensity of his. 'I wrote it there because I wanted you to know that I meant it, but you saw it as just another sign of my twisted humour and arrogance.'

'You're the most insensitive brute on this earth,' Lizzy shook out at him.

'*Ti amo*,' he said again, deeply, doggedly. 'You tell me I am too old for you and I agree, yet still I blackmailed you and I married you and I want to stay married to you.'

'I'm the same age as Bianca—what's the difference?' She frowned irritably, picking out the only part of that she wanted to argue with.

The look on his face altered. He tugged until she landed in quivering shock against his chest. Opening her mouth to protest, she saw what was coming the quivering second before his mouth landed like a burning brand on hers. And it wasn't a quick demonstration of male desire either, it was hot and it was hard and it probed and seduced every dark corner of her mouth until she knew she would have fallen down if he had not been holding her up.

She barely registered the gasp that rippled through their captive audience. People—*refined* people—drinking in the sight of Luc De Santis making passionate love to his wife!

'That is the difference,' he husked when he eventually set her mouth free.

But Lizzy shook her head. 'You're a taker, Luc,' she whispered unsteadily. 'If I let you you'll just keep on taking and taking until there's nothing of me left. You were cruel that night, you know?' She threw her clenched, shaking fist at his chest. 'And you did it deliberately. You believe a quick note left propped up against the kettle was going to put that right?'

Someone somewhere murmured something. Lizzy turned her head; she saw the sea of faces looking at them. Her mouth wobbled, lips burning and pulsing, she released out a small sob, then broke free of him and just ran.

And she actually made it as far as the grand hall before he caught up with her and scooped her right off her feet. 'You can use your fists on me again in a minute,' he gritted out and she fought him. And he turned and headed for the lift.

One brave hotel employer dared to try and stop him. 'She's my wife,' he announced as if that meant everything. 'You don't come between a man and his wife!'

And he stepped into the lift.

The last image Lizzy carried with her as the doors closed on them was an unrestricted view across the great hall and into the dining room where everyone was on their feet and staring at them.

'I hope you enjoyed causing that awful spectacle!' she choked out. 'Now put me down!'

'Not in this life,' Luc responded. 'You refuse to listen. You are an unforgiving harridan. You don't care what you make me feel. You love me but you don't *love* me!'

It was a distinction that made Lizzy stop fighting him so she could try to work it out. The moment she relaxed in his arms he let her feet slither to the ground. The doors to the lift parted as if he'd planned it. And maybe he had, Lizzy wouldn't put it beyond his capabilities. He dragged her out by the clamp of fingers he had around her wrist. The slide of a plastic key and she found herself standing in the most palatial suite of rooms she had ever seen.

The door closed, she heard the lock hit home. At last he let go of her and walked away. He was stiff with anger, she could see it pulsing from every part of him. He hooked up a bottle of something, poured some into a glass and downed it in one swallow, then finally turned.

'What else do you want from me?' he demanded, spreading his arms open wide. 'I let Bianca go. I married you as soon as I could arrange it. I put my pride and my reputation on the line for you. How many hints do you need before you stop being blind and see why I did these things?'

Lizzy tried her best to make her dizzy head think clearly, but all it was doing was soaking up his tense posture, the streaks of dark colour across his cheeks. He was angry—yes. He was defensive—yes. He was tall and dark and unbelievably more gorgeous to her than ever because he was finally opening up—for her.

Her fingers made a fluttering gesture, then came together across her front beneath the point where her heart was rattling around in her chest like an overexcited pup.

'Ti amo?' she dared to ease out.

He tensed—all of him tensed, then he gave a curt nod of his head. 'From the first time our eyes met in London,' he admitted. 'It came as a severe shock to me. I thought it was because you reminded me so much of *nonna*, but the feeling did not go away and I wanted it to. My life was already mapped out. I was betrothed to Bianca—'

'And sleeping with Bianca,' Lizzy put in huskily.

'What do you want me to say?' he demanded heavily. 'I'm a thirty-four-year-old man and I did not embrace celibacy while getting to this age.'

'I didn't think you did,' Lizzy said stiffly. 'I just didn't—'

She stopped, taking a bite out of her bottom lip because she knew what she had been about to say sounded stupid and immature and totally unfair—but she just hadn't thought about Bianca with him in that way. She didn't even know why it should matter to her so much yet it did.

'With Bianca it was just—'

'Don't,' she choked, not needing to hear him compare the two of them as if they were—

'No,' he sighed, hunching his shoulders and turning away from her, his stance weary and bleak.

Then— 'No,' he said again and spun back to face her again. His chin jutted and his expression turned fierce. 'I am going to say it,' he insisted, 'because I think it needs to be said. Bianca and I were engaged to be married so of course we were intimate. This is the twenty-first century, *cara*, an age in which most women expect their relationships to be intimate! But the intimacy stopped when I met you,' he admitted. 'A fact which probably contributed greatly to Bianca taking other lovers.'

He saw Lizzy's shocked expression and smiled cynically. 'Our decision to marry had nothing to do with love, *cara*.

Bianca was telling the truth when she called it forming a dynasty. She had the right name and she was beautiful.'

He paused, the words catching in his throat. 'But I made a big mistake,' he continued then. 'In my arrogance, when I didn't bother to look for the right woman because I believed I did not need to with Bianca there in the wings of my life, I did her no favours, or myself, by accepting what fate had handed to me on a plate. Then I met you and I was way too attracted to you to be fair to anyone. The way you just had to keep looking at me fascinated me. I watched for you doing it and arrogantly took it as my due without bothering to analyse why I liked to feel your eyes on me.'

His eyes blazed a golden trail across her pale, still face.

'Your hair fascinates me,' he murmured softly. 'I love its colour and the way it does its own thing and you don't care. I love your long, womanly shape and your soft, womanly curves and I miss you when you are not curled against me in our bed. I miss being able to fall asleep with my hand filled by the warm softness of your breast, or waking up with your mouth a brush away from my mouth and your hand claiming possession of *me*. You want to hear more?' he flicked out tautly.

Like a mouse mesmerised by the big jungle cat, Lizzy nodded.

'Okay,' he said and took in a deep breath. 'I *hate* the way I took your innocence. It plagues me constantly that I was so tough on you. I never want to see a look on your face like the one you wore when Bianca told you she was pregnant by me. And I *despise* that cheap excuse for a dress you are wearing because I can't see your beautiful figure through it and I *want* to see it. I want to lust after you even if you never let me touch you again. And I adore—' his voice softened and grew silky '—the way you're standing there lapping all of this up because you believe you deserve it when you *know* retribution is going to come at you for being such a greedy—' he took a step forward '—selfish, unforgiving woman with sex on her mind.'

'We don't have sex. We make love,' Lizzy corrected.

'Ah.' At last the strain relaxed from his face. 'So you admit you get the difference.'

Reaching up, he took hold of a fistful of her hair and tugged. Her head went back, exposing the length of her creamy throat to him and locking her eyes with his.

'Green,' he said. 'You're dying to rip my clothes off.'

'I want your baby,' she whispered.

And his golden eyes turned black, the studding power of the lion in him surging to the fore on a hot adrenalin rush as he dealt wih the rear zip to her dress.

The cheap black fabric fell away whilst her fingers were busy with the buttons on his shirt. He lost the jacket. Warm dark skin as taut as leather and clouded by dark virile hair brushed the backs of her fingers as she worked. She felt muscles flinch and flex as she worked.

And he didn't break contact with her eyes as she did it. He did not claim her waiting mouth. He just built on the pulsing sexual tension because—that was how they liked it, singing along wires pulled taut through the rushing heat of their blood.

His shirt was cast aside, her dress along with it. She unclipped her bra and discarded that too—and still they made no physical contact other than his fist in her hair and her hands now dealing with the clip and zip of his trousers.

But her lips had started to tremble and his eyes had gone from black to flames of burning gold. 'Take the shoes off yourself,' she tremored.

As he obediently heeled the first shoe off, one of her hands slid around his neck and the other slid inside his loosened trousers. Stretching up on tiptoe, Lizzy placed her lips against his ear.

'*Ti amo*,' she whispered and felt his response run like Martha's rum through his body. It raced along the place her hand was holding, and raged like fire across his face.

'*Ti amo*,' she whispered again across the burning temptation of his lips.

Then her hands squeezed—both of them, the one holding the velvet-smooth power of erection captive and the one clasped around his neck so she could bring his mouth into full, hungry contact with her own hungry mouth.

'I hope you appreciate you are going to pay for that,' he muttered tensely when she pressed her teeth into his warm bottom lip.

'Just something else I owe you,' Lizzy sighed mock tragically. 'Five and a half million kisses, a few De Santis cubs and one sexy bite of your lip.'

'You will never pay me back in this lifetime,' he declared confidently as he picked her up in his arms and walked through to the bedroom and tumbled her down on some really decadent-looking four-poster bed that knocked spots off the one in the Caribbean because of its heavy drapes in a dark red fabric and the matching cover that made her skin look so pearly white and clashed so alarmingly with her corkscrew hair.

But Luc loved what he was seeing—Lizzy saw it blazing like golden fire in his eyes.

'I give you leave to try,' he invited as he stripped the rest of his clothes off, then dealt with what else she had left on with the cool economy of a man who knew how much he was exciting the woman he was about to throw himself down on top of.

'Do I get to start soon?' she quizzed innocently.

'*Sì.*' He made the long snaking stretch with his body until he completely covered her. 'I will keep an account.'

* * * * *

THE GREEK TYCOON'S
UNWILLING WIFE

Kate WALKER

Kate Walker was born in Nottinghamshire, but as she grew up in Yorkshire she has always felt that her roots are there. She met her husband at university and she originally worked as a children's librarian, but after the birth of her son she returned to her old childhood love of writing. When she's not working, she divides her time between her family, their three cats and her interests of embroidery, antiques, film and theatre and, of course, reading. You can visit Kate at www.kate-walker.com.

For Michelle Reid.
A great writer, a great friend, whose support
and whip-cracking was invaluable to me
as I wrote this.

CHAPTER ONE

THE villa looked just as she remembered it.

Or rather, Rebecca acknowledged to herself, it looked just as it had always appeared in her dreams. Because the truth was that she had actually seen so very little of it on that one day she had ever spent inside it.

The one day that should have been the start of her honeymoon.

The one day of her marriage.

They had arrived just as the sun was setting and so she had only had the briefest glimpse of the huge, elegant, white-painted building, the sweep of the bay behind it blue and crystal-clear. But it seemed that that had been enough to etch the image onto her mind with perfect clarity so that the memories that had surfaced in her sleep were far more detailed and accurate than she would ever have imagined she could describe when awake.

Clearly the eyes of happiness recorded things much better than vision that was blurred and distorted by tears. Because that was how she remembered her arrival at the Villa Aristea, and then, just a few short hours later, her departure from it. She had reached the tiny island in the heights of delirious happiness, and left it just a few short hours later in the very depths of despair.

She hadn't even had time to unpack her case. Rebecca shivered in spite of the heat of the sun on her back as she recalled the way that Andreas had picked it up and flung it out of the door in a blazing, black rage. She had been so sure that he would have flung her out after it that she hadn't stayed even to protest, but had fled in a rush, trying to convince herself that discretion was the better part of valour and that she would do better to wait until he'd calmed down before she tried to explain the truth. At least then she might have a hope that he would listen.

She'd waited. And waited. But it had seemed that Andreas would never, ever calm down at all.

Until now.

'Is this the right place, *kyria*?'

Behind her, on the steep, curving road, the taxi driver stirred restlessly in the afternoon heat. He was clearly anxious to get back to the tiny village and into the shade once again.

'Oh, yes,' Rebecca assured him hastily, opening her bag and rooting in it awkwardly, hunting for her purse and thumbing through the unfamiliar notes she'd acquired in a rush at the very last minute, hunting for one that looked something like the amount on the meter. 'Yes, this is the right place.'

It was impossible not to contrast the shambles and discomfort of her arrival today with the way she had first visited the Villa Aristea barely a year before. Then she had travelled in the greatest possible comfort, flying to Rhodes in Andreas' private jet and then being ferried in a helicopter across the sea to this island that was little more than a dot in the ocean.

And she hadn't had to lift a finger. Everything had been arranged for her. Everything planned to be the end of a perfect day and the start of a perfect marriage.

Except, of course, it hadn't worked out at all that way. That day had been the start of nothing and had brought the end of her ill-fated marriage before it had even really begun.

Except in one way…

Bitter tears burned at the backs of her eyes as she was forced to remember how Andreas had so ruthlessly made sure that their marriage could not be dissolved easily and swiftly.

'There will be no annulment,' he had declared coldly and harshly, making it plain that that was what had been at the back of his mind all the time. He hadn't wanted her for himself any more, but he had made so sure that she could not be with anyone else for as long as he could keep her from it. 'If you want your freedom, you will have to go through the full legal procedure.'

'*If* I want my freedom!' Rebecca had flung at him, blinded by pain and desperate to get out of there before she had broken down and let him see just what he had done to her. '*If*! I wouldn't come back to you if you crawled over broken glass to come to me to beg for my return.'

He'd tossed aside her furious protest with an indifferent shrug of one powerful shoulder, a look of scorn on his beautiful face.

'You'll come crawling to me before I ever even think of you, if only because you need money for something. I'll be willing to bet that you'll come looking for cash before the year is up.'

'Never…' Rebecca had begun, desperate to stop him from thinking of her like this. 'I'd rather die.'

He'd scorned that declaration too, swatting it away as if her fury were just a buzzing fly that had annoyed him.

'You'll be back—because you can't help yourself. You'll want to get your greedy, grasping hands on as much as you can before our marriage is finally over and done with.'

'*Kyria…*'

The taxi driver was still hovering, trying to give her change, it seemed.

'Oh, no…'

Rebecca waved him away, trying to find the strength to smile in spite of her memories.

'Keep it. Keep the change.'

She might need him later, she told herself. Sooner, rather than later, if this interview didn't go well. But certainly at some point soon, she would need a taxi to take her back down to the ferry and it was as well to keep this man friendly as it seemed that he ran the only firm on this island.

She barely heard his thanks or the roar of the car's engine as it swung out into the road and set off down the hill again. Her gaze had gone back to the big, carved wooden door before her and her thoughts to the night, a year ago, when she had crept away from this place like a beaten dog, with her tail well and truly between her legs.

'You'll come crawling to me before I ever even think of you…'

The brutal words echoed again and again inside her mind, making her head ache, and her thoughts blur. She had come crawling to him in desperation, because only desperation could drive her to fulfil his prediction, make the callous words come true when she had vowed that it was the last thing on earth that she would ever want. And she *was* desperate.

But desperation wasn't why she was here.

The terrible news about her baby niece had driven her to write that letter to Andreas, expecting only ever to receive the curtest of replies from him—if in fact he replied at all. She hoped for, prayed for a cheque that would help them out of the terrible fix they were in—a cheque that she had promised him that she would pay back if it was the last thing she did. But she had definitely not dared to hope for anything else.

Certainly she hadn't dared to hope that he would actually see her, or speak to her. Let her put her case in person.

And of course he hadn't.

The formal letter had come almost by return of post.

She was asked to meet with his lawyer. To state exactly why she needed the money and on what terms. And when he had the details then Mr Petrakos would consider her request.

She had been still reeling from the curt coldness of the single typewritten sheet when the telephone had rung.

'Andreas…'

For the first time in almost twelve months Rebecca had let his name slip past her lips, whispering it aloud in the still, hot air, silent except for the buzz of insects amongst the flowers.

She hadn't even been able to say it when she had heard the unknown, accented voice at the other end of the phone ask to speak to Mrs Petrakos. In fact it had taken the space of several stunned heartbeats to even remember that Mrs Petrakos was her own name. She had gone back to using her maiden name after the brutally abrupt end to her marriage and had tried in all ways possible to put the fact that she had ever been Rebecca Petrakos, however briefly, out of her mind for good.

'Come on, Rebecca, *do something*!'

She spoke the words out loud, striving to push herself into action instead of standing there, foolishly, frozen to the spot. She seemed incapable of movement now that she was actually here.

She'd moved fast enough when she'd finally absorbed the phone message from Andreas' PA. Just to know that her husband had had an accident had been bad enough. At the words 'car crash', her blood had run cold, making her shiver in shock as the terrible truth hit home.

A devastating crash. His car brakes had failed and he'd gone off the road, into a tree. He was lucky to still be alive. But he had escaped, though badly battered and bruised—and now he was asking for her.

Asking for her.

As they had done back home, those words now pushed Rebecca into action, taking her towards the door, her hand lifting to tug at the ornate bell pull that hung beside it, hearing the sound jangle loudly deep inside the house.

Andreas had been asking for her, the voice at the other end of the phone had said. Did she think she could come to Greece? Would it be possible for her to come to see him?

Becca hadn't needed to *think*. There had been no doubt at all in her mind and she had given her answer even before she had time to consider whether it was wise or not. But the truth was she didn't care.

Andreas had been in a crash, he was hurt—injured—and he was asking for her. She had barely put the phone down before she had dashed upstairs to start packing.

Of course, the journey to Greece had given her too much time to think. Time to go over and over and over the conversation in her head and find all sorts of possible things to worry about and fret over.

What had happened in the accident and how badly hurt was Andreas? Why did he want to speak to her when for almost a year he had kept his distance, maintaining a total silence, with no contact at all, apart from that single stiffly formal letter that she knew he had got his secretary to write and had simply scrawled his name at the bottom of?

But it had been enough to know that Andreas had asked for her. And there was no way she was going to turn her back on him.

She was so absorbed in her thoughts that she barely noticed the big door swing open and jumped, startled, when a voice exclaimed in surprise.

'*Kyria* Petrakos!'

It was Medora, the elderly housekeeper who Andreas had said was the closest he had ever had to a mother. Medora, who had been the one person she had spoken to on that terrible day she had spent at the villa, before Andreas had so unceremoniously thrown her out. The one person who had had a smile for her then and still had now, it seemed.

'Welcome! Come in! The master will be so happy to see you.'

Would he? a little, niggling voice questioned in the back of Becca's thoughts. Would Andreas truly be glad to see her? She had started out on this journey so determined and full of confidence, but somehow along the way all of that courage had seeped away.

What if it had all been a terrible mistake? If Andreas had not been asking for her at all but for someone else? Or what if…?

Her heart clenched at the thought of the possibility that Andreas had asked for her all right but that he had done so for reasons that were far from kind or even friendly. What if his motives were simply to add to the misery he had heaped on her a year ago?

'*Kyria* Petrakos?'

Another voice, a male one this time—the voice from the telephone call—broke into her thoughts, making her turn, blinking hard in the shadowy hallway after the brilliance of the sun outside. A young man, tall, dark, was holding out his hand to her.

'My name is Leander Gazonas. I work for *Kyrie* Petrakos. It was I who telephoned you.'

Leander's handclasp was warm and firm, reassuringly so.

It drove away some of the doubts and fears in Becca's thoughts, and replaced them with new confidence and hope.

'Thank you for getting in touch with me. I came as soon as I could.'

'So would you like a drink—or a chance to freshen up? Medora will show you to your room.'

If a room had been put at her disposal then it seemed that, for the moment at least, Andreas was not just going to turn round and reject her again. But where was Andreas himself? How was he?

'If it's all right, I'd like to see my…'

The word died on her tongue and she found herself unable to actually say 'my husband' out loud.

'I'd like to see Mr Petrakos, if that's possible.'

If there was anything that brought home to her just how ambiguous her presence here was, it was this. The way that she was standing here, in the hallway of the home of the man who was, legally at least, her husband, waiting for an invitation to move into the house, while somewhere else in the building Andreas, the man she had promised to love, honour and cherish—and who had made the same vow to her—was…

Was what? Why was she being kept here, waiting like this? What had happened to Andreas? Where was he? Something about the look in Leander's eyes made panic rise in her throat.

'Is my husband all right? Where is he? How is he?'

'Please don't upset yourself, Mrs Petrakos.'

The tone was soothing, obviously meant to calm, but still there was something about the man's expression, his careful control of his words that set her nerves on edge. It was obvious that there was something he was holding back.

'Your husband is as well as can be expected. But he is still under a physician's care. So perhaps it would be best if…'

'No! No, it wouldn't be best—I want to see him now!'

Becca actually flinched at the sound of her own voice. It was too high, too sharp, too tight—too *everything*—and she didn't need the change that moved across the young man's face, tightening every muscle, pressing his lips together, to tell her that she had overstepped some invisible mark, one she hadn't been fully aware of. She didn't have the right, the position, in this household, to make demands like that. She had no idea what orders Andreas had given before his accident or even after it. She didn't even know whether he had given this Leander permission to contact her or if the young man had done it on his own initiative. And if that was the case…

'Please…' she added, unable to erase the raw note of desperation from her tone. 'Can I see my husband now?'

She saw doubt in the face before her and was about to give in to the despair that swamped her. But then, just as she was debating whether to open her mouth and plead or simply to try to push past him and head into the house—she could remember much of the layout of the place from the brief time she had spent in it in the past—Leander obviously reconsidered.

'Very well—if you will come this way.'

He would never know, Becca reflected, just how difficult she found it to keep behind him as he made his way up the wide, curving staircase and along the landing. With anxiety chewing at her thoughts, she wanted to rush ahead to get to Andreas' room before he did. It was only when Leander came to a halt outside an unexpected door that she was thankful that she hadn't. Because Andreas had obviously decided not to stay in the room that had been his when she had been at the villa before. The room that would have been *theirs* if the marriage hadn't broken up as soon as it had begun. And as her footsteps slowed and stopped she knew that she should be grateful.

How could she ever have gone into *that* room, with all the memories it held? How could she have coped with the past being thrown right into her face as soon as the door opened, and she saw the bed on which Andreas had made her his?

Made her his and then rejected her without a second thought.

It would destroy her, she knew. Already the way that her heart was beating high up in her throat was choking off the air to her lungs and making her head swim so that she felt faint.

So she could only be grateful when Leander opened the door to a room she had never been into and stood there waiting for her to come past him.

Becca's legs felt weak beneath her, shaking in apprehension as she forced herself to walk into the room. What would Andreas look like? What sort of a mood would he be in? He had been asking for her, yes—but *why*?

The image of her husband's dark, furious face, the black eyes blazing, the beautiful, sensual mouth drawn into a hard, slashing line floated in her mind so that for a few moments that was all she saw when she was actually standing in the room. It obscured her vision, covering the reality of the man in the bed.

But then she blinked and saw Andreas for the first time since he had slammed the door in her face almost twelve months before.

The bruises were the first things she noticed. Bruises that marred the smooth, olive-toned skin, turning it black and blue in a way that had her drawing in her breath in a sharp hiss. His eyes were closed, lush black lashes lying in dark crescents above the high cheek-bones, and a day or more's growth of beard darkened the strong line of his jaw.

Shock at the sight of him lying there so still and silent made her gasp. Her vision that had cleared for just a brief moment blurred again as tears of horror filled her eyes.

'He's unconscious!'

She didn't care that her distress showed in her voice, that the edge of fear sharpened it.

'Asleep,' Leander reassured her. 'He was unconscious for a time, but the doctors wouldn't let him out of hospital until they were sure he was on the mend.'

'Can I stay—with him?'

She didn't know what she might do if Leander refused permission. She didn't think that her legs would support her if she tried to walk out of the room. She could still barely see, and the fight to force back the tears, refusing to let them spill out down her cheeks, was one that took all her concentration.

'*Kyrie* Petrakos asked for me,' she added hastily when she saw that the younger man was hesitating. 'I promise I won't wake him—or do anything to disturb him.'

At last he nodded.

'He did ask for you,' he said, indicating a chair with a wave of his hand. 'But I should warn you that the blow to the head has left him with some memory problems—the doctors believe they will be only temporary. So he may be a little confused when he wakes. Would you like a drink sent up?'

'I'll be fine,' Becca assured him hastily, squashing down the weak thought that a cup of tea might warm the sudden coldness of her blood, give her a strength she so much needed. What she needed more was to be left alone, to have time to catch her breath, mentally, since the telephone call had rocked the balance of her world so desperately.

As Leander left the room she sank down thankfully into the chair he had indicated, her legs giving way beneath the weariness that was both mental and physical, her eyes fixed on the still form of the man in the bed.

She had promised not to wake him, not to disturb him, but

the truth was that he was disturbing her for all he lay so silent and unmoving. The sight of Andreas, whom she had last seen so tall, strong and proud, lying still and pale in the bed was almost more than she could take.

But it was worse than that.

She'd spent the last year telling herself that this man had been a mistake, one she deeply regretted, but she was over him. It had taken just one glance at the man in the bed, at the dark, stunning profile, the broad naked chest where the bronzed skin showed livid, disturbing bruises, ones that made her heart clench just to see them, to rock that belief in her head. If she had seen him standing, if her first awareness had been of the powerful, forceful man he was, the man who had used her and then thrown her out of his home, perhaps it would have been different. This man was too quiet, too vulnerable.

Too deceptively vulnerable, a warning voice sounded inside her head. Because at any other time, vulnerable was not a word she would ever associate with Andreas Gregorie Petrakos.

'I hate him.'

In a low, desperate whisper, she tried the word hate out for size, feeling it strange and alien on her tongue. For almost a year now, she had used it every day in connection with Andreas' name. Used it and meant it.

'I hate Andreas Petrakos,' had been the first words she had said on waking and often the last ones that had been on her tongue at night. They had replaced and reversed the ones that had been there before, in the brief time before her marriage, when she had whispered to herself how much she loved this man, afraid to voice the thoughts aloud for fear that she might be tempting fate and the happiness she dreamed of would evaporate just as a result of saying them.

She shouldn't have bothered, Becca told herself bitterly.

She hadn't tempted fate but the cruel blow had fallen after all. Andreas had never loved her as she had loved him; in fact, his marrying her had only been an act of revenge.

The man in the bed sighed, stirred, muttered something, immediately drawing her eyes to his face once again. Had those heavy, closed eyelids flickered once or twice, or was she just deceiving herself?

Just the thought of it made her heartbeat kick up several notches, making her blood pound in her ears.

What would she do if—when he woke? When he spoke?

And what about these 'memory problems'? How much had they affected him? Knowing Andreas as she did, she could just imagine how difficult he would find any limitation to his awesome mental abilities. He would hate it and it would chafe at him like a net thrown over a wounded lion, holding him captive. He would rage against it, and Andreas in a rage was a terrifying sight.

But perhaps more importantly, she should also consider what this news meant for her. Would Andreas even remember that he had asked for her? And what had been on his mind when he had?

The long-fingered hand that lay on the bed had definitely twitched, flexing briefly as he sighed again. There was a long, angry-looking scratch running from the base of his ring finger right to his wrist and it pulled on something deep in her heart to see the raw tear in the beautiful, bronzed skin that seemed so very dark in contrast to the soft white cotton of the coverings.

Becca bit down hard on her lower lip to hold back the faint gasp that almost escaped her and she fought to push away memories of how it had felt to know the touch of that hand, have it caress her skin, rouse her to heated longing...

'No!'

She wasn't going to let herself go down that road. To do

so would destroy her even before she'd spoken to Andreas, or found out just why he'd asked for her. And she was having enough trouble holding on to her self-control as it was, with the bitter memories that assailed her at just being in this house.

The *bittersweet* memories—because some of them she could never deny had been so very sweet. She had been so idyllically happy when she had arrived at the villa. So happy that she had thought that her heart would burst from sheer joy.

But that had been before Andreas had taken that loving heart and ripped it into tiny pieces.

'*O opoios...*'

There was no mistaking it this time. Andreas had murmured the words, rough and low, but he had spoken. His eyes remained closed but his head stirred restlessly against the pillows as he swallowed, ran his tongue over his dry lips.

'*O opoios...*?' he said again, his voice grating as if he hadn't used it for a long time.

'Andre…'

Becca's voice matched his for hoarseness and lack of strength. She felt as if all the blood had drained from her body at the sound of that once so dearly loved voice that she hadn't heard for a year.

'Mr Petrakos…'

That brought his eyes open in a rush, huge and dark, turning her way, frowning as he tried to focus on her face.

What could she see in them? It certainly wasn't welcome— but was it anger or rejection, or…?

'Who—?'

He heaved himself up on the pillows, propped himself on one elbow as he stared into her face, and the cold glare from his deep-set black eyes warned her that she was in trouble.

'So tell me,' he said slowly and clearly in English, 'just where the hell have you been?'

CHAPTER TWO

'SO TELL me, just where the hell have you been?'

He'd spoken in English, Andreas realised, but he had no idea why. Somehow when he'd opened his mouth, the words had just come out in that language, and he hadn't even really thought about it.

So what did that mean?

Ever since he'd come round from the coma into which he'd fallen after the accident, nothing had been clear in his thoughts at all. He hadn't even been able to remember his own name or where he lived, and it had taken a couple of long, hellish weeks for anything that he was told to stick inside his battered brain.

He'd been thrown about the car quite violently, and he'd hit his head hard, they'd told him. He was lucky to be alive, so a few scrambled thoughts, some hazy memories were not unexpected. Hazy he could cope with, scrambled too. It was the blank, empty hole where most of his memory of the past year or so should be that was really disturbing him.

But the doctors had had an answer for that, too. It would come back, they had assured him. In its own time. He just needed to relax and wait.

The problem was that no one told him how long he had to wait. Or what the hell he did if it didn't come back at all. The last thing he felt was *relaxed*.

And they never told him how to handle situations like this. Like waking up in his own room with a beautiful woman sitting in a chair, watching him.

A beautiful woman he remembered from before the gap in his mind.

She was of medium height, as much as he could tell, and with a neat, slenderly curved figure in a blue and green print dress under a short white cotton jacket. Her hair was almost as dark as his own, shaped in a neat, short feathery cut that framed the heart-shaped face, emphasising the high cheek-bones and the rich curve of her soft mouth. But where the eyes that he saw in the mirror every day were black too, hers were a soft, washed-looking pale blue, the colour of the sea out in the bay on a cool, shadowy day.

'You *are* Rebecca, aren't you?' he demanded again when the woman didn't speak but simply stared at him with wide, stunned-looking eyes.

'Yes, I'm—I'm Becca... Rebecca.'

The words were English and on the soft, hesitant voice the accent seemed to fit as well. So somehow he'd been right when he had spoken to her in English.

He didn't even really know why English, only that it had felt so right.

And something to do with this woman whose face had been the first thing that he had focused on when he opened his eyes. The woman who, he had to admit, had sparked off the first moment of real, sharp, intense interest he had felt since the day he had come round after the accident to a world turned upside down. At least he was still aware of the appeal of a beautiful female face, he thought bitterly, the sharp twist of desire reminding him that, no matter what was wrong with his mind, he was still functioning as a *man* for the first time since regaining consciousness.

And the amazing thing was that he could remember *her*. So she belonged in his life from the time before his memory had been wiped away.

Becca—Rebecca Ainsworth. The woman he had met at a party in London and who had knocked him for six from the moment he had first set eyes on her.

And the woman he must still be having a passionate relationship with—*Theos*, but he hoped it was passionate!—or else why would she have turned up here like this?

'So what took you so long?'

The look of shock combined with blank astonishment on her fine features told him better than his own ears how aggressive and hostile he had sounded. That was the result of the sudden, violent tug of attraction throwing him off balance with its hint of how things had once been—in the life he could no longer remember.

'Forgive me,' he added automatically. 'I don't find it easy living with everyone knowing more about me than I do myself. It's just a relief to see a familiar face.'

But then something about the way she looked, some movement of her head, a flash of wariness in her eyes, hastily concealed, set his nerves on edge and had him clamping his jaw tight shut on the anger that almost escaped him.

Had he got things wrong? Was Becca here because of what was still between them or had Leander decided to call her as a way of getting round the doctor's unwelcome suggestion that he have a nurse? If that was the case, then the way that

Andreas' explicit instructions had been so blatantly ignored made anger well up inside him.

'We are still together, aren't we? Or are you just here as the damn nurse?'

'Am—I…?'

Becca's thoughts spun as she saw the way that Andreas' face had changed. It seemed as if in the few brief moments since he had opened his eyes and focused on her sitting there, watching him, he had swung from one extreme of mood to another with such devastating speed that she had difficulty interpreting his feelings or keeping up with each new change.

Disbelief she had been prepared for, suspicion too. After all, they had parted on such terrible terms that she couldn't imagine that he would truly be happy to see her, even though she had been told that he had asked for her. The last memory she had of him was of him standing in the doorway of his villa, this villa, watching her walk away, his face set into stony, un-yielding lines, rejection stamped into every muscle in his tautly held body. She had known without even glancing back that his arms were folded tight across his broad chest, his powerful body filling the door space, blocking it, so that there was no hope of her getting back into the house if she had been foolish enough even to try.

But she hadn't tried. Even if she had wanted to, she knew she would be a fool to consider it. One glance into those cruel black eyes, seeing the hatred and the dark fury that had burned there, had been enough to keep her feet moving doggedly forward, even though tears blinded her eyes until she could hardly see the path in front of her. And even without that black fury, she had vowed that she was never going back. Never.

'I married you for sex—for that and nothing else,' he had said, and from somewhere deep in her soul she had dragged up a fierce, savage hatred for Andreas. A hatred that burned away all the love she thought she had felt for him and left it shrivelled into ashes in what remained of her heart. She had clung on to that hatred, and fuelled it by reminding herself over and over and over just what he had said, the way he hadn't believed her.

And that hatred, that fury had been enough to get her out of there and into the taxi that he had called to take her away.

It was only when the car had rounded the corner out of sight of the villa that she had let the bitter tears fall.

But it seemed from his behaviour now that Andreas remembered nothing of that. It was the only explanation she could think of for the way he was behaving.

Memory problems, Leander had said and, tense and jittery with nerves, she hadn't thought to ask for details of what had happened. Now it seemed that she might have to face the fact that to Andreas she was the woman he had known—what? A year before? Fifteen months? It couldn't be much more than that because they had married after only four months together.

But it seemed that that wedding and the dreadful events that had followed it had been wiped from his mind. He obviously recalled nothing about their break up—or the reasons for it. So how was she to cope with that—and how was she to behave now?

'Well?'

The question was snapped out curtly. She'd hesitated too long. Patience had never been a virtue that Andreas Petrakos held in high esteem and it seemed that that at least hadn't changed.

'*Has* Leander brought you in to act as the nurse they threatened me with?'

'Do you see having a nurse to look after you as a threat?' Becca hedged, unable to control the way an instinctive smile curled up the corners of her mouth.

Of course Andreas saw the idea of having a nurse to look after him as some sort of imposition—a threat. He'd hate the thought of needing to be looked after in any way at all. And his pride would make him fight against the prospect of that happening.

The look her instinctive teasing brought her stabbed like a stiletto. Not because of any anger in it, but because there was a gleam in those deep black eyes that told her he'd caught the faint shake of laughter in her words, the twitch of her mouth.

It was an expression that forced memories from the back of Becca's mind where she had tried to hide them away for so very long. Memories of a time when she had thought that she couldn't be happier; when she had believed that this stunning, devastating man had actually loved her as much as she had loved him. She had been very definitely and very bitterly disillusioned.

'I told the doctor I didn't need any nurse fussing over me.'

'But you haven't—been well.'

To her despair, her voice caught on the words, something sharp and uncomfortable twisting in her heart at the thought of the powerful, muscled body before her being bruised and torn in the car accident she had been told about. Even as she spoke, he shifted uncomfortably, and the movement revealed more bruising, this time along his ribs, and down to the lean waist.

She would feel that way about anyone who was injured, she tried to assure herself. All that it was was a natural compassion for anyone who had been hurt. There was nothing left in her heart to make it any more.

'The hospital believed I was well enough to be sent home, and I do not need any further attention!'

'Not even from someone who doesn't fuss?'

What *was* she doing? Becca's thoughts reeled as she heard what she'd actually said. She'd practically offered to take on the job of caring for him. And to her horror that was what Andreas obviously thought too.

'You're saying you'll never fuss over me?'

The beginnings of a smile tugged at the corners of his mouth, put a gleam in those deep, dark eyes. He couldn't be *flirting* with her—could he? The contrast with the memory of the way that she had last seen those black eyes, burning with an icy flame of hatred, made her shift uncomfortably in her seat.

'No...'

Too unsettled now to sit still, Becca got to her feet, wanting to move restlessly about the room, then suddenly thinking better of her actions and returning to perch awkwardly on the arm of the chair.

'I...I'm not saying that.'

'Then what are you saying?'

Andreas' tone had sharpened as his eyes followed her uneasy movements.

'I'm not...'

The words shrivelled into nothing, drying her mouth so that she had to slick a nervous tongue over her parched lips as she tried to find some sort of answer to give him.

She didn't know this Andreas—or, rather, she had known him once but so briefly and so unbelievably that she had to struggle to remember it.

He hadn't flirted with her when they had first met. Then he had been focused, determined, his devastating personal power concentrated totally on her, so strongly that she had found it almost impossible to breathe.

Certainly, it just hadn't seemed possible that this stunning man, this multi-multimillionaire with everything in the world that he wanted—a hundred times over—and every woman in the world prepared to fall at his feet could possibly want anything to do with plain, simple, unimpressive Rebecca Ainsworth.

And it seemed that Rebecca Ainsworth was whom he remembered. Not the fact that she had ever become Rebecca Petrakos. She didn't know what she could tell him about what had happened in the time he couldn't recall, but there had to be something. If she announced now, starkly and matter-of-factly that she was his wife—his alienated wife, the wife he had thrown out of his home with the furious order never, ever even to think of coming back there—did she even know if he would believe her?

She remembered once being told how an amnesia victim 'forgot' the time they didn't *want* to remember. That the condition could be as much psychological as it was physical. And if that was the case, had Andreas forgotten her because he couldn't bear to remember that they had been married? Some time soon, inevitably, he must get his memory back properly. And then he would know only too well just who she was.

Her heart lurched painfully at the thought. But still she wasn't brave enough to give him the truth and risk her instant dismissal.

'Andreas, you know I'm not one to fuss unnecessarily,' was all she could manage uncomfortably.

'Then I'm glad you're here to save me from someone who might.'

Andreas' tone said that that was the end of the matter, no chance of discussion, and she was still wondering just how she could take this any further when he shifted in the bed, pulling himself up even more against the pillows.

'Come here.'

It was pure Andreas; pure command. If he had snapped his fingers he couldn't have made it any more autocratic. In spite of herself, Becca pushed herself up from the arm of the chair, turning towards him, then hesitated when she saw the way that the powerful hands had closed over the bed coverings, about to throw them back.

'What are you doing?'

Her voice went up at the end of the sentence, revealing her shock and unease. When they had been together Andreas had always slept naked and the thought that he might reveal more of his powerful body than he was doing already made her blood run hot and then cold as if she was in the grip of some dangerous fever.

'I have to get up.'

The black eyes that met her shocked blue ones were wide and steady. No trace of anything other than straightforward openness lurked in their depths and his mouth showed no hint of quirking into any sort of a smile. Any double meanings or ulterior motives were in her own mind, her uncomfortable conscience making her edgy.

'And as I'm not yet as steady on my feet as I'd like to be, it might be advisable if my nurse—you—was close at hand in case of any problems.'

At least he was wearing pyjama trousers, Becca realised on a shudder of relief as the way that Andreas flung back the coverings revealed his long legs covered in navy-blue cotton. But with his chest and arms bare, there was still far too much of the beautiful olive-toned skin on display for her personal comfort.

Before the accident, he must have been working out more than ever because every inch of his upper torso was taut and toned, the muscles sharply defined, and there wasn't an ounce of spare flesh on the powerful ribcage, the narrow waist. The soft hazing of jet-black hair reminded her painfully of the way that she had loved to smooth her fingertips over its softness, feeling the contrast between it and the satin skin beneath.

Should she offer a hand to help him? Her pulse jerked at the thought of his fingers closing over hers, her throat drying painfully so that she had to swallow hard to relieve it. After all these months apart from him, she had managed to convince herself that her response to Andreas' hardcore male sexuality had been a form of mental aberration, a brief spell of madness that had taken her over, driving her out of her sane mind and into a world in which her normal, controlled responses no longer ruled her actions.

But now all she had had to do was to come into his presence once again—to move closer at his arrogant command—and suddenly it was all happening all over again. It was as if she breathed in the intoxicating drug of seduction simply by being in the same atmosphere as him, drawn to him irresistibly, her senses drugged into instant submission. And coming close to him only made it so much worse. She could catch the intimately personal scent of his skin, see the way that the sunlight glinted on his silky black hair as he moved his head...

'Here...'

Her voice was gruff and ungracious, made that way by the discomfort of her thoughts as she held out an arm to offer him support. Just at the last minute she suddenly had a loss of nerve that had her angling it so that her forearm, covered in the white cotton of her jacket, came closest to him rather than the bare skin of her hand.

'Thank you...I think.'

Andreas' tone of voice, the slightly cynical twist to his beautiful mouth, told her that he had noticed her hesitation, and the careful adjustment, and misinterpreted her reasons for it.

'You were not joking when you said that you don't intend to fuss.'

'I'm sorry—I…'

Whatever she had been about to say vanished from her mind as she felt him take hold of the support she offered, strong fingers closing around her upper arm, the heat of his palm searing her skin through the soft cotton. It was as if he had attached a live electrical lead to her skin and the resulting current had raced along every nerve, fusing her thoughts. And when he put his weight onto his grip and got to his feet she was lost completely.

'Andreas…'

His name left her lips in an involuntary gasp as a response burned its way up to her brain and flashed heated memories that she had tried to erase onto a screen in her mind. From nowhere came images of the way that he had touched her before, the effect that the feel of his hand on hers had created—the things that it had led to. Her skin tingled in response to those imagined caresses, her mouth dried in wanting, longing for the feel of his lips on hers, and a rush of liquid heat flooded into her innermost core.

Without being aware of it she swayed towards him in a moment of desperate weakness, only catching herself as the movement brought her so close to the lean, powerful body that she could catch the scent of his skin, still warm from the bed, inhale the clean, masculine essence of him and feel it burn all the way down her senses. The hyper-efficient air-conditioning in the room became less than useless as a fire of response raged through her body.

The truth was that a tiny part of her wanted him to realise who she was—wanted to have the real facts out in the open and done with. But at the same time she was terrified of the repercussions of that, personally and healthwise. Until she knew just what had been said about this memory loss that Andreas was suffering from, whether it was temporary or permanent, and what the doctors had recommended, she didn't dare take any risks. And on a personal level, as soon as he realised who she was then how would he react? Would he even let her stay or would he throw her out of the house as he had done barely a year ago, with the words, 'If I never see you again it will still be too soon,' echoing in her ears?

'Becca…'

Andreas' tongue seemed to curl around the syllables, turning them into a very different sound from the one she was used to. Hot tears burned at the backs of her eyes, threatening her hard-won composure with the memory of hearing him say her name in that special way as she had lain in his arms, her head pillowed on the broad expanse of his chest, hearing the heavy thud of his heart slow gradually from the hectic pace created by the fierce passion of their lovemaking.

She didn't know if her own heart was jolting in sensual response to her memories, his touch or panic-stricken fear of the possible repercussions if—when—he realised how their relationship had changed from the one he believed it was.

'Becca…' he said again and her shocked senses, dangerously alert to everything about him, caught the change in tone, the slight thickening of his accent on her name, the faint roughness of his voice that told her without words that his mood had changed.

Curiosity had given way to interest, annoyance blending into awareness so swiftly that only someone who knew him well would notice.

But Becca knew this side of the man too well. It was the

Andreas she knew more than any other. The sexually driven man who had taught her all she knew about passion, about desire—and most of all about pleasure. She knew that when his eyes darkened so much that they seemed all black, when his voice rasped in his throat in just that way, that he was turned on, hotly aroused by what he saw.

And she had enough experience of seeing this response to know when it was directed at her.

'An—Andreas...' she tried, her voice shaking and sounding almost as rough as his.

He shook his head, slowly, silently, his eyes dropping down to watch her mouth as she spoke.

And she knew that look too. Knew the way his own mouth had opened very slightly, the slow, heavily indrawn breath. He wanted to kiss her. Wanted it so much that it absorbed all his thoughts, took all his concentration.

He wanted to kiss her and she wanted him to do just that.

Her whole body was one stinging burn of awareness from the toes that curled inside her soft leather sandals to the prick-ling lift of each tiny hair on her scalp. She barely felt the point at which his hand was clamped around her arm, the warmth of his palm lost in the rush of heat that scoured her skin, strip-ping away one much-needed protective layer and leaving her raw and yearning beneath.

But who would he be kissing? The woman he had once asked to be his wife, then flung his wedding vows in her face as he rejected her and forced her out of his house before they had even been married for twenty-four hours? The woman he couldn't remember. Or would he kiss the girlfriend—the mistress—he believed she was? The woman he didn't remember ever asking to marry him.

And if he did kiss her would the moment that their lips

touched jolt something in his brain, loosening whatever blockage kept him from recalling her?

She would risk it, she knew. From the moment that he had touched her, she had been lost. Adrift on the heated sea of physical hunger that he had always been able to wake in her.

She wanted him to kiss her. Wanted it so much that it was like a thundering, pounding refrain inside her head, so heavy and loud that she felt sure he must either hear it declared out loud, or read it burning behind the eyes she couldn't find the strength to drag away from his stunning face.

Kiss me.

She could almost believe that she'd said the words herself, they sounded so loud and clear in her thoughts.

Please kiss me.

Andreas drew in a breath, heavy and low, then let it out again in a sigh. His head was angled slightly to one side, his gleaming black eyes hooded under heavy lids, the lush, thick lashes brushing his cheeks for a moment as he looked down, taking in her upturned face in a single, sweeping glance.

'Beautiful…' he murmured, his voice even huskier than before.

'I…'

Becca tried to speak and failed, ending up with her mouth slightly open simply because she couldn't make herself close it. She felt as if she was surrounded by Andreas, by the warmth of his body, the scent of his skin. Just inches away from her she could see the way his powerful chest rose and fell with each breath he took, almost hear the beat of his heart underneath the smooth, olive-toned flesh. It was as if the world had ceased to exist. As if there was only the two of them and the heated, sensual bubble they had created around them.

With that black-eyed gaze holding her still, frozen hypnotised, he lifted his hand and touched the backs of his fingers to her skin at her temple and then trailed them slowly down her cheek, tracing the line of her jaw, her chin. When the strong fingers reached her still open mouth, moving over the outline of her lips, it was all that Becca could do to hold back a moan of response. The temptation to part her lips even more, to let her tongue slide out and curl over that stroking fingertip, to feel the slightly salty tang of it on her tongue, remember how it had been to taste him all over, anywhere—everywhere—was almost irresistible.

But just as she drew in her breath, taking some of the essence of him in with it, fighting the primitive, carnal hunger that had suddenly reached out to enclose her, she hesitated for a second, for the space of a single heartbeat, suddenly terri-fied, painfully, cruelly aware of how far from wise such an action was.

And the next moment she could only be grateful for that sudden flash of control, of self-preservation. Because unex-pectedly that stroking hand slowed, stilled, and then was abruptly snatched away, the rush of cold air where its warmth had once been and the sense of loss cruel enough to force her to bite down hard on her lower lip to hold back the cry of shock that almost escaped her.

'I think not,' Andreas said sharply, the tone of his voice putting distance between them more effectively than the single step he took, backwards and away from her. 'This is not a good idea.'

While she was still recovering from a rejection that had had as much emotional force to her as a cruel slap in the face, he turned on his heel and strode away from her, flinging open a door in the opposite wall that obviously led to an *en suite* bathroom.

'I need a shower—I'll come down when I'm ready. Get

Leander to show you to a room. We'll talk about how we handle this later.'

Just like that, she was dismissed and he strode into the bathroom, the door slamming behind him. A moment later she heard the key turning firmly in the lock as if he felt the need to make very sure it was secure against...

Against what? Did he think that she might actually try to go in there after him? That she was weak enough, foolish enough—*desperate* enough to try to follow him to fling herself into his arms?

Just what had she shown in her face when he had touched her? How much of herself, of her innermost thoughts had she given away? Knowing that he didn't remember the truth about their relationship, had she been stupid enough to let her expression reveal the pain it had brought her in the time he couldn't recall?

Or perhaps his sudden reaction just now was because he was *beginning* to remember?

Becca found that she was trembling all over, her legs shaking beneath her so that she didn't feel they could support her any longer. Weak and unable to keep herself upright, she sank down onto the bed, covering her face with her hands. But her respite was brief because almost immediately she jumped up again, unable to bear the way the sheets were still warm from his body, still imprinted with the scent of his skin.

She could still feel him all around her, enveloping her in warmth. In her memory she could taste his kisses on her lips as strongly as if he had actually kissed her just now and not just dismissed her without a second's thought. But in her mouth the sense of rejection was bitter, reminding her cruelly of how she had once felt when he had denounced and banished her from his life on the black day that had been their wedding day.

If I never see you again it will be too soon.

The words rang inside her head, reminding her of the pain and disillusionment she had felt at that time. The same hurt and bitterness that she was risking feeling all over again just by being here.

'Oh, Becca, Becca, you *idiot!*' she reproved herself harshly as she moved as far away from the bed as she could.

She had trapped herself well and truly and the only way to get out of this was to admit to Andreas just what had happened...

'Oh, no...'

The words escaped from her lips in a whisper at the thought of confronting the cold, heartless anger she knew her husband to be capable of if she told him the truth. And besides, hadn't she read somewhere that it was foolish, even dangerous to tell someone suffering from amnesia the truth about their situation? It was forbidden, wasn't it? And she certainly wasn't about to take the risk of confronting Andreas with something he couldn't possibly want to know.

But he *had* asked for her.

That was what Leander had said, wasn't it?

Wasn't it?

The truth was that she was so emotionally battered by everything that had happened in the last few weeks that single events were beginning to blur into one big, confused and confusing mass. She had barely recovered from the curt, totally businesslike reply Andreas had sent to her first enquiry before the phone call about the accident had come through, and as soon as she had heard that she had been on the plane out to Greece, to this tiny island that Andreas called home—and that once she had hoped, dreamed would be her home too.

She couldn't remember too clearly the actual words that had

been used. But there was no way she would be here now if Andreas hadn't actually given his permission for her to be here.

But had that been before or after he had lost his memory? And was it the lover he believed she still was that he had asked for—or the wife he had rejected so completely?

Behind the door of the bathroom, the noise of the shower running jolted her back to the present, dragging her thoughts in the last possible direction that she wanted them to go. It was impossible to hear the driving sound of the water and not think of the times when she had had the freedom to join him in the shower, to share the hot water as it pounded down onto Andreas' hard, lean body, cascading over the bronzed skin, flowing down from the broad, straight shoulders, past his narrow waist, over the tight curves of his...

'No!'

Becca shook her head sharply as the word escaped her, just the image of what she was remembering enough to drive her into motion, pushing her towards the door as fast as she could go.

'I can't take this—can't do it...'

She would find Leander, explain that there had been a mistake. A terrible mistake.

And then she would get out of here.

She would run from Andreas as she had run a year before. Putting as much distance between him and herself as she possibly could.

She would run and run and she would never come back.

She should never have come back. Never, ever have come back to the island, to the villa—to the man she had once loved so deeply and so desperately.

What could have possessed her to even think that she could talk to him, persuade him to listen to her, to help her...?

She was almost at the top of the stairs when the word

'help' sounded in her thoughts again, stopping her dead, reminding her of the real reason why she was here. The reason she had forgotten.

Oh, how could she have forgotten Macy? And most of all, how could she have forgotten little Daisy?

Daisy was just a baby—and her life, her tiny, precious life, depended on the way that Becca acted now.

Without her help, Daisy would die. And Becca had promised that she would do anything she could—everything she could—to help.

Standing with her hand on the newel post, fingers clenching tight over the polished wood, Becca sighed, half turned, looked back at the still slightly open door into the bedroom from which she had just fled in a panic-stricken rush.

She had promised—and she would keep that promise, no matter what it took. She needed Andreas' help and she would have to get that help, whatever she had to do to get it. She had no choice.

If the only way she could stay in the villa, the only way she could get close to Andreas and stay there until at last he remembered who she was and what she had asked of him—the money he had promised to provide—was to pretend to be the mistress that he believed her to be, then she was going to have to do it. She would play the part to the best of her ability and pray that it wouldn't take too long for Andreas' memory to return.

She had to—for Daisy's sake.

Drawing in a long, ragged breath and letting it out again on a heartfelt sigh, she made herself place first one foot on the staircase and then another, straightening her shoulders, holding her chin up high as she headed downstairs.

CHAPTER THREE

ANDREAS turned up the power and the temperature on the shower so that it pounded down savagely onto the top of his head, thudding onto his skull, leaving him incapable of thinking.

At least that was the plan. But somehow, when he needed it most, the plan didn't seem to be working.

He wanted to forget about the moments out in his bedroom when he had touched Becca.

When he had wanted to do so much more than touch. Certainly much more than fasten his hand around hers, or to stroke his fingers along the peachy softness of her cheek.

He had wanted to kiss her so badly. The hunger to take her lips with his had been like a nagging ache throughout his whole body, adding further discomfort to the already painful bruises that made his muscles throb, tugged at his ribs when he drew in his breath sharply. He wanted to hold her, caress her. He had felt his heart kick up, his blood pulse through his veins.

He had felt himself come alive for the first time in days.

In the days that he could remember anyway. The days that had registered in the void that had been his mind since he had come round from the unconsciousness that that car crash had put him into.

And for the first time since the accident he had felt like a man again, passionate and burning with a hot, hungry desire.

But a desire he really shouldn't give in to.

'Hell and damnation!'

Andreas swore viciously and reached up to change the temperature of the water yet again, shuddering as this time an icy blast thundered onto his soaked hair, his bare shoulders. A long cold shower was what he needed to cool the heat in his blood, the fire that threatened to destroy his ability to think at all.

Any desire he felt would be crazy, stupid—madness to act upon, no matter how strongly he felt it, how urgently it called to him to appease it. He didn't need any further complications in his life. Things were already complex enough.

Wasn't it bad enough that he couldn't remember anything about the past twelve months? That anything he had learned about that year, and his accident, was something that he had had to take on trust, both in the hospital and since arriving home?

Home.

This time Andreas snapped off the shower completely and stepped out of the glass-walled stall, shaking his head like a big, angry dog, trying to drive away another flurry of unwanted thoughts that assailed and tormented him.

'Home!'

He flung the word like a curse at his reflection in the huge, steamed-up mirror, scowling blackly into the dark blur of his eyes as he did so.

This *was* his home; he knew that at least. But from the moment that he'd arrived at the door, he had had the appalling feeling that something was very wrong. And that feeling had stayed with him as he'd walked through the house.

What he'd not been prepared for was the sheer wave of desolation that had overwhelmed him at just the thought of going into the obvious room, the master bedroom. There was no way he'd been prepared to admit to it, so he had turned instead and headed for the bedroom that was furthest away from it.

Which was why he had ended up in here.

Shaking his head again, he snatched up a towel and began to dry himself, his movements rough and almost aggressive as if he could wipe away the frustration of his lack of memory along with the water drops.

'Damn!'

An unthinking movement caught the towel on a particularly dark-coloured bruise, making him draw in his breath in a sharp hiss between his teeth. But the stab of pain was easily dismissed, pushed out of his mind. It would heal. Another week or so and he would be back to normal. In his body at least.

But what about his mind?

Another string of curses, darker and even more vicious, spilled from his lips as he considered the prospect.

Without a memory or any knowledge of what had happened in the past year, how could he even think of any sort of relationship with a woman, even just the physical one that his hungry senses had been urging him on to? How could he ever allow himself any sort of emotional life when he knew nothing about the past one? He'd recognised Becca—remembered how he had felt about her. But what stage was that relationship at now?

That was certainly not a question he was ever going to ask Leander. There were some things that were too personal even for a personal assistant.

Flinging the wet towel away and snatching up a black towelling robe, Andreas shrugged it on and belted it tightly around himself, ignoring yet another protest from his bruised ribs.

He couldn't stay in here a moment longer. He twisted the key savagely to unlock the door, his fingers closing tightly over the handle until the knuckles showed white.

Becca was too much temptation for him to be able to face the thought of her staying in the house when he wasn't able to act on the sensual provocation she offered simply by existing. Just the memory of the way that his blood had heated in his veins as he'd touched her cheek had enough sting to make him fling open the door with unnecessary force.

'This isn't going to work...'

The words died on his lips as he took in the empty room, the door out onto the landing standing slightly open, showing which way she had gone.

So at least she'd done as she was told. He had been so sure that she would ignore his instructions and that when he opened the door he would find her still there, waiting for him, possibly even determined to tuck him up in bed again...

'I'm—not one to fuss unnecessarily...'

The memory of Becca's voice, soft and unexpectedly husky, speaking the words cut through another flare of sensual heat that surged along his nerves at the thought of being tucked up in bed by the lovely brunette, feeling her cool, soft hand on his brow, her fingers at his wrist checking his pulse. Immediately his pulse throbbed, desire giving him a hard, cruel kick low down in his body.

If it was this bad now, then how would it be if she stayed? What sort of 'rest and recovery' as ordered by the doctors would be possible with images such as that blazing inside his head? How could he live every day with her when just the sight of her woke a carnal hunger that he could barely restrain?

And how could he give in to that hunger when he didn't know

a thing about the missing months they must have spent together? It was better if she left, at least until he recovered somewhat.

His mind made up, he strode to the wardrobe, began pulling out clothes—a shirt and jeans—taking underwear from a drawer. He pulled on his clothes, and then headed down the stairs, bare feet padding silently on the polished wooden steps. The afternoon was coming to an end, the fierce heat of the day easing a little.

It was the sound of her laughter that caught him first. A light, bubbling sound, it seemed to reach out into the atmosphere and curl around his senses, soft and low. Just for a moment his footsteps slowed, bringing him to a halt a couple of stairs from the bottom as he paused, allowing himself to reconsider.

So what was wrong with a little flirtation—a sensual distraction from reality? They were both adults and she was as attracted to him as he was to her. She hadn't pulled away from his touch, in fact she had wanted more from him. He had seen it in her eyes. In the way that that luscious pink mouth had parted on a faint gasp. So what if he couldn't offer her a future? He didn't think she'd care about that. She'd obviously stayed around for the past year, so she must be happy with what they had.

Her laughter came again, but this time something in the sound grated on him. It sounded different, changed. Was that a flirtatious note that had slid into it?

From nowhere it seemed as if a cloud had invaded his mind. His mood changed, shifted, darkened, his whole body stiffening in the aggressive reaction of a bad-tempered dog that had just seen a stranger invade his territory.

Slowly, silently, he took a single step downwards towards the hall.

From this position he could see into the room, see where Becca was sitting at the table, a glass of some clear liquid in her hand. She was leaning back in her chair, looking so very much more relaxed than at any moment in his room upstairs. Her dark hair fell in seductive disarray around her beautiful, animated face. She'd taken off her lightweight jacket too and it hung, half on and half off the back of the chair, one sleeve dangling onto the floor. She was looking at someone else, those stunning, sea-coloured eyes fixed on whoever it was opposite her, across the table. And she was smiling.

That smile caught on Andreas' nerves. Caught and held and twisted. He found himself torn between two totally contrasting sensations. In one moment he experienced a real delight in seeing that smile, seeing the way it lit up her face, the way it curved the fullness of her lips, softening the kissable mouth and making it infinitely more tempting than before, and at the same time endured something else. That 'something else' was a feeling that was the total opposite of delight, totally at war with pleasure. Without knowing where it had come from, Andreas suddenly found that he was filled with a black fury, racked with a terrible sense of hatred that had him clenching his hands into hard fists at his sides, biting down fiercely on his bottom lip to stop himself from speaking and letting the savage anger that crouched inside him out into the open.

'I never thought of it that way,' Becca said and even her voice was very different from the way it had sounded before. It was light and easy, relaxed and touched with a hint of flirtatious teasing. 'But now that you've explained it—it makes total sense.'

'Of course it does,' a second voice put in. A deeper, thickly accented voice. A male voice and one that Andreas recognised at once.

It was Leander's voice. Leander his PA. Leander, his young, tall, dark and handsome PA.

A terrible sense of jealousy ripped through him, driving away all sense of rationality, all hope of calm. His jaw tightened, clamped into a thin, hard line until it ached and he could feel the rage rising in him like lava in a volcano, boiling up to the surface and threatening to spill out over the top, engulfing everything in a blazing, burning flood of fire.

Another slow, silent step downwards moved him to a position where he could see fully into the room. He could see where Leander lounged against the wall, long legs crossed at the ankles, dark face smiling, a glass in his own hand.

'Never argue Greek legends with a Greek,' the younger man said now, waving his drink in the air to emphasise his point, his smile seeming to Andreas' watchful gaze to be intimate, almost conspiratorial.

'I won't,' Becca said and the gleam of amusement in her face, the smile she directed at Leander twisted a knife deep inside Andreas.

He could feel his head start to pound, his breath becoming raw and uneven. He didn't ask himself where the rage was coming from, just accepted it as right, as the way he should feel. Wasn't this why he had told himself she had to go? That she was trouble if she stayed around?

He'd had enough.

Taking the last two steps down in a single jump, he marched into the room, his black mood showing in every stride, every movement. His attention totally focused on Becca, he saw the way that her head swung round, eyes widening in sudden confusion.

And guilt? Perhaps there was a touch of it. Certainly her face went white enough to make it seem that way.

'OK, that's it,' he snapped, watching her eyelids flutter, her long dark lashes dipping to conceal her gaze just for a moment in a reaction to his appearance that she couldn't disguise.

'It's time you left. Time you were out of here—*now*,' he added more forcefully when she simply sat back in her chair and stared at him, her mouth very slightly open, those beautiful eyes now blinking hard in shock as if she couldn't believe what she was hearing.

'But…'

'Andreas…' Leander put in but Andreas ignored him and addressed his words straight into Becca's stunned face.

'Did you hear what I said?'

'Oh, I heard all right…'

Becca was having to struggle to keep control of her voice enough to answer him. Her heart had lurched so hard, so violently when Andreas had come into the room that just for a moment she had thought she might actually faint from the shock of it. But even as she recovered a whole new tide of emotions had swept over her, a sense of apprehension so fierce as to be almost total panic being uppermost amongst them.

What was happening? Why was Andreas behaving like this? Earlier that afternoon, upstairs in his room, he had been distant it was true, but polite enough. Now he was in a dark, icy rage, his handsome features set into a mask of total hostility and rejection that made the panic come worryingly closer, her heart fluttering disturbingly and her thoughts whirling out of control.

Had he remembered what had happened? Had something she'd done betrayed her so that Andreas had realised the true situation between them and had now come downstairs in savage rage to turn on the wife he had rejected so brutally twelve months ago and force her out of his home once again?

'But I've only just unpacked.'

'Then pack again,' he commanded, eyes like cruel lasers fixed on her confused and worried face.

She knew this mood of old and it frightened her. When he was like this, then Andreas had no intention of yielding anything—he would not be swayed in any way. Harsh memories of the way that he had flung almost exactly those words at her a year before now resurfaced and threatened to take all her emotional strength away at a blow.

At last the haze in her mind was easing enough for her to be able to see him clearly but just the sight of him was enough to rock her composure once again.

His pure white shirt was worn casually loose, clinging to broad, straight shoulders and falling softly over the leather belt at his waist, the narrow hips. The fine cotton contrasted sharply with the hardness of taut muscle underneath, the pale colour throwing the golden tones of his skin into sharp, devastating contrast. His jeans had been worn and washed so many times that they were faded and rubbed, actually beginning to rip in places, and clinging with an almost sensuous closeness to the long, powerful legs. The hems were frayed where they fell over long, narrow feet, the toes curling slightly on the polished wooden floor. He looked much more like some untamed, unsophisticated Greek shepherd, or perhaps a fisherman, rather than the urbane and powerful multimillionaire he actually was. And, when he was dressed as simply and as casually as this, it was the sheer physical power of the man that hit home hard and strong, knocking her off balance fast with his appeal to the most primitive, most basic part of her female nature. Her blood was pulsing in her veins so much that she almost missed it when he spoke again.

'Pack up and get out.'

'But you said—'

'I know what I said and I've changed my mind. I don't need a woman in my life and certainly not one who's going to spend her time flirting with the rest of my staff.'

Flirting...

Well, at least there was one tiny hint of something that might give her a hope that all was not lost. Flirting, he'd said. So if a touch of jealousy was his problem, then perhaps the game was not up after all. Perhaps there was still a chance that he hadn't realised the truth about who she was.

It would be a bitter irony if he had. After the moment of weakness when she'd fled the bedroom in a panic, she had finally managed to get a grip on herself. It was the thought of Daisy that had done it. The memory of the tiny, frail little body she had last seen inside a hospital incubator, wires and tubes seeming to be attached to each tiny limb, to every inch of the baby's skin. She could still hear in her head the doctor's voice, giving them the terrible, the soul-destroying truth.

Daisy was a desperately sick little baby. To save her life she needed a vital operation—an operation that was so new, so experimental that only one surgeon in America had ever performed it successfully. If they could find the money...

Becca shuddered inwardly as she recalled the overwhelming despair that she and Macy had suffered at that moment. There was no way...no way but one.

Daisy's plight was what had brought her to speak to Andreas in the first place. Surely, even hating her as he did, her ex-husband could not harden his heart against the tiny girl. If only she could stay here long enough for him to regain his memory so that she could ask him for help. That image had stiffened her spine and brought her downstairs fired by a new determination to succeed. It had even given her the courage to tell Leander a version of the truth. That Andreas had been asking for her and so she was here to take care of him.

To her delight and amazement Leander had not only supported her idea, he had even got straight on the phone to the agency to tell them the nurse they had been asked to provide would not be needed.

'After all,' Leander had said, 'who better to care for a man than his wife?'

Leander, Becca decided, had a strong sentimental streak in him. But, as he had never met her when she had been in his employer's life, then he obviously didn't know that sentimental was the last way that Andreas would feel about his particular wife. But she didn't disillusion him. Having Leander on her side was more than she could hope for, and just that one small gesture of support had made her feel that she could stay. That she might just be able to handle this—and hope to save baby Daisy as a result. She had even started to relax just a little.

But that had been before Andreas had appeared in the room, stiff-necked and scowling, with dark fire in his eyes, and ordered her to pack up and go, destroying all her hopes in a single moment.

'I wasn't flirting.'

Somehow she imposed the control she needed over her voice and made it sound calm and just a trifle indignant. She had to keep the pain of the last eleven months out of her voice. That would give her away for sure.

But Andreas' current lover—the mistress he assumed her to be—would feel much more able to cope with his temper and his jealousy.

'No?'

The mocking lift of one black eyebrow questioned her response in a way that almost shook her confidence. But she couldn't let him get to her. For Daisy's sake she had to be strong—for Daisy's sake she had to make sure that she stayed here.

'No!'

The forceful emphasis got his attention, making those deep-set eyes widen just for a moment before his handsome features settled back into their expression of cynical scepticism.

'Can I point out that you were the one who told me to come downstairs…?'

The affronted tone was a good idea. It was quite clear that he hadn't expected her indignation and was decidedly taken aback by it.

'The one who lo…'

No, don't mention the locked door or protest about it—that would take things to a deeper level. One that was clouded by the past between them that he remembered nothing about.

'The one who told me not to fuss.'

That actually won her a tiny sign of acknowledgement from the dark, distant man before her. Not a nod, that would have been too much of a concession, but the proud head inclined faintly to one side and something flickered in the black eyes that might have been respect.

'*Kyrie* Petrakos…'

It was Leander who spoke, inserting his words carefully into the tensely silent stand-off that had come between them. He said something in Greek, speaking swiftly and, Becca thought, rather nervously. Obviously Leander felt that his job was on the line—so would he continue to support her?

Andreas' response was in the same language, sharp and obviously dismissive—a dismissal that was repeated when the younger man hesitated, looking distinctly uncomfortable and unsure.

'It's all right, Leander,' Becca put in, turning to him, wanting to reassure him. 'You don't have to worry about me.'

Out of the corner of her eye she could sense Andreas' head snap round, feel the dark fire of his eyes burning into the back of her head as she spoke, and she could see the reflection of the furious glare in the concern on Leander's face. But she made herself smile, pretending at a composure she was far from feeling.

'Really...' she said. 'This isn't your problem.'

As she watched Leander leave, the silence behind her seemed to grow all the more ominous, all the more oppressive, and she held her breath as the door swung to after him, waiting for the inevitable explosion that she had sparked off with her response.

CHAPTER FOUR

To HER astonishment it didn't come. Instead there was a faint, soft sound. The sound of Andreas drawing in his breath and letting it out again in a deliberate attempt at control.

'So who put you in charge?' he drawled cynically. 'Who gave you permission to give my staff orders?'

'Not orders.'

Becca caught her own breath, aiming to match his cold-toned restraint as she made herself turn round, coming to face him. She wouldn't let his imposing stature, the arrogant set of his jaw, or the cold light in his eyes overawe her. If she did then he would win and she knew that Andreas Petrakos had never lost this sort of a battle in his life. He hadn't almost tripled the family fortune in his thirty-three years by being anyone's pushover, least of all any woman's. But she had to manage this somehow; had to win herself at least permission to stay. The repercussions for Daisy if she didn't were too terrible even to consider. She wasn't going to let herself even imagine the possibility of defeat.

'You'd already told him to leave. I was just making sure that he didn't feel obliged to stay to protect me.'

'You understand Greek?'

Just for a moment Andreas sounded so taken aback that Becca actually allowed herself the smallest hint of a smile. Typical male—typical *Greek* male, she told herself. He made assumptions from his lordly position in charge of everything and was stunned to find that perhaps those suppositions and his assessment of the situation were not quite as perfect as he believed.

'I don't have to know precisely what words you used to know just what you meant,' she pointed out. 'So tell me, do you always order everyone around as if they were a dog that was yours to command?'

'Leander values his job too much to do anything stupid.'

'Leander knows that you're in a vicious mood and liable to bite his head off if he didn't do as he was told. You surely didn't really think that I was flirting with him? You have to know that…'

Yikes, no!

Mentally Becca screeched to a halt, slamming the brakes on the foolishly betraying words she had almost let slip. Don't go down that road—just don't!

Had she really been about to say to Andreas's face that he had to know that when he was in a room—anywhere nearby—any other man just didn't have a chance? That beside his incandescent male sexuality, every other male within a hundred miles became just a shadow of himself, fading into insignificance beside Andreas?

'I have to know that what?' Andreas enquired with silky menace when she caught herself up, biting hard on her foolish tongue. His brilliant dark eyes had narrowed sharply, the look he turned on her from them shrewdly assessing, and to Becca's horror she felt a rush of embarrassed heat flooding her cheeks.

'That I'm with you,' she managed to force out.

Her voice grew stronger as she recalled her thoughts of moments before, putting them into words to get herself out of the hole she had dug for herself. If she was his current mistress, then she would probably laugh off Andreas' over-reaction just now.

'And even if you don't want anyone to fuss, if you're de-termined to dismiss your staff like that, then someone needs to keep an eye on you.'

'And you're happy to do that?'

'Of course.'

Did his question mean that perhaps he was reconsidering? That he would let her stay after all? Behind her back, Becca crossed her fingers secretly. She didn't know what she would do if Andreas still insisted that she leave.

'You should sit down.'

She waved a hand towards the nearest chair, cursing the way that, in her own eyes at least, her fingers' unwanted tremor gave away too much to that cold-eyed scrutiny.

'And would you like something to drink? Water? Coffee?'

'Wine?'

It was a deliberate provocation and a wicked gleam in his black eyes told her that he was testing her. But he moved towards the chair just the same.

'You're just out of hospital after a nasty accident. Do you think wine is a good idea? How about thinking of some-thing else?'

'I would but you'd probably veto that as well,' Andreas tossed at her surprisingly lightly, but Becca noticed that he took the seat she'd indicated all the same.

He sank down into it with every appearance of ease and lounged back, stretching out his long legs and crossing them at the ankles. He looked as if he was simply relaxing but there was a slight tightness to his mouth, a shadow on his skin that reminded her he was still convalescent. Pushing back her own chair, she got hastily to her feet.

'I'll get you some water, then.'

'If that is all that you're offering…'

Andreas' reply stopped her in mid-flight to the kitchen, and she froze for a moment before she turned slowly back again. Had she heard right? Was that note in his voice what she thought it had been?

Was it possible that Andreas was actually *flirting* with her?

She realised what had happened. She had taken the route in the conversation that she would have done when they were together and an argument had broken out. She had stood up for herself, refused to give in to his anger, then she had moved the subject away and on to another topic entirely—and Andreas had followed her. Just as he had used to do when they were together, he had let himself be eased out of his bad mood and into another, very different one.

But was this different mood any less dangerous than before?

There was one thing she did know and that was that the way to make Andreas reveal his hand when he was determined to keep it hidden was to challenge him—call his bluff. And although he might not remember her or their life together, this was still Andreas, wasn't it? She had to know where she stood and she thought she knew the way to go about it.

'Water…' she said firmly, hoping she sounded more confident than she actually was as she headed into the kitchen.

He didn't need a drink—well, definitely not water, Andreas reflected as Becca marched into the kitchen, hunted around and found some bottled water in the fridge, but if she wanted to get him water then he was quite happy to let her. Anything so that he could watch her, enjoy the sway of her hips in the

delicate blue dress as she walked, the way her breasts swung
gently as she bent down to look in the fridge, the neat, precise
movements of those soft hands—the hands he still remembered resting on his when she'd stood beside his bed—as she
twisted open the bottle of water.

The truth was that he enjoyed sitting here and watching her
move around his home, letting her take care of him. He was
even enjoying his body's instinctive reaction to having her
around. The insistent clamour of his senses, the way he
became hard just watching her might be frustrating and uncomfortable on one level, but at least he felt alive in a way
that he hadn't known since the accident. She was a hell of a
lot more attractive than Leander or Medora, his devoted but
matronly housekeeper. Medora might be the closest thing he
had ever had to a mother, but she wasn't a delight to watch
like this woman.

This beautiful woman.

This beautiful, sexy woman.

This beautiful, sexy woman whom he wanted more than…

Hell and damnation, how could he say that he wanted her
more than he had ever wanted her in the time they had been
together, when he only remembered the smallest part of that
time? The first weeks after they had met. And the most vivid
memory he had of that time was of wanting this woman in
his bed, just as he did now.

So was anything different in any way? He just knew that
he wanted her so badly that it had made him act like a fool.

Andreas sighed and raked both his hands through his hair
as he went back over the way he had behaved, the way that
he had lost his temper so completely when he had seen Becca
with Leander. Seen them talking together—laughing—
flirting, he had believed. His anger had been like a red mist

before his eyes. A burning mist that had pushed him into action without stopping to think.

But now that he'd calmed down he was going to have to apologise to his PA for snarling at him like a savagely jealous dog guarding a particularly juicy bone.

Andreas' mouth twisted wryly.

Jealous?

Was that how he felt when he was jealous? The problem was that he had nothing to compare it with. He couldn't honestly say if he had ever felt like that before. Had he ever been reduced to that sort of fury because he thought someone else had what he wanted? Had he set out to ruin a good thing because he felt so savagely angry?

Because Becca could be a good thing. He didn't need to have any past reference points to tell him that; the effect that she had on him—on his body—on his senses—in the present was quite enough.

And he didn't need telling that that was why he had been so blackly angry. Because he wanted her so damn much that it had clouded his judgement.

He'd make it right with Leander tomorrow. But he'd also make it clear that the younger man should keep his hands off. Becca was *his* and he wouldn't allow anyone else to interfere.

She was coming back towards him now, the glass in her hand, and if the back view had been good then the front was so much better. The determination in her walk drew attention to those slender, curving hips and under the soft cotton her even softer breasts moved in a way that made his mouth dry. Her head was held high, stubborn little chin tilted deliberately and the fire in her eyes made him smile to himself at the enticing prospect of the battle to come.

'Your water.'

Becca thrust the glass at him without finesse or ceremony and only the fact that his reflexes were swift and accurate stopped it from upending all over him.

'I prefer it in the glass,' he murmured drily, earning himself an expected glare of reproof that made those sea-coloured eyes flash like polished gems. The trite cliché 'You're beautiful when you're angry' hovered on his lips but he swallowed it down with a sip of the water, opting for not provoking her any further, and murmured carefully polite thanks instead.

'You're welcome,' Becca retorted in a voice that made a nonsense of the courteous reply. 'Enjoy your drink.'

It was as she swung away from him, turning on her heel with a dismissive little gesture of one hand, that he suddenly had the clear idea that he knew exactly what she was going to do. Her determined steps towards the door confirmed as much, making his lips twitch in suppressed amusement.

'Are you going somewhere?'

She spared him another of those swift, flashing glares over her shoulder.

'To my room—to pack, seeing as you've made it so plain that you don't want me here. It would have been easier if you'd told me *before* I emptied my case.'

He let her get right to the door, waiting a carefully calculated moment, watching for the almost imperceptible hesitation in the fingers that reached for the handle...closed over it...flung it open...

'You can stay,' he said quietly, stopping her dead halfway out the door.

For a second or two he thought she hadn't heard. Her foot was actually still held out in front of her, preparing to take the next step. But then, very slowly and silently, she lowered it to the ground, and stood still.

'What did you say?' she asked, not looking at him but staring straight ahead of her, into the now shadowy hallway.

'I said you can stay.'

For a moment Becca couldn't move. She felt as if she didn't know what to think—how to think. She had the strangest feeling as if time had suddenly gone backwards and she and Andreas were back in the past, in the time when they had been together, before they were married.

Her strategy had worked exactly as she had planned it would. She had called his bluff, made it appear that she was about to leave, and he had let her get so far and then called her back. He was going to let her stay.

She should feel triumphant—she should feel happy. Andreas' change of heart meant that she could have a hope of talking to him about Daisy—about the money so desperately needed to give her baby niece a chance of life. But she only knew a tiny glimmer of triumph and her other feelings were so complicated and mixed up that they kept her frozen, her eyes wide and sightless. Before she could talk to him about Daisy he would have to recover his memory and the momentary glimpse she had just had into a past where they had been together—*happy* together—tore at her heart with the reminder of how it would be when he recalled the truth. He had thrown her out of the house, out of his life, because he believed she was only after his money. The thought of his reaction when he learned that she was only here now because of money again drained the blood from her limbs, making her legs tremble beneath her.

'Becca? Did you hear what I said?'

She had hesitated too long, arousing Andreas' suspicions. Out of the corner of her eye she was aware of the fact that he had got up from his chair, looked as if he was about to come towards her.

'Yes, I heard.'

Slowly she turned back to face him, her expression carefully blank.

'You want me to stay as your nurse or as…?'

She couldn't find a word to express the alternative—lover—partner—mistress—*wife*?—and so she just let the sentence trail off unfinished.

'As whatever you want.'

Then an arrogant flick of his hand dismissed the question.

'Definitely not my nurse! You know what I think of that idea. So why don't you just stay—as my guest? Then if you think you need to keep an eye on me you can.'

'And what would I do the rest of the time?'

'Oh, I feel sure that we will think of something.'

'Like what?' Becca demanded, eyeing him warily.

A note in his voice told her that the flirtatious mood of a short time before had not, as she had thought, evaporated when she'd called his bluff by heading for the door. In fact every instinct she had ever had where this man was concerned was screaming at her that the lazy sensuality of his smile was deceptive in its indolence. The black eyes might be hooded and partially hidden under heavy lids but she could see enough of the gleam in them to know that his thoughts were not on the idea of her taking care of him—in the nursing a convalescent meaning of the words, at least.

'Like this,' Andreas murmured with misleading softness and before she was even aware of the fact that he had anything planned, or could even think of taking any avoidance moves, he took several long, firm strides forward, covering the distance between them in a matter of seconds.

This time she had no warning. This time there was no change in his voice, no hint from the look in his eyes. This time he took her completely by surprise and so instantly had the upper hand, with total control over the situation.

'Like this,' he said again, low and rough.

His hand came under her chin, holding it tight. He lifted her face towards his and his mouth came down hard on hers, taking it in a burning, searing kiss that made her thought processes stop dead, then shatter into a million tiny fragments.

She couldn't think; she could only feel. And what she felt was heat. The heat of his mouth, his breath on her skin. The heat of his arms coming round her, that long, powerful body so very close to hers. But it wasn't just a physical heat that blazed through her. There was the burning fire of response, the sensation of her blood temperature climbing higher and higher with each accelerated beat of her heart. Her whole system was going into meltdown, her mind seeming to cease to exist, her nerves, her skin, even her bones becoming molten with desire so that she sagged against him, unable to hold herself upright, and it was only the strength of his support around her that kept her from collapsing in a trembling and abandoned heap right at his feet.

'Andreas—' she began against the pressure of his lips, but the attempt to speak, to try to form some sort of protest that she was incapable of sustaining, gave him the opportunity he was waiting for.

In the moment that her mouth partly opened, Andreas seized his chance and deepened the kiss with sensual deliberation. Her parted lips were crushed even more under the passion of his, his tongue sliding into the exposed warmth, the soft moisture, tangling with hers in an intimate dance that made her senses swoon, had her fingers closing over his arms, clenching tight.

But this time it wasn't the need for support that had her

holding him close, as close as she could. This time it was pure physical need that made her clutch at him this way. The need to feel his lean, hard frame against hers, feel the pressure of the strong bones of his chest, his ribcage against her breasts, the curve of his pelvis cradling her hips. And because of that closeness there was no way she could be unaware of the swell of his forceful erection, hot and hard against her, communicating need and passion in a way that no words ever could.

Cold need and heartless passion.

The icy little voice of reason slid into her mind, stopping the heat of her reaction dead, so fast that it made her head spin.

Andreas Petrakos was totally capable of coming on full and hard with his mouth, his tongue, his body, when no part at all of his mind was involved—and least of all his *heart*!

Hadn't he shown that when he had brought her here the first time, just after their marriage? When he had brought her into the house, barely stopping to shut the door as he went through it. When he had kissed her as they mounted the stairs and taken her into the bedroom, his mouth practically welded to hers. And with his hands hotly, hungrily busy on her body, finding the fastenings of her clothing blind, dealing with them with rough haste, discarding them like a Hansel and Gretel trail leading from the hallway to his room.

And in that room he had made the hottest, most ardent, most passionate love in the world to her, waking a matching hunger in every inch of her quivering body, showing her pleasures she had never believed possible, taking her to heights of ecstasy she had never known before.

Before dropping her right down to earth again with a sickening, agonising thud, just a few, devastatingly short hours later. She still had the scars on her heart where his black cruelty had slashed into it.

And with the memory everything inside her froze in an instant. The rush of heat that had flooded her body ebbed away as fast—faster—than it had come, taking all the passion with it.

'Becca?'

Andreas had sensed her withdrawal, her stillness, and his kisses stopped, adding another terrible sensation to the thousands of whirling feelings in Becca's head and in her heart.

'No...'

It was all that she could manage and it was just a whisper. A thin thread of sound that did nothing to express what she really felt deep inside: the searing agony of loss, the desperation of knowing that she was so weak—too weak—the bitter despair of knowing that Andreas had only to touch her, to kiss her and she had fallen into his arms, into his control like a foolish child, one that had not yet learned that fire burned—again and again and again.

'No...' she tried again, managing to make it actually sound like a word this time. But she still couldn't put any real force into it. She still couldn't make it sound like the word that was ringing inside her head, screaming to be heard.

No, no, no, *no*! that voice said. Loud and clear and savagely honest. A voice that no one could doubt she meant.

But that voice was the voice of panic. The voice of pain. The voice of the woman who had once loved this man so desperately that she had rushed into marriage with him without stopping to think. It was the voice of the woman whose heart he had broken. The voice of the woman whose love had turned to hatred in the black, terrible moments as she forced herself to walk away from him—fighting a cruel bitter war with her longing to turn back, to see him just once more.

It was the voice of the woman that she couldn't let Andreas see.

Not now, not ever, at least until he had his memory back and he knew once more who she was. Not until she had had a chance to talk to him, to ask him for help for Daisy. To save the baby's life.

And even then she couldn't—wouldn't ever let him see just what he had done to her. She couldn't let him begin to guess how much he had destroyed her life.

And she most definitely couldn't do it now.

'No?'

For a moment she thought it was still her own voice screaming inside her head. But then on a jolt of her heart, she realised that it was Andreas and that he had put a darkly questioning note onto the word.

One that meant she had to find an explanation for her sudden change of mood. A reason why she had been a willing, an eager partner one moment and then slammed the brakes on hard the next. And even in her own mind, looking at her actions, she saw with a shiver how her behaviour might be interpreted. How it could seem that she didn't know her own mind or—worse—was some sort of tease who had now decided to call a sudden halt.

CHAPTER FIVE

'You—upstairs—you said you thought this was a bad idea.'

Looking into his face, she felt her heart skip a beat as she saw the way he frowned, the black, straight brows snapping together over the brilliant eyes. Eyes that she could see were burning with frustration, with refusal to admit the need to stop. For a second she thought that he was going to argue with her but then, slowly, he nodded...

'It is a bad idea when I don't know who I am or the first thing about our past together. And you're not going to tell me about that, are you?'

That at least was easy to answer, but still Becca couldn't find any words, only managing a silent shake of her head as a reply.

'I understand. I know the doctors have said that it's better I wait for things to come back by themselves—if they come back. And that does complicate matters.'

He might be agreeing with her but he still wasn't letting her go. And somehow the fact that he wasn't actually kissing her made the way he was holding her so tight, so close, even more intimate than before.

His voice might be calm and civil, his expression controlled, but there was nothing remotely restrained or civilised in the swollen flesh that pressed so hard against her. And equally primitive was the hungry reaction that was raging through her as senses and nerves tantalised awake by the touch of Andreas' hand, the force of his kiss, were forced to adjust to the sudden loss of the heated pleasure, and protested wildly at having to do so.

'But only in that way.'

Black eyes blazed down into Becca's upturned face, the heat in them seeming to scorch her skin and making her shift uneasily from one foot to another. Andreas' intense gaze flickered for a moment as he watched the small movement, but he didn't release her or adjust his position at all. If anything he held her tighter. So tight that she could hear the heavy, powerful thud of his heart so close to her cheek, echoing her own restless pulse rate that refused to settle down into normal again.

'In every other way it felt right. So right that I don't want it to stop…'

He was drawing her close again but then, for a moment, his voice hesitated, that intent focus of his eyes seeming to blur and look clouded.

'Andr…' Becca began then let the rest of his name evaporate in a rush of sheer panic. Her heart seemed to stop, actually stand still and then lurch back into movement at a violent, uneven pace as the reason for his sudden abstraction hit home like a blow to her mind.

Was he remembering her? Starting to recall anything about his past—and about the part she had played in it?

Upstairs, in the bedroom, in the moment she had known that he wanted to kiss her and before he had run his hand down her cheek in the gesture that had torn at her heart, he had had just this sort of a look on his face. His eyes had seemed to become unfocused then as if his thoughts were not on the present but somewhere else, in the past, in the life he could not remember.

And that was what she wanted—wasn't it?

Wasn't it?

Or was it?

She needed him to know what had happened between them before she could even start to have a hope of asking him for help. Before she could tell him about Daisy and the vital operation the baby needed. And if kissing her—more than kissing her—jolted his memories back into place then why not go along with it, at least for now?

'That's better,' she heard Andreas murmur and knew that, in spite of herself, the direction of her thoughts had brought her closer to him, made her body soften against his. And when his hand slid under her chin again, lifting her mouth to his once more, she had no strength to fight him.

Or, rather, she had no strength to fight herself. This was what she wanted after all. There was no way she could deny it any longer. This was what her awakened senses demanded, what they yearned for. She needed his mouth on hers, needed the hard, intimate pressure, the warm, slick exploration of his tongue. And as his hands began to move over her she knew she needed that too. Everything inside her that had been folded tightly in on itself, closed off, shut away, now seemed to slowly unfurl, like a flower opening to the sun. And in just the same way that the flower instinctively turned towards the greatest, most glorious, most powerful source of heat and light, so without being able to stop herself she swayed towards Andreas, pressing herself against those caressing hands, writhing under the pleasure of his touch.

Murmurs of delight she couldn't hold back escaped her lips

in the brief moments that he allowed her to breathe and his name was a sigh on her lips, breathed into his mouth so that he swallowed down the sound as he took possession of her lips again.

'You see,' he murmured, husky and soft, letting that tormenting mouth slide along the line of her jaw so that she lifted her chin to tauten the muscles there, feeling it more intensely as he kissed his way to the most sensitive spot just under her ear. 'This is right. So right.'

One of those caressing hands had moved to her neck now, tangling in the soft hair at the base of her skull, twisting, tugging, pulling her head backwards so that he exposed the whole of her neck and the long, fine line down to her shoulder and the valley between her breasts that lay in the deep V-neckline of her dress. Becca's head swam as she felt the heat of his breath, the soft, tantalising caress of his mouth as it moved down into that warm valley of her cleavage.

'I want you...'

She felt as well as heard the words. They feathered over her skin, humid as the breath that seemed to slip inside her bra, coil around her nipples, making them tighten into stingingly aroused peaks that yearned for a touch that was harder, more forceful than a whisper of heated air.

'I want you,' he said again.

And she wanted him. The need was a heavy pulse between her legs, a throbbing demand from every aching nerve end along her body. Who cared if the sensual memories hidden in Andreas' numbed brain took him back into the past they had shared? So what if the touch of her lips, the taste of her skin, woke him to a recollection of exactly who she was and what she had been to him? He had to remember some time, it was inevitable. And surely it was better that he remembered sooner rather than later so that the truth was out in the open and they could renegotiate from there?

But the real truth was that she couldn't stop herself. And as her body rediscovered the pleasures she had thought she had forgotten she knew that she wanted this. She *needed* it. She had been dying inside for almost a year for the loss of it.

This *was* right, her sensual instincts told her. This was what had always been right between them. In Andreas' arms she had always felt that she was where she belonged, that she had come home. This was the one thing that had never gone wrong between them; the thing that had still been there at the end when it seemed that everything else had gone, been destroyed by hatred, distrust and cruel rejection.

Rejection.

The word was a cold, hard, vicious blade that slashed through the heated delirium inside her head, breaking open her sensual fantasies and making the wild, foolish dreams evaporate, once more letting in the icy winds of reality and self-preservation.

What was she doing courting that rejection all over again? Could she go through that pain, that loss, that terrible, terrible devastation a second time? It had almost destroyed her the first time and yet here she was risking her heart, her soul, all over again.

She couldn't do this just for the pleasure, for the physical satisfaction it would bring. It would destroy her if she did. But Andreas could. He had already done so once and she had no doubt that he could do it again. Whether his memory returned or not, he could take her, use her, take all she had to give and then turn and walk away without a backward look.

And the dread that brought made her stiffen against his stroking hands.

'Andreas…' she tried but he wasn't listening. His mouth was still caressing her skin, his hands moving down over the soft blue skirt of her dress, over her hips, inching the material upwards as they did so.

'Andreas—stop!'

Driven by rising panic, she twisted away from him sharply, fear giving her strength she didn't know she possessed. The force of her reaction took her halfway across the room before she came to a halt and was able to face him, eyes wide, her breath coming in raw, uneven gasps.

She couldn't really see him, her gaze was blurred and unfocused, and she was grateful for the way that hid the reality of his expression from her.

'No,' she said breathlessly, struggling for control. 'No, it isn't right—it can't be right! This isn't going to happen—I won't let it happen.'

'*You* won't let it happen?'

Andreas' voice was a cynical drawl and one dark eyebrow lifted in mocking response to her outburst.

'Lady, you are fooling yourself if you expect me to believe that.'

'Of course I expect you to believe it! I—'

'But I don't. I don't believe a word that comes from your lovely mouth.'

'You—you don't?'

Andreas shook his head in firm response to her shaken question. Her vision had cleared now and she could see his face. Immediately she wished she had the comfort of the protective blur back when she saw his burning eyes fixed on her face in a look of pure scorn.

'You expect me to believe your cowardly little protest when I know the truth?'

'Oh, so you're a mind-reader now?'

No—defiance was a bad move. She saw it in his face, in the way that those beautifully shaped lips clamped tightly together over some savage retort that he had hastily caught back.

'I don't need to read *minds,*' he bit out. 'But I am pretty good at understanding body language. Unfortunately for you. Because your body was speaking the truth—the truth you're now trying to pretend never happened.'

'I— No— I'm not pretending!'

'You're either pretending now or you were then—you can't have it both ways, Becca. So which one is it?'

Oh, how did she answer that? How did she tell him something that explained her behaviour and yet didn't give her away completely? The only thing she knew was that she couldn't let him believe that she had simply been leading him on—that was the course most likely to have Andreas demand that she leave right here and now. And then she would never be able to help Daisy. And saving Daisy's life was uppermost in her mind right now.

'All right—I'm sorry…'

She actually held out her hand towards him, as if pleading with him, begging him to take it. But the way that he watched the gesture, regarding it coldly with blank and unresponsive eyes, brought her up sharp. Becca felt as if she might just as well have slammed her hand against a hard brick wall and had to struggle to resist the temptation to snatch it back and cradle it against her as if his wintry response had actually hurt her physically.

'I'm sorry…' she said again, fighting to find something she could say.

'You said that already,' Andreas flung back, folding his arms across the broad expanse of his chest as his dark head went back, black eyes searing over her in a look of supreme contempt as he looked down his straight slash of a nose at her. 'Try something else. Sorry for what?'

'For—for overreacting.'

It was the only thing she could think of. The truth—or at least as close to the truth as she dared to go—seemed to be the only way to handle this. In any case, the partial truth was the only thing she trusted herself to be able to say without making it painfully plain that she was actually lying.

She'd hoped that that would be enough but, from Andreas' set, unyielding expression, it was far from adequate. If anything those folded arms tightened expressively and his upper lip actually curled in an expression of arrogant scorn.

She was going to have to try harder to convince him.

'I—I do w-want you.'

Really, there was no point in denying that. Her response to him had made it only too plain and she would only incense him further if she tried to pretend otherwise. If there was one thing that Andreas hated it was lies. A miserably cold, sneaking shiver went down her spine as she recalled the one time she had tried to keep the truth from him. She hadn't actually *lied* but she might as well have done. The fallout had been as bad as if she had.

'Then what are you doing over on the other side of the room while I'm here?'

'Because—because...'

Desperation brought inspiration and she hurried the words out, needing them to be said so that she could see if they had the effect she hoped for—the effect she prayed they would.

'Because you were right—it isn't a good idea. It isn't sensible...'

Andreas rolled his eyes in an expression of exasperation.

'And we must always be sensible, mustn't we?'

'Well, you've just had a terrible accident.'

'So now you're back to being my nurse again. I told you I hate a fuss…'

'I'm not making a fuss! I'm trying to be careful—for your sake as much as mine.'

That caught him unawares, bringing his head up in a rush.

'Me? What do I…?'

'You have amnesia.'

Becca spoke the words as slowly and as emphatically as she dared. She needed to get this through to him. If she did, then she might have a chance of staying, of working things out. Of waiting until his memory came back. And then she might have a chance of asking him to help Daisy.

'I know I have amnesia,' Andreas snarled. 'I can't forget that I do! Everything else I try to remember and I can't. The fact that I can't remember…'

He slammed the heel of his palm into his forehead with a brutal thumping sound that made her flinch inside.

'That's what I can't forget.'

'Oh, don't—please don't. Can't you see that this is why it has to be this way—because you can't take the risk?'

'You mean you can't—'

'No—you!'

Shaking her head violently, Becca took a single involuntary step towards him, then the look in his eyes, the dangerous way they flashed made her reconsider hastily. Abruptly she came to a halt again, only metres away from him, but the expanse of polished wooden floor now seemed like a wide, gaping chasm, one she knew they could never really ever bridge.

'You're the one who has the most to lose here if we—if we…'

'Lose?'

His harsh crack of laughter had no humour in it.

'From where I'm standing, I get what I want. The only thing that's interested me—excited me—since I woke up from that damn coma.'

'The only...' Becca whispered, unable to believe what she had heard. 'Me?'

'You,' Andreas confirmed roughly, with a brusque inclination of his head. 'Who did you think I meant? I was talking about excitement and pleasure—passion—something that makes life seem like it's worth living after all and not just the huge empty space where my mind—my memories—used to be. And you—you say we have to be sensible.'

He spat the word out as if it was a vile epithet.

Twice Becca opened her mouth, trying to find an answer for him, and both times her voice failed her, managing only a pathetic squeak that didn't even form a syllable, never mind a whole word.

Go to him, the irrational, emotional part of her brain was screaming. Go to him and accept what he's offering—while he's offering it. You want that excitement—you need that passion—you could enjoy—oh, dear God, more than enjoy—that pleasure. What are you doing, standing here when...?

'But we do.'

Becca couldn't believe she'd actually said what she had. Until she'd actually heard the words spoken out loud she had no idea that she had even planned to say them. She certainly hadn't thought about them rationally. She didn't even *want* to say them. But she had to. There was no other way to handle this.

'We do have to be sensible. At least you do.'

'Don't hide behind excuses. For some reason you won't admit, you're scared and you're trying to run...'

'Oh, no. No, I'm not.'

At least this time her voice had the conviction of truth. She couldn't run away. If she did she would let Macy and Daisy down. She saw Andreas' proud head go back, his eyes narrowing assessingly.

'You don't know what might have happened in your life—what you might…might find out when your memory comes back. Things that could change the way you feel about everything.'

'About you?'

Andreas' tone was sceptical.

'I doubt very much that anything could change the way I'm feeling—the hunger that's eating me up inside.'

It was purely a physical hunger—a sexual hunger—that he was talking about, Becca reminded herself miserably. There was nothing emotional about it at all. And he probably spoke the truth. Nothing had ever lessened the savage desire he had always had for her. Even when he had hated her most, he had still wanted her. The first and last thing he had done in their short-lived marriage had been to take her to bed.

But she knew just how much things would change if—when—he knew the truth about the way their relationship had ended. And she couldn't bear to think of what might happen then.

'Then—then what harm can it do to wait? You know what they say about anticipation adding to the pleasure…'

'On that point, you might be right.'

'You know I am.'

She didn't know quite how she'd done it, but somehow she'd managed to put a flirtatious note into her voice. And as she saw Andreas' expression change, the dark tension easing from his face, his eyes, she didn't know whether to feel relief or a terrible sense of fear at the thought of what she was building up for herself in the future. She might be able to persuade him now, to make him ease up, relax a little. But when his memory returned and he found out the truth, then...

Her blood turned cold at just the thought.

But she had no other possible route she could take. If she was to help Daisy at all, she had to do it this way. It was either that or leave the tiny girl to die. And that wasn't going to happen, not if she could possibly do anything to stop it. She would do whatever she had to do now, and take the consequences later when, inevitably, it all blew up in her face.

She was forced to acknowledge to herself that the thing she both most feared and most hoped for was all tangled up so that she couldn't possibly extricate one part of it from the other. Before she could ask for his help, Andreas needed to regain his memory and so she had to stay here until that happened. But when he did get his memory back he would also remember who she was and the way they had parted and then all hell would break loose.

And the real problem was that she was having to fight herself as well as Andreas. The truth was that she wanted to be in his arms as much as he wanted her there. She wanted his kisses, his touch...

Whatever else had died between them, the burning passion had not. It had brought them together, rushed them into bed, into marriage, and it was still there. It still blazed white-hot between them. Andreas had only to touch her and she went up in flames. But it hadn't been enough to hold them together before—and it wouldn't be enough now. Andreas might give her body the most glorious pleasure she had ever known but he had also broken her heart and sexual ecstasy was not enough to compensate for the pain and desolation that had followed. Andreas had been the love of her life and with every day—every hour—she spent with him she risked subjecting herself to that heartbreak all over again.

'All right.'

It was the last thing she expected Andreas to say so she actually felt her jaw drop a little when he spoke, her eyes blinking sharply in shock.

'All right?' she managed and got an unsmiling nod in response.

'We'll wait—a while. You could be right and the delay—the anticipation—will whet my appetite. I reckon you'll be worth waiting for.'

If he expected an answer to that, then he was going to be disappointed, Becca admitted to herself. There wasn't a single word she could find in her head, or form on her tongue. All she could manage was an incoherent little sound that might or might not have been agreement.

'But I won't wait for ever. I'm not a patient man, Becca. When I see something I want—I go for it.'

'I—understand.'

How could she not understand? She knew exactly what he meant; exactly how he was. Hadn't she been on the receiving end of all his forceful charm, his potent sexuality, once before? When Andreas Petrakos saw something he wanted he got it—no question.

And as if to prove it, to verify her thoughts, Andreas suddenly lifted a hand and crooked one finger in the most arrogant, supremely confident gesture, beckoning her to come to him. And from the look on his face he had no doubt that she would obey.

He was right. She could explain to herself, justify her actions, by saying that she was playing it safe, treading carefully. But if she did she would be lying to herself, stark onesty forced her to admit. She obeyed Andreas' autocratic ummons, moving across the floor to him without a word or esitation simply because she had no choice. She *had* to go o him; she didn't have the strength to resist. And as his arms ame round her again she knew she was lost, lifting her face or his kiss even before he had bent his dark head towards hers.

The kiss made what little remained of her thought processes swoon. It seemed to draw out her very essence, heart nd soul, taking them into his possession until she felt that she vould be nothing without him, unable to function, unable ven to exist on her own. She was floating, drifting, with no ense of direction or thought.

'So you'll stay,' Andreas murmured, his voice low and ensual, rich with total confidence, total conviction that he vas going to get his way.

'Yes.'

There was nothing else that she could say but even as she poke Becca had the terrible feeling of water, deep, dark and old, closing over her head, drowning her. But there was no ope of turning back.

'Yes,' she said, soft and low. 'Yes, I'll stay.'

CHAPTER SIX

'SO HOW long, exactly, did you foresee this "being sensible" to last?'

Andreas stretched lazily in the sunshine, noting with satisfaction that the rawness of torn muscles, the ache of bruising, was easing more with each day. If only he could say the same about the blank space where part of his memory should be. That and the burn of frustration that nagged at him all day, every day, simply because Becca was around.

At least the last few days had given his body a chance to heal physically. He would never admit it but the accident had taken more out of him than he liked, so spending time showing Becca around the island, taking her to his favourite restaurant, walking along the shore, had filled in the days of convalescence and stopped him climbing the walls with boredom.

Becca stirred her head against the cushions of the sun lounger next to him and opened those blue-green eyes in a look of such sleepy sensuality that it had his body hardening and aching in a moment, straining against the black stretch fabric of the swimming shorts that were all he wore. She was dressed all in white today in a loose sleeveless top and cotton trousers that were cut off short, revealing her slender calves and ankles.

'How do you feel?' she asked and in spite of her attempt to look relaxed he could hear the note of constraint in her voice that was always there when he moved the conversation away from the ordinary, everyday subjects they talked about.

Just what was it she was so uptight about? Was there something she was hiding? Something she didn't want him to know? It gave him the most disturbing feeling that the one person in the world he felt really comfortable with—someone he knew he had shared the missing part of his life with—might be deliberately holding something back from him.

'I feel fine! Never better!' he snapped, the edgy feeling getting the better of him, and he watched the change in her eyes, the way that the warm sensuality died, turning instead to a careful, defensive distance. Silently he cursed himself for his over-hasty reaction.

'And the doctor said you were OK at your check-up this morning?'

'You mean he didn't give you a full report? After all, your role as my nurse seems to be the only one you're interested in fulfilling.'

'I thought you'd done away with that idea? To tell you the truth…' Becca pulled herself up against the wooden back of the lounger so that she was sitting upright and looking him straight in the face '…I'm not at all sure what you want from me.'

'You know only too well what I want.'

Andreas made no attempt to disguise the blatantly sexual double meaning behind his words.

'How I want you—where I want you.'

There was that wary flicker in her eyes again. A momentary glance into his face and then away, fast, to stare out at the horizon. She affected an intense interest in the ocean that lapped lazily against the shore beyond the sunlit terrace.

'I thought we—agreed to take that slowly.'

'We agreed to be sensible. It's not the same thing.'

'To me it is. For one thing, I have no idea whether you have anyone else in your life—and you can't promise that you don't,' she pointed out.

'But if we're a couple…'

'I've been in England a long time…' Becca hedged.

So that was it. They'd been apart, and she wasn't sure she could trust him. That he could understand.

'There isn't anyone else in my life.'

'And you can swear to that, can you?'

'Well, for one thing I think she'd have turned up by now if there was someone. She'd have heard of my accident. And for another, then Leander would have told me if I was married or anything stupid like that.'

Now what had he said to make her mouth tighten as if against something she'd thought better of saying? And her eyes had moved to the swimming pool, studying the water there as if she had never seen anything like it before.

'And I doubt if Medora is going to sit back and watch me make a fool of myself over you if she knows I was committed to anyone else.'

'So that's what you think you're doing, is it?' Becca's tone was tart. 'Making a fool of yourself?'

'How the hell should I know?' Irritation at the way she wouldn't look at him, as much as at her tone, roughened the edges of the words. 'I don't know if I've behaved—or felt—this way before.'

He *couldn't* have felt this way before, he'd decided that already. If he'd ever felt this heat of desire for a woman, the sort of burning hunger that made his days impossible to get through without being with her, seeing her, touching her, and

turned his nights into sweat-drenched, sleep-deprived endur-
ance tests, then surely he would remember *that*?

And how could he wipe away the memory of the brief
moments of restless sleep that he'd finally managed? Sleep
in which his dreams were so vivid, so hot, so passionately
erotic that they were almost unendurable. And yet waking to
find that they had only been a dream had left him gasping for
breath and struggling to regain any trace of his lost control.

He couldn't have forgotten those feelings. Not if he had
ever experienced anything like them for anyone else before.

'And I believe that in England you have some saying about
kettles and pans…'

'Pots,' Becca corrected automatically, still using that stiff
little voice that scraped over his nerves. 'Pot calling the kettle
black—so what has that got to do with me?'

She sounded so English, so controlled, so *sensible* that it
set his teeth on edge and made him determined to shake her
out of that mood. He wanted back the Becca he had seen under
the prim and proper exterior on the day of her arrival. The
sensual Becca, the hotly responsive Becca. The Becca whose
soft, full mouth had felt so wonderful, tasted so delicious
under his. Whose firm, high breasts had fitted so perfectly into
his hands, the tight nipples pushing against the palms. The
Becca who would have been in his bed there and then if she
hadn't had ridiculous, apprehensive, *sensible* second thoughts.

'You say you don't know if there's anyone else in my life
but I could say the same about you.'

'About me?'

That edgy look was back, making him think even more of
words like guilt and concealment—and *lies*.

'Are *you* a free agent? Is there anyone else in your life?'
he pressed.

'Oh…'

For a second she looked blank, and then he noticed that her white teeth were digging into the soft fullness of her lower lip, worrying at the soft skin that only moments before he had been imagining kissing.

'Becca?' Suspicion darkened his voice on the question.

Was this what she wasn't telling him? Was the reason she wanted to be 'sensible' because there was another man in her world? Someone she didn't want to tell him about?

'Is there—?'

'No!' she said firmly and hastily—too firmly, too hastily so that instead of putting his mind at rest it put him more on edge than ever. 'No—there's no one.'

'Are you sure?'

That brought her head round, dark hair flying, chin coming up defiantly as she met his assessing stare head-on.

'Of course I'm sure!' she declared. 'There is no man in my life but you!'

It was what he most wanted to hear, so why did he sense something like the crawl of small, icy feet down his spine in spite of the heat?

'Good,' he said, reaching out to touch a hand to her cheek and hold her there, sea-coloured eyes locked with black. 'Just make sure it stays that way. I have exclusive rights to my women. You're mine and only mine…'

Under the touch of his fingers her face jerked just once as if in rejection of his comment. Her eyes opened wide and that determined little chin lifted even higher.

'You don't have any rights to me—not yet.'

'Not *yet*,' Andreas agreed, a slow, appreciative smile curling his mouth. She was gorgeous when she was like this— wonderfully sexy with the mutinous spark that lit those fantastic eyes, the wash of colour that flooded her cheeks. 'I know—we're taking this slowly…being *sensible*.'

He drawled out the word deliberately, putting every ounce of contempt he could into each syllable.

'But not for long. I could make you forget about that need for caution you think is so important.'

Another jerk of her chin, a lift of her smoothly arched brows, challenging the truth of his assertion, making his smile widen ever more.

'You know I could,' he murmured softly, leaning even closer so that his mouth was just inches away from the soft, rebellious pout of her lips. 'It would only take a minute. Not even that.'

She had frozen now, nothing moving but her eyes as they watched him warily, waiting to see what he would do next.

'All I'd have to do is to lean forward, just the tiniest little bit…'

He suited the action to the words, only just catching the tiny faint sound of her swiftly indrawn breath as he did so. Her eyes widened just a little bit more but she stayed where she was, though the pink tip of her tongue slid out and slicked over her lower lip in an uneasy, betraying gesture.

The movement and the slight film of moisture it left on her mouth was a temptation that Andreas couldn't resist. He'd waited too long for the taste of her mouth on his all over again. He wanted it again and he wanted it now.

Reaching up a hand, he curled it round the back of her head, fingers sliding into the silky dark hair, cupping the fine bones of her skull as he drew her near to him and took her mouth. Her lips were as soft and delicious as they had been before and she yielded to him with a soft murmur that made his senses give a hard, painful kick in response.

To hell with being sensible. This was what he wanted.

What he needed. Her mouth opened under his and with a sense of triumph he moved in closer.

And felt the faint, unmistakable shiver that ran through her body as she fought for control. It was there and gone again in the space of a heartbeat but he had felt it and recognised it for what it was.

He could kiss her out of it, he knew that. It wouldn't take much; she would be his if he only insisted, pressed a little more. But it was the fact that she had reacted in that way, that she still felt that restraint she talked about that stopped him dead in his tracks. She was still determined to keep him at arm's length for her own personal reasons. And that realisation destroyed the sensual mood completely.

With a savagely muttered curse in his own language he wrenched his mouth away from hers, pulling his head back to stare down into her dark, shocked eyes.

'Andreas...' Becca began and the shake on the sound of his name was the last straw.

Swearing brutally, he tore himself away from her, taking several swift, strong and almost blind strides across the tiled surround of the pool and diving head first into the cool water, plunging way down into the clear blue depths, driving himself as hard and as far as he could.

Becca watched him go through eyes that were blurred with sudden tears. She knew what had made him react like this, the tiny shudder of panic she hadn't been able to control, but that didn't mean that she understood quite what state of mind had influenced him. Was it fury—cold-blooded anger at the way that she was still determined to hold on to the idea of being sensible? Or was it an attempt to cool himself off literally?

Whatever his feelings were, they were wild and fierce and he was having to fight to bring them under control. That much was obvious from the way he was powering down the swimming pool, face down, black hair clinging to his skull, muscular arms and legs pushing him through the clear water at a speed that gave Becca a momentary pang of concern for any possible after-effects from the accident. The bruises from his injuries might be fading, but was it safe for him to subject himself to such a physical test?

But even as the worry crossed her mind she saw that Andreas was already slowing his furious pace. He eased up, continued to swim for a while but at a much more sedate speed and eventually came back to the side of the pool just beside where she stood. Slicking back his soaking black hair with a powerful hand, he supported himself on strong arms as he trod water, looking up into her watchful face, dark eyes narrowed against the sun.

'And now I suppose you're going to say that, as my nurse, you can't approve of my behaviour just now?' he commented cynically. 'Isn't this your cue to tell me that it wasn't at all sensible—?'

'I wouldn't dare say anything of the sort!' Becca flung back at him, the uncanny way that he had almost read her mind unsettling her even more. She might have been thinking it but she certainly wasn't saying it, not knowing the reaction she would undoubtedly get.

She just hoped that Andreas would believe that irritation was uppermost in her mind and so accept it as the explanation for the way her voice went up and down in the most embarrassing way. She had felt bad enough a moment earlier and the thought that he might recognise her response as one of purely physical awareness of the body floating lazily in the water, the tense muscles in the hard forearms, the glisten of water drops on the bronzed skin was more than she could handle right now. The drenched black hair clung so close to his scalp that it formed a severe frame for those devastating features, emphasising wide, carved cheek-bones, the long, straight nose, hard jaw and almost shockingly softly sensual mouth. Her pulse was already racing in double time, making her heart catch tight in her throat. She couldn't take another of his sensual onslaughts on her, any more of those devastating, breath-stealing, soul-destroying kisses.

'I'm glad to hear it,' Andreas retorted drily, hauling himself up onto the side of the pool and sitting on the edge with his long legs dangling over the side, feet in the water. 'Because you seem so determined to revert to the nursing role that I was beginning to wonder if perhaps we ought to discuss your salary.'

'I don't want that!'

Sheer horror and the knowledge of just what she was hiding pushed the words from Becca's mouth in an urgent rush. Scrambling down beside him so that she was on a level with him, she caught hold of his arm, looking earnestly into his face.

'You don't have to pay me! After all, I'm not doing anything to earn it…'

Her voice trailed off in shivering embarrassment as she felt a tide of heated blood flood her face, making her cheeks burn at the thought of the other way that her words might be interpreted.

'I didn't mean… You don't have to pay me to…'

Oh, hell, she was making matters so much worse. Her tongue seemed to have swollen to twice its size, tangling up in her mouth so that she couldn't get another syllable out, either to explain or to apologise. And the lazy smile that crossed that hard-boned face only made matters worse, the laughter in his eyes mocking her confusion and embarrassment.

'Not pay perhaps, but I have a reputation for generosity to my mistresses.'

My mistresses.

If he had fired an arrow straight at her heart, piercing it brutally, it couldn't have had a more painful effect than just hearing him speak so casually.

My mistresses.

That was all he thought of her as; all she would ever be; all he wanted her to be. Andreas only thought of her as someone with whom he wanted a sexual relationship—a mistress, nothing more. And he had said mistresses—using the plural. Which meant that he thought in terms of more than one relationship, of women who had come before her and… Her throat closed up, making it difficult to breathe… Women who would come after her.

And since their wedding day?

There was the burn of hot tears at the backs of her eyes as she forced herself to face an even less bearable thought. The idea that once he had rejected her, he had replaced her with someone else—maybe more than one someone else. How soon after her broken-hearted departure had he brought a new woman into the house that was supposed to have been her marital home? How quickly had he found someone new to warm his bed, fill his days?

How many of them had there been since she had been driven away from him?

The tears that stung at her eyes welled up even more, fighting for release. And with grim determination Becca fought them back, struggling to force them down, refusing to let them fall. But she could only manage the control she needed by gritting her teeth, refusing to blink, swallowing as hard as she could.

'Becca?'

She wished she could say something—anything to make

him look away. Preferably something light and throwaway that would distract him, make him laugh, direct that too intent, too searching scrutiny somewhere else. How could she recover her composure, get back her self-possession when he was watching her as if she was some particularly fascinating specimen under a microscope? One he wanted to dissect and analyse completely.

She knew that her cheeks were burning painfully. The struggle to fight back the tears had added to the already embarrassed colour in her skin. Mortified beyond bearing, she lifted a hand and brushed it across her face, praying that the small gesture would at least break the focus of that concentrated stare.

'You're hot,' Andreas said quietly, the note of concern in his words almost destroying her completely. 'And no wonder when you're wearing too much clothing.'

If there had been the slightest trace of a sexual intonation in what he'd said, anything that had made her think that he was deliberately putting a double edge onto the phrase, then Becca knew she would have totally lost control. But the note of genuine concern destroyed her composure in a totally different way.

'Why don't you put on a swimming costume and spend some time in the pool? You're clearly not used to this sort of heat and the water would cool you down.'

It wasn't the heat of the sun that was disturbing her, Becca admitted to herself. It was the subtler, more sensual warmth of his body so close to hers that she could smell the intimate, intensely personal scent of his skin, topped with the tang of the water that still clung to it. That and the heat of her own response, the honeyed sense of need that flooded her body, pooling moistly at the junction of her thighs.

A swim would be just what she needed. It would ease the burn of hunger, soothe the ache in her body. But there was one very practical problem.

'I don't have a swimming costume,' she managed, casting longing glance at the cool, fresh water as it lapped against the clean blue tiles of the pool. 'I—never thought that I would need one when I came here. And to be honest, I never thought I'd stay this long.'

She could have bitten out her tongue as soon as she'd spoken, realising too late how close she'd come to giving away the truth that she was not really the person he'd believed her to be. But Andreas hadn't noticed the slip, too intent on his own train of thought.

'That's not a problem. I can soon provide you with a costume. There's one in the pool house over there.'

A wave of his hand indicated the small stone-formed building that provided a changing room and a shower for those who used the pool.

'I saw it hanging up there when I went in this morning. It should fit you. Why don't you go and try it on?'

And come back here, wearing it?

Becca's mind quailed at the thought. Just the idea of sitting here beside him, lying in the sun or swimming in the pool close to him in some sleek, close-fitting Lycra costume made the tingling worse, bringing it close to the sensation of an electrical shock running over her skin. If someone had left it here then it was probably one of those mistresses he had spoken of. In which case, was it likely that the costume was anything more than a few skimpy pieces of material, precariously held up by a couple of shoestring straps?

And yet the idea of getting away for a moment, going into the pool house to be by herself, as she had hardly been at any moment over the last three days, except when she had retired to bed, suddenly seemed such an appealing idea. She could hide away there for a while, regain her composure, gather her strength. And then maybe she'd be able to cope much better than she had been doing until now.

'I'll do that,' she said, fighting with herself to make sure that she got to her feet slowly, trying desperately not to make it look as if she was running away even though she knew deep in her heart that that was what she was doing.

'I'll be back in a minute.'

And the costume? she asked herself as she padded on bare feet across the stone-paved terrace, heading for the pool house. Well, if it fitted—and was in any way modest—then she might risk it.

She'd make up her mind when she saw it.

But when she saw the pale lavender swimming costume hanging on a peg in the small changing room the effect of it was like a sudden blow to her heart, stilling its beat and leaving her standing staring in blank and stunned disbelief, unable to think at all.

It couldn't be. It just couldn't be, was the phrase that repeated over and over inside her head, making the real world fade from her awareness into a buzzing, whirling haze in which the only real thing was the sleek, small item of clothing before her.

'It can't,' she said, shaking her head in shock. 'It *can't* be.'

Because the costume she now held in shaking hands was the one that she had worn herself on the single day she had spent in the villa as Andreas' wife.

CHAPTER SEVEN

T STILL fitted her.

That was a shock. She knew she had lost weight in the ten and a half months since her wedding and that she was no longer the relaxed, happy-go-lucky person she had been before she had met and married Andreas Petrakos.

But the lavender swimming costume still fitted almost perfectly. There was so much Lycra in the material that it clung to her new, more slender shape, the low neck exposing softer curves, the high-cut legs revealing slender hips and thighs that had been so much more rounded when she had first worn it.

Looking at herself in the full-length mirror that hung on the wall of the changing room, Becca smoothed hands that were none too steady over the clinging material and tried to remember the Becca who had looked into the same mirror not quite a year before. Then her eyes had been sparkling with delight and the sensual satisfaction of having just made wild, abandoned, passionate love with her brand-new husband. And there had been a wide smile on her mouth that she had felt sure was going to be there for ever and that nothing would ever erase it.

She couldn't have been more wrong.

Barely two hours later she had been on her way home, leaving her married life lying in pieces behind her.

'Love!' Andreas' harsh voice, with its cruelly cynica
emphasis on that vital word, echoed down from the pas
sounding so loud and clear inside her thoughts that she almos
believed for a moment that he had come into the room an
thrown the word at her.

'I don't love anyone—least of all you! I doubt if I'r
capable of the feeling...'

They had arrived on the island late in the afternoon afte
the flight from England. Becca was still floating on a clou
of happiness after the delight of their wedding, the bliss of th
thought of being Andreas' wife. And she truly was his wife
He had wasted no time in making sure of that. They had bee
barely through the door before he had carried her upstairs t
his bedroom, stripped her of the elegant trouser suit she ha
worn for travelling and made passionate love to her with al
the ardour and the heat of which he was capable.

Later, when Andreas had reluctantly been obliged to go t
his office to deal with a fax that had come through unexpect
edly, Becca had changed into the lavender-coloured one-piec
swimming costume and headed for the pool.

'I'll join you there as soon as I can,' he'd promised.

He was much longer than she had anticipated. She wa
tired and bored, and thinking of getting dressed again befor
he came back onto the terrace where he stood, hands on hips
his face almost white with some fierce emotion that made hi
eyes glitter like polished jet.

'Get dressed.'

It was an order, an autocratic command delivered with
such savagery that her blood ran cold, icy pins and needle
prickling her skin in spite of the heat of the day.

'I want to talk to you.'

The words had barely left his lips before he turned on hi

el and walked away, either not hearing or deliberately
rning a deaf ear to her shaken question, her nervous request
r an explanation as to his sudden change in mood.

She hardly dared take the time to dry herself thoroughly,
scarding the swimming costume and hauling on jeans and
T-shirt, pushing her feet into flip-flops, barely pausing for
eath as she almost ran from the pool house and into the
fice, where Andreas was standing by the window, silhouet-
d against the setting sun, as he waited for her.

'What's happened? Is there something wrong?'

'You tell me.'

There was nothing of the ardent, caring husband in his
ne; nothing of the passionate lover who had torn himself so
luctantly from her arms and from their bed just a short time
efore. What could have happened to have changed his mind
d his mood so terribly?

'Andreas? What's happened? What's this about?'

'You tell me what it's about. Tell me about Roy Stanton.'

He flung the name at her like a weapon, watching through
arrowed eyes so that he caught the way she flinched, the
dden step she took backwards in uncontrolled shock.

'So you do know the name, then?'

It was too late to deny it. Her reaction had already given
er away.

'How—how did you…?'

'How did I find out?'

An arrogant flick of his wrist tossed away the question as
obvious that it didn't need an answer.

'An investigation into these things is easy to arrange.'

'You—had me *investigated*!' She sounded as appalled as she
lt. And she felt even worse when Andreas shrugged off that
uestion too, with even less concern than he had given the first.

'I have every right to know what my prospective wife i
doing with the small fortune I've given her. And I do no
believe that you have the right to judge my actions when wha
you did was give that money to some other man. Or are yo
claiming that that's not true?'

'No…'

Becca sank down onto one of the wooden benches in th
changing room as the bitter memories of that day took all th
strength from her legs. Andreas hadn't given her a chance t
explain. He had bombarded her with questions like som
brutal counsel for the prosecution, demanding answers to
new one even while she was still stumbling over the answe
to the last. And all the time she had been bound by the promis
she had made to Macy. The promise to her newly discovere
sister. The sister she had never known she had until just a fev
short weeks before.

At first Macy had wanted nothing to do with her but the
suddenly she had phoned, asking to meet, asking for help. Bu
she had made Becca promise that she wouldn't tell a soul.

'No, I'm not claiming that.'

'You gave this man money?' Andreas had thundered. 'A
the money I gave you, by the look of it.'

'You said it was mine!'

'You know damn well that I gave that to you to buy you
wedding dress and anything else you wanted for—'

'Are you saying that the dress I wore wasn't good enough?
Becca rushed in, jumping to the defensive in a panic as sh
struggled to think of some explanation she could give him.

Her mind was reeling in shock at just the thought tha
Andreas had found out about Roy Stanton. There was n
reason at all that he should even know the man's name. An
so she tried to stall him, using any argument she could t

distract him while she tried to work out just what was happening and how she could possibly answer him at all.

But going on the attack was the wrong move—the worst possible move of all. From being icily angry, Andreas' temper went into meltdown, blazing fierce and furious as a forest fire, engulfing everything that stood in its way. And before she knew what was happening, it seemed that *he* was accusing *her*. But of what she was not quite sure.

'The dress was fine—as far as it went. But it could have been more—should have been more...'

'Should have! So now I have to wear what you order just to make sure that—that what? That I didn't show you up by not wearing something suitable to match your status? Is that it, Andreas? Are you angry because I didn't marry you in a couture gown—a designer original? One that would show my family—your friends—how wonderfully you can provide for me? That you can give me a fortune to spend on a single dress for a single day...'

'A fortune that you gave to another man.'

'I had my reasons!'

'And what were they?'

And that simple question brought the whole argument to crashing halt. The words died on her lips, crushed back down her throat as if someone had put a gag right over her mouth and tied it so tightly that she had no chance of saying word in her own defence.

Because the truth was that she was gagged by her promise to Macy. She had sworn on everything she held sacred not to say word. Not until Macy was safe. And when she had discovered that her already emotionally vulnerable half-sister was also very newly pregnant that vow had become even more important. So, even though it tore at her heart, she had to hold to that promise.

'I—can't say.'

'Can't or won't?' Andreas snarled and the savagery of his tone had her flinching back, terrified of his rage, the flames of fury that blazed in the darkness of his eyes.

'Andreas—please…'

How had this happened? How had the wonderful, blissful mood in which they'd reached the villa been turned into this terrible horror, this brutal tearing each other apart?

'It was just money…'

'My money—the money I gave you. And you gave it to him…'

And then she thought she could see what was happening. In a sudden rush of understanding, she felt she knew just why he was so angry—what had got to him so badly. She had always known about the dark shadow over Andreas' past. The fact that his mother had only married his father for the money he had, the lifestyle he could give her, and when Alexander Petrakos had lost much of his fortune through some rash and ill-advised stock-market gambling Alicia had taken off with his wealthier cousin, turning her back on her five-year-old son without a second thought.

Then later, when Andreas himself had rebuilt the Petrakos fortune so that it had more than doubled the original amount, Alicia had turned yet again and tried to come back to the son she had abandoned over twenty years before. As a result, Andreas had always been wary of being used in the same way as his father. The slightest suspicion that any woman in his life might be a gold-digger meant that she was dropped so fast she never had time to even try to change his mind.

So if Andreas thought—or even suspected—that she had married him for his money…

'Andreas, don't...' she tried again. 'It doesn't have to be this way.'

There had to be a way that she could reach him. A way that they could talk this out. If she could just calm him down, make him see that things could be put right. And then she'd talk to Macy, get her to see that she couldn't keep her promise. She had to tell Andreas—he was her husband.

'Doesn't it?'

'No—not if you love me...'

A sharp pain in her fingers jolted Becca back to the present, where, staring down at her hand, she realised that she had been twisting the stretchy material of the swimming costume round and round until it had tightened about her fingers, digging into the skin.

But the tight physical pain was as nothing when compared to the one in her heart as she remembered Andreas' reaction to her stumbling attempt to put things right, or at least bring about a truce between them.

'Love!' Andreas' harsh bark of laughter had been cruel and totally without any humour in it. 'Love? Who brought love into this?'

'But you—I—you married me...'

'Not for love!' he flung the word in her face. 'I don't love anyone—least of all you! I doubt if I'm capable of the feeling. I married you for sex—for that and nothing else. No other woman has ever made me feel as hot as you do.'

It was as if some freezing iceberg had suddenly enclosed her so that she could see and hear but she was incapable of moving and, for now at least, the terrible cold had deadened all feeling so that she was numb right through to the soul. Even her heart hardly seemed to be beating at all.

'S-sex?'

'Yes—sex. That thing we just enjoyed upstairs.'

'I didn't enjoy it.'

'Liar.'

She wouldn't have enjoyed it, couldn't have enjoyed it if she'd known that he had been using her as cold-bloodedly and cruelly as it now seemed. If their whole marriage had been based on a lie and not the real love she believed it to be.

'You had no right...' she began but her frozen tongue wouldn't form the words. Her lips were so stiff they felt as if they were carved from wood.

'No right to what?'

Andreas' expression was carved from a similar block of ice as the one that seemed to enclose her. His jaw was taut and rigid, eyes freezing black pools.

'To marry me if you felt that way. You have nothing to give me!'

'Nothing!'

His laughter was so hard that it seemed to splinter in the air around her, making her wince away from the shattered fragments that threatened her face.

'Take a look around you, *agape mou.*'

One long fingered hand waved in a gesture that took in the luxurious room, the beautiful pool out beyond the patio door and the view of the sapphire-blue ocean beyond that again. 'You call this nothing?'

Nothing without love.

'Isn't this enough?'

'Quite frankly, no.'

Bitterness made her say it. Agony pushed it from her lips in a cold, tight voice that didn't sound at all like her own.

'I expected more from you.'

'You expected... Well, you can expect all you like but you'll get nothing else from me—nothing.'

'You think I'll stay for that?' she asked.

'I don't think you'll stay for anything. In fact, let's make this easy for you—let me help you on your way.'

Marching into the hall, he flung open the big wooden door, letting in the warm evening air where the shadows were now gathering.

'Andreas, you can't do this! You married me today—we—we've just consummated our marriage.'

But what sort of marriage was it when the man she adored had just baldly announced that he didn't love her?

'If you divorce me then it will cost you even more...'

It was meant to bring him to his senses. To get him to see that if she was only after him for his money, then he was going the right way about making sure that she got as much as she could possibly want. Surely the thought that she would get half of his vast fortune would make him stop and think and see where he was going wrong.

Thinking looked like the last thing that Andreas was capable of. And stopping was obviously the last thing that was on his mind. She'd never seen him like this before in her life. She could almost see the red mist of fury behind his eyes, and his dark face was so contorted into a snarl that she barely recognised him as the man she had loved so deeply. The man she had vowed only that morning to love, honour and cherish.

The man who had vowed the same while all the time he had a lie in his heart. He hadn't meant a thing.

'I married you for sex—for that and nothing else.'

He didn't love her. Did she really want to be married to a man who felt that way, no matter how much she cared about him? What sort of a marriage would she be tying herself to?

'Andreas, I'll be entitled to half of everything you own—and I'll take it.'

She wanted to shock him; prayed it would bring him to hi senses. Perhaps she could…

'It'll be worth it to get rid of you.'

Whirling round, he snatched up her suitcase, which sti stood at the foot of the stairs where he had deposited it on thei arrival. With a violent movement he tossed it out of the doo and then turned back to face her, challenge stamped into ever hard line of his dark, savage face.

'Now, are you going to follow it or do I have to throw you out myself?'

It was then that Becca gave up, gave in. She had no more fight left in her, and besides, she didn't know what she wa fighting for.

Was she going to beg—to plead with him to let her stay' Even if she managed to convince him that she had marrie him because she loved him, what difference would it make' He had made his position brutally plain. He had married he for sex and that was all. He wouldn't care if she loved him— the only thing he gave a damn about was his money.

Drawing herself up to her full height, she imposed a contro on her quivering mouth, her burning eyes, that she didn't know she was capable of. She didn't know how she *looked,* but she knew how she wanted him to think she *felt* and prayed she wa communicating that with her demeanour, her expression *Please* let it show in her eyes. She was determined not to let single tear fall, no matter how bitterly they stung at the back of her eyes, how hard she had to fight not to blink them away

'Oh, I'm going—don't worry. There's nothing here to sta for. I think I've got all that I wanted from this relationship.'

'Oh, I'll just bet you have. But don't think you'll be abl to go for any quickie divorce. There will be no annulment— I've already made sure of that.'

Something in his voice caught on the raw, bleeding edge

f Becca's heart, making her see just what was really behind
he callous declaration.

He'd known already, she realised. Somehow, though God
new how, he'd found out about Roy Stanton before their
marriage. And, thinking that he would trap her in a marriage that
meant nothing to him, he had gone ahead and married her after
ll, knowing all the time that he was going to let it come to this.

Becca had no more fight left in her. All she knew was that
he had to get out of here right now, before she broke down
ompletely. If she let Andreas see how much she was hurting,
hen he would know that he'd won.

Somehow she made herself go past him to get to the door.
'he faint brush of her arm against his as she passed almost
ndid her, making her body run hot and then shiveringly cold
s if she was in the grip of some terrible fever. She could only
ray that her legs would hold up beneath her until she was
ctually out of the door and heading away, far, far away from
he villa. She made it outside and into the warmth of the
light, where, thankfully, the darkness hid the misery in her
ace, the tears she was fighting a losing battle to hold back.

It was then that Andreas flung his final, unbelievable
omment after her.

'Well, money I'll give you—but nothing else. Not a damn
hing else.'

Marching with her head down, her eyes blind, fighting a
bitter little battle with herself not to give in, Becca couldn't
believe what she'd heard. He couldn't believe that all she wanted
was money, and if he did then why on earth, even now, would
he say that if she asked for money he would give it to her?

In confusion and bewilderment she turned, forcing herself
o make one last, desperate attempt. But even as she swung
ound, it was already too late. Andreas had stepped back into

the house, and as she watched he slammed the door shut, hard
and fast, in her face.

She had to have heard wrong anyway, Becca decided. He
couldn't have said what she thought he'd said. It didn'
make sense.

But then nothing about this whole terrible evening made
sense. The day had started out so wonderfully, with so much
joy, so much hope. She had been looking into a great future—
and now all that potential was over, in the past. Instead, the
life she was facing seemed to have nothing to offer. And the
future she had dreamed of was dead and gone.

And so she'd made herself keep walking. Walking away
from the marriage she'd thought she was going to have. Away
from the man she'd thought she'd loved.

The man she now tried to convince herself that she hated.

She'd walked away from the house, dragging her case with
her and trying to hate him. She'd made the long journey home
back to her stunned family, her bewildered friends, needing
to hate him if she was to survive.

And the truth was that coming back here had proved to her
in the most painful way that she hadn't succeeded.

She couldn't hate Andreas, in spite of a year of trying; it
just wouldn't work. She was still every bit as much in love
with him as on the day that she had married him.

CHAPTER EIGHT

ANDREAS was sick and tired of waiting.

How long had it been since Becca had headed for the pool house? And how long did it take to get into a swimming costume, for God's sake?

Or was there a problem? She had looked uncomfortable, edgy, when she had been sitting beside him on the edge of the pool. She'd definitely been too hot—and she had such fair skin...

The thought had barely formed in his mind before Andreas pushed himself to his feet from the sun lounger on which he had been relaxing and headed in the direction of the pool house himself, padding silently across the tiles on bare feet.

She was sitting on the wooden bench that ran along the white-painted wall. Her head was bent, her eyes downcast, staring at the floor, and her hands clasped together in her lap. She had changed into the costume and once again he was aware of the pallor of her skin, barely touched by the few days she had spent with him in the sun. And with the thought came a sudden vivid mental image of the two of them in bed together, her pale limbs entwined with his darker, stronger ones.

'What is it?'

Without thinking he spoke in Greek, the sudden burn of his libido too strong to allow enough thought for translation into English.

The sound of his voice brought her head up fast, sea-blue gaze locking with his in an instant. But there was something in that look that he didn't understand. Something new and different that told him without words that a change had taken place in the time she had spent away from him.

'Are you all right?'

'Yes, fine.'

The words sounded all wrong, strangely staccato and somehow unconvincing. And the smile that she turned on him flashed on and off like some neon advertising sign. As soon as it subsided, her face was stiff and unresponsive.

'Did it fit?'

It must have done—she was wearing the damn thing. So why was she sitting here, inside, instead of out in the sun?

'Well…yes…'

She gestured to herself with a hand that was not quite steady.

'I could get into it—but…'

The look in her eyes intensified, turned them into sea-deep pools under a sweep of dark, curling lashes. She seemed wary, as if unsure of how he was going to react.

Of course. She needed reassurance. She felt unsure of herself, of the way she looked.

'Stand up…let me see.'

At first he thought she was going to refuse and that she would insist on staying where she was. But then, slowly and reluctantly, she got to her feet and turned towards him. For a moment her hands fluttered nervously and then she forced them down to her sides, obviously having trouble submitting to his appraisal. Watching her, Andreas felt his heart take up a heavy, pounding beat, one that sent the blood rushing to his brain and set his thoughts swimming.

He hadn't realised quite what a spectacular body she had been hiding under the loose, floating dresses and skirts she had been wearing since she had arrived at the villa a few days before. It had been obvious that her shape was supremely feminine, curved in all the right places, but he hadn't been able to guess at *this*. If he had noticed the pallor of her skin a moment before, now he saw how the flow of her blood just beneath the surface flooded her smooth flesh with a soft pink glow that gave it a lustre like the finest pearls. Against that paleness, the gleaming darkness of her hair was shocking, especially when combined with the unique soft colour of her eyes.

Her shoulders were softly rounded, curving down to slender arms, and in the vulnerable hollow where they joined the base of her neck—one of the most entrancing parts of a woman, he had always believed—her pulse beat hard and fast, betraying the way she was feeling.

Just for a moment he caught her eyes, saw the way she was watching him and felt his own heart kick hard as her darkened gaze locked with his. Was she really so unsure of herself? He tried a smile, aiming for the encouragement he believed she needed.

'You look—beautiful.'

And he meant it. Meant it in a way that he would never have thought possible. It was as if, just for a moment, as she'd got to her feet something in the world had slipped, tilted, and then clicked back into place. But it wasn't quite the same now. Not quite as it had been before.

But for the life of him he couldn't say how.

He couldn't think about it now. He didn't *want* to think about it. What he wanted to think about was the woman who stood before him, tall and slender and so, so feminine in the clinging one-piece.

'Beautiful…'

Her legs were longer that he'd ever imagined, seeming to go on for ever from the high-cut legs of the costume, and the way that it clung to every curve, smoothed over the swell of her breasts, the neat indentation of her waist made his mouth dry with hunger. He wanted to reach for her, pull her towards him, enfold her in his arms and kiss her senseless.

Hell, he wanted to do so much more than that!

Something of what he was feeling must have shown in his face and he saw those rich lashes lift even higher as her wary eyes widened.

Her hands fluttered up again, came to rest above the scooped neckline of the costume, crossing over, covering the rich curves of her breasts and the shadowy valley between.

'No…'

His tone was sharp and, stepping forward, he caught hold of those concealing hands, pulling them away from her, gently but firmly. And although she tensed for a moment, clearly thought about resisting, she gave in and went with him, a faint sigh escaping her as her white teeth worried at the fullness of her bottom lip. A lip that he could see was trembling in spite of her efforts at control.

'No…' Andreas repeated, more softly this time. 'No, *agape mou*—never hide yourself from me. Never.'

'But—you—I…'

Her voice was just a breathless whisper and she seemed to struggle to get the words out. It wasn't just her lip that was trembling now; he could feel the faint tremors that shook the fine lines of her body as his arms came round her, supporting her when she seemed so nervous that she might actually fall

'No...' he said again, leaning forward to press the words against her mouth. 'Never be shy with me. Why would you want to hide such loveliness, when any man would delight in seeing you—holding you...?'

'I...'

Never be shy with me...

Becca barely heard the words above what seemed like the sound of a million buzzing bees inside her head, humming wildly and loudly as they whirled and twisted in a crazy flying dance that made her thoughts spin, her senses blur. Andreas thought that she was trembling all over because she was *shy;* because she was apprehensive as to what the man she was with would think of her when she first exposed her body in the clinging swimming costume to his assessing gaze. And he couldn't have been more wrong.

Or, rather, he was right but in a back-to-front sort of way.

She was nervous all right, apprehensive definitely, but not for the reasons he thought. Not because it was the first time he had seen her this way, wearing so little—but because of the exact opposite. Because she knew he *had* seen her dressed this way before and she didn't know if seeing her dressed in the costume again would remind him, jar loose whatever blockage was closing off his memory of the past from the reality of today, bring him back to himself in a rush.

And she was scared stiff that he was going to repeat his behaviour of that day and throw her out of the villa before she had a chance to talk to him, to even try to explain.

'Andreas...'

Her mouth was so dry with fear that his name had an embarrassingly squeaky sound, and she caught herself up, swallowing hard to try to ease the constriction in her throat.

'Thank you...' she managed, sounding better at least, but not much.

To her astonishment Andreas shook his head, sending the black hair, still wet from his swim, flying around his head.

'*Ochi*—no again.'

Somehow his use of his own language made his voice richer, deeper, more sensual, so that Becca caught in her breath as she heard it. And when he laid a single forefinger against her lips to silence her she felt her senses swirl again but in a very different way this time. The scent of his skin filled her nostrils, tantalising her nerves. She had to fight against the urge to open her mouth just so...and let her tongue slide out to curl around it, him, know the taste of his flesh on hers.

'I am the one who should be thanking you.'

'For—for what?' Becca questioned against his hand.

'For staying.'

'But you asked me to—and I was supposed to...'

'That is not what I mean.'

Looking deep into her confused eyes, Andreas moved the restraining finger, lifting it to the middle of her forehead and tracing his way along her hairline, stroking a gentle pathway round to her temple and down along her cheek, sliding it under her chin to lift her face to his.

'Don't you know that in a way you're the person I know best? The others—Leander, Medora—I don't remember the last year I spent with them—but that doesn't matter so much to me. We are as we have always been. But you—you're the one I feel I've come to know in the days you've been here. The one I've grown closer to. And I want to be closer...so much closer...'

'Oh, don't!'

The cry escaped her in a panic, before she had even considered what she might say if he asked her to explain her reasons for the protest. She couldn't let him go on like this—couldn't...

But Andreas wasn't listening and the next moment any chance she had of saying more evaporated in a rush as those strong fingers under her chin exerted just a little bit more pressure, tilting her face up higher, coming closer to his. And his mouth came down on hers in a kiss that stole all thought away and took her senses with it.

Andreas' kiss started out slow, almost light, but in the space of a heartbeat it had moved from gentle through enticing until it got to hungry and insistent. And in spite of her fears, or perhaps because of them, Becca found that she didn't have the strength to fight him. She didn't *want* to fight him. With the realisation of how much she still loved him right at the forefront of her thoughts, she gave herself up to that kiss, melting into his arms, feeling their strength tighten around her, holding her close.

She was pressed up against him, against the warm expanse of his naked chest, with her head resting on the hardness of his shoulder, under the smooth stretch of tanned, golden skin. The black haze of hair that covered his chest was soft underneath her chin and she sighed and rubbed her face against it, feeling it tickle her. Under the clinging swimsuit her breasts tightened and stung with need, the hardened nipples pushing against the constricting cloth, and desire was a heated, pulsing pool low down in her body.

'Becca...'

Her name was a raw sound on Andreas' tongue, thick and guttural, the sound of a hunger that matched her own.

This time when he took her lips again his kiss burned and demanded, his arms crushing her to him. And Becca went willingly, the thunder of need in her heart drowning out any weak voice of attempted caution. This was what she wanted; what she needed *now*. She didn't care about the past, had no thought of the future. What she wanted was right here in the present. Hers for the taking.

And she was going to take it.

She had spent almost a year mourning the loss of this passion in her life, hating the way that world seemed cold and hard and empty without it. Now she had one chance— probably one last chance—to experience the scalding pleasure of being here, where she most wanted to be, in Andreas' arms, with his kiss crushing her mouth, his hands hot and hard on her. And it was what she most wanted in all the world.

Those powerful hands were stroking over her skin, moving down along the straight line of her spine, leaving burning trails in their wake as if his touch was actually hot enough to mark her, brand her as his for all time to come. The feel of it made her moan aloud, arching her back like a small, sensual cat that stretched into a caress.

The movement brought her right up against him, against the heated swell of his powerful erection, a potent force that she felt almost as strongly as if she were naked, there was so little clothing to come between them. Just the heat of it made her breath catch in her throat and she swayed softly, turning her whole pelvis into a caress that had him snatching in air in a rush like a drowning man.

'Becca!'

It was half protest, half encouragement and he clamped his big hands on the tight curve of her buttocks, holding her still, but keeping her pressed hard and tight against his burning flesh.

The words he muttered in her ear were in thick, rough Greek, and so incomprehensible to her, but she didn't need to know the language to understand, at the most basic, primitive level, exactly what he was saying to her. And it was something she wanted to say right back.

'I want you…'

She choked it out, the knot of need in her throat almost preventing her from finding her voice.

'Want…want…want you!'

'*Nai…*'

His response was as rough-voiced as her own, but he didn't need speech to show her he understood—and shared—the yearning that was clawing at her deep inside. With a swift, sudden tensing of the powerful muscles in his shoulders and back, he swung her off her feet and up into his arms, turning towards the still open door behind him.

'Andreas…'

A sudden rush of embarrassment at the thought of being carried through the house like this brought his name to her lips.

'What if we meet Medora—or Leander—on the way?'

But Andreas shook his head instantly, dismissing her concerns with a smile.

'We're all alone,' he told her with a deep intensity that seared all the way along every nerve path until it made her toes curl tightly in response. 'No one will bother us. And I'm sure as hell not making love to you on the pool-house floor.'

Becca barely noticed the journey through the house—up the stairs. It was only as Andreas shouldered open a door and carried her over to the bed that she realised where they were.

The master bedroom. The room that should have been theirs when they were married. The room that she had never shared with him—at least to *sleep*. Had some unconscious part of his mind directed his footsteps this way, or was it simply coincidence?

The question left her head as soon as it had entered it

because in the same moment Andreas lowered her to the floor, sliding her down the length of his body as he did so. And before her feet had actually hit the ground, he had hooked his fingers into the thin straps of the swimsuit and peeled them off her shoulders, down to her waist...

His mouth followed the same path, kissing his way from the hollow where her hungry pulse throbbed, and down over the curve of her breast, making her catch her breath in shocked delight.

'I know, *kalloni mou...*'

She could hear the smile in his voice, feel it on the lips that caressed her skin, and her own mouth curved into a wide, brilliant smile of pure delight, her head going back as she gave herself up to his skilled caress.

'It's how I feel too. How you make me feel.'

His head was moving even lower now as the little that was left of the lavender-coloured costume was eased from her, his mouth caressing every inch of the creamy skin he exposed. When he paused to let his tongue slide into the shallow indentation of her navel, drawing a sensual circle all around it, Becca could not hold back a small cry of response, her hands coming out, clutching at his hair, twisting in the black, silky strands as she held him closer to her.

He was kneeling before her now, helping her to step away from the bundle of lavender Lycra, tossing it aside without even looking, his attention totally focused on pleasuring her. The feel of his kisses over the cluster of dark hair between her legs made her writhe in sensual anticipation in the same moment that she tugged at the hair she held, wanting him closer, needing more of him, his heat against her, the scent of his body enclosing her. She wanted him everywhere, all of him, and every kiss, every touch made her hungrier, needier than ever before.

'*Anypomonos*—impatient!' Andreas laughed, the warmth of his breath feathering over her skin, stirring the curls, whispering around the sensitised opening between her legs. 'But I like that in you. I like to know that you're as hot for me as I am for you.'

'Know it...' Becca managed in a broken whisper, feeling the flood of need moisten her most intimate core, her breath catching in her throat as he began to kiss her once more—but reversing his path this time, caressing up and up until that tormenting, knowing mouth was pressed against the warm underside of one tingling, aching breast.

'Know it...' she said again, this time on a heartfelt sigh. 'I want you—need you...'

Now that he was upright again she could touch him herself, release her grip on his hair, only to explore more of his powerful male body, letting her needy fingers wander over the hot, tight skin, smooth the potent muscles that flexed and tautened beneath her touch. She didn't know where she wanted him the most, his hands at her breasts, teasing the straining nipples into harder, tighter peaks, his mouth on hers, his slick tongue probing in heated imitation of the more intimate invasion she longed for. She wanted all of him, above her, on her—*inside her.*

'These will have to go.'

It was a muttered reproach as her fingers encountered the waistband of his shorts, tugging impatiently, pushing them down, a sigh of satisfaction escaping her as she exposed the smooth warmth of his waist, the firm, muscled stretch of his buttocks. But then, as the shorts fell to the floor and he kicked them aside, not taking his attention from the devastation his hands and mouth were working on her, she let her hands slide between them, closing over the hottest, hardest part of him and smoothing her thumbs down its straining length. Her heart kicked sharply, her own hunger growing, pooling hotly between her legs as she heard his groan of anguished pleasure.

'Witch!' he muttered hoarsely, tearing his mouth away from hers to drag in a gasp of much-needed air. 'Tormentor—temptress…!'

And with a hunger too strong for care, too ardent for gentleness, he half lifted, half pushed her backwards, tumbling her down onto the bed so that she landed on the pillows with a gasp, her legs splaying out from the shock of her landing.

Andreas came down beside her before she had a chance to recover. His hands reached for her breasts, cupping them and lifting them to his mouth, his wicked tongue encircling each pouting nipple in turn, drawing erotic patterns around them, making her squirm and sigh in restless need before he concentrated all his attention on one, drawing the distended peak into his mouth and sucking softly.

At the same time his long body moved over hers, powerful, hair-roughened legs coming between her splayed ones. Pushing them even further apart, he settled himself so that the heated force of his erection just touched the central core of her body, so near and yet so far from offering her the complete fulfilment that she yearned for.

'Andreas!' she muttered in impatient protest, clenching her jaw tight over the needy words that almost escaped her. She wouldn't beg… 'Don't tease…'

'Tease, *agape mou*?' he questioned softly, a wicked smile on his lips—but one that was belied by the haze of passion that clouded his eyes, the slash of heat that scored the wide cheekbones. 'What makes you think that I am teasing? I merely want to make sure that this is what you want. That—'

'You know it's what I want!' Becca clenched her hands into

tight fists and pounded them against the rock-hard wall of his chest so close above her. Andreas grabbed at the flailing hands, holding them round the wrists and bringing them down on either side of her, holding her prisoner.

'Do you?'

'Oh, I do—I do—I do—Andreas—please…'

'Ah, well, when you ask so nicely…'

Andreas shifted slightly, pushing himself closer, almost where she wanted him…and then pausing again.

'Andreas…' Becca began warningly.

'Then who am I to deny a lady?'

'You—!'

Whatever she had been about to say was broken on a sharp cry of fulfilment as Andreas abandoned all pretence at teasing and eased himself into her waiting, welcoming body in one long, hard thrust.

'Andreas!'

This time his name was a wild, keening sound of delight, one that was pushed back into her throat as his mouth clamped down hard on hers, his strong body moving against hers, setting up an erotic rhythm that made her pulses throb in heady delight. Closing her eyes tight, the better to enjoy the feeling, she arched against him, abandoning herself to the sensual pleasure of his possession.

In the space between one frantic heartbeat and the next the smouldering embers of need sparked into wild, burning flames of hunger. Hunger that knew no restraint, allowed for no holding back. Finding themselves free, Becca's hands reached for Andreas, clamped tight over those powerful shoulders, her nails digging into the warm flesh of his back, a sob of excitement escaping her as she gave herself up to the glorious sensations they were creating between them.

It was hard, it was fast, it was hot as hell, and it was taking her closer to heaven with each burning second that passed. She could feel the incredible tension building up inside her, climbing higher and higher until she thought she would scream aloud with the pressure of need. It was there in Andreas too, in the tautness of every powerful muscle, the raw, uneven sound of his breathing, the way that his powerful hands were clamped tight around her upper arms, almost bruising the tender flesh. The peak they reached for was so close—so, so close—and yet it seemed that she would never reach it. And then Andreas bent his head, catching one straining nipple in the heat of his mouth and suckling hard, nipping gently at the delicate skin and creating a stinging pleasure that took her right over the edge in an instant. The world disappeared, as she was whirled into a blazing oblivion, seeing nothing, hearing nothing, only *feeling,* feeling at the highest, wildest pinnacle of sensation that she had ever known.

Somewhere in the back of her mind she registered the harsh, primitive cry that told her that Andreas was with her in the most intimate way possible and she felt his hard body clench and tighten as he followed her out of reality and into the scorching ecstasy that had claimed them both.

For a long, long time they lay there, mindless, sightless, breathless, Andreas' wide chest heaving as he struggled to come back to reality. And only then did Becca dare to do what she most wanted as she folded her arms around his big, still shuddering body, feeling the aftershocks of pleasure pulsing through him as she held him close. Her heart clenched with bitter-sweet delight as, barely conscious, he turned his head and pressed the sweetest, most tender kiss on her cheek before he tumbled into sleep. And a moment later she followed him, still holding him in her arms.

She had no idea how long she lay there, blissfully unconscious, she only knew that at last, slowly and reluctantly, she
swam up from the dark waters of sleep and into the real world
again to find that beyond the bedroom window the sun was
already beginning to set. The brightness of the afternoon was
fading, and darkening shadows were starting to fill the room.
But they were as nothing when compared with the shadows
that were creeping into her mind and heart.

Beside her, Andreas still slept deeply, his head pillowed on
her arm, jet-black hair fallen forward over his wide brow, his
strong jaw starting to be darkened by a day's growth of
stubble. His breathing was deep and even and, encouraged by
the fact that he was so dead to the world and so had no idea
of what she was doing, she allowed herself just to lie there
and watch him, studying his sleeping face—his sleeping,
beloved face—so intently that it seemed as if she needed to
imprint its image on her mind, store it up there like supplies
hoarded carefully against a future famine.

And she might truly have to do that, Becca admitted to herself,
acknowledging with a desperate, sinking sensation of sadness
that after this there was no way things could ever be the same.

Sighing deeply, she lay on her back and stared up at the
white-painted ceiling above her, with eyes that fear and misery
made blind, the bitter tears stinging hard, fighting to fall.

'We can't go back,' she whispered to herself, recalling how
on the way upstairs she had been thinking how this one special
time with the man she loved could be so extraordinary, so new,
so fresh, so wonderful in a way that it could never be again.

Even if Andreas' memory never returned, there was no
way they could repeat that exceptional, unique and magical
moment of finding each other again in a way that almost
matched—and totally outclassed—the time that she had lost

her virginity to Andreas, just a few weeks after they had met. That glorious time had gone for good and things could never be as great as that again.

And the cold, creeping sensation of fear that ate into her heart forced her to face the truth and to acknowledge the worry that things could only go downhill from here.

Downhill to where? How far could things go? How bad could it be?

Beside her, Andreas stirred, muttering faintly in his sleep, the sound drawing her head round sharply to look into his face just as he stretched lazily and opened his eyes, his black gaze looking straight into her clouded blue one.

And what she saw in those dark depths made Becca's blood run icy cold in her veins as she realised that things could very definitely get a whole lot worse.

And they just had.

CHAPTER NINE

ANDREAS had been dreaming.

Deep in sleep, he had been in a world that was so very different from the hot sunny day he had known when he was awake. A cooler, greyer world, but one where his most vivid impression was of green—lush green grass, rich and smooth as velvet, that sprang under his feet as he walked towards the huge marquee tent that was set up right in the middle of the vast lawn.

Inside the tent there was the buzz of conversation, the clatter of glasses and every now and then a ripple of laughter. And his eyes, the blurred eyes he had in his dream, were assailed by the sight of hundreds of people, all crowded together. To his unfocused sight, the men were just grey or black blurs, the women multicoloured, bright and silky, so brilliant they made his head ache.

He didn't know what he was doing here. Didn't feel that he belonged. He only knew that this was where he had to be— that they all seemed to be expecting him, because they turned when he came in, all those faceless people, turned and lifted their glasses in a toast, cheering and saying, 'Congratulations, Andreas! Congratulations!'

To Andreas' horror the words felt almost like physical

scrapes against his skin, ripping away some much-needed protective layer and leaving him raw and disturbingly sensitive. They added to his sense of being in the wrong place, at the wrong time, with the wrong people. There was no one there he could recognise, no one he could turn to, to start a conversation with or even risk giving a smile.

Not that he wanted to smile at anyone. His mood was quite the wrong one for this happy, cheery gathering too. He felt more like a wild, hungry, savage wolf that had prowled into a gathering of birds of paradise and was hunting for just the right one to pounce upon, to tear to shreds with the teeth that were clenched tight inside his aching jaw. He knew just which one he was looking for, and he stalked amongst the happy party, struggling to control the ferocious snarl that threatened to escape him at any moment. She was there somewhere—instinctively he knew that his prey was female—she was there, and when he found her...

Suddenly the room fell silent. The buzzing, chattering, brilliant birds of paradise stopped moving, stopped talking, became totally still. And over at the far side of the marquee he could see her. Tall and slender—and totally in white... plain, simple, unadorned white from head to toe, in stark contrast to the colours all around him. When he saw her his tense jaw fell open for a moment as he snatched in a breath, then his teeth came together with a snap as he turned, headed straight for her. The crowd parted to let him through, a wide, clear path was opening up, taking him straight to her.

He couldn't see her face, not even the blur of pink that was everyone else. She was *white*. Nothing but white. Did she even have a face?

And then, as he came nearer, nearer, suddenly he could hear a single voice, a young, female voice, loud and clear and bubbling with contained laughter, barely held back.

'I do—I do—I do!'

'I do—I do—I do…'

The words repeated over and over in his head until his thoughts swam with the force of it.

'I do—I do—I do…'

And behind him the crowd murmured and laughed and broke into spontaneous applause. Applause that swung around and over the words, breaking into them but never quite drowning them out.

'I do—I do—I do…'

His head was aching from it, the pressure at his temples unendurable. He wanted to lift his hands and rub at them to ease the pressure but he found he couldn't do so. Something had them trapped, tying them down, keeping them from moving. He heard another voice groan aloud and realised with a violent shock to his system that it was his, and that the words he had been trying to form were the same as those in the laughing voice inside his head.

I do.

I *do*!

Rough and unclear, they were enough to make the white-clad figure before him turn sharply. Blinking hard, he found that his gaze would focus more, his vision sharpening just a little. She was wearing a veil, he realised. A long white, flowing veil that hid her face, concealing it completely. But when she saw him she smiled. He couldn't see the smile but he knew it was there. He could sense it with some primitive instinct that came to him with the dream. He knew that she smiled in the same way that he knew he didn't like the smile one little bit.

'Andreas…' she said and her voice was low, huskily se-ductive.

And then she threw back her veil and all he could see were her eyes—her amazing, pale blue eyes—sea-coloured eyes...

And in his head all that he could hear was that laughter filled voice saying yet again, 'Oh, I do—I do—I do...'

Becca!

The step he took backwards in his dream, the jolt it gave him, brought him awake in rush. Awake to a realisation that the deep green lawn, the marquee, the guests, were all a fantasy. Reality was that he was in his bed, in the villa, that the growing darkness of dusk was gathering round...

And that he was not alone.

He smelled her skin before he opened his eyes, inhaled the warm, intensely personal fragrance of her body, heard the soft sound of her breathing, and knew that some woman shared his bed. The scent of passion, too, was on the sheets, a wild intensity of sex, the after-effects of which still lingered in the heaviness of his limbs, the feeling of deep fulfilment, the strong reluctance to move at all. But at the same time something was nagging at his thoughts, taking him back into his dream for a moment and then out again, back into the present. Something that warned him he had to wake up, had to think, had to act.

With an effort he forced his heavy eyelids open and found himself looking straight into those same beautiful sea coloured eyes. The eyes of the woman in his dream. Eyes that were watching him with a look of wary apprehension in their smoky depths.

And the taste of betrayal was terrible and sour in his mouth.

'*Rebecca!*'

No one said her name quite like Andreas, Becca reflected privately. No one else put quite that exotic intonation onto the syllables, making it sound like a totally different word. And no one else had ever put such an icy tone into his use of her name, a freezing fury that made her feel as if she had suddenly stepped onto the most dangerous black ice.

'My darling wife—what the hell are you doing here?'

'I—should have thought that that was obvious.'

She regretted the words the minute she had spoken them. Regretted the stupid attempt at flippancy in her tone, the even rasher gesture of her hand that indicated the rumpled bed on which they lay, the disorder of the sheets, the crumpled pillows. It also, to her deep mortification, drew attention to her naked state, brought those frozen black eyes to skim over her body, seeming to sear the delicate skin as they went so that hot colour flooded her cheeks and in a moment of pure embarrassment she reached desperately for the nearest sheet.

'I think it's a little late for that now,' Andreas drawled in cynical contempt. 'Now that I remember my past, I have no recollection of immediate events...so....'

His eyes narrowed, his tone darkening.

'Are you going to tell me just what happened here?'

'You know what happened!'

He did—didn't he? Andreas had recognised her; he had called her his wife with that appallingly savage note in his voice. Somehow, something that had happened had jarred loose whatever had been blocking his memory and while he was asleep the scattered jigsaw pieces had been falling into place. But how complete was it? Did he remember *everything*?

And what picture did the completed jigsaw show?

'We—we made...'

'We had sex,' Andreas interrupted harshly as she stumbled over the words, unable to say 'made love' when confronted by his darkly scowling face, the contempt that blazed in the jet-black eyes. 'That much is obvious. What I mean is just what are you doing here in the first place? I told you to get out and stay out.'

'I know you did—but I—couldn't.'

'And why not? Don't tell me that you've come back to say you're sorry—that—'

'Of course not!'

Becca's total rejection of his challenge rang in her voice. How could he think that *she* had anything to apologise for? Andreas was the one who had declared to her face that he had only married her for sex.

'I thought not.'

Andreas flung himself off the bed and stalked across the room to where the black swimming shorts he had discarded with such eagerness—and her willing help—such a short time before lay in a crumpled heap on the floor. Snatching them up, he pulled them on, every rough, brusque movement speaking of hostility and aggression without a word needing to be spoken.

'Much as I love the image of you curled up in my bed with only a sheet to cover you, I think I would prefer it if you put some clothes on,' he flung into Becca's ashen face. 'I'd like to have this conversation without any unnecessary—distractions.'

'I can't.'

Becca couldn't allow her thoughts to dwell on the idea that the sight of her naked body could still 'distract' Andreas. It wasn't the effect she wanted to have on him. Or was it? Her body still sang from the sensual effect of his lovemaking—his attentions, she amended painfully. Her blood was still hot, her skin prickling with sensitivity so that just the feel of the finest cotton of the sheets against it was almost too much to bear. Her body ached in places, there were tiny bruised spots in others, but they were aches and bruises she didn't mind at all.

Her nipples were still tender, and the intimate spots between her legs still pulsed faintly with the aftershocks of passion. The thought of having to pull on the close-fitting Lycra swimsuit was frankly unbearable.

'The only thing I have to wear in here is that…'

An unwary wave of her arm towards where the lavender swimming costume lay in a similar state to his shorts let the sheet slip and she snatched it up again, clutching it to her as if it was a shield against those black, accusing eyes. She saw Andreas' mouth twitch in an almost-smile of the darkest humour, and shivered when she realised how bleak and stony his eyes remained, no light in them at all.

'In that case I prefer the sheet.'

No, he didn't, Andreas told himself reprovingly. The sheet was almost as bad as nothing at all. The fine cotton lay lightly over the slender lines of her body, clinging to the curves of her hips, the rise and fall of her breasts, defining them in a way that made his throat dry. And even beneath the white material, the faint dark shadow between her thighs was visible, reminding him of the way those curls had felt against the most intimate, most sensual parts of his body. Just recalling it made the roar of blood thunder in his head so that he could barely think straight.

OK, admit it, he told himself, you don't want to think at all. What he wanted was to throw himself down on the bed beside her, rip the sheet from her body and start to make love to her all over again. The taste of her lips, of her breasts was still in his mouth, her scent was on his skin, blending with his own into the most intoxicating perfume he had ever inhaled. It went straight to his head like the most potent *ouzo*, clouding it and making it spin.

When combined with the heat of pounding lust, it was a

brutally lethal combination, making him feel as if his head was a volcano where red-hot lava was just pushing to the top, waiting to explode.

No. He needed to keep a grip on himself, on his temper. He had to think clearly. His body, his senses, might be thrilled to see Becca again but common sense warned him to tread very carefully. If she was back then it was for her own purposes, and he wanted to know just what they were before he made a foolish move.

Another foolish move. She'd already got under his guard once, while his brain was scrambled from the accident. He wasn't going to let that happen again.

But just the sight of her made him so damn sexually hungry. After living for almost a year without her, he might have thought that he had forgotten the impact she had on his senses. But it seemed that she had only to walk back into his life and he was a slave to his libido like some horny adolescent in the throes of his first physical affair.

He might have thought that he'd have forgotten... *Hah*!

A harshly cynical laugh broke from him as he realised the bitter irony of what he had just thought. He'd spent the last months trying to force himself to forget that someone called Becca Ainsworth—Becca Petrakos legally, but very definitely not morally—had ever existed.

And failed miserably.

'Andreas?'

Becca was watching him—nervously, he could almost swear. He had never realised that she was such a good actress. But sitting there like that, with the sheet twisted tightly round her, those beautiful blue eyes wide in a damnably perfect face, she looked the picture of innocence. So innocent that he could almost believe in her himself.

This was the Becca he'd tried to push from his mind. But then the accident had done that for him by wiping her from his memory, and in the time that he had been out of it she had walked back in, cool as could be. And lied through her teeth to him.

And he had been fool enough to let his lust for her drown out all thought of common sense. One tug on the golden chain of sensuality that tied them both together and he had fallen straight into bed with her. Right where she wanted him, it seemed.

But why? What did she want from him? Not just sex, that was obvious. She had to have something else up her sleeve.

So what had happened between her and her precious Roy Stanton? Because something must have done to bring her here, like this, when she had vowed that she would rather die than come back.

'On second thoughts...'

He turned towards the door, where his black towelling robe hung. Grabbing it, he tossed it roughly in Becca's direction, not caring that it overshot by several metres and landed on the floor on the other side of the bed.

'Put that on. I've had enough of the sight of you.'

Liar, his conscience reproached him. Hadn't today—the past couple of days—taught him anything? He could never get enough of the sight of her, the feel of her, the taste of her. He doubted if he ever would. The truth was that passion made him a fool where Becca was concerned and that was a feeling he didn't like one little bit.

'And then we talk. You can start explaining just what the hell you are up to.'

'I'm not "up to" anything!' Becca protested, struggling to get off the bed and reach the black robe, while at the same time keeping the sheet securely wrapped around her.

'No?'

'No!'

'It seems that way to me. You surely don't expect me to believe that you turned up here out of love for me—to beg me to take you back? No—I thought not,' he added when he saw the way her face changed, her lips pinching tight together. 'So you've obviously come for something, and I want to know what.'

And when he did know he would take a great delight in throwing his rejection of her request right back in her face, Becca told herself as she tried once more to grab the black robe. She'd really messed up this time. What had possessed her to fall into bed with him like that, forgetting all about the reasons why she was here? She should have known that there was a chance that something like passionate lovemaking— passionate *sex,* she amended painfully—together with the fact that she'd been wearing the lavender costume that had practically been the last thing he'd seen her in, would be likely to stir his memories, if not actually bring them right back. She would never be able to forgive herself if she threw away Daisy's chance of the life-saving operation because of her own foolish passion.

She had the robe in her hand now, but when it came to pulling it on, while still holding on to the sheet that was wrapped round her, she found the situation was impossible. And it was made all the worse by the fact that Andreas stood dark and devastating, on the far side of the room, watching her through cynically amused black eyes.

'You might have the courtesy to look away,' she flung at him in indignation, knowing that the struggle she was having was making her face look pink and flustered.

'Why?' he shot back, leaning against the wall and folding his arms across his chest as he met her furious glare with icy calm. 'Did you do that for me? Did you look away when I got out of bed—or before that? Did you insist on covering your own eyes then?'

'That's different.'

'Is it? Then will you please tell me how? I'd like to know why it's fine for you to ogle me when I'm naked but not for me—'

'I did not *ogle*!' she flashed furiously.

'Seemed that way to me. I could almost feel your hot little eyes on me all the way across the room. But then I am not so much of a hypocrite as to pretend to a rush of false modesty so soon after I have been—what is it you say?—rolling around in the sack just a short time before.'

'It's not a pretence! I—I don't feel right that way. Not any more.'

'Not any more,' Andreas echoed darkly and the cynicism of his tone made her tense instinctively, waiting for the brutal lash of his tongue in quick response.

To her surprise it didn't come. Instead, Andreas' face closed up, setting hard and cold until it looked as if his features were carved from granite, his eyes just polished jet.

'My apologies,' he declared in a tone that made a mockery of the polite words. 'In that case, I will wait for you downstairs. I think we would both feel more capable of holding this discussion on more neutral territory. I'll make us some coffee—you'll be...what? Five minutes?'

That 'five minutes' was an order, not a suggestion, and, leaving Becca still fighting to find a way to respond that didn't make her look petty or weak, he turned on his heel and walked out.

She could almost hear the steady ticking of some imaginary stopwatch as she listened to his footsteps going down the landing.

CHAPTER TEN

SHE made it downstairs in seven minutes.

She had been determined not to let Andreas think that he could just click his fingers and she would jump to do as he said. But all the same, stirring it too much by keeping him waiting deliberately was not a clever idea. His temper would only darken by the minute and, as he had already started out with it almost as black as it could be, she didn't want to take unnecessary risks.

First she had had to go to her own room to find her clothes and snatch a quick shower. The extra seconds had ticked away while she had dithered over what to wear.

Just what did one wear to a sort of emotional trial? she wondered on a wave of near-hysteria. A trial in which Andreas was not only judge and jury but also very definitely counsel for the prosecution all at once. The lightweight sun-dress that was her first choice was discarded as being too revealing and frivolous. A white T-shirt and Indian print skirt went the same way when the button on the waistband of the skirt proved suddenly to be somehow too complicated for her unsteady fingers to fasten easily.

In the end she had kept the T-shirt and pulled on denim

jeans to go with it before deciding that enough was enough—
she'd made her point without risking him actually losing it
completely—and hurrying down the stairs after him.

Andreas was in the big sitting room that opened onto the
pool area. The first thing that Becca noticed about him was
that he too had taken a moment to dress and was now wearing
a short-sleeved black shirt, hanging open over his tanned
chest, and loose black linen trousers that hung low on his
narrow hips. Like her, he was barefooted, as he so often was
around the house.

He had opened the patio doors and was standing gazing out
at the glorious view of the ocean, but Becca had the distinct
impression that he didn't see anything but was intent on his
own thoughts. He had a mug of the strong black coffee he in-
variably drank in one hand, and another mug containing a less
potent version of the drink stood on the coffee-table behind
him. He didn't turn when Becca arrived, or make any sign of
having noticed that she was there, but continued to stare,
frowning, at the horizon until, after waiting a few moments
to see what he would do, she cleared her throat pointedly.

'You wanted to talk to me.'

His turn was slow, deliberately so, she felt and when he was
facing her he let those deep-set black eyes run over her from
the top of her head, still wet from her shower, down to her feet,
and back up again.

'*Déjà vu*,' he murmured on a note of irony. 'Haven't we
been here before?'

It was only then that Becca realised that they were in fact
both dressed as if for a replay of the dreadful scene on the
evening of their wedding day. The scene that had ended their
marriage. The recollection was enough to drain some of the
hard-won strength from her legs and make her think twice

about picking up the mug of coffee for fear that her hand would shake so badly it would give away the way her nerves were tying themselves into tight, uncomfortable knots in her stomach. Instead she perched on the arm of one of the big leather-covered settees, hoping she looked moderately at ease.

'So what are we going to talk about?'

Andreas took a sip from his coffee, stared down into the mug as if looking for inspiration in the dark liquid. The movement made Becca realise that, like her, he had snatched the time to have a fast shower before coming downstairs, his hair was still soaking too. But, unlike hers, the wet look flattered him, giving the blue-black strands a glistening sheen and a slightly spiky look that suited him, while her own heavily flattened, sodden rats' tails had quite the opposite effect.

'Why don't we start with you telling me just what was so important to you that you were prepared to sell yourself to get it?'

Becca was glad that she was sitting down. She felt sure that her legs would have gone from under her if she hadn't, with the cutting force of his attack. But even though she was sitting, she still clung onto the back of the settee for extra support.

'I didn't—I wasn't—I *didn't*!'

'Oh, so what are you claiming—that you didn't have sex with me just now, in that bed...?'

An arrogant tilt of his dark head in the direction of the ceiling and so the bedroom above them emphasised his point.

'I—you know I did.'

Did he have to keep saying 'have sex' in that brutal way? It reminded her too painfully of his cold-blooded declaration that he had married her for sex and nothing more.

'So you must have wanted to use that sex to get something from me.'

'No! No way! I never—I wouldn't...'

'Wouldn't you? Well, you do surprise me. So that leaves only one other possible alternative, and I have to say that I really never thought that you'd admit to that.'

'I'm not admitting to anything,' Becca growled. 'And what is the only other possible alternative?'

Andreas flashed her a wide, deceptively innocent look from huge, brilliant jet-black eyes.

'Why, the fact that you were so overcome with need—with passion for me—that you just couldn't help yourself. That nothing else in the world mattered but that we should come together in bed...'

'It wasn't that!'

'No? Then—to go back to my original interpretation of your actions—you *were* using sex to get something from me.'

'I wasn't—no! I didn't!'

'Oh, please, Rebecca!' Andreas exclaimed in exasperation. Coming to the table, he slammed his mug down on it with such force that some of the coffee slopped over the side.

'Credit me with a little intelligence. It's either one thing or the other. What other possible explanation could there be?'

The fact that she was head over heels in love with him, crazy about him in a way that made her a fool to herself, weakened all her defences and left her totally vulnerable where he was concerned. That she hadn't been able to say no to the thought of being with him just one last time.

'A mad moment?' she said flippantly, trying desperately to distract him from the way that he was thinking. 'After all, we were always good—great together that way. You said it yourself—no one ever made you as hot as I do.'

The way his black brows drew together in a dark frown alerted her to the fact that she'd said something he didn't like. And she winced inwardly as she realised just what it was.

He'd flung those exact words at her in the appalling row on the day of their marriage, destroying all her hopes and dreams in one blow.

I married you for sex—for that and nothing else. No other woman has ever made me feel as hot as you do.

'A mad moment, hmm…'

He had come too close. If she was not careful, then surely he would see the truth in her face, read it at the backs of her eyes.

'Mad, certainly, but not totally crazy.'

Andreas flung himself down into the chair opposite and sprawled back against the cushions, long legs stretched out in front of him, crossed at the ankles, elbows resting on the chair arms, long fingers steepled together under his chin.

'Which is what you'd have to be to have come here just for that.'

His brilliant black gaze seemed to sear into her skull, trying to pull out the truth whether she was prepared to give it to him or not.

'My, you do think a lot of yourself, don't you?' Becca used defiance to try to hide the way she was really feeling. 'Do you really think that I'd travel all this way just for a quick tumble into bed with you?'

'No.'

Andreas' wickedly slow smile told her how easily she had fallen into the trap he had dug right at her feet.

'I really do not think that—which is why I keep asking the question that you seem to want to go to any lengths possible to avoid. You're not drinking your coffee,' he added in a way that sounded like an afterthought but which left Becca very much afraid that he knew exactly *why* she wasn't drinking.

'I don't fancy it.'

'The coffee or telling me why you're here?'

'Either, if you must know!'

She really had to stop trying to be flippant. It was getting her nowhere and was obviously starting to rile him. The way that he compressed his lips into a thin, hard line told her that he was fighting to hold back the sort of acid retort that would be capable of flaying half the skin from her ears just to hear it.

'So what is it you have to hide?'

'Nothing—it's just…'

'Rebecca!' Andreas' tone was low, almost soft, but it was the softness of the hiss of a hooded python, just before it struck with deadly force, and it made Becca flinch inwardly simply to hear it. 'Tell me…tell me now why you are here or pack your bags and get out of my life—and this time make it for good.'

If she did that then she would never be able to help Daisy— and she would never be able to see him ever again. Right now, Becca couldn't begin to think which of those two possibilities hurt most. But then the truth was that when her heart was one mass of pain, how could she tell if any one particular spot was worse than any other?

'Can't you guess?' she muttered, low and uneven.

'I want you to tell me,' Andreas returned, face rigid, expression unyielding.

'Isn't it obvious?' she no longer cared if she sounded desperate; it was how she felt. 'You always said I'd come back for money and—well, here I am.'

'You came for money?' He actually sounded—what? He couldn't be disappointed but that was the note that was in his voice.

'Don't sound so surprised, Andreas—you always knew this would happen! You should have made that bet you wanted—the one where you said that I'd come looking for

cash before the year was up. Because you'd have been right.
Here I am and it's money I'm after.'

It was the only way she could get it out. She couldn't go
on her knees and beg. And for some reason she couldn't bring
herself to talk about Daisy—not yet. She didn't feel strong
enough, brave enough, to open herself up to him like that. Not
after all that had happened and the brutal damage he had in-
flicted on her heart. So she'd gone on to the attack, wanting
to lash out, repay hurt with hurt.

'Money for what?'

'Does it matter?'

'To me it does.'

'But you've been proved right. That should give you
immense satisfaction. I've shown myself to be the greedy—'

'It gives me no satisfaction,' Andreas cut in, cold and flat.
'No satisfaction at all. If you want the truth I would rather you
had stayed away for ever than that you turned up here like
this—for this.'

How the hell could anyone think it would give him satisfaction to be proved right like this? He had once loved this
woman, once wanted her to be in his life for ever—and she
had betrayed him even before the vows had been spoken.

Wasn't that what his dream had been about? About the way
that he had had warning of what she was really like and yet
had gone ahead with their wedding all the same. He had
wanted to believe in her, to trust her, to put his faith in the one
woman he had ever loved with all his heart. And so because
he had loved her he had married her, convinced that the
terrible things he had heard about her were lies.

And found out that they were the truth.

Did she think that he really would enjoy going through that
hell all over again?

'So tell me—what is it for? Have you gambled yourself into ruin? Spent a fortune you don't possess? Developed an appalling cocaine habit?'

'I would never do that!' Becca protested, looking horrified that he would even consider it. 'No, none of those.'

At least that was some sort of a relief. But it still left the other, less endurable reason why she might want the money.

'Then why do you want the money so badly? Who do you want it for?'

'Who?'

Becca's head came up and she stared into his face with obvious confusion clouding her eyes.

'Who would I—?'

'Let me make it plain so you have no chance of misunderstanding: tell me that this money is not for him—not for Roy Stanton.'

'Roy...no—no, it's not!'

It was almost convincing but he had seen the way that her eyes had dropped, just for a split-second, her sea-coloured gaze sliding away as she gathered herself, thought hastily and then nerved herself to face him again.

'It's not for him.'

Andreas couldn't sit there any longer looking into her beautiful face, into those wide, brilliant eyes, and know she wasn't telling the truth. He couldn't stand to watch those soft, full lips frame the lies that made his disgust a fury of rage inside his head.

He didn't want to remember the number of times he had kissed those lips, all unknowing of the lies that had come to them so easily. He didn't want to be tempted by the fact that all he had to do was lean forward, take that sexy body into his arms, press his mouth to hers, and in the fiery explosion of sensuality that was sure to follow they would both forget about the reasons why she was here, the past and all that had come between them.

If only he hadn't taken her to bed this afternoon so that the memory of the passion that could flare between them at a touch was now so fresh in his mind. He only had to look at her and his body ached with need; he was hot and hard just thinking of her. His hands yearned to touch, his lips to kiss, every one of his senses clamoured for appeasement of its hunger. He had tried telling himself that she was not as gorgeous as he remembered, but taking her again after so long had only made him realise how wrong he had been. Once had not been enough—it could never be enough. All it had done was to serve to make him realise how much he wanted her again and again, more than ever before.

The satisfaction he had known in her bed this afternoon had totally evaporated already. It had only been enough to show him that he could never, ever sate himself on this woman, if he was to spend a lifetime trying.

'Tell the truth, damn you!' The hungry demands of his body made his words harsher and rougher than before.

Flinging himself to his feet, he made himself move across the room, putting as much distance between himself and Becca as possible, pushing his hands deep into the pockets of his trousers to conceal the way they had clenched into tight, angry fists.

'Don't lie to me, Rebecca! Never lie to me—not if you want to have any hope of getting what you want.'

'I'm not lying.'

'You are if you tell me that Stanton has nothing to do with this.'

That got through to her. Her face went white, all colour deserting her cheeks, and her mouth fell open in shock. So he'd been right in his suspicions. It didn't make him feel any better to know it. Instead, he felt sick with contempt.

'I'll ask you again—does Stanton have anything to do with the reason why you want this money?'

How did she answer that? Becca thought miserably. Because she knew that just mentioning the name Roy Stanton was like setting a match to paper-dry tinder where Andreas was concerned, and she'd tried to dodge the truth once—not actually lying but avoiding answering with strict veracity as far as she could. Now that he'd changed the question, there was no hope she could do that again.

'Don't bother to say anything, Rebecca.'

She'd hesitated too long and Andreas had jumped to the inevitable conclusion.

'I can see your answer in your face.'

She would have sworn that it was impossible for Andreas' face to close up any tighter, his eyes to get any colder, or his expression any more distant, but somehow he had managed it.

'I think you've had a wasted journey, Rebecca. You should have stayed at home and spared yourself the effort of coming all this way for nothing. You might have thought that deceiving me into believing that you had come to look after me so that you could worm your way into my bed would enslave me sexually again so that I could deny you nothing—'

'It wasn't like that!' Becca protested sharply, but Andreas continued without pausing, speaking over her as if she had never tried to say a thing.

'Unfortunately for you, I got my memory back before you could really work on me, but I think you should know that you were foolish even to try. I don't put my head into that sort of noose twice.'

'I didn't...' Becca tried, but Andreas shook his head, his refusal to listen stamped into every line on his face.

'If you're wise, you'll leave it there, Rebecca. You will only make things so much worse if you continue.'

Pulling his hands out of his pockets, where they had been pushed deep all this time, he raked both of them through the black silk of his hair, ruffling it wildly, and Becca bit down hard on her lower lip as a sudden yearning desire to go and smooth it down for him caught her painfully on the raw.

Then he was speaking again, heading for the open patio doors as he did so.

'I threw you out of my life once because of him, and I'm quite prepared to do it all over again. In fact, I would prefer it if you left now. I'm going for a walk on the beach—and I don't want to find you here when I get back.'

'Andreas...' Becca tried but she was talking to his back. He was moving so fast, with such ruthless determination, that he was already outside, already heading away from her physically when he had been so distant from her mentally all the time.

She couldn't let him go. Not like this. If she did then any hope of saving baby Daisy were gone for good, and she would rather die than let that happen. She had to try and get him to reconsider.

'Andreas—please...'

But he continued walking, not even glancing round at her. His long, straight back was held so stiffly upright, his proud head so high, that she could almost see her words bouncing off the invisible walls of defence that he had built around himself.

'Andreas—don't...'

She stepped out after him into the heat of the sunny afternoon.

'The money's not for me—or for—for him...'

She didn't dare to actually speak Roy Stanton's name, knowing the incendiary effect it had on Andreas.

'It's for a child—a baby...'

He'd stopped at least. But she still had to get him to turn round. Right now he could still walk on—away from her.

'Please listen.'

He was turning. Slowly—but he was turning to face her. Her heart leapt with relief, leaving her breathless and shaky.

'A baby?'

He managed to inject the words with such scepticism, such disbelief that she fully expected him to fling a rejection in her face and move on. She had his attention for now; she had to hold on to it and make him understand.

'A little girl—Daisy—she's desperately sick and—'

'*Whose* baby?'

It slashed through her words as she struggled to get them out. And at the same time those blazing black eyes seared over her from top to toe, taking in her slender figure, lingering on her waist...

'No, not mine,' she hastened to assure him. 'Daisy's not my baby—though I love her as if she were. She—she's my niece. And I would do anything I could to help her.'

'Niece?' Andreas echoed as if he did not understand the word. '*Anepsia*? You do not have a niece.'

'Yes, I do—she's my sister's little girl. And before you say that I don't have a sister,' Becca rushed on when he opened his mouth, clearly planning to do just that, 'let me tell you that I do. A half-sister, that is. But I didn't know about her for years. I only found out about her—quite recently.'

She paused, waiting for Andreas to ask the next question, but he remained silent, hands on narrow hips, black eyes fixed on her face, obviously waiting for her to go on.

'You know that I'm adopted. That I was born when my biological mother was only sixteen? And my mum and dad adopted me as a tiny baby. I told you...' she prompted, needing some response from him before she could go on. She couldn't just pour the whole story out while he stood there, silent and withdrawn, as distant from her as if some huge cavern had opened up on the stone-flagged terrace, separating them from each other.

A faint, brief inclination of his dark head was all the acknowledgement Andreas made and then he was still again, obviously waiting for her to continue.

'I've been trying to find my birth mother—to see if I had any family. Blood family. I thought it was important to know.'

She couldn't tell him that this search had taken on a whole new meaning and importance from the moment that Andreas had asked her to marry him. That she had really felt the need to know about her family then, to know if she had some blood ties, someone who was linked to her that way. And deep down there had also been a secret, private need to know if there were any health problems she needed to take into consideration if she and Andreas were ever to have children. That was one concern that no longer mattered at all, she told herself miserably.

'I found that my mother was dead—and she'd never known who my father was. But I had a half-sister—Macy. I managed to get in touch with her—meet her.'

'And when was this?'

Becca bit her lip in discomfort. She'd known this question would come, but being prepared for it didn't make it easy to answer.

'Just before our wedding.'

'I see.'

Andreas took a step backwards, and the arms that had been at his sides were now crossed over his broad chest. He couldn't have put a distance between them more effectively if he'd tried.

'And you didn't think to tell me?'

'I—couldn't. Macy had—some problems and she made me promise not to tell anyone.'

Once, perhaps, she might have explained all this in detail to him. Once he would have been owed the full story. But Macy had been so insistent that no one should know. If she'd breathed a word, she would have lost the sister she'd just found. Macy had only just discovered about Daisy then. And the realisation that there was a baby on the way had made everything so much more urgent; made it so much more important that she stay in touch with her half-sister, and with the baby who was to become her darling niece.

And then Andreas had forfeited the right to know anything more about her when he had declared that he had never loved her and their marriage was only for sex before throwing her out of the house.

'I would have told my husband as soon as I could—but then you weren't my husband long enough for that to matter at all.'

Andreas actually flinched as the barb she flung at him went home, and just for a moment some emotion that she didn't understand flashed across his face. It was there and gone again before she had time to even try to interpret it and the stone-wall look was fully back in place again.

'So Macy is the mother of this Daisy?'

'Yes. And Daisy's just eleven weeks old—'

'And who is the father?'

The words seemed unnaturally loud in the silence of the sunny garden. The inevitable question. The obvious question. And one she would dodge if she could. She desperately wished that she could.

'Does it matter?' she hedged nervously, knowing as soon as she heard it that her voice gave her away, the way it broke in the middle, making it obvious that she had something to hide.

'The look on your face tells me that it does,' Andreas told her harshly, his tone as cold as ice. 'So tell me—who is the father of this baby?'

Becca's jaw seemed to have frozen stiff so that it was impossible to open her mouth to answer him, even if she had wanted to. And she didn't want to. Every time she tried to force herself to speak, she looked into Andreas' dark, shuttered face and a terrible sense of dread overwhelmed her. Bitter tears stung at the backs of her eyes and she blinked hard, trying to force them back. But she knew why they were there. Fear had put them there. Fear of what would happen as soon as she spoke.

She feared it for poor baby Daisy, who needed this man to help her so much—and yet who would probably be condemned not for anything she had done but for the simple biological fact of who her father was.

And she feared it for herself because she dreaded how she was going to feel if Andreas did reject her and walk away in a black, unforgiving fury as soon as she spoke the name that enraged him so much.

And she knew that he wouldn't let go of this until he knew.

'Becca...' Andreas' use of her name was a warning, but it was the fact that he had once more reverted to the shorter, more affectionate form of it that finished her completely. The tears she had struggled against wouldn't be held back any longer but flooded her eyes and a single one spilled out and ran slowly down her cheek.

'Don't ask me...' she whispered, and to her astonishment Andreas accepted her plea and didn't push her any more. But only because he didn't need to. Her response, the distress she couldn't hide, had given him her answer.

'Roy Stanton,' he declared, hard and flat. 'The baby's father is Roy Stanton.'

It was a statement, not a question, but still Becca had to give him an answer, though all she could do was nod silently, the ability to speak having deserted her completely.

'Roy Stanton,' Andreas repeated, the other man's name almost like a curse on his lips.

She couldn't read his expression through the blur of tears but she didn't have to. All she needed to know about his reaction was there in his voice, in the way he spat out the words.

And then it was as she had always dreaded it would be when, without another word, Andreas turned on his heel and walked away from her, striding fast and determinedly over the terrace and down the roughly carved steps that led from the cliff to the shore. Rejection and hostility were stamped into every line of his powerful body and she knew that if she tried to call him back he would refuse to even show that he had heard.

And besides, she couldn't find the strength to do so. She didn't know what she could say to change his mind, and even if she'd been able to think of anything her voice wouldn't work. So all she could do was stand and watch through tear-drenched eyes, staring after him until he disappeared from view.

CHAPTER ELEVEN

Down in the bay, a lively breeze was whipping up the sea into unruly waves. The water whirled and swayed, rising up into foam-topped peaks and then hurling itself against the shore in a swirling rush before ebbing back out again fast, in a way that had it sucking at the sand, drawing it back with it.

The atmosphere suited Andreas' mood perfectly. The restless movement all about him was in keeping with his own frame of mind, the way that he couldn't make his thoughts settle into any balanced pattern. Instead they swung from burning rage to icy cold and back again in every second that passed.

Roy Stanton.

He kicked viciously at the sand as the name burned in his mind, making him clench his teeth hard against the feeling.

Roy Stanton.

Almost a year before he had hoped that he had heard the last of that name. That the man who had ruined his life, and taken away the one thing of value he truly loved, was out of his life for ever.

Roy Stanton and Becca between them had destroyed his happiness, and when he had thrown her out of the villa on the evening of their travesty of a wedding day he had hoped—

prayed—that he would never, ever see or hear of either of them again.

And then she had turned up, needing money.

Money for a sick child.

Money for Roy Stanton's sick child.

Standing staring at the sea was doing nothing to ease the restless rage of his thoughts and Andreas set off along the edge of the shore, striding fast, splashing through the water, heedless of the way that the waves broke against his legs, soaking the fine linen of his trousers. He needed the movement to express his feelings, to ease the fury in his mind so that he could think.

There was one thing that stood out clearly. The baby was innocent in all this. How could he not help a sick child? That was not in question. But Roy Stanton…!

Obviously the selfish bastard had moved on from Becca to another woman—*Theos,* he'd moved to her *sister* and had a child by her! And Becca had wept at the thought of it.

Oh, she'd fought with everything that was in her not to show those tears, but he'd seen them sheening her pale eyes, swimming under her lids as she fought to blink them back. Stanton had taken her from him, he'd made her break her wedding vows before she had even spoken the words out loud in the ceremony, and then he had broken her heart by moving on to someone else and fathering a child on her.

And Becca had still come here to plead for help for that baby. Her sister's baby. Her sister's child with her own former lover. His stomach heaved at the thought.

Inevitably, his mind went back to the time just before the wedding. The last time that he had been truly happy. When his future had been like a glorious sun rising out there on the horizon. He was going to be married to the woman he adored.

She was his life and she loved him back—or so he had believed. Another few days, less than a week, and they would be together forever.

And then the phone calls had started.

Foul, sneaking phone calls that spoke of secrets and lies. The voice at the other end of the line had told him that Becca—his fiancée—wasn't the woman he believed her to be. That she didn't love him at all but was only using him; marrying him to get as much money from him as she could. Money that she was then going to share with her real lover…

And for a fee—a substantial fee—he would reveal the name of that lover. For now he would just give the initials. And those initials were RS.

Coming to a halt in his furious march over the sand, Andreas stared out at the horizon with unseeing eyes, shoulders hunched, hands pushed deep into his pockets.

He'd laughed. He'd actually laughed. The story was impossible to believe. He had trusted Becca. There was no way she was deceiving him. He'd slammed the phone down on the call; put it out of his mind.

Until the letter had arrived with a photocopy of a cheque. A cheque for the full amount of the money he had recently given Becca to help her pay for everything she needed for the wedding—right down to the last penny. And the cheque in the copy had been written in his fiancée's handwriting—and made out to one Roy Stanton.

That was when he'd called in an investigator. He'd wanted to get to the bottom of this, find out the truth.

There had been nothing to find, the man he'd hired had assured him. He'd turned up no evidence to link Rebecca Ainsworth to Roy Stanton. The phone calls had been traced to the same Roy Stanton, who was obviously at the back of all this.

Whatever Becca had paid him the money for, he'd obviously wanted more. But Andreas didn't give a damn about the money. He had plenty of that. It was only if the claims that Stanton was Becca's lover were true that he would have acted.

And so he'd put the matter out of his mind and gone through with the wedding. He wouldn't have been human if a doubt, a worry, hadn't flashed across his mind just once— but he pushed them away. One look at his bride's face had been enough to convince him that she was honest, innocent and as much in love with him as he was with her.

It was there in the way that she'd smiled at him, the way she'd looked deep into his eyes when she said her vows. And it had been there in the way that, in reply to the usual question 'Do you take this man…?' she had been unable to hold back in her reply, answering not just with the simple 'I do', but saying:

'Oh, I do—I do—I do…'

At least that was what he had thought. It was what he had wanted to believe too.

He had married the woman he adored; brought her here to his home on this tiny island that his family had owned for centuries, thinking that he could put it all behind him. He'd hardly been able to keep his hands off his beautiful bride, and had made passionate love to her just as soon as they had reached the house. Their marriage couldn't have begun in a more perfect way, he had told himself.

And then the photographs had arrived. The faxes had been waiting for him when he walked into his office. Sent by the investigator he had put on the case. Photos he couldn't deny, no matter how much he wanted to.

Stooping, Andreas picked up a flat stone and flung it into the sea, watching as it skipped its way over several waves, and then sank deep into the water, disappearing without a trace.

Becca hadn't been able to deny anything either, when he'd challenged her with Roy Stanton's name. She'd gone white, and he had seen the near-panic in her eyes. She'd never expected to be found out, that much was obvious. Had she really thought that she could hide her affair with the other man while being married to him?

Had she really thought that the money she could hope to give her lover would keep him by her side?

Because obviously, when she had returned home, her tail between her legs, without the huge financial settlement they must have been expecting, Roy Stanton had grown tired of her and his eye had started wandering. Or perhaps he had wandered even before then, and Becca had been duped all along.

Did she really care for him so much that she would come here, plead for money for his child? Or was the child now her uppermost concern? And if that was why she was here then why—*why*—had she gone to bed with him today?

Just remembering the experience of that afternoon, the passion that had blazed between them, made Andreas' blood pound in his veins, setting his whole body throbbing in recollection. He would pay any price to have that experience all over again.

Any price…

Daisy's not my baby—though I love her as if she were. She— she's my niece. And I would do anything I could to help her.

In the back of his thoughts he heard Becca speaking as clearly as if she had been standing behind him, whispering in his ear.

I would do anything I could to help her.

All right, let's see if she meant that…

Becca hadn't been able to move from her place on the terrace since Andreas had left her there. She had seemed to be frozen there, her legs unable to move, as she watched him walk away and out of her sight. And then she had sunk down onto one of the low stone walls that edged the terrace, shielding anyone on it from the long, sheer cliff to the sea, covering her eyes with her hands briefly as she faced the fact that she might have ruined everything. That she might have destroyed Daisy's one and only chance of help.

She didn't know how she was going to go back and face Macy, what she was going to tell her sister, if that was true. Macy was barely back on the straight and narrow as it was, and another setback could ruin everything. Brutal claws of anxiety clutched at her heart, making her wish for the relief of tears. But somehow the tears that had burned in her eyes so hotly before, now seemed to have vanished completely, leaving her eyes dry and uncomfortable.

And suddenly she knew why. Whatever had made Andreas walk off like that, it was nothing to do with Daisy. Andreas had been listening, his attention totally focused, when she had been telling him about Macy and her baby. It was only when the name of Roy Stanton had come into the conversation— when he had forced it out of her—that his mood had changed, become blackly savage, and he had turned and walked off without another word. Perhaps there was still hope—and if there was any sort of a chance, she wasn't going to let it go.

She had said that she would do anything she had to to save Daisy's life—and she'd meant it. She only prayed that Andreas would give her the opportunity.

The sun was setting by the time that Andreas came back from the beach. He appeared at the top of the cliff steps just when the burning red ball had hit the horizon, and his tall, powerful figure was silhouetted against it, like some demon appearing out of hell, making Becca shiver in dreadful apprehension in spite of the warmth of the evening.

He had made up his mind, that much was obvious. She could see it in the way he held himself, the tension in his shoulders, the set to his jaw that etched white lines of determination around his nose and mouth. His decision was made, and if he had decided against her then she doubted very much that there was anything she could do to change it for better or worse.

'You're still here,' Andreas said as he came within a few yards of her. It was a statement, not a question, and there was no way of judging his mood from it, or from his tone, so she simply nodded in agreement.

'I was waiting for you,' she said in a low, uncertain voice.

'Why?'

Why? There was an answer for that in her heart, but she had no idea whether she dared to risk giving it to him. But what else did she have?

Taking a deep breath, she forced the words out, fighting to control her voice so that she sounded so much braver than she felt.

'Because I know that no matter what you think of me—or—' her courage failed her at the thought of saying that provocative name '—or Daisy's father, you won't be able to turn your back on a child. You might hate me, but you won't let an innocent baby die if you can help it.'

If her words had been a slap aimed at his face, his head wouldn't have gone back any more sharply. Becca wished she could see his expression but the way he stood with his back to the sun threw his face into shadow and all she could spot was the way that he had closed his eyes just for a moment.

'We need to talk,' was all he said and he walked past her, into the house, not sparing her another glance but obviously expecting her to follow.

Which she did, of course. She had no other option.

In the sitting room, Andreas clicked on a single lamp but that was all. With some light still filling the room from the sinking sun, it was possible to move around, but not to see anything really clearly. But at the same time, the shifting shadows in the room were a sort of comfort, suiting Becca's mood completely. She felt as if she was groping her way forward, hoping that somehow she would end up in the place she most wanted to be.

Though the truth was that right at this moment she had no idea where that might be.

'I could do with a drink,' Andreas said abruptly, making her start in surprise. 'How about you?'

'I—Some wine would be nice,' Becca managed carefully. Perhaps the alcohol would relax her, ease her dry throat, help her handle what she felt was going to be one of the most difficult conversations of her life, second only to the appalling confrontation on the evening of her wedding day.

But that time she had been caught on edge, not knowing what was coming. This time she was desperately tense because she knew exactly what they had to talk about. Right at this moment she had no way of saying which situation was actually worse.

'White or red?'

Did it matter? She knew that he was just preparing the ground, so to speak. He was being polite, offering a drink, settling her down before…

Before what?

That was the really important question. The one she needed answering *now*. But she didn't dare to press the point, to risk pushing Andreas into saying anything he was not ready to say. And so she tried a small smile, almost managed it.

'Red will be fine.'

'I'll get it. I will be back in a moment.'

He was gone much more than a moment. How long did it take to find a bottle, open it—pour? Becca paced around the room like a restless cat, unable to settle, too uneasy to sit still.

Was he ever coming back?

It was as she thought the words that the door opened again and Andreas came back into the room. And at once for Becca it was as if the world had suddenly righted itself again, in a way that had nothing at all to do with the reason why she was here, the question she was waiting for him to answer.

The truth was that she was so desperately in love with this man that simply to be with him, in the same room, so that she could see him, watch him, know he was there, was enough for her. She could see how the burning light from the sunset fell on the raven's-wing darkness of his hair, burnishing it with glowing red tones, look into the blackness of his eyes and see their brilliance in spite of the shadows of the room. She could hear his soft breathing, the pad of his still bare feet on the wooden floor. And the ozone tang of the sea was still on his skin and hair from the time on the beach.

And from wanting things to hurry up, from needing an answer to her questions as quickly as possible, she suddenly knew an overwhelming desire to drag this confrontation out for as long as she could. She had just realised that this was probably going to be the very last conversation she ever had with Andreas. The last time she would be able to be with him and talk to him at all. After this, whatever his answer was, then they would go their separate ways. She would go home to England, to Macy and Daisy and some sort of life she would live there, and Andreas would stay here. And she would never, ever see him again.

The thought burned in her throat, closing it up so that she

had to struggle to breathe, concentrating so fiercely that she didn't hear Andreas speak even when he repeated the words more loudly.

'I—I'm sorry?'

'I said, would you like to sit down?'

Andreas gestured towards the settee with one of the wine glasses he held.

'Isn't it usual at this point to say—do I need to?' she managed, aiming for a joking tone.

But then she looked into Andreas' sombre, shadowed face and all trace of laughter, real or pretend, fled from her thoughts at once.

'Do I?' she asked on a note of anxiety.

'Sit down, Becca,' Andreas said and it was a command not a suggestion, one that had her slumping down onto the big leather settee without daring to protest or question any further.

'All right…'

Andreas sat opposite as he had before, placing both glasses of rich red wine on the table and pushing one towards her. Becca reached for hers, picked it up, then hesitated, looking down into the ruby-coloured liquid. She had the nasty feeling that if she tried to swallow it, her throat would constrict even more, choking her, and she would simply splutter the drink everywhere. With a faint sigh she set it down again and waited.

'So tell me about the baby. About Daisy.'

It was the chance she had wanted, that she had prayed for. But now that it was here she hardly knew where to begin.

But Andreas had used the baby's name. He'd called her Daisy. So surely he couldn't be going to turn his back on the little girl. Not when that seemed to mean that she was becoming a real person to him.

'I have a photograph—it's upstairs in my…'

She had been getting to her feet, anxious to go and fetch it, to show him her beautiful baby niece, but she stopped when he shook his head, sank back down into her seat instead.

'I want to hear about her from you.'

For a second Becca couldn't find the words, didn't know where to begin, but then she started hesitantly, and suddenly everything just came pouring out. How reluctant her sister had been to admit that she was having a baby. The way that Macy had neglected herself during her pregnancy...

'She's always been in danger of being anorexic and when she started getting bigger with the baby, she hated it. I tried to get her to eat, but she was always saying she was too fat. She never ate enough to keep herself alive, never mind let the baby grow healthy. Then she went into labour early—too early. Daisy was born prematurely...'

She choked off the words, unable to continue, staring in front of her with unfocused eyes as she remembered the tiny little scrap of humanity that the baby had been at that time.

'They managed to save her—but there are problems with her heart. We were told that the operation she needs isn't available in England—it's too new, too specialised. Before this babies like her just died—no one could do anything for them. But there's a surgeon in America who has been working wonders on tiny babies just like her. If we could just get him to operate on her.'

'And for that you need money.'

Becca could only nod silently, her heart too full for speech. Putting Daisy's plight into words like this had brought it home to her how desperate the situation was; made her remember just how fragile the little girl's life could be.

'And that is why you came to me?'

There was a note in his voice that she couldn't interpret, and his eyes were bleak as ice floes.

'I—I wrote to you about it,' she managed and Andreas nodded slowly.

'I remember that now—a letter that arrived just before the accident. Those days are still not clear.'

He frowned faintly, rubbing at his temples, obviously trying to recall things from before the car crash.

'The distant past is something I remember better. But I sent an answer, I believe.'

'Yes. You told me to get in touch with your solicitors—write down exactly what I needed and why and you would con—consider my request.'

That frown was back between Andreas' black brows, but it was more pronounced now.

'Then why are you here? Why didn't you just do that?'

'Because...' Becca began then broke off sharply as something Andreas had said a moment earlier hit home to her.

Those days are still not clear... The distant past is something I remember better.

Did he not remember that he had been asking for her? That was the one reason she was here. A reason that she had been forced to decide had just been Leander imagining things, because nothing in Andreas' behaviour seemed to fit with a moment like that.

But if he didn't remember...

'Because?' Andreas prompted harshly.

Leaning forward, Becca snatched up her glass of wine again and took an unwary gulp. It was enough to clear her head.

'Because I thought it was best to explain the situation to you face to face. You deserved that at least if you were going to help us.'

'But when you got here, you found that I didn't remember your letter—or you.'

'And so I let you think that we had never split up. I'm sorry,' Becca put in hastily and sincerely. 'I couldn't think of anything else to do.'

Andreas didn't seem to be listening. He was reaching into the pocket of his trousers, pulling out a folded piece of paper. He tossed it onto the table beside her wine glass.

'What's this?' Becca looked at him, puzzled.

'Open it and see.'

She picked up the paper with hands that shook, opened it with difficulty. But she couldn't make head or tail of the contents. Even when she held the document directly under the lamp, it still didn't make any sense and the words and figures on it—especially the figures—danced and blurred in front of her eyes.

'What is this?'

'Instructions to my bank—I faxed them just now. They will release the money—anything you need.'

'Anything I need…'

Becca couldn't believe that this was happening. Was it true. Had Andreas really said…?

'You're going to help?'

'I always said I would give you any money you needed.'

'Oh, thank you!'

It was hopelessly inadequate to express the way she felt. She wanted to dance for joy—she wanted to fling her arms around Andreas and kiss him…but a careful look into his dark, shuttered face made her rethink that idea hastily. Instead she reached out across the table and caught both of his hands in hers, holding them tightly.

'*Thank you*! Thank you so much!'

'My pleasure.'

The words meant one thing, but the expression in those glittering black eyes and the way that he pulled his hands from her grasp said something else completely and a lot of Becca's euphoria evaporated as he got up and moved away.

Of course—he was prepared to help Daisy, but not her. Though there was something he had said...

But before she could quite grasp what it was, Andreas had spoken again and his words pushed all other thoughts from her mind.

'So now you've got what you came for...'

How she wished that Andreas hadn't got to his feet because now he seemed to tower over her, dark and forbidding, as she registered what he had said.

She'd got what she'd come for and now he wanted her to leave. She'd been right that he couldn't let Daisy suffer for the division that had come between them, but his actions hadn't indicated any healing or even a hope of peace. He'd provided the money she needed; he wasn't offering her anything more.

'Of course.'

She stumbled to her feet in a rush, refusing to let the anguish in her heart show in her face. She might be falling apart inside at this speedy, cold-blooded dismissal, but outwardly she was determined to be as brisk and businesslike as possible.

'I'll leave at once. If you'd just give me time to pack, I'll be on my way. And if you call me a taxi—'

'No.'

It was hard and coldly savage, slashing into her words as she tried to get them out.

'No. That's not the way it's going to be.'

'It isn't?'

The sun was almost totally below the horizon now and the room so dark that she could scarcely see his face. But one last, lingering ray of light fell on the coldly glittering eyes, the start of his tightly clamped jaw. There was no yielding in him, no gentleness at all, and her heart quailed at the thought of just what he was about to say.

'You're not leaving.'

It was so unexpected that she almost laughed. But she caught back the betraying sound with an effort and managed to control her face so that the shocked astonishment she was feeling didn't show on it.

'Of course I am.'

She had to get home, tell Macy the wonderful news, get the hospital to put things in motion...

'You can't want me to stay.'

She blinked in astonishment as an autocratic flick of Andreas' hand brushed aside her protest in a second.

'That is where you are wrong, *agape mou*,' he told her with deadly intensity. 'I very much want you to stay.'

'But why...?'

'Oh, Becca, Becca...' Andreas reproved and the softness of his tone made an icy shiver crawl all the way down her spine. 'You are not so naïve that you have to ask that question. You know why I want you here, what I want from you.'

And of course she did.

'Sex,' she stated baldly and saw a frown draw his black, straight brows together.

'I prefer to call it passion.'

'You can call it what you like.'

The pain that was clawing at her heart made her voice harsh; the fight to hold back tears roughened it at the edges.

'But sex is what you mean and...'

Her voice failed her as a terrible truth dawned in her thoughts, the horror of it taking away all her strength.

'Is this about the money? Is this what you're demanding

in return for helping Daisy—your conditions for the loan? Is it what I have to do to ensure she gets the operation?'

She knew she was wrong as soon as she'd spoken. Even the shadows in the room couldn't disguise the way his head went back, the hiss of his breath between clenched teeth.

'What sort of a brute do you think I am?'

The vein of savage anger in Andreas' voice made her blood run cold. There was no room for possible doubt of his sincerity. But she didn't have the strength to take the words back, particularly not when his hand flashed out, clamped tight around her wrist and pulled her towards him with a rough, jerky movement.

'Your sister and her child, the money for the operation—money that is a gift, not a loan—all that is dealt with. You can get on the phone to your sister—to the hospital, tell them arrange everything—and then that is done. Finished. *This* is between you and me. And nothing is finished between the two of us.'

'But…' Becca tried to interject but Andreas ignored her weak attempt at speech.

'I let you go too easily the last time, and I've regretted it ever since. I've never been able to get you out of my mind. You've shadowed my days—haunted my dreams—and this afternoon in my bed reminded me of just why you have this effect on me. And it also told me that once would never be enough. I want so much more.'

Becca could only listen in dazed silence, struggling with the cruelly ambiguous feelings his words woke in her.

They should be complimentary. They should be what every woman dreamed of the man she loved saying to her. But she knew what he really meant and that destroyed any joy she might have wished she could find in what he was saying.

Money I'll give you but nothing else, he had flung at her, and now here he was, offering her nothing—nothing more than the cold-blooded passion he had for her, the purely physical need that he openly admitted was all he felt.

'And I know you feel it too. That's why I want you to stay. I'll make it worth your while. I'll give you anything you want—everything you want.'

I have a reputation for generosity to my mistresses. The words spoken outside by the pool—was it only a few hours ago?—came back to haunt her. And that was all she would be—his mistress. His wife in name but his mistress in reality. Because as his wife she should be loved, cherished—and she might hope to stay with him for life. As his mistress...

'How long?' she croaked out, her voice failing her. 'How long would you want me to stay?'

'For as long as it lasts. As long as it works. If we're both getting what we want out of this, then I don't see why it can't last...'

'Until we get each other out of our systems?'

Becca prayed that her falsely airy voice hid the agony that was squeezing her heart deep inside.

She would never get what she wanted out of this. Never. There was no hope of that, because what she wanted—what she longed for—was for Andreas to love her just as much as she loved him. And as she had given him her heart without hesitation or restraint in almost the first moment she had met him—and again here, when she had realised that she still adored him—there was no hope of that adoration ever being reciprocated.

Money I'll give you—but nothing else. Not a damn thing else.

And yet her body cried out to her to accept—her body and her weak, foolish heart that begged her to take this, take the little he was offering and accept it. It was better than nothing.

Better than having to turn now and walk away—knowing that if she did so there was no hope that he would ever let her back into his life again.

She couldn't do that. She had had to walk away from him once, and the moment that he had slammed the door behind her had almost killed her. She couldn't do it again.

I married you for sex—for that and nothing else.

And so when a weak, longing voice in the back of her mind whispered that Leander had said that Andreas had asked for her in the first few moments after he had regained consciousness— he had asked for her and perhaps…she pushed it away and made herself face the reality of what she was being offered.

And sex was all he wanted from her still. The thing that was different now was that she no longer had any illusions. She was no longer deceiving herself that Andreas loved her, she knew exactly where she stood, and in that knowledge was a desperate kind of strength.

In that moment the sun finally disappeared below the horizon, and the last rays of light fled the room completely so that there was only the small lamp in the corner to see by. And in the darkness it was easy to hide the way she was really feeling.

In the darkness she could step forward and put herself completely into Andreas' arms. With her face unseen, her eyes and their betraying message hidden, she could put her hand against the warm strength of his chest, whisper his name, the single word, 'Yes,' and lift her face to his for his kiss.

And when his mouth came down hard on hers then all thought stopped, only feeling began. And that was when nothing else mattered. Only this man for whatever time she might have with him. She would take that. And she would never let herself dream of more.

CHAPTER TWELVE

THE light of the full moon through the window made the bedroom almost as bright as day when Andreas finally gave up on any hope of sleeping and slid from the bed. Pulling on his jeans, he paused for a moment to look down at Becca's sleeping form, her body still curved as it had been when it had been pressed up against his, her face almost buried in the pillow.

She was completely out of it, lost in a world of total exhaustion, oblivious to anything. By rights he should feel that way too. The blazing passion between them had had full rein during the night, each hungry coming together more eager than the first, each tide of mounting pleasure stronger, each soaring, burning climax more mind-blowing than the one that had gone before. Never in his life had he known such pleasures, such delight in another person's body—in the gratification it could bring to every single one of his senses. And in the end it had been only exhaustion that had ended it. The exhaustion that had plunged Becca deep into the oblivion of sleep and left him lying awake and restless, staring at the ceiling as the moon rose high out in the bay.

At first he had had no idea why he too couldn't find the ease he needed in sleep. His body was sated, his clamouring senses quietened—for now anyway—but it was his mind that wouldn't let him rest.

It kept playing over and over again a snatch from the conversation that he had had with Becca days before. A set of words that were the reason for the way he was feeling, the cause of his unease.

'How long?' Becca had said. 'How long would you want me to stay?'

'For as long as it lasts. As long as it works. If we're both getting what we want out of this, then I don't see why it can't last…'

'Until we get each other out of our systems?'

The problem was, he reflected as he slipped out of the door and headed downstairs, he doubted that he would ever get Becca out of his system, no matter how hard he tried.

And God knew he had tried!

It had been a week now since she had agreed to stay, and every day it had seemed that instead of his appetite for her being blunted, it had grown until there wasn't a moment of his day, a single second in the night, even in his sleep, when his mind wasn't full of thoughts of her. It was worse than when he had thrown her out on the day of their wedding. At least then he had had no sight of her to remind him of how beautiful she was, no touch to bring home to him how fabulous she felt, no kiss to fill his mouth with her own essential taste. Instead, now she was always there, setting his senses on red alert, making him hungry again even in the moment of his greatest satisfaction.

If he had known that it would be like this, then just as he had told her to stay he might have hesitated, knowing that he was being a fool to himself to even consider it. He should have realised then that this would never be over, not for him; that he was only risking his peace of mind, his sanity, to take her back into his life again, knowing that one day she would walk out of it again.

She had been so determined to leave just as soon as she had the money she needed. She'd been on her feet and almost heading out the door when he had known that he could not let her go. He had wanted to have her, to hold her—and so he had damn nearly ordered her to stay.

'To have and to hold from this day forward until death us do part…' The lines from the wedding service haunted him as he made his way into his office, but he pushed them away, refusing to let them settle in his thoughts.

There was no till death us do part with Becca—she'd made that only too plain a year ago, when she had married him simply for his money while all the time conducting a passionate affair with Roy Stanton.

But now that Stanton was out of the picture…

Stanton *was* out of the picture, wasn't he? He had to be now that he had fathered Becca's sister's child.

Roy Stanton. The name tasted like acid in his mouth, making him want to spit as he unlocked the bottom drawer in his desk and yanked it open.

The file was still there. So often he had meant to take it out and shred it, burn the contents, but he had never quite managed to do it. Tonight he felt he could. He had to if he was to have a hope of moving forward.

Tossing it on the desk, he flung open the folder, flicked on a lamp and stared down at the photographs. It was a year since he had last seen them but they still had the effect of hitting him like a punch in his guts. The man he didn't know, though the investigator he had hired had told him that that was indeed Roy Stanton. And the woman's face was hidden so that she could be anyone. He had tried to convince himself that the investigator had been mistaken, that she was someone other than Becca. But the ring was the killer blow. There was no mistaking the ring on her hand.

It was the ring that had marked the betrothal of his great-grandmother to his great-grandfather, and had been passed down to him to give to his own future bride. He had put it on her finger himself when she had first agreed to marry him.

'What are those?'

The question came from behind him, making him start, spin round in shock. Becca stood in the doorway, her face pale, her eyes wide and her white cotton nightdress still floating round her from the effects of her movement, making her look like some ethereal spirit that haunted his home.

'Nothing important.'

His answer would be more convincing, Becca told herself, if it hadn't been so swift, so uneven, so blatantly obviously defensive in every way. Just the way he spoke and the look in those dark, dark eyes gave away the fact that whatever was in the file he had been looking at was very far from 'nothing important'.

'Just something I planned on shredding.'

'At three in the morning?'

'I couldn't sleep.'

'Neither could I—not after you left the bed.'

Of course, that wasn't the truth. She didn't know how long she'd lain there, alternately listening to Andreas tossing and turning, and knowing that he was lying far too still, trying so hard not to wake her. She didn't know what kept him from sleeping, and she'd been afraid to ask.

What if the week of total sensual indulgence had been enough for him? What if that was long enough to get her out of his system so that he was no longer getting what he had declared he wanted? Had his ardour cooled so fast that he was lying awake, wondering how to tell her?

When he'd crept from the room, she tried so hard to convince herself that wondering how to tell her wasn't Andreas' way. If he'd tired of her, he would tell her straight, no hesitation, no cushioning the blow. But even knowing that hadn't provided any comfort. In fact, it had only made things so much worse. If he wasn't trying to think of a way to tell her *that,* then what else was going through his mind to keep him on edge throughout the darkest hours?

She hadn't been able to stay where she was, with the space beside her in the bed growing colder with every second that passed. The feeling had reminded her too closely of the way she had felt when she had gone home after the disaster of their wedding day and had had to try to fall asleep in the bed that she had once shared with Andreas, knowing that she would never, ever sleep with him again. And so she had pulled on her nightdress and crept down the stairs after him.

But now she wished that she'd never done so. The look on Andreas' face, the sense of withdrawal that had hooded his eyes, tightened his jaw, worried her even more than his restlessness had done. There was something very wrong here and she couldn't begin to guess what.

And being in this room with him like this, in this incomprehensible mood, brought back unhappy memories of the way that he had confronted her here, on the night of their wedding.

'Then I should take you back there. I'm sure I can think of a way of helping us both to sleep.'

It was smoothly done. Almost convincing. But Becca's nerves were already on red alert, and, hypersensitive as she was to everything about Andreas, she caught the faint uneven-ness of his tone, the way his gaze had flicked to the file on the table and then away again.

There had been a file on the desk then too. In fact, she wasn't sure that it wasn't the same file.

'What *is* that?'

'Just business…'

His hand went out to close the file, but, alerted by his tone, Becca was there before him. Grabbing at it to get it from him, she sent it flying, the file, and the photographs it contained, falling wildly to the floor.

'Oh, I'm sorry…let me… Oh…'

On her knees beside the desk, she froze, staring down at the photographs in each hand.

'Who's this with Macy—and why do you have a picture of my sister?'

'Give them to me…'

Andreas had crouched down beside her, reaching for the pictures, but then he too froze, staring at her in blank confusion.

'What did you say?'

'Who's this?'

The look in his eyes made fear clutch at her heart. Just what was happening?

'No—the rest of it. "Who's this with…?"' he prompted.

'With Macy?'

Was that what he wanted? Or something else?

'If you want the man's name then I can't…'

'You don't recognise him?'

If the look in his eyes had been bad, then the raw urgency in his voice made her tremble.

'No—I—Andreas, what is this—what are you asking—what is this picture?'

He didn't answer but just held out his hand to take the photos from her. Then he gave her the other hand and helped her to her feet. All in total silence. When she was upright, he spread the photos on the desk and focused the beam of the lamp directly on them.

And waited.

This was important. No words needed to be used to tell her that. Andreas' silence and that wary, watching stance of his meant that she had to give the right answer. But what *was* the right answer?

There was only one way she could go with this.

The truth.

'I don't know what you want me to say, Andreas, but I'll tell you what I see.'

She touched the photograph lightly, her fingertip resting on the image of the slender, dark-haired woman.

'That's Macy—my half-sister—and that building behind her is where she has her flat. Or, rather, had her flat. Since she discovered she was expecting Daisy, she moved in with me and...'

Her voice trailed off as realisation dawned and suddenly she was looking at the picture again, knowing just when it had to have been taken.

'Are you telling me that that...' a wave of her hand indicated the man in the picture, small and slim and with a boyishly handsome but weak, self-indulgent-looking face '...is Roy Stanton?'

And that was the moment when she knew that something had really changed. Because when she looked into Andreas' eyes as she spoke the words she saw none of the anger, none of the hostility that her use of that name had always created, but instead there was a stunned expression in their darkness. And she could almost have sworn that there were new shadows under his eyes, giving them a bruised, exhausted look.

'How do you know that's your sister?' he asked now and his voice was so husky and raw that it made her wince. 'You can't see her face.'

'No, but I know the T-shirt she's wearing—and the shoes. Macy just *loves* the highest heels she can find. Of course, from the back she could almost be me but there's...'

The impact of what she'd said dried her throat, taking the words from her. In the half-light Andreas' face looked drawn and haggard, and that stunned look had given way to one of real horror.

'Is that what you thought, Andreas? Is that what—what someone told you?'

Once more she looked down at the photograph, seeing it this time as he might have seen it, if someone had told him that she was the woman in the picture.

A woman who had flung herself into the arms of the man with her. Into Roy Stanton's arms. A woman who had her own arms up and around his neck, one hand almost buried in the man's fair hair as she pressed her lips against his in an ardent, passionate kiss.

Almost buried. Because there was one finger that could be seen only too clearly. And on that finger was...

'She's wearing my ring!' Becca exclaimed.

'Forgive me.'

The words came together almost in unison, so that Andreas' voice clashed with hers in the same moment that she spoke. And for a second she couldn't quite register what he had said. But as she paused, a small, confused frown creasing the space between her brows, he spoke again, and this time there could be no doubt about what he said.

'Forgive me for ever doubting you. For thinking that she could be you. For believing you could be capable of marrying me for what you could get when really you were...'

He choked off the end of the sentence, too shaken to go any further.

'For... Is that what he told you I'd done? Oh, Andreas, I knew he was evil, but I never thought he'd take things that far.'

Her heart thudding in shock, she reached out and placed her hand over Andreas' where his rested still on the desktop. For a moment he showed no response, remaining absolutely still, but then his fingers curled around hers and held tight.

'Tell me,' he said softly.

'Just one thing first.'

She had to know. She had to ask. And his answer to this would mean so very much. It would mean all the world.

'Were you really going to shred these?'

Her answer was there in his eyes, in the expression on his stunning face. She didn't need any more but he gave it to her.

'Yes,' he said, his voice strong and firm this time, with no room for doubt in his tone. 'Yes, I was going to shred them— and burn them. And then—'

But Becca stopped him there, pressing a finger to his lips to keep back the rest of what he had been about to say.

'Later,' she whispered, looking deep into his eyes and willing him to believe there would be a 'later'. A much better, easier— please God—a happier time, when whatever he had been about to say could be spoken with no hesitation, no doubts.

'Let me tell you about my sister. The sister I should have told you about.'

She'd hurt him with that, Becca knew now. It had really stung that she hadn't trusted him enough. That she'd been so afraid of losing her one blood relative that she had kept

Macy's existence even from him. If they'd stayed together longer she would have told him.

And now she *could* tell him. There were none of the restrictions Macy had placed on her when they had first met. All the need for secrecy had gone now. So she could be as open as she wanted—as she needed to be.

So she launched into the story of how she had tried to find her birth mother, only to find that she had died just six months before. But there was a daughter, Becca's half-sister.

'Macy was barely nineteen then—and she was making a real mess of her life. She'd got in with a bad crowd, been in trouble with the law—she had a drug habit. I was so conscious of how good my life had been with my adoptive parents—how different from hers—so I begged her to let me help her. She promised me that if I'd stick by her—help her out—then she'd try to go straight. But to do that, she had to get away from everyone she knew. She made me promise not to tell anyone who she was or where she was. If I did, then she would just disappear and I'd never see her again. There was one man in particular—a man she owed money to. Lots of money.'

She paused, searching for the strength to go on, to bring that name into the conversation. But she didn't need to. Andreas was there before her.

'Roy Stanton.'

'Yes. They'd had a relationship—she was crazy about him, would do anything he asked. He'd got her hooked on drugs, and when she couldn't pay for more he loaned her the money she needed—but at a ruinous rate of interest. The debt had just mounted up and up, until there was no way at all that she could pay it.'

'So you paid it. Using the money I gave you.'

Becca nodded slowly.

'I'm sorry…' she began but Andreas stopped her urgent words with a gentle shake of his head.

'Don't be—it was the only thing that you could do. I understand. But oh, Becca, *agape mou,* did you never think what might happen? Rats like Roy Stanton are never satisfied, even when you've paid them off. They always want more. And if one source dries up, then they'll find another way to get the cash they want.'

Sorting through the photographs, he found another sheet of paper and held it out to her. Becca stared numbly at the photocopy of the cheque she had written to pay off Macy's debts.

'*He* told you—but you said…'

'I said I had you investigated and I did.' Andreas' tone was sombre, his eyes shadowed. 'I wanted to clear you for your own sake—so that there was never any need for doubt. But it wasn't the money that concerned me—you could have had all of that and more, and I wouldn't have given a damn. What I did care about was the rest…'

'The rest…' Becca echoed, her heart seeming to stop still in dread. Now they were coming to it and she wasn't at all sure that she wanted to know what was coming. 'What did he say, Andreas? Tell me!'

But even as she spoke she was hearing in her thoughts the words he'd said just a few moments earlier.

For believing you could be capable of marrying me for what you could get when really you were…

'He told you that we were lovers.'

She could see it all now. It was exactly the sort of thing that Roy Stanton was capable of. When she had paid off Macy's debts with the money Andreas had given her, he must have thought he was on to a good thing and moved from dealing drugs into a little—he believed—highly profitable blackmail. And it must have been Macy who had told him about Andreas.

'I think I know when this picture was taken,' she said slowly. 'In fact, it had to be then. I'd been visiting Macy and when I went to the bathroom I took my ring off when I washed my hands. By accident I left it on the side of the basin. I remember that when I went back to get it, Macy wouldn't let me in—she was flustered and obviously embarrassed. She obviously had someone in the flat, but I never thought...'

Becca's eyes focused on the picture of her sister. On the hand that was up and half-hidden in Stanton's hair.

'She was obsessed with him—could never say no to him. But she knew what I would think, so she tried to keep him hidden from me. When I asked about my ring—she took it off her finger! She'd found it in the bathroom and tried it on.'

'And that was the day that the investigator spotted them together.' Andreas' voice took up the story. 'I believed he'd done what I hoped for—that he'd found no evidence, cleared you completely. And so I married you and brought you here. I thought we were free of it all... The photographs were waiting when I went into my office.'

The horror of that moment was stamped so clearly on his strong features that Becca's heart twisted in a pale reflection of the pain he must have felt.

'And I thought it was just the money—Andreas, why didn't you show me the pictures then?'

She saw his answer in his eyes; in the pained glance he shot at the discarded photographs, with its dark echoes of what he had felt then, when he had first seen them.

'Because I couldn't bear to. I wanted you to think it was the money that mattered. I could not have shown you the photos. Could not have stood there while you looked at them and knew—as I believed you would know—that you'd ripped my heart out with your betrayal. With the thought that you loved someone else.'

Andreas shook his dark head in despair at his memories.

'I wanted you to leave thinking I hated you—not knowing how much I loved you, that in spite of everything I still loved you beyond bearing.'

'*Loved*?' Becca had to force herself to say it, to take the risk, though every nerve in her body clenched tight in fear that she might not hear what she wanted to hear most in all the world.

But Andreas didn't hesitate.

'*Love,*' he declared clearly and proudly, the emotion he was feeling burning bright in his eyes for her to see too. 'I still love you Becca, always will. I can do nothing else. You are in my heart, in my soul. You're part of me. With you I am complete. Without you I am only ever half a man.'

'And I love you, my darling. You're the other half of me.'

Her voice was breaking on the words and she couldn't have gone on. But she didn't need to. Andreas gathered her into his arms, holding her tight against him, and his kiss was all that she needed to know that nothing more had to be said. Or could be said. There were no words to describe the love that was in that kiss. The love that was hers now and for ever.

'So tell me,' she whispered when, safe in his arms, she finally got a chance to speak again. 'When you had shredded those photographs, what were you going to do?'

Andreas' smile was one of pure joy as he looked deep into her eyes.

'I was going to go upstairs and wake you, very gently. And then I was going to beg you to let us start again. I was going to tell you that I couldn't live without you. That even as I slammed the door behind you I knew that I'd made a terrible mistake—the worst mistake of my life—but I believed it was too late to take it back. That you'd been in my thoughts every day since you left. That you were the first person I thought of in the moments when I came round from the accident.'

'I know—Leander told me that you were asking for me. That's why I came here in the first place. Only by the time I got here, you'd lost your memory.'

'Perhaps that was some sort of defence mechanism. They always say that you don't lose your memory—you just don't want to recall what has happened. Perhaps I wanted to forget what a fool I'd been ever to let you go.'

Once more his arms tightened round her and his mouth came down on hers in a lingering, loving kiss that made Becca's senses spin in hungry delight.

'But never again,' Andreas whispered in her ear. 'I'm never going to let you go ever again. I want you with me all day every day so that I can spend the rest of my life loving you as you deserve to be loved. So that I can prove to you that you are the only woman for me.'

'And you are the only man I'll ever want,' Becca sighed. 'My husband, my soul mate, my love, for ever.'

* * * * *

THE SICILIAN'S
VIRGIN BRIDE
Sarah Morgan

Sarah Morgan trained as a nurse and has since worked in a variety of health-related jobs. Married to a gorgeous businessman, who still makes her knees knock, she spends most of her time trying to keep up with their two little boys, but manages to sneak off occasionally to indulge her passion for writing romance. Sarah loves outdoor life and is in an enthusiastic skier and walker. Whatever she is doing, her head is always full of new characters and she is addicted to happy endings.

CHAPTER ONE

SHE flew in at night, in a small private plane that she'd chartered using the last of her cash. The brim of her hat was pulled low over her eyes, concealing almost all of her features, and her hair was ruthlessly subdued and twisted out of sight. She wore a plain black coat over black trousers. No make-up. No jewellery. It was the outfit of a woman who didn't want to attract attention to herself. *The outfit of a woman who was hiding.*

Had the pilot looked closely he might have remarked on the ashen colour of her skin, or the slight shake of her hands as she clutched her one small bag. Had he looked closer still he might have seen the fire in her blue eyes and the determined jut of her chin. But he wasn't looking. He'd taken one brief glance at her as she'd boarded the plane and immediately lost interest. He'd been paid an enormous sum of money to do exactly that, but all the same Chessie sat rigid in her seat, unable to relax as she stared through the small window into the darkness. She'd refused the offer of refreshment with a brief shake of her head, unable to contemplate placing any further strain on her already churning stomach.

Any minute now they'd be landing in Sicily, and the thought made her feel physically sick.

Trying to slow her galloping pulse, she closed her eyes, leaned her head back against the seat and breathed deeply. *No one would stop her.* No one was expecting her.

It had been six months: six months during which she'd learned to live her life looking over her shoulder. No names. No identities. Everything paid in cash. She'd lived a completely anonymous life in order to protect herself.

But now she was back.

In Sicily.

For many, the Mediterranean island was a paradise.

For Chessie it was a prison.

Soon, she thought to herself, shifting restlessly in her seat. Soon she'd do what had to be done. But for now she just wanted to see her mother. It had been six months…

The co-pilot walked into the back of the plane. 'We'll be landing in five minutes, Miss Berkeley. Keep your seat belt fastened. The car is waiting for you, as you requested.' He spoke in heavily accented English, and Chessie replied in the same language, careful to conceal the fact that she was fluent in Italian. For a brief moment she contemplated what the pilot would say if he knew her identity, but then she gave a mental shrug, reassuring herself that there was no way the pilot could identify her. There was nothing in any of her documents that would betray her.

'*Va bene.*' The co-pilot nodded to her. 'Have a safe journey.'

A safe journey?

Discovering that her mouth was dry with fear, Chessie tensed as the plane landed in a series of gentle bumps, and then fumbled with her seat belt, lifted her overnight bag and forced herself to walk to the front of the plane.

It would be all right, she told herself firmly as she walked down the steps onto the tarmac, breathing in the scent of

Sicily and feeling the warmth of the night air close around her. Her father was dead. The funeral had passed. No one was going to be expecting her home. She'd sneak in and see her mother, and then leave.

And then she was going to sort out her life.

No more running.

No more hiding. If nothing else, the last six months had taught her that she was capable of so much more than she'd ever imagined.

In her state of high anxiety, the powerful headlights of the approaching car reminded her of searchlights. Trying to control her galloping imagination and her racing pulse, Chessie tensed as the vehicle purred across the tarmac and gently came to a halt beside her.

Anxious to avoid the attention of anyone who might be watching, she barely waited for the rear door to swing open before she slipped inside.

Only as the door closed behind her, sealing her in, did she realise that there was someone else in the back of the car, and her stomach lurched in a wild panic.

Oh, no, no, *no!*

Frozen by shock, she was unable to move. Unable to look. She didn't *need* to look. She *knew* who it was because she felt his presence with every bone in her body.

Rocco Castellani.

Billionaire and bastard.

Her husband.

Keeping an iron grip on his simmering temper, Rocco watched as she reached for the door handle—watched as she registered the fact that the rear of the car was locked, providing her with no means to escape. Beneath the brim of the hat he could see that her eyes held the panicky, frightened look of a hunted animal.

He'd underestimated her, he thought grimly, and felt a flicker of cynical amusement. Because, of all the women he'd ever met, Francesca was the only one who had ever managed to surprise him.

'*Buona sera, tesoro.* Welcome home.' He switched to English because that was the language they'd always spoken together, and saw the colour drain from her cheeks.

It was obvious that she hadn't expected him to be here, and her reaction intrigued him.

Was she really that naïve?

Had she really thought she could return to Sicily without his knowledge?

He waited for her to say something, but she didn't speak. Instead she sat in frozen stillness, clutching the edge of the seat, her chest rising and falling rapidly as she sucked in air.

If she'd been anyone else Rocco would almost have felt sorry for her.

But he was a long way from feeling sorry for his wife. Why should he? After what she'd done she was fortunate that he was even prepared to sit in the same car as her.

'You look surprised to see me.' With a huge effort he kept his tone neutral, careful to reveal nothing of his true feelings. 'Why? We're married, *tesoro.* Why wouldn't I be here to meet my wife on her return to our home?'

Finally she turned to look at him, and her eyes were stricken. '*How* did you know?' Her voice was little more than a choked whisper, and he had to strain his ears to catch her words.

'How did I know you'd be landing tonight?' The smile didn't come easily but somehow he managed it, along with a casual lift of his shoulders. 'Did you really think I wouldn't?'

You're my wife, Francesca. I care about everything that happens to you. Your father entrusted you to me and I'm responsible for your safety. It's a role I take extremely seriously.'

'Care?' Her voice recovered some of its strength. 'You don't care about me, Rocco. You don't care about anyone but yourself.'

Rocco leaned forward and removed the hat. Her dark hair slid from the inadequate clip and tumbled over her shoulders in curling waves. She looked incredibly young. Far too young to be so scheming.

'What a surprise you are,' he murmured thoughtfully. 'So much fire and spirit, and yet you keep it so well hidden. When we met before our wedding you barely spoke. I had to coax every word out of you. I thought you were impossibly shy.'

For a moment she just stared at him. 'You don't know me at all, Rocco.'

'Clearly.' He wondered if she even registered the irony in his tone. 'But I intend to work very hard to rectify that. In fact you should probably know that I now intend to devote all of my time to furthering our acquaintance.'

'No.' There was a note of panic in her voice, and she gave a quick shake of her head. 'You don't need to know me. And I don't want to know you either. I already know enough.'

She was a mass of contradictions, he thought to himself as he studied her. Infinitely complex. First impressions had suggested that she was gentle and timid and yet she'd proved herself to be wild and wilful. 'Your dark hair shows your Italian blood.' He leaned forward and gently wound a silken lock around his finger. 'But those blue eyes of yours show your English heritage.' She had huge sapphire eyes, and a soft pink mouth that was temptingly full. In fact, she was a vision of feminine youth and innocence. And yet he knew that her innocence was gone for ever. Lost to another man. Anger rushed through him, along with another infinitely more ugly and dangerous emotion.

Jealousy.

So this was how it felt, he mused, trying to detach himself from the hot burn of envy that licked at the heels of his iron self control.

This was how it felt to confront infidelity.

Something from his past—*something dark and dangerous*—flickered to life and he ruthlessly suppressed it, reminding himself of his golden rule.

Move forward. Always forward. Never back.

She might have lost her innocence but she was still his.

Her breathing was rapid. 'Don't touch me. I don't want you to touch me.' With a jerk of her head she moved away from his fingers and slid to the furthest corner of the seat, staring straight ahead, as if by not looking at him she could somehow deny his presence. 'I want to go to my father's house.'

Still struggling against a desire to flatten her to the seat and make himself the entire focus of her attentions, Rocco was silent for a moment, his eyes on her profile as he considered her request. 'Aren't you a little late? Your father is dead. The funeral was two weeks ago.' He softened neither his tone nor the harshness of his words, and yet there was no reaction from her. Nothing. It didn't fit, he mused as he watched her. The pieces just didn't slot together. 'As his only child, you didn't think it might be appropriate to show up and pay your respects before now?'

She turned to face him, and there was something in her eyes that he couldn't interpret. 'No,' she said quietly. 'I didn't.'

'Why not?'

There was a long silence—a long silence during which she simply stared at him with a blank expression in her eyes. Then she turned her head away. 'My relationship with my father is none of your business, Rocco. I don't owe you anything, least of all explanations. And I'm not here to see you. I came to see my mother.'

'Your mother has gone.'

'Gone?' There was shock in her voice and fear in her eyes. 'Gone where?'

'I really have no idea,' Rocco drawled, and she reached across the seat and clutched his arm with nervous fingers.

'Was she at the funeral? *I need to know if she was at the funeral.*'

'Yes. She left soon afterwards.' He watched as she sank against the seat, her eyes closed, her relief visible.

'Thank goodness,' she whispered. 'In that case you can stop the car. I'll get back on the plane and I won't bother you again. You can get on with your life.'

'I intend to. But I certainly won't be taking you back to the plane,' Rocco said smoothly. 'We have much to talk about. Welcome home, *tesoro.*'

She was still his, he reminded himself with grim determination.

Everything else was in the past, and he was a master at keeping his eyes fixed firmly on the future.

Much to talk about?

Watching her hope for a rapid departure from Sicily crash and burn, Chessie tried to think fast. *Why hadn't she anticipated this?* How could she have been so stupid as to imagine that she could arrive in Sicily and not be noticed?

At what point had she forgotten just exactly who her husband was?

They called him *il lupo*. The wolf.

He'd made his first million before he was even out of his teens, and then carried on amassing money with ruthless determination. As unpredictable as he was brilliant, he was also wild, ruthless and dangerously handsome. Chessie had once overheard a woman observe in dreamy tones that if the world were about to end, then she'd choose to spend her last night naked with Rocco Castellani.

He was the object of every woman's fantasies, and being this close to him froze her normally agile brain.

Watchful and unsmiling, he lounged back against the seat, his powerful body almost unnaturally still and Chessie found his iron self-control strangely intimidating. Everything about him was dark. His eyes, his hair and his simmering temper. She gave a tiny shiver, because he embodied power and authority, and she knew that this man wielded more influence than her father ever had.

He was the ultimate smooth operator, but she wasn't fooled by the sophisticated persona that Rocco presented to the world. The shockingly expensive hand-made Italian shoes, the exquisitely cut suit and the impossibly handsome face were nothing more than camouflage. A disguise designed to lull his opponents into a false sense of security. She knew that the charismatic smile that had seduced so many willing women hid a cold, tough streak that would have been the envy of the average barracuda.

It didn't matter how this man dressed, or how he appeared to others. She knew the truth.

Rocco Castellani was Sicilian. Full-blooded Sicilian. And Chessie was one of the few people who understood exactly what that meant.

You could wrap a tiger in a sheep's fleece but it would still be a tiger underneath.

His presence in the car was so unexpected that her cool determination deserted her. Her heart took off at an alarming pace and her insides suddenly churned.

'You can't seriously wish to continue with our marriage?' She must have misunderstood him.

The silence stretched between them and she stared at him in panicked silence, finding it impossible to read his expression and equally impossible to look away from his glittering dark eyes.

'Why?'

'Because our marriage is over.' *Because she'd left him.* What Sicilian would forgive that?

He gave a faint smile. 'It hasn't even begun, *tesoro.* Thanks to you, we have much ground to cover. I'm looking forward to it.'

Her heart was pounding like a hammer against her chest, and her whole body was gripped by a reaction so violent she thought she might pass out. 'What are you doing here? *Why* are you here? The papers said you were in New York.' *She'd been banking on it.*

'You should never believe everything you read in the papers, but I'm flattered to know that you've shown such an interest in my movements during your long holiday.' His voice smooth, his eyes still on her face, he issued a set of instructions to the driver before relaxing back in the seat. 'Clearly you were missing me. Don't be embarrassed. It's perfectly natural for a wife to miss her husband. I'm just relieved that we've now been reunited.' His tone was smooth and civilised, but Chessie felt her palms grow damp—because she wasn't fooled by his outward appearance of calm. Rocco was a deadly opponent, and she knew that her actions had put her in the role of adversary.

He had to be angry. She *knew* he had to be angry. And yet so far he hadn't even raised his voice

'H-how did you know I was on that plane?' Her stammer was back, and she wanted to scream with frustration. Why now? Why, when she needed every bit of her new-found confidence, did everything she'd learned over the past six months suddenly desert her?

'Why wouldn't I know?' His firm, sensual mouth flickered into a faint smile. 'After your father's death, your return to Sicily was inevitable. It was only a matter of time. Patience isn't my major virtue, but I struggled through.'

'I thought I— You didn't—'

'Since you didn't come home for the funeral, I assume you have finally returned because you are bored with your lover.'

'My lover?' She stared at him blankly, still trying to come to terms with the fact that he'd obviously been waiting for her return. 'What lover?' Still in shock, she couldn't look away from his penetrating gaze, and her voice was barely a whisper.

'You're my wife. From the moment we exchanged vows, my security team was briefed to watch you closely. So if you're trying to deny that you left our wedding with Carlo Mancini—' he gave a careless shrug, as if the matter was of little consequence '—then you're wasting your time. I hope you found him a satisfying sexual partner.' Something in the way he delivered those words increased her tension, and she remembered that one of Rocco's most deadly skills was his ability to think with a cool, clear head even when he was seething with anger.

And he *was* seething with anger. She sensed it. *Sensed his inner struggle.*

Unlike her father, Rocco had learned to control his unpredictable Sicilian temperament and use it to his advantage. Instead of confronting the enemy, he studied them, watching for weakness, picking his time to pounce and kill. She'd once read a profile of him in the financial pages of a quality newspaper that had described him as a master of strategy, a skilful tactician and a merciless adversary. He was a man who took no prisoners.

Except her. She had been earmarked to be his prisoner by virtue of their marriage.

It was one of the reasons she'd escaped. One of the reasons she'd taken off with Carlo. Carlo, her father's gardener, who had just happened to be in the right place at the right time. It hadn't occurred to her that Rocco would think they were lovers. In fact that assumption on his part was just another example of the differences between them.

She would no more take a lover on her wedding day than she would swim naked through a pool full of sharks, and the fact that he thought that she would said more about him than it did about her.

He was a man who didn't know the meaning of the word love. A man who had never cared for a woman in his life.

And she still couldn't believe that she was trapped in the back of his car. She'd been so careful…

'How did you know I was on the plane?' She blurted the words out before she could stop herself. 'I paid them in cash.'

'And I paid them more.' A bored expression on his face, he glanced at his watch. 'Your naïvety is incredibly touching. Did you really think I'd allow my wife to return to Sicily without the appropriate protection? I'm just pleased that you came home alone and didn't bring your boyfriend. That would have been embarrassing for all concerned.'

She curled her hands over the seat, her knuckles whitening, worry suddenly choking all her fragile confidence. He *seriously* thought that Carlo was her lover? Wasn't that just typical of the way the Sicilian male mind worked? Jealousy and possessiveness blinded reason every time, and she understood that his anger stemmed not from love but from the public dent to his pride.

He thought she'd lost her virginity to another man.

For a moment she sat there mute, so unaccustomed to standing up for herself that she didn't know where to begin. And then she remembered exactly what sort of man he was and felt courage flicker to life inside her. If she was going to fight then it had to be now.

Like a diver braced to enter deep water, she drew in a breath and plunged. 'I'm not coming back to you, Rocco. I don't want to be married to you. I want a divorce.' She'd rehearsed the words so many times that they flew from her lips with remarkable ease, and immediately she felt relief.

It was done.

No more lying awake at night, planning the best way to approach him. No more plucking up courage.

'How can you not wish to be married to me,' he drawled softly, 'when the very last time we met you were standing in front of a priest and saying yes to that very question?'

'That was when I thought you were a nice person.'

Amusement flickered in his dark gaze. 'Francesca, *tesoro*, I am a nice person,' he purred softly, thick dark lashes lowering slightly to conceal his expression. 'How could you think otherwise? I'm always kind to old ladies and children.'

'Y-ou don't know any old ladies or children.'

'But if I did—' he gave a dismissive shrug and waved a bronze hand expressively '—I would be kind to them.'

'And then you'd probably rob them,' Chessie choked, turning away from the burning dark gaze that churned her insides into a turmoil. 'You don't think about anyone but yourself.'

'On the contrary, I've thought of little but you since you walked away from our wedding. Do I need to remind you that you couldn't wait to marry me? You had stars in your eyes from the moment I proposed. You were madly in love with me.'

A hot flush of humiliation engulfed her body, and she opened her mouth to utter a denial but it wouldn't come. How could she give voice to such a blatant lie? She *had* been in love with him. It was just that love hadn't been part of her plan. To begin with, marriage to Rocco had just seemed like the perfect escape from her father. It had been a chance to finally gain the freedom she'd craved for so long.

And then they'd spent time together and she'd done what every other woman did when they met Rocco—fallen for his dark, dangerous charm. It was something that she'd never told him, and the fact that he'd *known* how she'd felt about him made her want to slide underneath the nearest rock with embarrassment.

How he must have laughed at her, she thought to herself, looking out of the window to hide her misery. Rocco was a man who had models and actresses competing for his attention. Why would a clumsy, awkward girl who'd never been allowed to travel out of her local village have had a chance of snagging his attention?

'I thought I was in love with you, yes, that's true. But that was before I understood the sort of man you are. I could never love someone like you.'

She blurted out the words, anguish almost choking her. She didn't want to betray just how much she cared, but she couldn't help it. She'd held her feelings inside for so long that her body and brain felt as though they might burst. 'You did what it took to make me say yes, but for you it was all a business arrangement, and that isn't the sort of marriage I want. I want the real thing!'

'The real thing?' The mockery in his voice revealed what

he thought of her statement. 'You're wearing my ring on your finger. How much more real does it get?'

'You just don't understand, do you?' She turned her head and forced herself to look at her husband. *The husband she'd run from.* 'It isn't about rings and vows, Rocco. That's all meaningless. It's about *feelings.* It's about caring and love— all the things you know *nothing* about.'

'And is that what Carlo offered you? Caring and love?' The sarcasm in his tone was the final straw.

'You are a total hypocrite! *Why* did I leave our wedding, Rocco? Have you even bothered asking yourself that question?' She saw his eyes narrow slightly but was unable to stop herself. The anger rose inside her, strengthening her shaking limbs and her flagging confidence. 'How *dare* you sit there and accuse me of having a lover, *mocking me,* when you had the gall to invite your g-girlfriend to our wedding? What sort of man does that, Rocco? What sort of man expects his girlfriend to watch him marrying another woman? What sort of man expects his new wife to entertain his mistress? Don't you have any feelings? Don't you have any morals—?'

She broke off, shocked by her own outburst and suddenly apprehensive. Living with her father, she'd spent her entire life biting her tongue, keeping her eyes on the floor and never answering back. Never before this moment had she spoken her mind. Instinctively she shrank back in her seat, but he made no move towards her, only continued to watch her, one dark eyebrow raised in sardonic appraisal.

'That is the longest speech I've ever heard you make,' he observed in a lazy drawl. 'When we spent time together before the wedding you were virtually monosyllabic. Impossibly shy. I had to work overtime to get any sort of response from you. You stared at the floor, the walls, the table—anywhere but at me. It's fascinating to note that you do, in fact, have an opinion.'

She blushed fiercely, knowing that what he said was true. Almost all their meetings had been carried out in the presence of her father, and she'd learned from bitter experience that it was safer to stay silent than risk incurring his anger. She'd learned how not to draw attention to herself.

'Well, I'm looking at you now and I'm speaking now,' she said, trying to keep her voice steady. There was no way she was going to show him how nervous she felt. 'And my opinion of you is rock bottom, Rocco. You measure everything in terms of profit. You don't do anything unless you gain something from it. And you don't care about people's feelings. I've had six months to think about what you did. You married me because you wanted my father's business. That was bad enough, but I thought that you at least had some respect for me. And then *you invited your mistress to our wedding*!'

The pain and humiliation still throbbed inside her like a raw and vicious wound.

'You're being extremely juvenile. There were two hundred guests at our wedding.'

'I don't care about the two hundred. Just about the one. The tall blonde one who couldn't put you down. Your girlfriend!'

'Ex-girlfriend,' he corrected her, with a faint frown. 'And I don't know what you're worrying about. She and I weren't together any more.'

'So why were you kissing her on the terrace?'

He suppressed a yawn, visibly bored by the conversation. 'I can't honestly remember. Some women are naturally affectionate. She was probably kissing me goodbye.'

Naturally affectionate? Chessie recalled the driven passion of that kiss—recalled the envy that had almost floored her.

Rocco had never kissed her like that. 'If you weren't together then why did you even invite her?'

His eyes grew suddenly cold. 'Your position as my wife doesn't give you the right to question my behaviour. Frankly, I don't understand what you have to complain about. I married you. You were the lucky one.'

It took a few moments for his arrogant statement to penetrate her brain. 'Lucky? Lucky?' She stared at him in disbelief, searching his bronzed, handsome face for some evidence of remorse or contrition. But there was nothing except confidence and authority. This was not a man given to questioning his own actions.

'Yes, lucky,' he drawled softly. 'I offered you something that I have never offered another woman.'

'And that was supposed to make me feel how, exactly?'

'Grateful?'

'Grateful?' She choked on the word. 'Grateful to be given the opportunity to share my husband with half a dozen others? Well, excuse me if I'm not displaying the correct level of gratitude!'

'I never would have guessed you had a fraction of this much passion locked up inside you. How intriguing. It does explain a great deal.' His gaze was thoughtful as he studied her face. 'But you probably ought to know that jealousy is not a trait that I find appealing in a woman. And your jealousy is ridiculous, given that *you* are the one wearing my ring.'

'I'm not jealous. To be jealous I would have to care, and I really don't care about you one little bit.' *Once* she had. *Once she'd been ecstatic at the thought of marrying him.* So excited that she hadn't been able to wipe the smile from her face. But that had all been a childish fantasy. The reality had proved to be entirely different. 'I wasn't jealous. I was humiliated.

Publicly. What was I supposed to do, Rocco? Was I supposed to look at all those women drooling over you and feel blessed? Is that what you're saying? I was expected to party with your cast-offs and smile because I was the chosen one? Is that right?'

He watched her through half-shut eyes. 'You're hysterical.'

'No, Rocco. I'm *not* hysterical. I'm thinking clearly for the first time in years.' And she no longer cared about the consequences of speaking out. Where had silence ever got her? 'Answer me one question. If you wanted to be with that blonde girl then why didn't you just marry her and have done with it?'

'Lorna is American. She wouldn't have made a suitable wife. She has her own business and she's very independent.'

'What sort of an answer is that?' Chessie gaped at him in disbelief. 'What you mean is that she had more sense than to marry you! So instead you thought you'd choose some dumb Sicilian girl who didn't know any better? Is that what you're trying to say? Well, someone should have reminded you that my mother was English, so my Sicilian blood is rather diluted. You made a mistake marrying me, Rocco. A big one.'

His hard gaze didn't flicker. 'I never make mistakes. You, on the other hand, made an enormous one by leaving our marriage. But you're back now, so you can start making amends. I've decided to overlook the fact that you're no longer a virgin. Play your cards right and I might even forgive you.'

Forgive *her*? She stared at him in helpless frustration. He didn't even believe he'd done anything wrong. Rocco Castellani was so used to treating women badly that he didn't even realise there was any other way. He was *just* like her father. A wife was someone to leave at home while he went out partying with other women.

'I'm sure you found plenty of willing females to console you.' Chessie was mortified to discover that she had a lump in her throat. Why did she care? Why did she care that their wedding had meant so little to him? It was over. Their marriage was over, and she felt nothing for him except contempt.

His eyes were cold. 'You agreed to the wedding. It was what you wanted.'

'That was before I knew the truth about you.'

'What truth is that?'

Her breath caught and for a moment she hesitated, almost too embarrassed to admit her own naïvety. But there were times for honesty, she reminded herself, and this was one of them. 'You and my father set me up. You both treated me like some sort of commodity.' She stumbled over the word and lifted a hand to her throat to try and slow her breathing. 'You bartered and bargained until you both got what you wanted. You made me think that you wanted to marry me, but I was nothing more than a bargaining chip. Not once did either of you stop to think about me. You didn't think about what *I* wanted. What *I* needed. It was all about *you*.'

And she'd been torn apart by their lack of care and their naked ambition.

'Plenty of marriages are arranged in such a way, and we were not strangers. You seem to be conveniently forgetting the time we spent together. We spent many hours getting to know one another.' He spoke the words with subtle emphasis, and she knew exactly what he was referring to.

That one occasion when curiosity had defeated modesty and common sense and she'd kissed him.

It had been an experience that had disturbed her sleep ever since. *The warm, sensual pressure of his mouth against hers. The slow, lazy stroke of his strong hand over her trembling thigh.* The sudden eruption of sensations in her body had been so shockingly exciting that she'd hoped that he'd strip her naked there and then and satisfy her female curiosity in full.

But he hadn't.

And now she knew why. He hadn't found her attractive. He'd married her for other reasons entirely.

But she hadn't been able to forget that one kiss, and even now her body flared hot at the memory and she felt her nipples harden. Without thinking, she let her eyes drop to his mouth, and she felt something warm and dangerous uncurl low in her pelvis.

Horrified by the almost painful intensity of her reaction, she lifted her eyes to his, saw the gleam of masculine understanding in his sardonic gaze and looked away quickly.

'I didn't get to know you at all.' Embarrassed by the reaction of her body, she was grateful for the black coat that covered her. 'You revealed nothing of yourself, Rocco. As far as you were concerned, those meetings of ours were no more than a job interview.'

'Job interview?' There was a trace of humour in his tone as he repeated her words. 'And what was the job?'

'Your wife. Salary: unlimited. Bonus and perks: amazing. Requirements: one meek, obedient virgin who will stay at home, do as she is told and never answer back.' She couldn't stop her gaze sliding to his mouth. *The same mouth that had kissed her just the once.* Then she remembered that it was also the same mouth that had been kissing his mistress on their wedding day. 'A girl who is prepared to be understanding and tolerant about your numerous affairs. Well, you chose the wrong woman for the job. I resign. Next time you marry, you might want to extend the interview process, Rocco.'

'Why would I want to marry again when I have a perfectly good wife sitting in front of me?' His silky observation caused a flicker of shock to whip through her body and she stared at him, careful to hide her consternation.

He was joking. He had to be joking. No way would a proud, arrogant man like Rocco allow his wife to leave on their wedding day and then take her back.

He was going to release her. She knew he would.

He would make it difficult and awkward, but eventually he would release her.

She'd finally be free.

'You're just saying that to punish me because your ego is damaged.'

His smile indicated just how much that statement amused him. 'My ego is completely intact. Why wouldn't it be?'

'You can't possibly want to stay married to me. We both know that you only married me in the first place because it was part of the deal you agreed with my father.' It felt so humiliating to admit the truth—*to admit that he hadn't found her in the slightest bit attractive.* Obviously that had been the reason that he'd held back when they'd kissed. He'd been postponing the moment when he'd have to make love to her. 'My father needed someone to run his company and you were the chosen one. And why were you chosen? Because you were the only man he'd ever met who was as ruthless as he was himself. Congratulations.'

Rocco raised an eyebrow. 'By *ruthless* I assume you mean possessing the ability to make a decision unaffected by emotions—a concept that most women find impossible to grasp.'

'Emotions are important, Rocco. You and my father each had your own agenda to follow. The only one that neither of you bothered to think about was *me*. All you thought about was your own greed.' And she couldn't believe she'd been stupid enough to fall in love with him.

'Your father's company was losing money, so I can hardly be accused of greed.' He gave a casual shrug. 'Generosity, possibly.'

Shocked into silence by that unexpected statement, Chessie stared at him. 'It was losing money?'

'Why does that surprise you? Your father's olive oil business was very much a local operation, and he had no idea how to expand or make himself competitive.'

'My father's business was successful.' She thought of all the important people who had come to the villa; *of the deference they'd shown towards her father.*

'Your father's business was corrupt and badly run,' Rocco interjected, his tone suddenly hard. 'His methods were locked in the Dark Ages. But I'm slowly rectifying that.'

Chessie shook her head, trying to take in the enormity of what he was saying. 'Are you seriously telling me that my father's business was failing?'

'You didn't know?'

'Why would I know? My father never discussed business with me,' Chessie said stiffly. 'I picked the olives and I did some of his secretarial work but he never shared the details with me. Had I been a boy it would have been different, but as it was—'

'—he had a daughter.' Rocco's gaze rested on her face thoughtfully, as if something had just occurred to him.

'I don't understand.' She stared at him blankly. 'If my father's company was such a disaster, why would you want it?'

'Call it a whim.' Rocco gave a faint smile that revealed nothing. 'A sentimental desire to have a touch of Sicily in my portfolio of companies.'

'You're about as sentimental as a man-eating lion.'

His smile widened. 'You think so? All right, in that case I

admit it may have had more to do with profit than sentiment. I have a talent for spotting commercial opportunities that others have missed.' His eyes were suddenly sharp, his tone crisp. 'Your father was losing business because of the weaknesses in his operation, not because of the produce. The oil is top quality. I've eaten in the best restaurants all over the world and I've never tasted better. I'm going to export the oil as a premium product.'

Chessie stared at him. She'd grown up with olives, and she was completely unable to get excited about them. Harvesting them from the bushes was hard work. 'The market is flooded with olive oil.'

Rocco gaze lingered on her mouth. 'Not *my* olive oil,' he said with gentle emphasis. 'There's always a market for the best, and extra virgin oil is the best.'

Wishing that he'd stop looking at her in that lazy, assessing way, Chessie felt her colour rise. 'That's a typically Sicilian male remark,' she muttered. 'Even the oil has to be virgin. And not just virgin, but *extra* virgin.'

He moved so quickly that she didn't see it coming. One minute he was lounging at a safe distance, the next his dangerously handsome face was close to hers. 'If I were obsessed with virgins,' he purred softly, 'then I wouldn't have gone to the trouble of drawing you back into the folds of matrimony once you'd lost yours.' He lifted a hand and slid his fingers over her cheek, forcing her to look at him. 'And if I were typically Sicilian I would have put an end to that spotty teenager you ran off with on our wedding day. I'm trying to be *incredibly civilised* about the whole thing, but, just for the record, it probably isn't a good idea to remind me that you were unfaithful. From now on it's a banned topic of conversation.'

Chessie stared at him, unable to move, hypnotised by the darkness of his eyes and the thickness of his lashes.

He was so good-looking it almost hurt to look at him.

Her heart pounded, and she struggled against an almost irresistible urge to press her mouth to his. 'Why did you marry me? It sounds as though my father should have paid *you* to take the business off his hands.'

For a moment he stared down at her in brooding silence, and she wondered whether he was feeling the same inexplicable urge as she was. Then he slid back along the seat, putting distance between them. 'I was ready for marriage. If I hadn't been then I would never have agreed to your father's demands, no matter how much I wanted access to his olive oil.'

He'd been ready for marriage? Chessie gaped at him, and thought of everything she'd ever read about him. His reputation with women was scorching hot. Rocco Castellani certainly wasn't known for monogamy. If he'd been ready for marriage, then he'd certainly hidden it well. 'So why didn't you marry one of your many willing mistresses?'

'What a quaint expression. Very Victorian England.' He gave a faint smile as he acknowledged the term. 'A mistress is for sex, *tesoro*. Metaphorically speaking, all a mistress is required to do is set fire to the bed. The position of wife, however, carries entirely different responsibilities, and for that I wanted a different type of woman. I wanted a Sicilian girl.'

'I'm half-English.'

'Your father was Sicilian and you were brought up in Sicily.' He gave a casual shrug. 'That's good enough for me.'

'You mean because I'm supposed to know what's expected of a Sicilian wife?' She straightened her back and lifted her chin, remembering all the times she'd rehearsed this scenario. 'Well, I've got news for you. I would make a really, *really* bad

Sicilian wife. You better divorce me quickly, Rocco, before I display too much of my English blood.'

His powerful frame stilled. 'One final time—I have no intention of divorcing you. Ever. I don't believe in divorce. You are my wife and you're staying as my wife. The sooner you get used to the idea, the more comfortable for both of us.'

CHAPTER TWO

'HE HAD no intention of divorcing her?

Chessie sat in frozen silence, wondering if she'd misunderstood him. *Hoping.* She'd always known that one day she'd come face to face with Rocco again, but she'd consoled herself with the knowledge that, however bad the confrontation, ultimately he'd agree to a divorce. His behaviour at their wedding had proved that he had absolutely no thought or care for her. That their wedding meant nothing to him in emotional terms.

He had the business now. Her father was dead.

Why would he possibly want to stay married to her?

'We can have a quick, quiet divorce,' she said quickly. 'I don't want any money or anything, and I won't make a fuss.'

'You can forget it,' he drawled, his eyes hard. 'There's no way I'm giving you a divorce. So if your lover is waiting in the wings to marry you then I hope he's a patient man.'

She opened her mouth to deny that Carlo was her lover, and then closed it again, her brain sprinting into overdrive.

Rocco was pure-bred Sicilian, driven by macho tendencies and a possessive nature designed to control and dominate.

Surely the one thing that would eventually push him

towards divorce was confirmation that she'd been with another man?

It was a high-risk strategy, but…

'Carlo and I don't care about marriage,' she said quietly, carefully watching his reaction. 'We just want to be together.'

Something hard and dangerous glinted in his black eyes, but when he spoke his voice was steady. 'Then you can resign yourself to misery, because as far as I'm concerned marriage is for life.'

'Why, when you say it, does that prospect sound so completely unromantic?' She gave a humourless laugh and shook her head slightly. 'I get a prison sentence while you go off and enjoy yourself. My father married my mother for "life" so I understand exactly what that means to a Sicilian man. Forget it, Rocco. Once, maybe, there was a chance for us. But you blew it when you invited that girl to our wedding. If you couldn't even manage to stay faithful on your wedding day, then what chance is there for us?'

'I don't think you're in a position to lecture me about morals,' he observed in a silky tone, and she closed her eyes briefly, aware that she'd fallen into a trap of her own making.

All she could do now was play on his possessive streak.

'I'm not a virgin. I've had sex, Rocco. Lots of it. Do you really want a woman who is thinking of another man?'

His powerful body stilled, and for a brief moment she wondered if she'd gone too far. 'That's in the past. It will take less than fifteen seconds in my bed for you to forget you ever knew anyone else,' he predicted with characteristic arrogance. 'By the time I've finished with you the only name you'll be crying out is mine.'

She blushed hotly, unutterably shocked by the vivid image created in her mind. 'I can't believe you just said that.'

'Try and be consistent, *cara mia*,' he advised in a silky tone. 'You can't flaunt your lover one minute and then pretend modesty the next. Make up your mind. Which are you? Virgin or vamp?'

Virgin, she wanted to shriek, but she knew that wouldn't help her case. 'You can't make me stay here,' she said in a strangled voice. 'I only came back to see my mother. If she isn't here then I'm leaving.'

'You're not leaving. You're my wife. And as soon as we reach my villa I'm going to remind you of that fact.'

Was he seriously going to overlook her claim that she wasn't a virgin?

No, that wasn't possible.

Her heart performed a series of elaborate acrobatics and suddenly she realised that she didn't have a clue what to do next. She wasn't used to playing games, least of all with men like Rocco. He was totally out of her league.

Suddenly she regretted the impulse that had driven her to lie. 'You're just trying to stake your claim, like some sort of male predator marking his territory. But you don't need to. I was lying when I said I had an affair with Carlo. The truth is that I hardly knew Carlo. I—I just said that because I thought it would make you divorce me.'

'Nothing will make me divorce you, and changing your story every three seconds isn't going to change that fact.' Rocco's eyes didn't shift from her face. 'I've already said that I don't want his name mentioned, but this once—just this once—we'll examine the facts together so that there can be no mistake. You ran away with him on our wedding day. You now expect me to believe that the relationship was innocent?'

'He gave me a lift, that's all. He was saving me!'

'Saving you?' One dark eyebrow rose in sardonic appraisal. 'From what, precisely, *tesoro*? A life of rich, pampered idleness? More money than you could ever dream of spending? A fleet of staff waiting to supply your every need?'

She gazed at him with frustration and disbelief. He was *exactly* like her father. He measured everything in terms of wealth and possessions. If it couldn't be bought, it wasn't worth having.

'I don't care about any of those things.' For a moment she was tempted to blurt out the truth. She was tempted to tell him that what she wanted most in life was freedom. But she knew that a man like Rocco Castellani would never understand. What could he possibly know about her life? What could he know about growing up as her father's daughter? 'I decided that I just couldn't be married to you.' *To a man who was so careless of her feelings.*

'You preferred to run off with a spotty teenager,' he observed, in a slow, masculine drawl that dragged at her nerve-endings. 'Did he satisfy you, *tesoro*? Was your first experience of sex the stuff of dreams? I remember that first time in your father's garden, when I kissed you. Or did you kiss me? I can't remember the exact circumstances. All I remember is your warm body pressing against mine, urging me on.'

He'd known.

The colour flooded into her cheeks and she felt a sudden heat in her body. He'd known *exactly* what that one, single kiss had done to her—how desperate and frustrated she'd felt. The knowledge that he'd understood her so well simply increased her feelings of humiliation. She'd made *such* a fool of herself. Once she'd believed that he found her attractive. She'd believed that he cared about her as a person. But then she'd discovered that he wouldn't have cared *who* she was.

The only thing he'd cared about was sealing the deal with her father and gaining a traditional, Sicilian wife.

It was her parents' relationship all over again.

Why hadn't she seen it sooner?'

Before the wedding she'd been dizzy with happiness. For the first time in years she'd seen a glimmer of light in what had been a bleak, dark future. She was finally escaping from her father. And she was marrying the man of a million women's dreams. Rocco was an international businessman. She'd finally get to leave Sicily. She'd travel. She'd have a life outside the villa.

Her battered confidence and her trampled self-esteem had made a brief recovery as she'd imagined her new life. No more being insignificant and lonely. As Rocco's wife she'd be welcomed everywhere. She was going to glitter and shine. All those skinny girls at the convent school she'd attended, who had mocked and teased her about her height and her curves, would stare in awe and envy as she married the most eligible bachelor in the western world.

Rocco Castellani had chosen *her*.

He'd looked beyond her tallness and her womanly figure and her hideously shy exterior and seen the woman she really was.

Or so she'd believed.

Remembering just how completely she'd deluded herself, she wanted to shrink with humiliation. How could she have been so pitifully desperate?

'Let's not play games. It's demeaning to both of us.' She could hardly bring herself to say the words. It was just so deeply embarrassing. 'You didn't want to marry me. Tell me honestly, Rocco, just how much did my father pay you to take me off his hands?'

His gaze didn't shift. 'I spend enough of my day talking about business. I don't want to do it with my wife.'

'Business?' Her voice rose and suddenly she forgot her nerves. '*Business?* This was our *wedding*, Rocco. It wasn't supposed to be about business. It was about two people pledging to spend their lives together.'

'I made that pledge.'

He made it sound like just another one of his deals, and she turned her head away so that the pain wouldn't show in her eyes. There was absolutely no way she wanted him to see just how much she was hurting. *Just how much the deal had humiliated her.*

'Fine. Well, my father gave you the company on our wedding day, so you got what you wanted.'

He gave a wry smile. 'So far I've spent twenty-three hours a day trying to unravel the mess that your father called a business. Things are finally showing a positive improvement. I'm now ready to turn my attention to our marriage.'

Chessie stared at him, hypnotised by the look in his dark eyes. Her heart skipped and danced and her thighs felt heavy. Something uncurled deep inside her, and she quickly dragged her gaze away from his, confused by her reaction.

She didn't feel anything, she told herself firmly. She really didn't. It was just that he was incredibly good-looking and it was hard to forget that. *Hard to look at him and not think about sex.*

Dragging her gaze away from his, she stared out of the window, suddenly aware that she'd paid no attention to her surroundings. From the moment she'd stepped into the car and seen him lounging on the seat next to her, her brain had frozen. 'Where are we going, anyway?'

'Home, of course. Where else would a married couple spend their time? We need somewhere that we can be completely alone and undisturbed.' His voice was a soft purr. 'My villa is the most private place I know. And you and I really do need privacy to get to know each other better, *cara mia*.'

There was no mistaking the implication behind his words, and she turned to him, a flush on her cheeks. 'Why? Is your current girlfriend busy?'

'That is an *extremely* childish comment.'

The car drew to a halt and Chessie realised that they were at a marina. 'Where are we?'

'You don't recognise it?' He gave a faint frown, as if surprised by her question, and she wondered what he'd say if he knew she'd never been allowed to travel further than the local village, deep in the Sicilian countryside.

'I've never been here.'

'That surprises me, because your home isn't far from here.' His eyes rested on her thoughtfully, and then he gave a tiny shrug as he named the harbour town. 'My villa is not on the mainland. It's just a short boat trip across the bay. Sufficient to remind you that there is going to be water between you and the rest of the world. Don't even think about returning to your lover.'

'You live on an island?' She hadn't even thought to ask. Her heart plummeted as her last hopes of escape evaporated in front of her hungry eyes. 'I don't want to be trapped on another island!' On an island she'd have no freedom at all. Everything she'd hoped to do, *the person she'd planned to be*—all that would be impossible. 'I've had enough of islands to last me a lifetime. I don't want to be surrounded by water! I want to go to the mainland and have new experiences. I want to—'

'Being in my bed is going to be an experience previously unmatched,' Rocco promised in a low, masculine tone. 'And I can assure you that our surroundings are entirely irrelevant.

All I really need is a locked door, behind which I can remind you that you're my bride. When I've finished with you the only thing you're going to want surrounding you is me.'

She swallowed hard, trying to ignore the burning heat that flared low in her pelvis. 'How can you say that?'

'Why not? It's the truth.'

'You have a ridiculously high opinion of yourself.' Her heart was thudding and her palms were damp. 'You really think you're the ultimate lover, don't you?'

A faint smile touched the corners of his hard mouth. 'I'm naturally competitive, that's true. I always have to be the best at everything I do. What's the point of doing it, otherwise?'

She struggled to keep her voice light. 'Well, much as I hate to dent your ego, Rocco, you ought to know that you do absolutely nothing for me. I prefer my men gentle.'

'I can be extremely gentle.'

A dangerous warmth spread through her limbs, and Chessie struggled to keep her mind on the facts. 'I'm really not turned on by arrogant Sicilians.'

'You're not turned on?' His voice was a deep, accented drawl, and he leaned towards her, his mouth hovering tantalisingly close to hers. His thick dark lashes lowered slightly, and the expression in his eyes was impossible to read. 'You're not at all turned on?'

'Not at all.' She pressed her thighs together ignoring the sudden heat that flared through her body. 'Not even the slightest bit. You do nothing for me.'

His eyes slid to her mouth, lingered there for a torturous moment, and then he smiled and leaned back against his seat. 'I don't know what that fumbling teenage boy of yours taught you, but by the time the sun comes up you're going to be helpless in my bed, *cara mia*. A shivering mass of female gratitude. You're going to plead for me again and again. Play your cards right and I just might indulge you.'

'You arrogant bastard!' Goaded past the point of reason, Chessie lifted a hand and slapped him hard across the face.

'*Madre de Dio.*' He caught her wrist in his hand, his eyes flashing with a volcanic fury that made her shrink away from him in an instinctive gesture of self-defence.

She couldn't believe the boldness of her actions. In fact, if it hadn't been for the hot sting of her palm and the livid streak of colour on his bronzed cheek, she might have thought that the violence had been all in her imagination.

How many times had she lain there at night, imagining what it would be like to stand up for herself? To be brave and bold? How many times had she imagined herself fighting back? Defending herself and her mother from her father?

In reality she'd only ever done it once, and her defiance had caused repercussions that she'd never forgotten. From that point onwards she had learned to stare at the floor so that the anger in her eyes would never show. And she'd learned to dig her nails into her palms rather than hit out.

Until today.

She braced herself for some degree of retaliation on his part, but, although Rocco's long, strong fingers wrapped around her wrists like bands of iron, he didn't hurt her.

'Let me go.' She tugged hard but he didn't release her. 'And don't expect me to apologise. You deserved that. I'm just amazed no woman has hit you before.'

'Clearly we're going to enjoy an extremely physical relationship, and that's fine by me.'

She yanked at her wrists, her expression frustrated. 'Let go of me! Even you can't force me onto that boat, Rocco! If you try and make me, I'll scream. I'll tell them you're kidnapping me. I'll—' The words died in her throat as his mouth came down on hers with purposeful intent.

The heat of his kiss deprived her of the power of speech and she sank against him, her hands clutching his jacket for support. She felt the intimate invasion of his tongue, the erotic brush of his fingers against her cheek, and the world spun and whirled into a vortex of sensuality from which there was no escape. The feelings released inside her were so incredibly intense that she couldn't think or breathe. Instead she tumbled down and down, falling deeper into a world where the only thing that mattered was satisfaction.

Attempting to relieve the throbbing, insistent ache between her thighs, she slid her arms round his broad shoulders and wriggled closer to him. His mouth still seducing hers, he slid an arm under her legs and lifted her onto his lap in a powerful movement, his arm anchoring her against him. Buttons sprang from her coat as he dragged it open, and then he ripped the thin fabric of her blouse with characteristic impatience.

'You're wearing far too many clothes,' he muttered against her mouth. 'Don't do it again.'

She opened her mouth to tell him not to order her about, but then his clever fingers brushed against her exposed nipple and she cried out as an agonising shaft of excitement pierced her body.

He muttered something in Italian, slid his free hand into her hair to hold her face steady, and claimed her mouth with his once again. This time the kiss went on and on, the excitement heightened by the skilled caress of his fingers. Drained of all resistance, Chessie tumbled further and further into the dark temptation of passion, and when he finally lifted his head she was dazed and shaken—too shaken even to summon a protest when he lifted her into his arms and carried her through the warm night air towards the boat.

Dimly she heard a male voice mutter a coarse observation in Italian, and she heard Rocco's lazy, masculine response.

'Rocco—' Her voice was hoarse, and she squirmed slightly but he held her tightly as he stepped onto the gangplank and issued a series of instructions in rapid Italian. Then he carried her below deck to an elegant living area.

'Sorry to interrupt the fun, but we need to make a move. We'll be on the island in less than twenty minutes. Then we'll be able to take up from where we left off.' Depositing her onto the sofa, he strode across to a cabinet and poured himself a drink. She couldn't help noticing that his hand was totally steady. In fact he looked cool and in control, as if he'd just completed a business meeting.

Unlike her.

She was horrified and confused by her reaction. She didn't like him. She didn't like a single thing about him. And yet when he'd kissed her she'd forgotten everything.

Was she really that shallow?

Infuriated with herself, and hideously self-conscious about the fact that she was now half naked, Chessie wriggled on the sofa and tried to cover herself by closing her coat over her torn blouse. It was only now that she realised he'd somehow managed to remove her bra, and her full breasts were spilling out of the flimsy fabric.

'You've torn my clothes.'

'Buy more. Or, better still, don't wear any. I'm going to be removing them anyway, and my villa is extremely private.'

'You expect me to walk around naked?'

He gave a shrug, casually indifferent. 'Naked works for me when we're the only two people around.'

But it didn't work for her. She hated her body and she always had. At school she'd been the opposite of all her stick-thin friends, and she'd died a thousand deaths from embarrassment. She'd longed to be flat-chested and slim-hipped, but had been blessed with the complete opposite.

Still shivering from the effects of his kiss, she watched in silence as he drank from his glass, trying to ignore the insistent throb of her body. *What had happened to her?* One minute she'd been ready to scream, and the next she'd been unable to string a sentence together. How pathetic was that?

She was furious with herself for reacting in such a predictable way!

'So I'm your prisoner now?' Her voice was hoarse and her fingers clutched the front of her coat together.

'No, *cara mia,*' he said softly, lifting his drink to his lips. 'You're my wife, and I want you to remember that fact and start behaving accordingly.'

Her chin lifted. 'Did *you* remember it at our wedding?'

'My girlfriend isn't here now,' he pointed out. 'So you have me all to yourself. You can look forward to being on the receiving end of my undivided attention.'

She sank back onto the sofa, her heart pounding. She didn't *want* his undivided attention. The thought brought turmoil to her insides. She sought comfort from the knowledge that Rocco was a businessman of international repute, and he hadn't gained that reputation by sequestering himself on a remote Mediterranean island. Sooner or later he'd leave, and so would she. *In the opposite direction.* Even if she had to swim, she wasn't going to stay trapped in Sicily. 'When are you returning to New York?'

He gave a faint smile. 'When I'm bored with sex?'

'If you expect me to believe that you're prepared to

abandon your business in favour of our marriage, then you must think I'm stupid.'

'I didn't say anything about abandoning my business.' There was amusement in his gaze. 'This is the age of technology and hi-tech communication, *tesoro*. I have everything I need to work from the island. For the next few weeks nothing need disturb us, except perhaps the need to eat in between bouts of passionate lovemaking.'

She scrambled to her feet, thoroughly unsettled by the gleam in his eyes and the smile on his lips. 'How can you talk about it so casually? Marriage to you is having a good, obedient wife who is going to stay at home and keep the fire burning.'

Rocco studied her face for a moment and then put his drink down. 'And what is marriage to you?'

'It's a partnership. It's about respect and lo—' She broke off, realising that speaking the word 'love' in front of a man like Rocco would just be to risk exposing herself to ridicule. 'Lots of things like that,' she finished lamely.

'Respect? Is that the same respect you showed me when you left our wedding with another man?' Rocco's voice was deceptively calm. 'For your information, my staff are very excited about welcoming my new bride onto the island. Please remember that.'

In other words, she wasn't to embarrass him.

A thought suddenly occurred to her and she frowned. 'But surely they know we've been separated for the past six months? Everyone knows we haven't been together.'

'No one knows.' He drained the glass. 'I returned to New York the night of our wedding. Everyone, including your father, assumed you were with me.'

'My father thought I was with you?'

'Of course. You gave no thought to anyone but yourself

when you ran off that night.' His voice hardened. 'Your father was in poor health, and yet you left without a word. He died without being given the opportunity to say goodbye to you. Family should be the most important thing in the world, and yet you didn't even attend his funeral.'

Chessie stood still, frozen to the spot. Rocco Castellani had no idea. *He had absolutely no idea what her life had been like.*

She sank back onto the sofa, staring into the distance.

'It is a little late for guilt, *tesoro*.' Rocco's voice penetrated her thoughts. 'Your father is gone. It is too late to make amends.'

'Make amends?' Her voice cracked as she tried to speak. She ought to tell him. She ought to tell him what sort of man her father had really been. But she couldn't even bring herself to speak of it. She was so used to keeping her thoughts completely private that she had absolutely no idea how to confide in anyone, least of all an arrogant Sicilian who was exactly like her father in almost every way. For all she knew, he might approve of her father's conduct.

Suddenly depression and panic mingled inside her.

Marriage to Rocco had freed her from her father, but now she was essentially a prisoner again. Passed from one ruthless man to another.

What was the phrase they used? Out of the frying pan into the fire?

She was only too aware that the flames were well and truly licking around her ankles, waiting to consume her.

'Rocco—'

'The past is behind us. All that matters now is the future.' He reached out a hand and hauled her to her feet. 'We've arrived. Welcome to your new home. The sun is rising and I have some important calls to make. I had to leave New York in rather a hurry. Go to bed and get some rest. You're going to need it.'

CHAPTER THREE

ROCCO toyed with his second glass of wine, watching his new wife across the table that had been laid on the terrace, careful to conceal the anger and frustration that simmered inside him.

They'd arrived at his villa just as the sun rose above the horizon, and he had left his bride sleeping and spent the day trying to unravel the millions of problems that had developed since his departure from New York. He was on the verge of closing another major deal, and his senior executives were in a state of high tension. Whichever way he looked at it, it wasn't a good time to be closeted in Sicily.

Neither was it a good time to risk leaving his bride.

He sensed instinctively that if he left her she'd run again. Or worse. She might contact her lover. Who would have thought she'd be this complicated?

Rocco ground his teeth angrily and topped up his wine glass.

She was a mass of contradictions.

To look at her she seemed innocent and incredibly young. Her dark hair was caught up by a ribbon at the back of her head, and her clothes were extremely demure and wouldn't have looked out of place in the convent school she'd supposedly attended. On the surface she appeared to be the woman he'd chosen to marry. Modest. Warm. A good girl. The perfect wife.

Not someone who would run away with another man on her wedding day.

But since he'd apprehended her at the airport he'd seen an entirely different side to her. Gone was the shy, tongue-tied young woman he'd had to coax into speech. That version of Francesca had been quiet and subservient, pathetically grateful for his attentions. In her place was a fiery, defiant young woman who clearly had a mind of her own. It was as if she'd suddenly discovered that she had an opinion and was determined to express it.

He'd definitely underestimated her, Rocco conceded. Something he never did. But it wouldn't happen again. Already he'd made complex arrangements to guarantee her security. His wife wouldn't be travelling anywhere without his agreement.

He was still smarting over the fact that she'd managed to disappear for six entire months.

Within moments of her stepping into the car with Carlo Mancini, he'd received a full report from his security team. Unfortunately not full enough for him to be able to prevent her departure or track her down.

They'd lost her.

She'd somehow managed to blend into the background and elude his usually eagle-eyed security team.

Rocco gritted his teeth as he reflected on how many staff he'd fired over that incident.

His expression grim, he stared moodily into his wine glass and recalled the occasion when Francesca's father, Bruno Mendozo, had first mentioned marriage to his daughter. Rocco's immediate impulse had been to recoil and renegotiate terms. It was true that he'd been contemplating marriage, but he'd definitely been going to select his own bride. But then he'd met Chessie and realised that she'd be perfect for his needs. In fact she'd been *exactly* the sort of woman he would have chosen himself. She'd dressed modestly, worn no make-up, and had obviously been not in the slightest bit interested in flirting. She'd lived her life in Sicily and she'd been a virgin. All his. And she had clearly been completely starstruck by him. What more could a man want from a wife?

Deciding that this was one business deal that was looking better by the minute, he'd agreed to the terms.

Looking at her now, dressed in a high-neck black top that drained the colour from her already pale cheeks, he wondered just what lay beneath that flawless skin and innocent expression. Was she missing her lover?

The thought of his wife with another man incited an attack of jealousy so fierce that Rocco wrestled with a sudden urge to splay her flat on the terrace and drive all thoughts of Carlo Mancini from her head. Later, he promised himself as he drained his glass. Later he'd take her to bed.

And she wouldn't be thinking of anyone but him.

Chessie poked listlessly at the food on her plate, her appetite gone. She couldn't believe she was back in Sicily with Rocco.

How had her life gone so horribly wrong? After all those years with her father, didn't she deserve her freedom?

After the short boat crossing, she'd spent the day lying on a huge bed, staring at the ceiling, too stressed to sleep, trying to summon up another escape plan. But so far she'd failed to come up with anything remotely workable.

It was too far to swim, and Rocco's staff were hardly likely to offer her a lift to the mainland.

She lifted her head and stared at the horizon. Beyond the

vine-covered terrace was a stretch of fine golden sand and then the sea. It was exquisitely beautiful, but she didn't notice. All she saw was the isolation. *There would be no escape from here.* The fire and resolve drained out of her, leaving her in a state of despair.

She had to get back to the mainland.

Staring at her plate again, she knew Rocco was watching her.

She could *feel* him looking at her with those dark, dangerous eyes. *Those stormy, passionate eyes that reflected the bad boy that he was.* One look from those eyes was enough to persuade the most virtuous of women to think extremely bad thoughts.

And she didn't want him in her thoughts at all.

She didn't want to think about his reputation with women, or the fact that she was trapped here with him, and she certainly didn't want to think about that kiss on the boat.

The kiss had confused her, because at the time it had felt like everything even though she knew it had meant nothing. She wasn't the sort of woman that Rocco Castellani normally glanced at once, let alone twice. Suddenly she had a clear vision of the blonde-haired slender girl who'd been wrapped around him at their wedding. If that girl was an example of his usual taste in women then it was no wonder that he kept reaching for his wine, she thought miserably. Her body was so far from his idea of feminine beauty that he probably had to get himself drunk in order to carry out his promise of taking her to bed.

How had this happened?

How had she ended up married to Rocco Castellani?

She put her fork down and picked up her wine glass, her mind drifting back to the day her father had told her of his plans for her wedding…

* * *

'Well? Aren't you going to say anything?' Bruno Mendozo's voice was harsh and impatient. 'Are you mute?'

No, she was shocked.

Chessie stared hard at the floor, knowing better than to look her father in the eye. Cringing with embarrassment, she curled her toes inside her flat, practical shoes. *Oh, dear God, her father was going to try and buy her a husband.* And not any old husband, but Rocco Castellani. Could there be anything more humiliating?

She didn't need to think about the taunts of the girls who had attended her convent school to know that nature hadn't been kind to her. True, she had blue eyes, but her hair was the colour of a raven's wing and her body had carried on growing in every direction long after others had stopped. Fully aware of her own deficiencies, she didn't need to study herself in the mirror to know that she was about as far from Castellani's normal choice of woman as it was possible to be.

He'd turn her down, of course. Why wouldn't he? Why would a sophisticated businessman like Rocco Castellani ever agree to marriage with a girl like her? A girl who'd never been allowed to travel further than the village? And the most humiliating thing of all was that deep in her pocket, carefully folded so that no one would see it, was a worn picture of him. She'd cut it out of a newspaper a year earlier and hidden it under her pillow. It had been a foolish, childish thing to do, but Rocco had a face and body that had fuelled a million female fantasies. He was just so impossibly handsome. The stuff of dreams. And dreams were all she had, because her life was totally barren and empty.

He was her Mr Darcy, her Heathcliffe and her Mr Rochester all rolled into one.

A man no woman had ever held onto.

In a world that increasingly encouraged a man to get in touch with his feminine side, Rocco Castellani was unashamedly masculine.

But Chessie hadn't cared. In fact she'd been drawn by his raw masculinity, his dangerous reputation and his bold refusal to please anyone but himself. The wife of a man like that would travel and see the world, and she'd lain awake at night thinking about what it would be like to be desired by someone like him. But she was mature enough to know what it was about Rocco that really drew her, and it wasn't his wealth or his looks. It was his strength. Rocco Castellani was tough and powerful and entirely indifferent to the opinion of others. And he was the only man she'd ever met who had what it took to stand up to her father.

And now her father was telling her that he'd set her up for the most humiliating rejection of all. He was telling Castellani that he had to marry her. But she knew that no price her father paid would be enough to persuade a man like Rocco to spend his life with someone like her.

And his rejection would be the ultimate humiliation.

'Go and brush your hair,' her father ordered, his black eyes filled with contempt. 'He'll be here in the next five minutes and he wants to meet you.'

Chessie stared at her father in horror. Brush her hair? Rocco Castellani was a man who dated models and actresses. What difference was it going to make whether she brushed her hair? What she really needed was to lose six inches in height and two stone in weight in the space of the next five minutes.

With an anguished glance at her mother, who was silent as usual, Chessie slid out of the room and returned to her bedroom. She splashed her face in the bathroom, and was just reaching for a comb when she heard the throaty growl of a powerful car approaching the house.

Sneaking to the window, she watched with a mixture of resignation and fascination as a sleek black sports car came to a halt outside the house and Castellani stepped out of the driver's seat.

Il lupo, she thought weakly as the comb slipped through her fingers and fell to the floor. The wolf. Wasn't that what the business pages called him? He attacked failing companies and either broke them up or turned them, depending on which was likely to make him the most profit. He was a risk-taker: bold, ruthless and fearless.

And he was the most amazing-looking man she'd ever seen.

His hair was glossy black, and gleamed under the powerful Sicilian sun. A pair of dark glasses covered his eyes, but she knew that they'd be dark, too. He was over six foot in height and powerfully built, with a lithe, athletic body that was designed to meet the most extreme physical challenge, and he wore his masculinity as easily as he wore his clothes. No woman could look at him and not want.

And then there was her...

Turning to look at herself in the mirror, Chessie suppressed a groan. How was he going to react when he saw her? He was probably going to pass out with shock and laughter that anyone would even *suggest* that he should marry her.

Suddenly she wished her wardrobe were full of sexy clothes, like the ones she knew other girls wore when they went out, but everything she owned was shapeless and dark. Her father didn't allow her to wear anything that might attract attention to her full figure. There was only one word to describe her, and that was 'frump'.

Wondering whether she had time to start digging an escape

tunnel, she went downstairs with a feeling of dread, preparing herself for humiliation.

Rocco Castellani was talking to her father in Italian, and they broke off when she entered the room.

Her father introduced her, and Chessie stood in anguished silence, not knowing what on earth she could possibly say to redeem the situation. If Rocco Castellani had any sense, he'd run while he still could.

But he didn't run.

He stood there, legs planted firmly apart in a stance as confident as it was aggressively masculine. Finally he broke the silence. 'Your gardens are beautiful,' he observed, in a velvety tone that heated her insides to melting point. 'Perhaps Francesca could show me around?'

Her father frowned his disapproval of that suggestion. 'I'll arrange for someone to accompany you.'

'That won't be necessary.' Rocco looked up and there was steel under his smile. 'Your daughter will be safe with me.'

Safe. *Safe?* Chessie clamped her lips together to stop herself from screaming with frustration. She didn't want to be safe. She wanted to escape from the repressive confines of her narrow, small little world. She wanted to *live*. She wanted to discover the true meaning of the word passion. If Rocco Castellani felt even remotely tempted to make a serious pass at her then that was fine with her.

All the other girls she knew had started experimenting with boys and sex while still at school, and here was she at the ripe age of twenty-one, not even allowed to go for a walk with a man unless someone was watching! Rocco was going to think she was a schoolgirl, and what man in his right mind wanted to marry an awkward adolescent?

Perhaps her father had realised that, because he finally

agreed and they walked together in the garden. Rocco totally relaxed and at ease; herself dying in a thousand agonies of shyness and embarrassment. But, instead of appearing bored, Rocco went out of his way to show her kindness. He gently probed and questioned until finally she was forced to abandon her tortured silence and answer him.

And he made her laugh. Twice. Which felt amazing, because she couldn't remember the last time she'd actually found anything in her life worth laughing at.

It was the first of several meetings, and each time Rocco insisted that they spend time alone, and each time he made her smile. By their fourth meeting she'd decided that he was the nicest person she'd ever met, and by their fifth meeting she was in love with him.

All the same, on the day that he asked her to marry him she stared at the ground, painfully self-conscious, unable to believe she'd actually heard him correctly.

'You're asking me because it's what my father wants.'

'If you think that then you don't know me at all,' he said, in that slow, lazy drawl that always made her nerve-endings tingle. 'I've never in my life done anything to please anyone but myself. I'm congenitally selfish.' He slipped a hand under her chin and lifted her face so that she was forced to look at him.

Chessie felt her insides tumble. He was asking her to marry him because it was what *he* wanted? 'I'm not the right sort of woman to be your wife.'

'You're *exactly* the right sort of woman to be my wife. If you weren't then we wouldn't be having this conversation now.'

She looked at him with disbelief. Rocco Castellani seriously wanted to marry her? 'Why?'

The look on his face indicated that he wasn't accustomed to explaining himself. 'Because we can have a good marriage,' he said, with arrogant self-assurance. 'We make each other laugh, and you are everything I want in a wife.'

She wanted to pinch herself and beat herself with sticks, just to see whether she'd wake up from the dream. She was the girl everyone at the convent had laughed at. She was frumpy and awkward. And yet this god among men had chosen her. *Rocco Castellani.* Suddenly she wanted to drag him into the middle of the village, just so that she could tell everyone and show him off.

'Francesca?' There was amusement in his tone. 'I'm waiting for an answer. Is it yes?'

An answer? He wanted her answer? Since when had a man ever cared about her opinion on anything? 'Yes,' she replied in a shaky voice. 'Yes, of course.' How could she contemplate a different answer? Suddenly the world seemed accessible. With him she could lead the sort of life that had only ever been in her dreams.

And they'd be happy.

No more agonising loneliness.

No more isolation.

She was finally going to *live*.

Chessie brought herself back to the present and realised that Rocco was still watching her. She gave up on the plate of food in front of her. Somehow just being with him had wiped out her appetite.

Her stomach churned and flipped in a way that she didn't recognise.

'Eat something.' He leaned forward and topped up her glass. 'Starving yourself isn't going to solve any of your problems.'

Neither was putting on any more weight. Painfully conscious that she was already several stone heavier than the woman he'd danced with at their wedding, she once again wished she were flat-chested. She wore baggy tops in dark colours, but still it wasn't possible to entirely conceal her shape.

'I'm really not hungry." She cast a sideways glance towards the villa, but there was no sign of the staff. 'I need to know where my mother is. Will you find her for me?'

'What makes you think I would I be able to do that?'

'You're Sicilian. You have influence, I know you do. You could find her if you wanted to.'

He helped himself to more wine. 'She should have stayed in the family home, mourning your father.'

'Don't *ever* judge my mother.' Forgetting her churning stomach, Chessie rose to her feet, her legs shaking. 'If you knew what she had put up with for all those years, you'd recommend her for a sainthood.'

Rocco's eyes lingered thoughtfully on her face. 'I'm starting to gain the impression that your father wasn't the easiest man to live with. Sit down, Francesca. Tension at the meal table gives me indigestion.'

She remained standing, her fingers gripping the table, her cheeks pink from the wine. 'You can't just—'

'Chessie.' His voice was level. 'Sit down.'

She sat, her heart thumping at his more informal use of her name. It was the first time he'd called her anything other than Francesca, and on his lips the shortened version of her name sounded—intimate?

'Do you get a thrill out of ordering me around?' There was a long silence and his eyes held hers. A powerful bolt of electricity stabbed through her body.

'I fully intend to show you what gives me a thrill as soon as I've finished my dinner,' he informed her in a silky tone, and she sank further into her seat.

'If you're talking about sex again then you ought to know that I have absolutely no desire to go to bed with you.'

He smiled. 'Of course you do. You're desperate to go to bed with me, but you're still sulking about Lorna. You can relax. I'm not with her any more. That relationship is over.'

Chessie gasped at his monumental lack of tact. 'And that's supposed to make me feel better?'

'Why wouldn't it? My relationship with Lorna was purely physical, and it's finished. Before our wedding.' Clearly believing that those facts made everything all right, he gave a careless shrug. 'So you really have no need to be jealous.'

'I keep telling you that I'm not jealous. I just don't like you!' She shook her head in disbelief. 'You say that your relationship was purely physical, but is it ever more than that for you? Do you ever actually *like* the women that you have affairs with?'

'Of course.'

'Have you ever been in love?'

Rocco muttered something in Italian that she didn't catch. Then he leaned forward, a slightly mocking gleam in his eyes. 'Grow up,' he advised, in a silky tone. 'You're in the real world now. Relationships between adults are complex and are carried out on many levels.'

'From what I can see, yours are carried out on only the one level,' Chessie muttered. 'And that's horizontal.'

Rocco lifted a hand in a dismissive gesture. 'And what's wrong with that? We both know you've done exactly the same thing, so stop acting like an outraged virgin. From this point onwards the past is forgotten.'

Suddenly she wished she hadn't told that lie about Carlo, but at the time she'd seriously believed that he'd reject her if he thought she'd been with another man. 'I don't find you attractive and I have no desire to go to bed with you.'

He reached for his glass, his expression amused. 'Fifteen seconds,' he said softly, raising the glass in a silent salute. 'That's all I need to make you change your mind. Possibly less.' His gaze dropped to her mouth and she felt a burning heat rush into her pelvis.

'Maybe I'm going to be the first woman to reject you. Did that thought ever occur to you?'

'No.'

She wished he'd stop looking at her mouth. Nervous and unsettled, she reached for her wine glass. Didn't people drink when they needed courage? Well, she needed a mountain of the stuff. She sipped cautiously, and then sipped again, pleasantly surprised by the flavour and the scent. Several mouthfuls later, her head started to swim. 'This tastes really good.'

'You're not supposed to drink the entire glass in one mouthful.'

'I'm thirsty.' She drained the glass. 'Is there any more?'

'Not until you've eaten some food.' Rocco slid the bottle out of her reach and she frowned at him, wondering why everything suddenly seemed fuzzy.

'Stop bossing me around.'

'Then stop acting like a child,' he advised, and she looked away, unable to stand his scrutiny any longer.

'Stop studying me. You'd drink too if you were in my position.'

'And what position is that?'

Should she confess that the thought of taking her clothes off in front of him made her want to die of embarrassment? No. Wasn't a lack of confidence supposed to be unattractive? Well, she was unattractive enough already, without adding to her problems. 'This isn't exactly a relaxed situation, is it?' she mumbled, letting her hand fall from the glass. Suddenly she felt exhausted. The stress of the flight, being met by Rocco, the discovery that her mother had left Sicily. It was all too much. 'I'm really tired. Am I allowed to go to bed?'

There was a brief silence while he studied her. 'This is your home,' he said evenly. 'You do as you please.'

Did he really expect her to believe that? She looked at him suspiciously, feeling suddenly dizzy. 'You mean, as long as it's something you approve of?'

'Of course.' He gave a faint smile and rose to his feet. 'Fortunately, going to bed is something that meets with my approval. I'll show you the bedroom.'

'I know where the bedroom is.'

'Today you rested in one of the guest rooms. Tonight you sleep in our bed.'

He guided her through the palatial villa, up a wide curving staircase and into a huge, airy bedroom. White filmy curtains floated in front of glass doors that opened onto a terrace.

'Oh—this is lovely.' Her legs feeling ridiculously heavy, Chessie wandered outside and swayed suddenly. 'My head feels sort of swimmy. It must be the wine.'

'You only drank one glassful.'

'Well, that's one glassful more than I've drunk in the rest of my life,' she slurred, and gave a sigh of relief as he swept her into his arms with a muttered imprecation. 'Thank you. That's so much better than walking.'

Her head swam as he laid her on the bed, and she opened her eyes and stared up at his bronzed, handsome face, noticing the firm lines of disapproval around his mouth.

'You're probably worried that you've married an alcoholic,' she mumbled sleepily as she rolled onto her side. 'But don't worry about it. Tonight is actually the first time I've ever touched alcohol, and the way my head is feeling now, it's definitely going to be the last.'

'The first time?' His voice was loaded with disbelief, and she gave a soft smile and closed her eyes, the world still spinning.

'Mmm. My father didn't approve of women drinking. Actually, he didn't approve of women at all—other than the ones he cheated on my mother with. A bit like you, really.' The pillow was incredibly soft. 'This is sooo comfortable. Night-night.'

Pacing the terrace outside the bedroom, Rocco tried to contain his mounting frustration.

She'd had one glass of wine and she was asleep on the bed. Just where exactly had he gone wrong?

Francesca Mendozo should have been the perfect wife.

When he'd first met her, she'd been discreet and painfully well mannered. She had been gentle, compliant, and she'd looked at him with a flattering degree of admiration. In fact she'd been so visibly amazed at his proposal of marriage that Rocco had been entirely sure that his choice of wife was nothing short of perfect. She was sweet, and the excitement she'd shown when he'd kissed her had been pleasantly surprising. Recalling the unexpected thud of lust that had overtaken him during that one steamy encounter in the garden, Rocco frowned. He'd always suspected that his new bride had hidden passions.

He just hadn't expected her to display them to another man.

Rocco paced back across the terrace. Normally he prided himself on his level of self-restraint, but since his bride had reappeared on the scene he had fast been discovering that his threshold for explosion was lower than he'd thought.

He was fighting a continuous battle with a vicious jealousy that tormented his every waking moment. And he didn't want to feel like this. *He of all people should be aware of the destructive nature of that particular emotion.* The fact that she was no longer a virgin was irrelevant to their future.

He needed to put it behind him.

The fact that she was far from being the sweet-natured, easy-going girl he'd thought he'd married, and that she was proving more of a challenge to handle than his most difficult takeover bid, shouldn't matter.

But, however hard he tried, he couldn't ignore the fact that since her disappearance she appeared to be an entirely changed personality. In fact he was fast coming to the conclusion that Chessie was very possibly the most complex and contradictory woman he'd ever met.

One moment she was yelling at him in a storming temper, displaying all the characteristic signs of female jealousy, the next she was curled up on the bed in a ball, more child than woman.

And not once had she flirted with him or tried to please him in any way.

Rocco let out a long breath and jabbed his fingers through his hair, wondering why women couldn't be more straightforward.

None of this was turning out the way he'd planned.

When he'd made the decision that it was time to turn his attention to creating a family, he hadn't realised how complex and time-consuming the project would be. It should have been easy. Given the number of women who had dropped him hopeful hints about being on the receiving end of a proposal of marriage, he'd had no clue that the process would be anything other than entirely simple.

But handling Chessie was proving to be anything but simple, and he had absolutely no doubt that, given the chance, she'd be on the run again.

It was all about ego, he reminded himself. Despite her traditional Sicilian upbringing, Chessie was clearly super-sensitive about competition. Seeing Lorna at the wedding had dented her pride.

Resigning himself to the fact that marriage was clearly nowhere near as straightforward as he'd anticipated, Rocco lined up the facts and analysed them, treating the current problem in the same way that he treated any problem. He looked for solutions.

Like any complicated project, his marriage was going to need his personal care and attention—for the immediate term at least. But he had no doubt that if he concentrated his mind he would have his new wife eating out of his hand after just a couple of nights.

Checking his watch, he took the steps down from the terrace and strode over to the part of the villa that he'd had converted into a suite of offices.

The night was still young and his bride was asleep.

He might as well make a few calls to New York and see how the deal was progressing—to ensure that when his wife awoke he could devote his full attention to her.

CHAPTER FOUR

CHESSIE woke with a pounding headache and a spotlight glaring into her face. 'Oh, please will someone turn that light off,' she groaned, rolling onto her stomach and burying her face in the pillow.

'It's the sun,' came a cool, male voice from right beside her, and suddenly she was aware that the sheet was somewhere round her ankles. Cool air washed over her skin, and she realised that she was wearing only her underwear.

With a gasp of embarrassment she grabbed at the sheet and pulled it upwards, but it tangled in her legs, and it took several strong yanks on her part before she finally managed to cover herself to her satisfaction.

'What happened to my clothes?'

'I removed them five seconds after you fell unconscious,' Rocco drawled in a mocking tone. 'I have to confess that alcohol makes you a less than stimulating dinner companion. Tonight, remind me to give you water.'

Still struggling with the disturbing knowledge that he'd undressed her, Chessie sat up, clutching the sheet to her chin. 'It wasn't the alcohol. It was just lack of sleep. I was tired.' She stared at him, her eyes suddenly wide as she watched him remove his tie with a few careless movements of his long fingers. 'It's morning. Why are you undressing?'

'Because I haven't been to bed yet, and I don't intend to come to bed with you while wearing a suit.' He dropped the tie over the back of the nearest chair and shrugged off his jacket.

'Come to bed with me...' She clutched the sheet even tighter. 'We can't have sex now. It's daylight.'

The careless lift of his broad shoulders indicated that he considered that fact to be entirely irrelevant. 'I've been tied up in meetings all night, otherwise I would have been lying by your side, waiting for you to wake up. I've never been wedded to the idea that sex can only take place in darkness.' He removed his watch and placed it on the nearest table, then slowly undid the buttons on his shirt. 'Daylight works for me.'

'When it comes to sex, I suppose just about anything works for you,' she mumbled, horrified at the thought of him making love to her in broad daylight. It was her worst nightmare. Still clutching the sheet against her breasts, Chessie skidded back in the bed so fast that she almost bounced off the headboard. 'Look, we're really not doing this.'

'If you're worried about staying faithful to your lover, then I can assure you that after today you won't even remember his name,' Rocco informed her with characteristic confidence as he dropped the shirt and reached for the zip of his trousers.

Chessie averted her eyes, her cheeks scarlet. She'd never seen a male stripper before, but she was sure that Rocco would be up there with the best. Undressing in front of an audience clearly wasn't something that disturbed him in the slightest. But if she'd had a body like his, maybe she'd have been equally relaxed about revealing it.

She was unable to stop herself sneaking another look.

Dark hairs formed a shadow across his bronzed chest,

shading perfect musculature. He was all hard lines and powerful masculinity, and she couldn't help comparing him with the pictures of Renaissance sculptures she'd seen in books. A Michaelangelo or a Donatello, designed to capture the strength and muscular perfection of the male form. Only Rocco was no god cast in bronze. He was flesh and blood and very much alive.

As the zip descended she saw that the dark hairs trailed downwards, leading the eye to the significant bulge of masculinity that pressed against his silk boxer shorts.

Chessie gave a gulp and looked away quickly. This was definitely the point where she was supposed to tell him again that she hadn't actually slept with Carlo. To pretend to be experienced in bed was just asking for trouble, given her complete lack of knowledge in that direction.

But to confess to being a virgin would be to admit that no one had ever found her remotely desirable before now, and she just couldn't bring herself to say that aloud. It was obvious from the fact that he'd invited his mistress to their wedding that he didn't find her particularly desirable either, and she had no intention of reminding him of her deficiencies.

Surely she'd be able to pretend that she'd done it all before?

His boxer shorts slid to the floor and she suddenly found her gaze riveted to her first sight of an aroused male. Her heart flipped and her anxiety levels soared.

'Are you going to let go of that sheet?' He joined her on the bed and firmly prised the sheet from her lethal grip.

She spotted the loose black top she'd worn the night before lying on the floor, and wriggled across the bed to make a grab for it.

'What are you doing?' Lean, bronzed hands grabbed her around the waist and hauled her back into the centre of the bed, ignoring her quest for modesty. 'You're not going to need that.'

'I was just going to put my top on.'

'What would be the point of that?' he asked softly, stroking her tangled hair away from her face in a supremely confident gesture. 'When I'd only have to take it off again?'

'Listen—' her voice was shaky '—it's time to stop fooling around. I'm not the sort of woman you normally sleep with. We both know that.' He was probably going to take one look at her and lose his erection, she thought miserably, as she slunk as far under the sheet as she possibly could.

'Stop talking about other women.' A note of exasperation in his voice, he prised the sheet away from her hands for a second time and pushed it out of reach. 'I'm with you now, and that's all that matters.'

Aware that his gaze had dropped to her breasts, Chessie felt hot, burning colour flood into her cheeks. If intense embarrassment could have shrunk her breasts then her chest would have been flat.

The silence seemed to extend for ever, and all the fight went out of her while she waited for him to say something derogatory. 'Stop looking at me. I know I've got the wrong sort of body,' she mumbled finally, trying to wriggle away from him.

He held her firmly, a strange look in his dark eyes. 'The wrong sort of body? What's that supposed to mean?'

Was he going to make her spell it out? 'We've already established that I don't look anything like those models you usually date. I'm fat.'

'*Not* fat,' he assured her in husky tones, pushing her gently onto her back and sliding a leisurely hand over the soft curve of her abdomen. 'You have exactly the *right* sort of body. It's perfect.'

Perfect? Chessie opened her mouth to argue with him, but he chose that precise moment to close his mouth over her right nipple. She gave a soft gasp, her body arching off the bed in an involuntary movement as hot flames of lust shot through her. His tongue flicked and teased, and the sensations intensified to almost unbearable proportions. She gave a low moan, her eyes drifting shut as her whole body was racked by an excitement so powerful that she dug her nails into the smooth skin of his bronzed shoulder.

'We shouldn't be doing this—'

'We're married,' he purred. 'And we should have done this six months ago.'

He turned his attention to her other breast, and the insistent throb between her legs became an almost agonising ache. Chessie shifted against the sheets in an attempt to ease the growing tension inside her, but he spread his hand over her shifting pelvis and held her still.

'Rocco—' in the grip of feelings that she didn't recognise, she gasped his name, and he gave a low laugh and covered her body with his in a lithe, powerful movement that left no doubt as to who was in control.

'You like that, no?' He made a rough sound and brought his mouth down on hers, at the same time sliding his hand underneath her and cupping the rounded curve of her bottom. 'You feel fantastic. I knew from the first moment I saw you that sex with you was going to be incredible.'

He had? He'd really thought that? She tried to hold onto that thought, but the erotic stroke of his tongue inside her mouth and the touch of his skilful fingers sent her body surging at breakneck speed along a road of sensual discovery.

Suddenly there was nothing in her world but the physical reaction of her body. Her pelvis throbbed and ached, seeking a deeper satisfaction, and she was dimly aware of the friction of rough, male body hair against sensitive female skin. He was all hard, strong muscle against her soft, rounded curves. Then he shifted slightly and she felt his hand move, felt the slide of his fingers exploring her intimately.

'Oh—' it was the first time any man had touched her there, but his touch was so sure and confident that her resistance evaporated in an instant. Unfamiliar sensations racked her body, and she cried out in shock, instinctively tried to move her hips, but he anchored her with the weight of his body and continued to kiss her until her world was spinning and indistinct.

'Does that feel good, *cara*?' The soft purr of his voice against her ear barely registered against the practised skill of his fingers. 'Do you like that?'

'It feels amazing and I think I want—I need you to— Rocco—' She sobbed his name and dug her nails into the smooth, bronzed skin of his shoulder, and he gave a husky laugh that resonated with masculine satisfaction.

'Any time you want me to stop you only have to say so.'

'Stop? No, don't stop,' she gasped against his mouth, lifting her hips in a frantic attempt to relieve the almost unbearable building of tension.

'What is it you want, tesoro? This?'

With single-minded purpose he shifted her position slightly, pushed her thighs apart, and entered her with a decisive masculine thrust.

The size and power of him stole the breath from her body, and as he slid an arm under her hips and thrust deeper she gave a murmur of protest.

Instantly he stilled, tension visible in his handsome face as he looked down at her. 'I'm hurting you?'

Afraid to move in case it made the pain worse, she lay rigid, staring up at him. 'What makes you say that?'

There was a gentle humour in his eyes as he stroked her tangled hair away from her face with a surprisingly light touch. 'Possibly the fact that your nails are drawing blood from my shoulder?'

'Oh—' she let her hands fall to her sides. 'Sorry.'

'Has anyone ever told you that you're crazily mixed up?' His expression thoughtful, he studied her for a moment, and then his hand slid into her hair and he lowered his head and took her mouth. 'Kiss me,' he urged softly against her lips, his voice hoarse with restrained passion. 'Kiss me, *tesoro*, and everything will be all right. Trust me.'

Feeling the rough scrape of male stubble over the sensitive skin of her face, she opened her mouth under the demanding pressure of his and gave a low moan as he took control. His kiss was slow and purposeful, designed to arouse and excite, and she squirmed against him as her insides turned to liquid and drove coherent thought from her head.

She forgot that there'd ever been pain, because suddenly her body was consumed by pleasure.

He withdrew slightly and entered her again, and this time all she felt was the most wickedly delicious sensation of fullness and male possession. She felt his hands on her hips, felt him subtly alter her position, then surge inside her with sufficient care and control for her sudden gasp to this time be one of ecstasy. Her whole body was on fire, burning up with a desire that she hadn't even known existed, and when Rocco lifted her, plunging deeper still into her silken core, she gave a sob of desperation, utterly consumed by the strength and skill of his possession.

Excitement flowed through her in hot, greedy waves, and

she gasped his name and arched into him, moving her hips to the rhythm he'd set.

Sensations overwhelmed her body—sensations that she didn't recognize—and she gave a sob of disbelief as she shot into a climax so breathtakingly intense that her world suddenly splintered apart and her body throbbed around the powerful thrust of his. The pulse of her body went on and on, and then she heard his harsh groan and felt the sudden increase in masculine thrust as the strength of her orgasm drove him into his own.

Eventually the storm eased, and Chessie lay with her eyes closed, feeling the intimate throb of his body joined with hers, shocked and dazed by what had happened to her. *She hadn't known.* Even in her wildest dreams she hadn't been able to imagine that it would be like that. *It was so much more than a physical experience. It was an overwhelming connection and a closeness that couldn't possibly be expressed by words.* And the closeness astonished her.

She was used to being solitary.

All her life she'd been a private person. Her father had held her at a distance and discouraged friendships. Unbearably lonely, her relationships had been with books, her friends the characters living inside them.

But this—she felt the warm, sluggish afterglow of incredible sex and gave a faint smile—this was the real thing. No amount of fictional description had prepared her for the overpowering satisfaction that came with real human intimacy. *Man-woman intimacy.*

It was only now, with her body trembling under his, that she knew what it was like to truly share. *To give all of herself to another person.*

She lay still underneath him, reluctant to move, wanting

desperately to prolong the perfection of the moment. Trapped by the weight and power of his body, she listened as his breathing slowed, felt the roughness of his chest brush the smooth silk of her skin as he moved. Suddenly the harshness of real life seemed like a distant place. Held like this, her body warm and throbbing with unfamiliar sensations, she suddenly couldn't remember why she'd wanted a divorce. She forgot why she'd wanted her freedom so badly. *Why would she want anything more than this? What more was there?*

When he eased out of her and rolled onto his back she wanted to hold onto him and beg him never to move, but her tongue wouldn't form the words. She had no idea how to behave after such a cataclysmic assault on her senses. Had he felt it too? *Had it affected him the same way?* Unable to resist the temptation to look at him, she turned her head and felt everything inside her dissolve into liquid longing.

He was indecently handsome.

Unable to help herself, she let her hungry gaze move over the hard, masculine planes of his profile and linger on the strong lines of his darkened jaw.

As if sensing her scrutiny, he turned to look at her. 'Don't *ever* let me think that you slept with another man again.' His voice had a hard edge, and hinted at a boiling cauldron of emotions fiercely suppressed. 'I could have killed him.'

Basking in the aftermath of sexual perfection, braced to hear something suitably romantic, Chessie felt the warm, soft feeling evaporate inside her. 'Wh-what are you talking about?'

'Mancini.' Rocco lay on his back. He made no attempt to cover himself, totally unselfconscious about his nudity. 'Either he's useless as a lover, or you were lying to me about what happened. Until this morning you were a virgin.'

Her expectations of hearing soft, romantic words well and

truly crushed, Chessie felt the colour flood into her cheeks. This wasn't the conversation they should be having. 'I tried to tell you the truth—'

'But only after you'd first told me a lie. Just for the record, telling your Sicilian husband that you're sleeping with another man is a dangerous game, *tesoro*. Don't risk it again.' He rolled onto his side and looked down at her, the fire in his eyes fading to slumberous satisfaction. 'But I'm pleased you were a virgin. *Extremely* pleased. In the circumstances, I might just forgive you for running away.'

Forgive *her?*

Chessie lay in bemused silence, searching those stormy molten eyes for some hint of gentleness. *Something that reflected the deep emotional intensity of their lovemaking.* They'd just shared something impossibly intimate. Where were the words of affection that were supposed to follow? 'Is that all you have to say? Is that all you care about? My virginity?'

'Is that so surprising?' His satisfied smile was all male, and he slid a bronzed hand over the curve of her hip in a sensual gesture. 'You're my wife, and I've never been any good at sharing. I was trying to be relaxed about it, but I have to confess that it was an uphill struggle.'

Her body responded instantly to his touch and she felt a warm, heavy feeling spread across her pelvis. 'You're unbearably possessive.'

'Thank you.' He moved his hand, sprang out of bed, and prowled towards the bathroom, gloriously naked and totally indifferent to the fact. 'Best remember that before you accept any more lifts from strangers.'

She lay still for a moment, thrown by the fact that he'd taken her criticism as a compliment, trying to ignore the dangerous throb in her body. Then disappointment rose inside her, swamping her fledgling happiness.

This was her first sexual experience and he knew it. And had he said one single romantic thing to her? Had he uttered one gentle word? No. It was obvious that the entire episode just been about his need to make her his. So much for closeness and intimacy. And so much for her ego. He probably hadn't even noticed her body. For him it had been about nothing more than possession.

Unbelievably crushed, Chessie lay still.

Then she felt determination grow inside her—a determination that had been nurtured by her six months away from her father. No man was going to treat her badly again.

She slid off the bed and made a grab for his discarded shirt. Her hands shaking, she pushed her arms into the sleeves and gathered it around her. Then she followed him into the bathroom, walking through the door just in time to see him hit a button on the wall that sent jets of water pouring onto the tiled floor.

'I want to talk to you.'

'Talking after sex is an overrated pastime,' he drawled as he reached for a towel. 'I prefer just to enjoy the physical.'

'Well, that's pretty obvious.' The reminder that none of the feelings she was experiencing were new to him simply increased her misery. 'I think your bedroom technique needs work.'

He turned, treating her to an uninterrupted view of his gloriously male body. Suddenly her fingers itched with the need to draw him, and she took an involuntary step backwards, almost blinded by his physical perfection. She'd sketch him in pencil, using strong, bold strokes… She looked away, knowing instinctively that no artist, not even Michelangelo or Da Vinci, would be able to do justice to the masculine power of his body. A drawing would always be two-dimensional, and even a sculpture wouldn't be able to faithfully reproduce the glossy curves of hard, strong muscle.

Ominously still, Rocco watched her for a long moment, his dark eyes glittering with incredulous disbelief. '*What* did you say?'

She swallowed hard, trying not to be intimidated by the power and strength of his physique. 'I said that your bedroom technique needs work.'

'You've just had an incredible orgasm—I suspect the first of your life. I left you limp and exhausted on the bed.' His voice was low and deadly, his eyes glinting dangerously. 'Just what exactly needs work?' He prowled over to her, and she gave a soft gasp and averted her eyes from the curling dark hairs that shaded his broad chest.

He was too close.

'It wasn't the sex, it was afterwards,' she muttered, her cheeks burning hot as fire as she concentrated on the tiles. 'You didn't say anything—nice.'

'*Nice?*' He sounded genuinely confused. 'What do you mean by nice?'

'You didn't say anything personal. And if you didn't find me attractive then it's your own fault. I warned you not to do it in daylight,' she said, and there was a long silence.

'What does daylight have to do with anything?'

She bit her lip. 'If you'd waited until dark, you wouldn't have been able to see my body.'

'Which is precisely why I chose full sunlight,' he responded in a silky tone, sliding a hand under her chin and forcing her to look at him. 'Why wouldn't I want to see your body?'

Did he need her to spell it out? 'I'm not your usual type. I thought perhaps you—'

He interrupted her. 'What would you change about your body?' He spoke in his usual tone of command. 'Tell me. I want to know.'

'Oh—well, that's obvious.' She tried to look away from him, but his fingers held her fast, preventing her from moving. 'I'd have smaller everything. Smaller boobs, smaller hips, shorter legs—'

'Then it's fortunate for me that you're not in a position to alter what nature has given you.' He released her chin, caught the hem of his shirt and pulled it upwards, resisting her feeble attempt to stop him. 'Your body is perfect, *tesoro*. I would change nothing except your continued desire to cover it up.'

Perfect? He'd said that once before, and she hadn't believed him then, either. Instinctively she tried to shield herself with her arms, but he gave a soft laugh and took her wrists, forcing her to loop her arms round his neck.

'Don't,' she whispered. 'You can't possibly like my body.'

'You need further proof?' Sliding his hands around her waist, he hauled her against him in a decisive movement, and she felt the hard thrust of his erection pressing against her.

Her gasp of shock was muffled by the demanding pressure of his kiss.

'Convinced yet, *angelo mio*?'

Dizzy from the unexpected assault on her senses, she tried to remember what their conversation had been about. 'So if you find me attractive then why did you leap out of bed so suddenly?'

'Because I can't be in bed with you and not make love.' He gave a slow, sexy smile and stroked her hair away from her face. 'And it is too soon for that. I don't want to hurt you, so I decided to take a long, cold shower as an alternative.'

'Oh.' Her eyes flitted to the shower and she noticed the distinct absence of steam. He was taking a cold shower?

When he'd left the bed so quickly he'd been thinking of *her*? In a *good* way?

'And now I have a question for you,' he said softly, sliding a hand over the soft curve of her bottom with almost arrogant assurance. 'I want to know exactly who made you think you are fat?'

'I don't know.' She gave an embarrassed shrug. 'The girls at school. My father. Myself, looking in the mirror. Everyone, I suppose.'

He frowned sharply. 'Your own father knocked your confidence?'

'I think it would be more accurate to say that he attacked it with a cricket bat,' she said flatly, and then realised that she'd probably said too much. She frowned slightly, astounded by her own behaviour. *After twenty-one years of keeping her mouth clamped shut, she suddenly seemed to be speaking her mind at every possible opportunity.*

His eyes rested on her face, his expression thoughtful. 'I see. Well, your father was wrong, and I never want to hear you speak of yourself like that again. Your body is perfect in every way. There is absolutely nothing I would change.'

Softened by the compliment, and the unexpected gentleness in his eyes, she let her hands trail downwards, loving the satiny strength of his shoulders. 'Nothing? You really mean that?'

'Absolutely.' He murmured the words against her mouth. 'You are everything I want and I'm going to prove it to you. Again and again, *tesoro*.'

And he did.

The next two weeks passed in a blur of sexual ecstasy, and it became increasingly obvious to her that Rocco just couldn't leave her alone. All night, every night, he made love to her, ignoring her inhibitions and her insecurities, taking such obvious pleasure in her body that it was impossible for her to feel anything other than completely desired. And it felt fantastic.

And if he wasn't exactly affectionate, he was extremely complimentary about her body, and she told herself that it was a start. Rocco clearly wasn't used to expressing his feelings, and she had some sympathy with that because neither was she.

They'd learn, she told herself as she lay in a satisfied stupor two weeks after she'd arrived back in Sicily. Together, they'd learn.

She knew he cared about her because he showed her that he did, and for the first time in her life she felt good about herself.

She felt attractive.

She felt sexy.

She felt like a woman.

When it came to sexual Olympics, Rocco definitely took the gold medal. His energy levels and stamina were nothing short of awesome.

Each day now followed the same pattern. He'd work in the suite of offices that took up one wing of the spacious villa, and then he'd spend the entire night making love to her before rising at dawn to begin another working day. His schedule was punishing, and when he ate and slept she had absolutely no idea. A small, nagging part of her wished he'd spend more daylight hours with her—*wished that they shared more than mind-blowing sex*—but then she reminded herself that he was a billionaire, and billionaires didn't make their money by lounging around all day, even if they *were* newly married.

On more than one occasion it crossed her mind to wonder *why* a man so wealthy continued to be so driven in his working habits, but she didn't have the opportunity to ask because their relationship didn't include time for conversation. And that was fine, she told herself. Didn't lots of relationships begin life focused on sex and then move on to deeper, more lasting emotions?

And as for her own feelings—being with him was the first real adventure she'd had in her life. Rocco made her feel feminine and desirable, and he knew things about her body that came as a complete surprise to her.

Her burning desire for freedom had retreated into the recesses of her mind, and her entire focus was their relationship.

Every night he strolled into their bedroom like a warrior claiming the spoils of battle, and every night her resolution that this was the night they were just going to cuddle up and talk lasted less than ten seconds.

Their relationship was basic and primitive, but it was also sensitive and caring, and she no longer had any doubts that he found her attractive. In fact she was becoming increasingly convinced that he actually *liked* her. Why else would he spend hour after hour making love to her? He couldn't leave her alone, and she just loved the fact that he clearly found her so addictive.

It was only a matter of time before the closeness spread into other parts of their lives, she assured herself. He'd take her with him on business trips abroad; they'd travel and they'd spend time exploring together.

Rolling onto her back and feeling the faint protest of her aching body, Chessie gave a satisfied feminine smile. He might not have said that he loved her, but he *definitely* loved her body, which was a start. Over and over again he'd tell her that she was perfect.

Perfect.

She rolled the word around in her head and smiled a satisfied. The fact that he just couldn't stop having sex with her delighted her. He made love to her repeatedly, night after night, telling her that he found her completely irresistible, and for the first time in her life she was starting to feel confident about the way she looked.

And he hadn't spent a single night away from her since they'd arrived on the island, she reminded herself, hugging the knowledge to her like a warm blanket. Since he'd deposited her in his bed on that first night, he clearly hadn't felt the need to see other women.

In fact she was coming to the conclusion that she'd been wrong in thinking that he was like her father.

Entirely wrong.

It was true that Rocco was strong and tough, but he was also sensitive to her needs, and they were becoming closer with each passing night of passion. Had her father spent every night in her mother's bed? No. She knew for a fact that he hadn't.

Feeling confident that it was only a matter of time before Rocco found that he couldn't go a whole day without seeking out her company, Chessie slid out of bed, took a quick shower, and then dressed and reached for her bag.

She'd taken to spending her days on the beach, catching up on sleep and indulging in her secret hobby. Drawing. She no longer had to hide what she did, because Rocco had better things to do than rifle through her things as her father had habitually done. Most days she swam; sometimes she just lay there, drawing and dreaming of Rocco, thinking of the night ahead.

But today, as she settled herself on her rug on the sand, she felt ridiculously unsettled.

She missed Rocco.

Glancing at her watch, she realised that it was barely afternoon. Hours yet until he'd arrive in their bedroom.

Unless she went to see him. And why shouldn't she? Why should it always be Rocco who took the initiative?

Feeling incredibly daring, she gathered up her things and walked back to the villa, slowly plucking up the courage she needed to go and see him in the wing of the villa that he used as an office.

To her surprise, it was a hive of activity.

Four extremely pretty girls were clearly snowed under with work in a light, airy office, and beyond them, in a much larger glass-fronted room with a breathtaking view of the sea, was Rocco.

He was perched on the edge of his desk, cradling the telephone between his shoulder and his ear, in the middle of what was clearly a heated exchange. The perfect white of his rolled-up shirtsleeves contrasted with the bronze of his forearms, and the fluid, demonstrative gestures he made with his hand indicated his growing frustration at the direction of the conversation.

For a moment Chessie paused in the doorway, captivated by the width of his shoulders and the command in his voice as he issued a string of complex instructions down the phone. And then his eyes lifted and he saw her.

'I'll call you back.' He replaced the phone, cutting the connection without apology or visible sign of regret. His eyes were hard, his expression businesslike as he focused on her dishevelled appearance. 'Has something happened? Is something the matter?'

It was a reflection of their marriage, she acknowledged ruefully, that he would associate her presence with a problem. Apart from their physical relationship, they never spent time together. They never usually even saw each other during the day. But she was about to change all that. She was about to move their relationship to a different level—give him the nudge that he needed.

Suddenly she wished she hadn't come straight from the beach. She should have stopped to change. Not that her wardrobe was exactly extensive, but she was suddenly horribly conscious that her beach clothes were creased.

'Nothing's the matter.' How could anything be the matter when the incredible night they'd shared only hours earlier was still replaying in her head? 'I just wanted to see you. To talk.'

'Talk?' He repeated the word as if it were something foreign that he didn't recognize, and then he straightened and walked towards her. 'What about?'

He was so tall, she mused dreamily. Six foot two at least. *He was the only man who'd ever made her forget her own height.* With him she no longer felt like a displaced giraffe, and she had no need to hunch or wear flat shoes.

Chessie linked her hands together, wondering how to revive the intimacy that had enveloped them both during the previous night. She just wanted him to say something soft— something affectionate that would prove that he cared for her. *But he wasn't great at that,* she admitted with a faint frown. Rocco was more about action than words.

Realising that his staff were probably listening to every word, she glanced over her shoulder. 'Can we close the door?'

'I'm working, Chessie.'

Trying not to be discouraged by his businesslike tone, she reminded herself that he hadn't been expecting to see her, and probably still had his mind on his phone call. 'It's just that I wanted to talk to you. In private.'

He studied her face for a moment, and then the hardness of his gaze was replaced by something softer. The tension in the air was replaced by a sense of anticipation. He strolled the length of his office and slammed the door shut with the flat of his hand. 'We have privacy,' he announced in a silky tone. 'And I am looking forward to hearing what it is that you have to tell me.'

'You're not angry with me for disturbing you?'

'Some things are worth being disturbed for, and this is certainly one of them.' He walked back to her, a smile on his face, and she felt the warm flood of relief spread through her limbs. She'd been right to come. He *did* care for her. It was just that he wasn't used to being interrupted in the middle of his working day, and he obviously found it hard to express his feelings. Clearly he needed a little prompting.

'I wanted to talk to you. I couldn't wait until tonight.'

'That's understandable,' he purred, lowering his mouth to hers in a brief but lingering kiss. 'Why wait when you have something important to divulge? I'm glad you came.'

Suitably encouraged, Chessie smiled up at him. 'I want us to spend more time together.'

'Of course you do—and we will.' His own smile was indulgent. 'Family trips. Picnics. I sense that your own father was very strict with you and had very little to do with your upbringing. You needn't worry. I think it's very important for a boy to have a male role model, and I intend to be a very involved with my son right from the beginning.'

His son? She stared at him blankly. 'What are you talking about?'

'You are trying to tell me that you're pregnant. You needn't worry. I'm delighted by the news—and of course I've been expecting it.'

He thought she was *pregnant*? 'Wh-why would you be expecting me to be pregnant?'

'Why else have we made love all night, every night for the past two weeks if not to make you pregnant?' He gave a careless shrug. 'Creating a family is what our marriage is about. It's fantastic news. I'm really, really pleased, *tesora*. You're a clever girl.'

She gaped at him in disbelief, his words echoing in her head. A flashback to endless ecstatic sex suddenly careered through her mind. 'This past two weeks...' Her voice almost failed her, because a horrifying, alternative scenario that she hadn't previously contemplated was forming in her mind. 'You were trying to make me pregnant?'

'Of course.' His faint frown revealed that he considered her question superfluous. 'What else?'

What else? She wanted to ask him about passion and desire, but her mouth wouldn't form the words. Instead her brain sifted through the information at her disposal. 'Y-you told me my body was perfect.'

'And it *is* perfect. How could you doubt it?' He stood back from her, his eyes dropping to her full breasts and then moving lower still, to the curve of her hips. 'I've told you that over and over again. Everything about you is designed for motherhood. Your hips are perfectly curved—designed for bearing children.'

Designed for bearing children? He thought her body was perfect because *it was designed for bearing children?* Not because she was sexy and irresistible?

The fragile shoots of her confidence snapped, and for a moment she was so shocked she couldn't think, let alone speak.

'I need to sit down,' she croaked weakly, and instantly his arm came around her and he guided her to the squashy cream sofa in the corner of his office.

'Of course you do.' His tone was smooth and concerned. 'You need plenty of rest, and I'm very sympathetic. From now on I'll leave you alone at night. You can sleep.'

It was the last thing she'd wanted or expected to hear, and

she sat down on the sofa with a plop, her legs shaking too much to hold her. Her mouth was suddenly dry, and she had to lick her lips before she could form the words that needed to be said. 'You didn't come to bed every night because you found me attractive but because you wanted us to have a baby?' Slightly dazed, she mumbled the words almost to herself, as if by voicing the truth aloud she might be able to make sense of it. 'You didn't really like my body?'

'How many times do I have to say it? I think your body is perfect.'

'P-perfect for producing an heir,' she stammered, feeling the anger rise inside her. 'That's different to finding me attractive.'

'If I didn't find you attractive,' he drawled, 'I wouldn't have made love to you four times a night for the past few weeks.'

Five times a night, she thought to herself, but she was too stunned to correct him. 'And it didn't occur to you to discus it with me?'

'What is there to discuss?' He frowned. 'Pregnancy is a natural conclusion of marital sex.'

Marital sex? 'In the Middle Ages, maybe,' she said, hearing her voice rise and not bothering to do anything about it. 'But not now. Women have jobs, Nowadays women plan their families with their partners. They both decide when to have children and how many to have.'

'And so have we.' He gave a casual shrug. 'Given that you don't have a job, and we have no financial constraints, I'd say loads and straight away.'

'Oh, would you?' The shine in her eyes betrayed her growing outrage. 'And do *I* get any say at all in this?'

His glance was impatient. 'There are absolutely no reasons why we shouldn't have as many children as possible as *soon* as possible. You're young and healthy and you were born to be a mother. Why wait?'

Still coming to terms with the fact that his obsession with her body had nothing to do with lust and everything to do with his desire for a child, Chessie swallowed and tried to force her voice past the lump in her throat. 'Have you any idea how I feel right now? Any idea at all?'

'Blessed?' Obviously sensing that he was facing a problem that as yet remained beyond his grasp, Rocco was suddenly watchful. 'There are millions of women who would kill to be in your position.'

'There are also millions of women who would kill *you* for placing them in my position,' Chessie muttered through gritted teeth, her nails digging into her palms as she struggled to control her emotions. 'If I was the violent type, I think you'd be dead on the floor by now.'

'I'm sure that's just your hormones,' Rocco offered helpfully, and Chessie rose to her feet, so incensed that she was ready to thump him and take the consequences.

'You don't have a clue, do you? You just don't know what's going on in my head.'

'No man would ever be optimistic enough to pretend that he understands what's going on in a woman's head—especially when that woman happens to be pregnant,' Rocco assured her in his characteristically lazy drawl. 'And I don't believe in investing time in losing situations. We don't have to understand each other to be married.'

'But it would be a start, don't you think?' Chessie stared at him in helpless frustration. Not only did he know *nothing* about her, he didn't seem remotely interested in finding out. It was obvious that he believed that she was here to produce children. Nothing more. That was her job description.

'Did it ever occur to you that I might have plans that don't include children?'

His eyes narrowed. 'Such as what, precisely?'

'I want to travel, I want to live my life—*I want a job, Rocco.*' There. She'd said it, and suddenly her heart was beating so fast that she wondered whether she might faint. 'I want to work.'

His eyes were suddenly cold. 'Why would you possibly want to work when you have access to more money than you could ever need?'

'It isn't about the money. It's about self-esteem and enjoyment—about being like other people and—' *And she wanted to do something with art.* She broke off, her outburst quashed by the hardness of his eyes. 'I'm trying to make you understand.'

'Understand what? That my wife doesn't want children?'

'I'm not saying that I don't want them,' she said quickly. 'Just that I don't want them quite *yet.* I suppose I assumed it was something we'd talk about. Didn't it occur to you that there are other things I want to do first?'

'Why would it? I haven't been using any contraception and you haven't once protested,' he drawled, his eyes intent on her face. 'You're very pale, and obviously upset. You need more sleep than you've been getting. You're tired. I'll have a doctor flown in this afternoon to check you out, and I'll stop disturbing your nights.'

He wasn't listening to her. 'You mean, having managed to sow your seed, you no longer have to expend all your energy trying to make me pregnant?' Chessie said stiffly, still recovering from her sudden realization that they had used no contraception. 'Well, I hate to disappoint you, but there's no need to waste the doctor's time. I'm not pregnant. And I'm not hormonal, Rocco. I'm just really, *really* angry.'

He stilled. 'You're not pregnant?'

'*Not* pregnant.' She repeated the words slowly, so that there could be no misunderstanding. 'I'm not having your baby, so if that's really your aim then you still have some *serious* work to do. Perhaps you'd better make it six times a night, just to be sure?'

His eyes were suddenly cold. 'You disturbed my working day in order to tell me that you're *not* pregnant?'

'No, I *didn't* interrupt your working day to tell you that I'm not pregnant! The subject of pregnancy hadn't even crossed my mind until you brought it up! I didn't come here to tell you *anything*. I just wanted to—' She broke off, anger and frustration giving way to helpless misery. How could she possibly confess that she wanted to spend more time with him when he clearly didn't share the same emotion? She wanted to leap on him and hurt him for being so *incredibly* insensitive.

It was obvious that he didn't care for her at all, and the fact that for a while she'd really believed that he did made her want to sink through the floor with humiliation and self-loathing.

She'd done it again.

Been taken in by Rocco's fatal charm; made a fool of herself over him in the same way that dozens of other women had before her.

She'd believed that he was something he wasn't. *She'd believed that he'd cared.* The moment he'd taken her in his arms she'd started thinking love and romance, and he'd been thinking sex and babies.

Stupid, stupid, *stupid*.

Determined to leave the room before she embarrassed herself in front of him, Chessie scrambled to her feet. 'This is a pointless conversation. I need to go,' she muttered. 'No doubt I'll see you later, for another determined baby-making session.'

'Sarcasm doesn't suit you.' His hand closed over her shoulder and he turned her back to face him. 'You're not leaving until we reach a satisfactory conclusion.'

'This isn't a business deal, Rocco! And a "satisfactory conclusion" to you is just getting your own way. You railroad everyone who stands in your way, but you're not doing it with me!' Her heart thumping, she lifted her chin. 'I'm your wife, and we're supposed to be a team. I will not allow you to bully me.' She'd made that promise to herself, and she intended to keep it.

Rocco stared at her with mounting disbelief. 'I am *not* bullying you,' he ground out with raw emphasis. 'And we *are* a team.'

'How can we be a team when we never talk?' Oh, what the heck? She might as well tell him the truth. Tears smarting in her eyes, she lifted her chin and stared him in the eye. 'That was why I came here. To try to introduce something into our relationship apart from the physical. Do you realise that in the past two weeks we've hardly exchanged a single word? I wanted us to spend time together, which is something we never do—and I've just discovered why. You're not interested in talking. In fact you're obviously not interested in me at all. You say that you want a wife, but when have you spent a single minute with me?' She gave a short, humourless laugh. 'My role is simply to provide you with a son. You just want to make me pregnant—which explains why I never see you during the day and why you spend the entire night competing for the title of super-stud.'

Looking like a man trying to stand on shifting ground, Rocco ran a hand over the back of his neck. 'There's an element of truth in what you're saying, but you're twisting it to make it seem bad. I can see that you're upset—'

'Really? You can tell that just by looking?' Chessie tossed

her head angrily and her dark hair spilled down her back. 'Then you're more sensitive than appearances would suggest.' She went to stalk out of his office, but he caught her by the arm again, and swung her round so that she was forced to face him.

'I see you as the perfect mother for my children,' he growled, incredulity and frustration lighting his dark eyes. 'What bigger compliment is there for a woman?'

'Oh, let me see…' She blinked back the tears that threatened. 'Finding a woman irresistible, interesting, stimulating company—those would all be bigger compliments.'

'Not from where I'm standing.'

'Let me ask you something, Rocco—and I want you to give me an honest answer. Do you ever look at me and want to rip my clothes off and take me there and then just because you can't help yourself?'

'What sort of a question is that?'

'A perfectly reasonable one. Answer me, Rocco.' Her voice was hoarse and she stepped closer to him. 'Do you find me *sexy*?'

'This is *not* the sort of conversation I expect to have with my wife.' The chill was back in his eyes and she turned away, helpless with exasperation and so miserable she just wanted to lie down and sob.

'Forget it, Rocco.' Her voice was choked. 'It's a shame we didn't have this conversation earlier—because it's perfectly clear to me now that we both expect entirely different things from marriage. I'll leave you to get on with your work. It's clearly all you care about.'

CHAPTER FIVE

SHE didn't mean anything to him at all.

Nothing.

Chessie stuffed clothes into her bag, crying so hard that her head throbbed and her face was blotched.

It was just as well Rocco didn't want a sexy wife, she thought to herself as she fumbled for yet another tissue and blew her nose, because at the moment she was as far from sexy as it was possible to be.

And the worst thing was that it didn't even matter. Clearly she could have had the physical attributes of an oil tanker and he wouldn't have cared, providing she gave him a son.

She'd been flattering herself that he found her irresistible, and now she had discovered that when he'd said her body was perfect what he really meant was that it was *perfect for having babies*! Not perfect for sin and seduction! He just had a burning desire for children, and for some reason she was the one chosen to help him fulfil his ambition. He saw her as a wife and a mother rather than as a voluptuous sex siren.

She felt totally and utterly deflated.

On impulse she abandoned her packing, stripped off her

shapeless dress and stood in front of the mirror in her underwear. What did he see when he looked at her?

Full breasts. *Child-bearing hips.*

Brushing the tears from her cheeks, she turned sideways and stared at her outline. He'd chosen her as a wife capable of breeding a family, not as a life partner he could love, cherish and have fun with. *Share with.*

And yet why should his attitude surprise her. *Why?*

He was Sicilian and she'd always known that.

Wasn't that the whole reason she'd run in the first place?

How could she have forgotten?

Tears still soaking her cheeks, she slid back into her dress and sank onto the edge of the bed, forcing herself to face the painful truth.

He didn't love her and he'd never love her.

For him, their relationship was all about having babies. Creating a big, noisy Sicilian family full of big, fat sons groomed to carry on the macho tradition.

She blew her nose hard, and then looked up as the door crashed open and Rocco strode into the room. Strands of glossy dark hair fell over his bronzed forehead and his dark eyes glimmered with volcanic fury.

'Go away—' She scrunched the tissue into a ball and turned her head to hide her blotched cheeks. She didn't want to give him the satisfaction of seeing her crying. 'I don't have anything to say to you.'

'And yet you came to my offices so that we could talk, did you not?' He pushed the door shut, and suddenly the enormous bedroom seemed impossibly claustrophobic.

'Just leave me alone,' she muttered, sliding back onto the bed and drawing her knees up against her chest. 'I don't like you. I wish I'd never come back to Sicily.'

'I would have tracked you down.' She felt the bed move as he sat down next to her. 'If this marriage of ours is ever going to work, you have to stop running away.'

'I'll stop running away when you stop giving me cause!' She lifted her head and glared at him, suddenly indifferent to her blotched cheeks. 'Do you want to know why I left the night of our wedding? Because I suddenly discovered that you are *exactly* like my father.'

The anger in his eyes was replaced by wary incomprehension. 'Francesca—'

'They were all talking about you—did you know that?' She blew her nose again, and then wiped her eyes on the heel of her hand. 'I was standing there, in my stupid frothy wedding dress, thinking I was the luckiest girl in the world, and I heard them talking. A whole group of them.'

'Who?'

'You should know! You've obviously slept with all of them,' she muttered, covering her face with her hands as she recalled the conversation. 'They were talking about *me*. They said that you'd married me because I was meek and compliant and that was what you wanted in a wife. I think the exact quote was, "No modern woman in her right mind would marry a man like Rocco, rich and gorgeous though he is."'

'They were clearly jealous because they hadn't been offered the opportunity,' Rocco said smoothly, prising her hands away from her face with determination. 'Look at me, Chessie!'

'They said that Lorna had nothing to worry about because you'd carry on seeing her after we were married.'

'They were *trying* to hurt you,' Rocco breathed, but Chessie shook her head.

'They didn't know I was there.' She abandoned the

crumpled tissue and yanked another from the box. 'But I decided that I'd find you and talk to you about it.'

Rocco tensed and released her hands. 'So why didn't you?'

'I did! And you were on the terrace, laughing with Lorna and kissing her.'

'I've known her a long time.'

Chessie covered her ears. 'I don't want to know. I really really don't want to know. I just want you to agree to a divorce.'

'You're being ridiculous. Lorna and I were not together in the way you mean. And those women were just being spiteful.'

She dropped her hands and looked at him. 'I watched the same thing happen to my mother,' she whispered, and his mouth tightened.

'*What* did you watch happening to your mother?'

'I watched my father slowly break her heart and then her spirit. My mother was his wife, and yet she shared nothing with him. There were no romantic gestures, no caring. Nothing.'

'It was your mother who encouraged you to run away that night, wasn't it?'

Chessie nodded. What was the point in lying? 'She wanted me to do what she'd never had the courage to do. Have a life of my own. She gave me the money I needed to make a fresh start, away from my father.'

'And Carlo? I know that you didn't sleep with him, but were you close?'

Chessie hesitated. 'He was my father's gardener,' she admitted finally. 'I barely knew him, but he was leaving to take a job in Rome and my mother had enough money saved up to persuade him to give me a lift as far as the ferry.'

'He dropped you at the ferry? That's all?'

'That's right. After we docked he drove off. I didn't see him again.'

There was a long silence while Rocco digested this piece of information. Then he rose to his feet in a fluid movement, his broad shoulders tense as he paced the length of the room. 'I thought you had a relationship with him.'

'No. Before that night we had exchanged fewer than ten words.' Why was he still dwelling on her relationship with Carlo? Chessie gave a humourless laugh as she studied the tension in his frame. Because he saw her as a possession and all he cared about was keeping his possessions exclusive. How could she have believed that Rocco genuinely liked her? He might be a different generation from her father, but in terms of attitude, no progress had been made. 'Your problem is that you're living in the wrong era. You'd be entirely comfortable in the Stone Age, living in a cave with a willing woman waiting by the fire to greet you after you've cleaned your weapon after a day's hunting.'

He turned, one dark brow raised in question. 'And what's wrong with that?'

She glanced at him in disbelief. 'Haven't you ever heard of evolution? Man has moved on, Rocco.'

'Which is why you're now living in a villa and not a cave.' He waved a hand as if to prove his point. 'You have a beautiful home.'

He just didn't get it. Tears threatened again, and she covered her face with her hands. 'Just get out, Rocco.' She felt the bed move slightly as he sat down next to her once again.

'Whatever you may think about me, I do *not* like seeing you this upset,' he breathed, pulling her hands away from her face and forcing her to look at him. 'I can see we've had a major misunderstanding here, but we can fix it.'

'We have different personalities,' Chessie said thickly,

reaching for yet another tissue and blowing her nose hard. 'I don't see how we can ever fix that.'

'Different personalities is good,' Rocco assured her, a faint smile touching his hard mouth as he scrubbed away her tears with the pad of his thumb. 'If we were the same then we'd clash all the time.'

Chessie sniffed. 'We *are* clashing.'

'No, we're not. We've just had a slight difference of opinion.' He dismissed it with a careless wave of his hand. 'Whatever you may think, I want our marriage to work.'

'Our marriage will never work.'

'It will work.' His rough, sexy voice made her nerve-endings tingle, but she rejected the sensation.

'How?' Her tone weary, she shredded the tissue clutched in her hands. 'I just can't begin to understand you, and it's perfectly clear that you can't begin to understand me either. And, given that we only ever meet to procreate, that isn't ever going to change.

'Children should be *part* of a relationship, not the whole reason for it. Our marriage isn't what I expected. There's no romance! No sharing!'

He looked at her stack of books on the table next to the bed, scanning the titles. 'Perhaps you should remember that the success of romantic fiction usually lies in its ability to transport the reader into a fantasy world.'

'A fantasy world? Why does a good relationship have to be a fantasy?'

'I'm just saying that you shouldn't be taken in by fiction. A relationship based on respect and understanding is far more successful than one based on physical lust. I've had those, and they've never lasted long,' he assured her, clearly oblivious to the depressing effect his words had on her.

She didn't know which was more upsetting—his tactless reminder of his numerous previous relationships, or the fact that he didn't see her as a candidate for physical lust. She wanted him to desire her! 'We have completely different aspirations and expectations,' she said flatly, and he shrugged dismissively, as if her observation posed no great problem.

'Then we will work to understand each other. You're obviously saying that you need more traditional romantic gestures, and I'm sure I can oblige—so you can unpack your bag.' He checked his watch and rose to his feet in a fluid athletic movement. 'And now I have to go back to work. I'm expecting a call from Tokyo.'

'I thought we were talking—'

'We've talked, and I've got the message. You don't want to have children immediately. Despite what you think of me, I can understand that. You're still very young. So we'll wait. And I'll be more romantic. Get some sleep. You must be very tired.'

After all that baby-making, Chessie thought to herself, but bit her lip to stop herself saying the words aloud.

It was obvious to her now that he had very fixed ideas about her role as a wife and mother, and they didn't coincide with her own. But how could she even begin to explain that she wanted him to find her sexy when that clearly wasn't what he looked for in a wife?

She stared at the bag she'd packed.

At least he'd bothered to come and talk to her. That was a start, wasn't it?

She sank back against the pillows, exhausted from the all the emotions, and she was still lying there when the first bunch of flowers arrived, exotic and confident.

Rocco's housekeeper Maria brought them into the

bedroom suite, with a beaming smile and a warm look of approval in her brown eyes.

'Beautiful, aren't they?'

Chessie stared. They *were* beautiful. And ordering them must have been the first thing Rocco had done on his return to the office. Despite her reservations about their relationship, she was touched.

'Was there a card?' Had Rocco included a few affectionate words? Her heart gave a little skip of anticipation, but Maria shook her head.

'No card.' The housekeeper arranged them in a vase and placed them in the centre of a table. 'They look beautiful there.'

'Yes. You're sure there was no card? No message?' *Nothing personal?*

'Flowers say a great deal all by themselves,' Maria said dreamily, and Chessie pulled herself together with an effort, trying not to be disappointed.

'You're right, of course.'

The second bouquet arrived half an hour later, and from then on one arrived every hour, on the hour, until dusk fell. By the time she'd eaten her lonely supper on the balcony, every surface in the room was crowded with scented blooms.

'Good job I don't suffer from hay fever,' Chessie murmured as she cleaned her teeth in the bathroom and then slid into bed.

But he was clearly making an effort, and she appreciated the gesture. And if a tiny part of her would have preferred just one bunch of flowers and a thoughtful note, another part reminded her that Rocco wasn't great with words and at least the flowers were a start. At least he was trying.

And she'd show him that she could try too. She'd unpacked her bag, and tonight she'd thank him. Properly. And this time their lovemaking would have absolutely nothing to do with making babies.

She lay in bed, hardly able to breathe as she waited for him to stroll through the door.

Tonight, she thought to herself, *everything is going to be different.*

It was going to be special.

She rolled over in the bed, her newly awakened body humming with delicious anticipation.

CHAPTER SIX

THE phone woke her from a fitful doze.

'How were the flowers?' It was Rocco, his voice smooth and supremely confident.

One glance at the bed was enough to confirm that she'd spent the night alone. *He hadn't come to bed.*

'Where were you last night?' Struggling to throw off the cloud of sleep, she rubbed her eyes. 'You didn't come to bed.'

'I left you to sleep.'

She felt the dull ache of disappointment. 'I—I was expecting you. I thought we could—' She broke off, suddenly realising that she had absolutely no idea how to tell her husband that she'd wanted sex. She'd never flirted with a man before, let alone seduced anyone. How was she supposed to tell him that she needed to know he found her attractive? 'You usually spend the night with me,' she muttered lamely.

'You don't want children yet, and I'm trying to respect that,' Rocco replied immediately. 'I'm happy for you to spend some time getting used to married life. Of course when you think you're ready just say the word and we'll be burning up the sheets in an instant.'

Discovering that there was nothing like anger and frustration for providing an effective wake-up call, Chessie sat up in bed. 'So what you're saying is that you don't want to spend the night with me unless we're making a baby.'

'Francesca—'

'You're supposed to have a PhD in women, but you don't know *anything*.' Her passionate declaration was greeted by a tense silence.

'You are making no sense at all,' he growled. 'You said you weren't ready for children so I'm staying away from you. I'm being thoughtful.'

Which basically meant that he didn't find her attractive. If a man found a woman irresistible, surely by definition he wouldn't be *able* to stay away?

Chessie flopped back against the pillows, too demoralised to argue.

'The flowers are lovely,' she said finally, deciding that she ought at least to acknowledge the gesture. 'There seems to be every type of bloom ever grown.'

'Good. My assistant wanted to know your favourite, and I didn't have a clue so she decided it was safest to order everything.'

Chessie closed her eyes, wondering if he even realised what he'd just said. His assistant. So the gesture hadn't even been his own. She could almost see him ticking the boxes. Romantic gesture means flowers. 'They're great.'

'She suggested that I ask you your favourite for future reference.'

'Deadly Nightshade,' Chessie muttered under her breath. 'So that I can crush it into your drink and poison you.'

'You're mumbling. I can't hear you properly.'

'Roses,' Chessie said flatly. *Maybe she could stab him with the thorns.*

'I'll tell her. At least now you can see that I'm capable of romance.' His tone was businesslike. 'There are some matters which require my personal attention over the next few days, so I left the villa yesterday. I'll see you when I'm back.'

'Right.' What difference would it make, Chessie thought numbly, when she didn't see him anyway?

'I think you should go shopping. Just speak to Max, my head of security. He'll arrange it. Feel free to spend my money.'

On what? she wanted to ask, but bit her lip 'Thanks.'

'When I come back, we'll talk again.'

'Right.' Chessie wanted to scream at him that she didn't *want* to spend his money or talk. What was the point of talking when they were on a completely different wavelength? She wanted *passion*! She wanted hot, steamy sex with a man who desired her so completely that he couldn't remember his own name, let alone the fact that he had business commitments.

But Rocco didn't associate her with hot, steamy sex. He didn't see her as a lover, and the word romance didn't enter his vocabulary. He saw her as a wife.

How was she ever going to change that? 'Where are you, anyway?'

'I'm in Florence. I hope to be home in another two days.'

Florence? Chessie felt the envy bubble up and swamp her as she thought of all the books she'd read and the art she'd studied in so much detail. 'You lucky thing. I'd love to see Florence,' she said in a husky voice. 'How long are you going to be there?'

'Not long enough for sightseeing. Another time, maybe. I'll bring you here and we can go shopping.'

Why would anyone want to visit Florence and waste time shopping? Chessie wondered. All she wanted to do was enjoy the art and architecture.

Reminding herself that he did have a job to do, and

couldn't be expected to act as tour guide, she didn't voice her disappointment. 'You poor thing, having to work so hard.'

At least he was making an effort, she told herself as she replaced the receiver and flopped back against the pillows. And he was obviously thinking of her. When he arrived home she was going to find some way of persuading him that fun in the bedroom didn't have to be restricted to making babies.

Suddenly hungry, Chessie sprang out of bed, showered, dressed and wandered through the cool, airy villa to the large, spacious kitchen.

The room was empty, but a half-drunk cup of coffee was on the table, and a television was on in the corner of the room with the sound muted.

Chessie reached for the coffee pot, and then froze as pictures of Rocco appeared on the screen, apparently leaving a Florence nightclub, his arm around a sexy, sleek blonde in a skirt so short it barely covered her bottom.

It wasn't Lorna. Which meant that he was with someone new.

This was the news. Which meant that the picture had been taken the previous evening. When he'd supposedly been in Florence on business.

Business?

She stared at the blonde.

When he'd told her that he was working she'd believed him, but instead—

She sank onto the nearest chair, struggling to breathe. She'd done it again. Believed in him. Believed that in his own way he cared about their marriage. *Given him the benefit of the doubt.* But his assistant had sent the flowers and he wasn't working hard at all. He was partying with another woman— an extremely sexy woman—while she, his wife, sat at home waiting for him to return.

How could she have been so stupid?

At what point had she forgotten that Rocco was Sicilian? When he'd said that she could postpone having children, she'd assumed that he intended to use the time to improve their relationship. Instead of which it was obvious that she was just supposed to do her own thing while he went out and enjoyed himself. And when she was ready to have children, he'd come back to her and perform the necessary biological function.

She ground her teeth with frustration.

When had he ever taken *her* out? When had he ever shown any inclination to spend time with *her*? It was obvious that if he wanted fun and enjoyment then he'd choose another woman.

He was her father all over again.

Her father had married her mother and then proceeded to spend their entire married life sleeping with other women. Marriage for him had been the respectable, socially responsible way of bringing children into the world while enjoying yourself on the side, and clearly Rocco was the same.

Wife. Mistress. Two separate roles with entirely different briefs. Her job was to stay at home, with her good, childbearing hips, and breed and feed their children. The mistress's job was to have endless sex for pure pleasure and indulge in other fun pursuits.

Unless she could persuade him to change his attitude.

Chessie glanced down at herself, trying to see herself through his eyes. Shapeless skirt. Shapeless top. Perhaps it wasn't entirely his fault that he didn't see her as a sex siren. If she wanted Rocco to see her as sexy then surely the first thing she had to do was actually try and *look* sexy? If she wanted him to look at her differently then she had to start looking like a woman he might choose to date—and she certainly didn't at the moment.

Casting her mind back to the girl on the television, she mentally evaluated the outfit she'd been wearing. Short skirt, high heels, revealing neckline. Hair loose and sexily dishevelled. At least she didn't need to be ashamed of her height. It didn't matter how high her heels were, the one thing she could guarantee was that Rocco, with his impressive build, would be taller than her.

Still in a daze, she stood up and walked back through the villa.

'Is everything all right, *signora*?' Max, the security chief at the villa, looked at her with consternation. 'You look very pale. Can I get you a glass of water?'

On the verge of confessing that she didn't need a glass of water, she needed a new wardrobe, Chessie stopped herself and thought quickly. 'Rocco said you'd be able to arrange a shopping trip before my journey to Florence?'

'You're joining him in Florence, *signora*?'

'In time for a night on the town,' Chessie said with a smile. 'I'm supposed to ask you to sort everything out. I'm meeting him at his favourite nightclub tonight. It's called—it's called…' She pretended to flounder and Max quickly supplied a name.

'That's right.' Her smile widened. 'That's the one. Perfect.'

'Do you want me to arrange for you to fly to Florence, *signora*?'

'I certainly do, Max.' She beamed gratefully. 'But do you know what? We need to go via some *seriously* expensive shops. Would you believe that I don't have a single suitable thing to wear?'

'I'll make the necessary arrangements.'

'And, Max—?' Chessie licked dry lips, trying to look casual. 'Do you happen to know a good hairdresser?'

'Of course.' Unconcerned by the request, he gave a nod. 'I'll arrange that too.'

Trying not to mind that Max had obviously been required to make similar arrangements for other women, Chessie smiled. 'Thank you.' She bit back a sudden impulse to grill him on her husband's favourite type of woman.

'I'll arrange for someone to pack your things, *signora*.'

Chessie opened her mouth to say yes, and then closed it again. 'Don't worry about packing, Max, because I'm going to have *new* things,' she said sweetly, suddenly remembering Rocco's claim that she had access to his immense wealth.

He'd probably made that statement safe in the knowledge that her taste didn't run to the glamorous.

Which meant that he was in for a shock.

Not only was she going to show him that her taste was perfectly capable of running to the *extremely* glamorous, but she was also going to teach him that it was possible for one woman to play a great number of parts—including wife *and* mistress.

'You're sure this skirt isn't too short?' Four hours later, Chessie scrutinised her reflection from every angle, feeling horribly naked and self-conscious. It was like wearing underwear and very little else. Did women really go out looking like this? She had an uncomfortable vision of herself being arrested for indecency and Rocco refusing to bail her out because he didn't recognise her as his wife.

'You have legs that most women would kill for, *signora*. Why cover them up?' The stylist fussed around her, narrowing her eyes as she assessed the finished result. 'There aren't many women who can wear that particular skirt, but you're one of them. And that halter top is perfect on you. It actually provides all the support you need while looking incredibly glamorous.'

Glamorous? *Did* she look glamorous? Unconvinced,

Chessie tilted her head left and right, examining the sparkly silver material that was cut to expose a tempting amount of cleavage. 'My father would have fainted on the spot if he'd seen me in this outfit—'

'Everyone's father would faint at this outfit,' the stylist drawled, a wicked smile in her eyes as she slipped several bangles onto Chessie's slender wrist. 'It isn't designed for fathers. It's designed for lovers, with sex and seduction in mind.'

Sex and seduction.

Wasn't that exactly what she wanted?

Certainly it was exactly the sort of outfit that one of Rocco's skinny girlfriends might wear. Mindful of that fact, she asked the question that was preying on her mind.

'Does it make me look fat?'

'Fat?' The stylist looked genuinely startled by the question, and then gave a slow smile. 'Well, you've got a body, if that's what you mean, but fat? No. You curve in all the places that really matter to men. Be prepared to be besieged when you walk into that nightclub.'

Besieged? Chessie frowned slightly. She didn't want to be besieged. She just wanted Rocco to notice her.

'Now I just need to have my hair cut.'

'Not cut,' the stylist urged hastily. 'Just trimmed. The length is fantastic. You just need some layers and texture to soften the effect.'

Never having been near a hairdresser, Chessie didn't have the first clue what the other girl was talking about, and in the end she just put herself in the hands of the hairdresser and crossed her fingers. He, in turn, ordered a deep conditioning treatment and then proceeded to cut soft layers into her hair until it fell around her face and over her shoulders in a seductive curtain.

Amazed by how different she looked, and unable to stop peeping at herself in the mirror, Chessie sat passive while someone did her nails and make up.

If this was how long Rocco's lovers took to get ready every time they went out, she thought to herself, then it was little wonder that they didn't have time for more serious commitments or a job. Being beautiful was definitely a full-time occupation.

Finally she left the salon and slid into the limousine that was waiting for her. But as they drove through the outskirts of Florence, Chessie felt her new-found confidence drain away.

It was all very well, dressing in a seductive way, but she had to learn to behave in a similar fashion and she wasn't sure she was up to it. She kept tugging at the hem of her skirt, and checking her cleavage to check she wasn't displaying too much.

Trying to boost her flagging confidence, she reminded herself that she looked *good*. In fact she couldn't wait to see Rocco's face when he realised that his wife was capable of being a sex siren. Comparing the way she looked now with her usual appearance, she came to the uncomfortable conclusion that it probably was her fault that up until now he'd only ever thought about her in the role of mother. After all, she'd hardly given him cause to think differently, had she?

But things were about to change.

When he saw her he was going to realise that his wife was also a living, breathing, sexy woman.

Their whole relationship was about to change for the better.

All the same, when the car finally drew up outside the nightclub that Max had assured her Rocco would be frequenting that night, she felt almost sick with nerves.

Hoping that she wouldn't fall and break something vital trying to walk in her ridiculously high heels, Chessie reached for her bag. 'Don't wait for me,' she told the driver as she slid gingerly from the car, 'because I'm going to be a while.'

She teetered past the man policing the door and picked her way carefully down the marble stairs that wound into the darkness of the nightclub. Lights swirled, music pounded, and for a moment she just stopped and stared, amazed by the frenetic atmosphere. As her eyes adjusted to the lack of light, she noticed that the club was quite large, with a central dance floor surrounded by a seating area, and an ultra-modern-looking bar made out of glass and chrome.

Fascinated by the vibrant energy of the people on the dance floor, Chessie watched with admiration and a touch of envy as a woman lifted her arms high and swayed her hips in blatant invitation to her partner. Wondering what it would be like to be that uninhibited, Chessie watched a few others, seeking clues as to how they managed to dance in the heels.

'Fancy joining them? I can't believe someone as beautiful as you can possibly find herself without a partner, but I'm more than willing to oblige,' came a slurred male voice from beside her, and she turned to find herself uncomfortably close to a tall, handsome Italian man.

'Oh, no—I'm not on my own.' Realising that his eyes were fastened on the dip in her cleavage, she struggled against the impulse to cover herself. 'I'm with someone.'

'And he left you alone?' He moved closer. 'Is he a fool?'

'I—He—' Chessie's eyes slid back to the crowd and she felt a rush of relief as she saw Rocco saunter onto the dance floor. Relief turned to sick disappointment when she saw that his hand was locked around the wrist of a very beautiful blonde. Was it the same blonde he'd been with the previous night? Chessie narrowed her eyes. Same blonde. Different outfit.

'I see him.' A spark of anger igniting her flagging courage, she clutched her bag tightly and walked onto the dance floor, weaving her way through swaying couples until she reached Rocco.

He hadn't seen her approach, and was smiling down into the teasing blue eyes of his blonde companion, the warmth of his gaze unmistakable.

Ignoring an impulse that told her to just run and hide, Chessie sucked in a deep breath, reached up and tapped him on the shoulder. 'Excuse me.' Her voice barely carried over the throbbing music, but he turned instantly and stilled, his blank, discouraging look giving way to recognition.

'*Francesca?*' Even above the music she could hear the shock and disbelief in his tone. '*What* are you doing here?'

Prepared for a look of stunned admiration, and seeing something entirely different in his eyes, Chessie felt her courage falter. 'I was missing you.'

For a moment he didn't reply, and she watched as he inhaled deeply and took a good look at her. His eyes rested on the silky conditioned length of her beautifully cut hair before travelling slowly down over her bare shoulders, her exposed cleavage and the long length of sheer-stockinged leg. Shock turned to incredulity, and then to glowering disapproval.

Only when his eyes reached her vertiginous heels did he finally recover his powers of speech.

'*What* have you done to yourself?'

It wasn't the question she'd been expecting. 'Dressed up?' She could barely hear him over the pounding music, but it was obvious from the thunderous expression in his eyes that he was less than pleased with her appearance. Suddenly her confidence died a dramatic death.

Which bit of her outfit wasn't right?

A surreptitious glance behind him was enough to confirm that his companion for the evening was dressed in a similar manner, although admittedly on her the clothes looked different. But surely that was because the girl was extremely flat-chested and slim-hipped?

Chessie bit her lip. She could change her outfit, but she couldn't change her curves.

'Rocco—' Clearly resenting the competition for his attention, the girl curled perfectly manicured red nails over his arm. But he shrugged her away impatiently, his eyes still on Chessie.

'This place isn't appropriate for you.'

'Why not?' Her gaze challenged him, the spark in her eyes concealing the distinct quake in her stomach.

He was about to answer, and then something over her left shoulder made his face darken alarmingly. Wondering what could possibly have triggered such a volcanic response, Chessie turned to find the man she'd met at the entrance hovering behind her. He ignored Rocco and gave her a suggestive smile.

'How about that dance? Looks like your partner already has his hands full, so you might as well make do with me.'

She opened her mouth to refuse, and then closed it again. She was standing in the middle of a dance floor making a complete fool of herself over a man who didn't care about her. At least dancing with someone else would help to restore her dignity. 'Why not?'

The man reached out to take her hand, but Chessie felt strong fingers bite into her shoulder and she was jerked backwards into Rocco's hard, muscular body.

'She isn't dancing,' he said icily. 'And she's with me.'

The blonde girl shot Chessie a malevolent look and stalked off the dance floor, but Rocco seemed oblivious to the fallout of his actions. Instead he released Chessie and shrugged out of his jacket, his eyes fixed on her beautifully made-up face. 'Put this on. Now.'

'I most certainly will not. It doesn't match what I'm wearing and it will cover up my new clothes.' Chessie moved slightly, so that the jacket slid into a pool on the floor.

'That's the general idea,' Rocco said through gritted teeth as he stooped to retrieve it. 'I *want* to cover you up. You're making an exhibition of yourself.'

'What about the girl you were with? Wasn't *she* making an exhibition of herself?'

'She isn't my wife.'

'Thanks for reminding me,' Chessie said flatly, and Rocco's eyes smouldered with building anger.

'I *won't* discuss this with you here. We're leaving.'

'Leaving?' Chessie stepped away from him. 'I'm not leaving. I've only just arrived, and you haven't even danced with me yet!'

'I'm not dancing with you when you're dressed like that. You're attracting enough attention without moving around.'

'What do you mean "dressed like that"? This is the way you like your women to look, Rocco. I look *exactly* like your girlfriend—except that I'm bigger in certain places over which I have absolutely no control.' With the help of the ridiculously high heels she could almost look him in the eye. 'I don't understand what's wrong.'

A muscle flickered in his lean, bronzed jaw and his dark eyes glittered dangerously. 'I don't like the way you look.'

Something died inside her. 'Well, I can't do much about that,' she mumbled, glancing towards the man who'd asked her to dance. '*He* didn't seem to find me repulsive.'

Rocco's dark jaw tensed and the expression in his eyes was menacing. 'Call me old-fashioned,' he growled, 'but I don't want my wife to be considered an object of lust by other men.'